MW01232305

Fantasies Collide Vol. 5

The Make 100 Kickstarter Series

Dean Wesley Smith's Make 100 Challenge

The First Thirty-Three

The Second Thirty-Three

The Final Thirty-Four

Colliding Worlds

A Science Fiction Short Story Series

by Kristine Kathryn Rusch and Dean Wesley Smith

Vol. 1, Vol. 2, Vol. 3, Vol. 4, Vol. 5, Vol. 6

Crimes Collide

A Mystery Short Story Series

by Kristine Kathryn Rusch and Dean Wesley Smith

Vol. 1, Vol. 2, Vol. 3, Vol. 4, Vol. 5

Fantasies Collide

A Fantasy Short Story Series

by Kristine Kathryn Rusch and Dean Wesley Smith

Vol. 1, Vol. 2, Vol. 3, Vol. 4, Vol. 5

Also by Dean Wesley Smith

THE POKER BOY UNIVERSE

Poker Boy

The Slots of Saturn: A Poker Boy Novel

They're Back: A Poker Boy Short Novel

Luck Be Ladies: A Poker Boy Collection

Playing a Hunch: A Poker Boy Collection

A Poker Boy Christmas: A Poker Boy Collection

Ghost of a Chance

The Poker Chip: A Ghost of a Chance Novel

The Christmas Gift: A Ghost of a Chance Novel

The Free Meal: A Ghost of a Chance Novel

The Cop Car: A Ghost of a Chance Novella

The Deep Sunset: A Ghost of a Chance Novel

Marble Grant

The First Year: A Marble Grant Novel

Time for Cool Madness: Six Crazy Marble Grant Stories

Pakhet Jones

The Big Tom: A Packet Jones Short Novel

Big Eyes: A Packet Jones Short Novel

THUNDER MOUNTAIN

Thunder Mountain

Monumental Summit

Avalanche Creek

The Edwards Mansion

Lake Roosevelt

Warm Springs

Melody Ridge

Grapevine Springs

The Idanha Hotel

The Taft Ranch

Tombstone Canyon

Dry Creek Crossing

Hot Springs Meadow

SEEDERS UNIVERSE

Dust and Kisses: A Seeders Universe Prequel Novel

Against Time

Sector Justice

Morning Song

The High Edge

Star Mist

Star Rain

Star Fall

Starburst

Rescue Two

COLD POKER GANG

Kill Game

Cold Call

Calling Dead

Bad Beat

Dead Hand

Freezeout

Ace High

Burn Card

Heads Up

Ring Game

Bottom Pair

Also by Kristine Kathryn Rusch

THE FEY SERIES

The Original books of The Fey

The Sacrifice: Book One of the Fey

The Changeling: Book Two of the Fey

The Rival: Book Three of the Fey

The Resistance: Book Four of the Fey

Victory: Book Five of the Fey

The Black Throne

The Black Queen: Book One of the Black Throne

The Black King: Book Two of the Black Throne

The Qavnerian Protectorate

The Reflection on Mount Vitaki: Prequel to the Qavnerian Protectorate

The Kirilli Matter: The First Book of the Qavnerian Protectorate

Barkson's Journey: The Second Book of the Qavnerian Protectorate

(coming 2023)

THE RETRIEVAL ARTIST SERIES

The Disappeared

Extremes

Consequences

Buried Deep

Paloma

Recovery Man

The Recovery Man's Bargain

Duplicate Effort

The Possession of Paavo Deshin

Anniversary Day

Blowback

A Murder of Clones

Search & Recovery

The Peyti Crisis

Vigilantes

Starbase Human

Masterminds

The Impossibles

The Retrieval Artist

THE DIVING SERIES

Diving into the Wreck: A Diving Novel

City of Ruins: A Diving Novel

Becalmed: A Diving Universe Novella

The Application of Hope: A Diving Universe Novella

Boneyards: A Diving Novel

Skirmishes: A Diving Novel

The Runabout: A Diving Novel

The Falls: A Diving Universe Novel

Searching for the Fleet: A Diving Novel

The Spires of Denon: A Diving Universe Novella

The Renegat: A Diving Universe Novel

Escaping Amnthra: A Diving Universe Novella

The Court-Martial of the Renegat Renegades

Thieves: A Diving Novel

Squishy's Teams: A Diving Universe Novel

The Chase: A Diving Novel

Maelstrom: A Diving Universe Novella

Writing as Kris Nelscott

THE SMOKEY DALTON SERIES

A Dangerous Road

Smoke-Filled Rooms

Thin Walls

Stone Cribs

War at Home

Days of Rage

Street Justice

AND

Protectors

Writing as Kristine Grayson

The Charming Trilogy, Vol. 1

The Charming Trilogy, Vol. 2

The Fates Trilogy

The Daughters of Zeus Trilogy

Fantasies Collide Vol. 5

A Fantasy Short Story Series

Dean Wesley Smith
and Kristine Kathryn Rusch

WMG
PUBLISHING

Fantasies Collide, Vol. 5

Published by WMG Publishing

Cover design by Allyson Longueira/WMG Publishing

ISBN-13 (trade paperback): 978-1-56146-866-9
ISBN-13 (hardcover): 978-1-56146-871-3

Due to limitations of space, expanded copyright information can be found on page 449.

Contents

Dark Fantasy

Kristine Kathryn Rusch

Oh, jeez, here's the problem. Both Dean and I are good at dark.

As I skim the table of contents for this volume, I realize that many of our darkest tales aren't even in here. I think we both shied away from including the stories that make us shudder.

What we did put in this volume, though, are some truly disturbing tales. From my "Children of the Night," which is the basis for my novel *Sins of the Blood,* to Dean's "I'm Her Dead Husband," these stories bother us. I have no idea what the effect will be on you.

I do know that some of these stories were written in anger. ("Killing The Angel of Death" comes to mind.) Others were written as a simple assignment by a now-forgotten anthology editor. Those stories are always the surprising ones, because we (the authors) never really expect the story to take that sideways turn.

And yet it does.

The bulk of Dean's most disturbing stories take place on Bryant Street. When I see a manuscript from him with the subtitle "A Bryant Street Story," I brace myself. Something strange, fantastical, and a little bit upsetting will happen in those pages.

I think that's probably the best way to describe all of the stories in this volume. Strange, fantastical, and a little bit upsetting.

If you want strange, fantastical, and a little bit uplifting, pick up the first volume in this five-book set. That's where we go light.

Here, though? Here we're looking at everything from the angel of death (three times!) to immortal assassins. Yeah, there's a lot of death here. But a lot of suspense and heart as well.

I'd say enjoy, but I really mean brace yourself. You're in for a truly enlightening ride.

TEN STORIES

BY

DEAN WESLEY SMITH

Best Eaten On A Slow Tuesday

Dean Wesley Smith

Best Eaten On A Slow Tuesday

Mark Estes stared at the sugar cookies in Heaven's Bakery window. The grains of white sugar seemed to catch the light of the sunny, spring day at just the perfect angle, making the cookies almost twinkle in happiness.

Cookies could be happy, couldn't they? They made him happy just looking at them.

The sidewalk in front of the bakery smelled like fresh bread, drawing unsuspecting passersby like him to the evil trap of sugar cookies and a promise of how they would melt in his mouth with their joyous sweetness.

He knew he would be transported to his own heaven if he could just bite into one or two of them.

No, maybe in the end a half dozen or so.

No. No. He would need a dozen.

A baker's dozen.

Thirteen of the little bastards would give their lives to his taste sensations and they would die happy doing so. He wouldn't even share them with his mistress, Candy. He would eat them before he got to his secret penthouse apartment for their normal Tuesday lunch romp on the

Posture Perfect Mattress. Neither Candy nor his annoying diet-master of a wife, Beth, would ever know.

Secret cookies were a lot better than flaunted cookies.

Both Candy and his wife stayed with him because of his money. And his power. He had no doubt they were both afraid to leave him. And they should be. He hadn't gotten to where he was at in the world without a few broken bones and bodies in his wake.

So if he wanted to spend some money on sugar cookies, screw Candy and his wife and his stupid doctors.

Cookies were worth it.

Good food of all types was worth it.

He just loved to eat, almost more than anything else in the world.

He hitched up his silk pants and checked his suspenders to make sure neither had come loose under his silk jacket. He seemed to be gaining a little weight, so he was going to need to get new suits this week. As long as he kept his suits fitting his 400 plus pounds, no one would notice he was still gaining weight.

He glanced around, feeling slightly guilty, but not enough to turn away from the wonderful bakery smell. Then, as he started for the front door, his phone rang.

He pulled it from his pocket and glanced at it. Only three or four people on the planet had his private number. Shit, it was Brenda, his secretary. She had strict orders to never call him on Tuesday and Friday lunch breaks unless it was an extreme emergency.

He answered, "Yeah. Better be good."

"Sir," she said. "I have really bad news."

"Go ahead."

She took a deep breath. "A dozen sugar cookies will kill you this afternoon at 3:15 p.m. exactly."

"What?" he asked.

"Don't have the sugar cookies, sir," Brenda said. "Just go have sex with Candy and come back to the office. I beg of you."

He actually sputtered.

Mark Estes, one of the most powerful men in all the city prided himself in not being caught unaware or surprised.

And he never sputtered.

Never.

He clicked off the phone without another word, then made sure the tracking on the GPS was switched off, then he turned the entire phone off and stuck it in his pocket.

Then slowly, he stood in front of the window with the plate of sugar cookies and studied the neighborhood around him, looking for anyone suspicious, or anyone watching him.

Third Street was wide, with cars parked on both sides and two lanes of traffic headed east in the middle. As was normal for midday, the traffic was heavy, mostly cabs, and the sidewalks had a fair share of people focused on getting somewhere and ignoring everyone else.

A number of office buildings towered over the street, with storefronts, delis, and restaurants lining the sidewalk on both sides. His office was on the top floor of a building two blocks from here. His company owned the entire thirty-story building. His secret penthouse apartment was still another three blocks away.

On bad weather days he had his limo driver take him the five blocks, but today because the weather was nice, not too hot, not too nasty, he had decided to walk.

His business was the importing of condiments for half the country. He was rich beyond his imagination and had seldom cared what anyone thought or said about him. Or his massive weight.

At five-eight, four hundred pounds made him look round and more powerful than he already was.

All he cared about was getting more power, bossing around other people, eating great food, and having sex like a whale of a bunny.

So how did Brenda know he was going to buy cookies and what was all this scare crap about the cookies killing him at a specific time?

He liked Brenda, he trusted Brenda. Maybe it hadn't been Brenda who had made that call.

In this modern world, anything was possible, especially with the Democrats in charge. He had sure donated his fair share to some questionable Republican candidates. Maybe that was what this was all about.

He shook his head. No one scared the condiment king off his cookies.

He took out his phone, clicked it on, and called his office.

Brenda answered.

"How did you know about the cookies?" he asked.

"What cookies?" she asked.

"Did you just call me a minute ago?"

"No, sir," she said. "I respect your orders to not be disturbed."

"Thank you," he said. "I will be back by 3 p.m."

"Very good, sir," Brenda said.

He clicked off his phone again.

So he had been right, it hadn't been Brenda who called him. He would get his security people on it when he got back to the office. He had some top-notch people working in his tech department. They would be able to tell who had hacked his phone.

He glanced at the plate of sugar cookies once again. The little bastards called to him even more. He needed to buy two dozen, keep a dozen for snacking in his office.

He again started for the door of the bakery and his cell phone rang again.

But it couldn't ring. It had been turned off.

He pulled it out of his pocket.

It wasn't turned on, but it was ringing anyway.

Now that was some fancy hacking skills.

"What do you want?" he said to the phone without putting it up against the side of his head.

Text instantly appeared on the screen. "Don't eat the cookies. They will kill you at 3:15 p.m."

"Fuck you," he said to the phone, walked three steps and tossed the phone as hard as he could at the pavement in the gutter. Then he stepped on it with his polished new shoes, smashing the damaged phone into bits.

A couple walking past gave him a wide berth and muttered something about anger management courses loud enough for him to hear.

He stood on the edge of the street between a parked Ford Taurus and an old pickup truck with most of its paint missing. He was panting and he could feel his heart racing.

When he got back to his office, he would have a team of tech experts track through that private phone account. No one hacked him like that. No one.

Suddenly, at that moment his stomach rumbled.

He glanced back at the bakery and the cookies in the window. The fresh bread smell seemed to have gotten stronger.

He needed cookies, then sex.

In that order.

And that's what he got.

In that order.

He made it back to his office with the second dozen cookies in a white bag just five minutes after three. Candy had been her own wonderful and energetic sex partner, letting him mostly just lay there while she did all the moving around his bulk.

He liked that.

And he had flat loved the cookies. They had delivered on their promise of life-altering sweetness and melt-in-your-mouth death.

He had savored them, eating the last one while on the elevator to his apartment.

Although, after the cookies, the sex, and the walk back to his office, he was feeling a little washed out. Luckily his afternoon was pretty light on appointments.

Brenda nodded to him as she handed him his messages as he walked past and into his office.

He had dropped into his chair before he realized someone was sitting across the desk from him.

It took him a moment to recognize the large bulk of his best friend Benny Nieto. The two of them had come up through school together, both built businesses, and remained fast friends through it all right up until the day Benny had died two years before of complications from diabetes. He had only been fifty-two.

Benny's death had caused Mark to cut back eating for a short time, start walking more, and get a physical. It was during that physical that Mark had learned that he was also diabetic.

Beth, on hearing that news, had become a tyrant around food, as she said, trying to keep him alive.

After a few months of food hell, he had just decided to play along, but not bother.

"You're not here," Mark said to Benny.

"Yeah, I know, I'm dead." Benny said, biting into what looked like a huge peanut butter cookie.

"So I know you're dead and you know your dead, how come I can see you?"

Benny shrugged letting the flesh on his massive shoulders jiggle like he was experiencing an earthquake. "I'm just waiting for 3:15 so we can get the hell out of here and go have dinner."

"Ghosts eat?" Mark asked, ignoring that time thing again.

"The restaurants on the other side are to die for," Benny said, then realized the bad pun and laughed, again sending waves of flesh bouncing around his body.

Mark had no doubt that Benny had gained some weight since dying. A lot of weight, actually. Hundreds of pounds, maybe.

"So it was you that tried to get me to not eat the cookies?" Mark asked.

"Sure was," Benny said. "If you hadn't eaten those cookies, you could have gone on banging good old Candy for another six years before the heart attack finally got you."

"But how?" Mark asked.

"The overload from the cookies to your system is going to shut you down in about three minutes. You die almost instantly."

Mark felt a bolt of terror surge through his body. "Any way out of this?"

"Nope, not after you ate those cookies," Benny said. "Suicide by sugar. But I bet they were good, huh?"

Mark ignored him.

"Sorry old friend," Benny said. "We both picked this path through the world and out the door. We knew what we were doing. And you enjoyed those cookies, as much as all the other meals and desserts you have eaten. We both traded off years of life for food. Sometimes I think it was worth it."

"Only sometimes?" Mark asked, glancing at his watch.

"The food is great on the other side," Benny said. "You'll see in just a minute."

"But it has its problems?" Mark asked.

"Oh, sure," Benny said, finishing off the peanut butter cookie. "No hookers and no money, so no woman on the other side is interested in anyone our size except the really creepy ones with some really sick stuff going on."

"Okay," Mark said. "So what's the downside?"

Benny held up his hand. "Say goodbye to that living body."

Mark suddenly felt a sharp pain run through his entire body and the next thing he knew he went face-first into the expensive cherry wood of his desk.

Then, he stood up and moved to one side, feeling almost exactly the same.

His human body was solidly encased in his big chair, his face slack-jawed and his eyes open, staring into nothingness.

Mark looked down at his ghost body. He was still wearing his silk jacket and pants, held up by suspenders.

Benny slowly pushed himself out of his chair and stuck out his hand. "Welcome to the other side."

Mark shook it. "Thanks for coming to meet me."

They both stood there staring at Mark's body for a moment. He didn't feel at all sad about dying. He felt nothing, actually.

Benny handed him a peanut butter cookie and Mark took a bite. The taste was heavenly, even better than the sugar cookies that had killed him.

"Does all food on this side taste this good?" he asked.

"Sure does," Benny said. "You up for getting some lunch?"

"I am," Mark said.

Benny shifted his massive bulk toward the office door. "Follow me."

"We can't just jump to where we want to go?"

Benny laughed. "Nope, we walk everywhere. And it doesn't help us lose a pound either."

"Is that the downside you mentioned?" Mark asked as they made their way past Brenda, who was staring at her computer screen and didn't notice the two large ghosts.

"Nope," Benny said. "The downside is that we use no energy, burn no fat or calories when we move around or just exist each day. But we take in calories when we eat."

Mark shook his head. He wasn't understanding at all what Benny was getting at.

Benny finally reached the staircase and walked through the door.

"No elevator?" Mark asked.

"Can't," Benny said. "Elevators, cars, trains, nothing works for us. We walk. And let me tell you, it took me all morning to climb these stairs to meet you."

"Thanks," Mark said.

"Don't mention it," Benny said. "That's what friends are for."

"So besides the walking and not burning any calories, what's the downside you mentioned?"

"For a time I thought of it as an upside," Benny said. "On this side of death, we don't pee or crap."

"That's a downside?" Mark asked. At 400 pounds, both of those bodily functions had become chores.

Benny made the ten steps down to the first landing and stopped, panting and red in the face.

Mark felt the same way. Going down stairs was almost as hard as climbing them.

"Think it through," Benny said. "All in, nothing out."

"You mean we are just going to get fatter?"

"Unless you don't eat anything at all," Benny said. "But I don't think I could spend eternity doing that unless I was forced to."

Mark sat down on the steps and stared at his best friend. What Benny was saying was finally dawning on him.

"We're going to eat and get so fat we can't move around anymore because we don't burn calories and can't pee or shit," Mark said. "Is that what you are saying?"

"Yup, spot on the nose," Benny said.

"And then we spend eternity as giant blobs of flesh only thinking about food, but having no way to get any. Right?"

"That's how I read it as well," Benny said.

Mark just put his head down and covered his face with his hands.

He could feel he was hungry. He wanted another peanut butter cookie. More sugar cookies. Steaks, seafood, you name it, he wanted it.

He craved it.

And the feeling was very real.

He pushed the feeling away as best he could and tried to think. He had died and now, to keep his ability to even begin to move around as much as he did now, he had to stop eating.

Period.

Or he could eat until he could never move around again and then never eat after that, craving food for all eternity.

This was hell. He had no doubt.

He always sort of knew this was where he might head considering many of the things he had done to get ahead. But he had always kind of hoped there wouldn't be either a heaven or a hell.

He had been wrong about that.

"Any out you can see on this?" Mark asked.

Benny shook his head. "There are massive piles of human flesh all over the place, existing where they fell and couldn't get up."

"Oh, Jesus," Mark said.

"He doesn't live in these parts," Benny said. "But what's even worse are the poor souls who got sent here on the other side of things."

Now Mark was confused.

Benny clearly saw that.

"You'll understand when we get to the street. The people who are in this place who were focused in life only on staying thin with the same passion that we ate don't get fat here. They burn calories when they move around, but take no calories in no matter how much they eat."

Benny just shuddered. Exactly the opposite of what was going to happen to them.

"Piles of living human bones litter the street as well," Benny said, shaking his head in disgust. "Nothing but skin covering bones. They just stay where they fell when some muscle finally got eaten away from starvation."

"So we are all destined in this hell to go one direction or the other?" Mark asked.

"Got it in one," Benny said.

Mark felt his stomach rumbling. “So you say the food is great here?”

Benny nodded, smiling. “Memorable.”

“Memorable enough for the memories of the food to last for eternity?” Mark asked.

Benny made a motion to indicate his huge mass of flesh. “I’m betting on it.”

Mark could either go on a strict diet and never eat and retain the right to move around or he could eat and then remember each meal off into eternity.

Short-term gain, long-term loss.

That’s how he had gambled with his life when alive. He could see no reason to change now.

This was hell. Of that there was no doubt.

But at least the food was good.

And the cookies heavenly.

I'M HER DEAD HUSBAND

DEAN WESLEY SMITH

One

Tall glass, ice, peach schnapps, orange juice, red straw, and a thin slice of orange.

I finished the Fuzzy Navel and slid it toward the woman across the polished wood bar. "Two-fifty," I said, using my bar towel to wipe water spots off the surface.

I was always wiping up something. This bar might be a smoke-filled dive, but as long as I worked here it was at least going to be a clean, smoke-filled dive.

She dug in her large brown purse, obviously unused to paying for a drink. The older balding guy beside her was making no move for his wallet. He hadn't said a word, but he stood beside her as if they were together.

After bartending for ten years, since my last year in college, I knew, at a glance, which people belonged in a bar and which didn't. But way back on my first night I would have bet anything this lady didn't belong in The Continental Lounge.

And I would have been right.

The older guy she was with was another story. He looked vaguely familiar and a bunch washed out, as if he had spent half his life drinking.

I wouldn't have been surprised to see him sliding drunk off of any bar stool in town.

I watched her while she dug for the money. Her dark red hair was conservatively fixed close to her head and pulled back tight. She kept her elbows tucked against her sides, as if opening them up might let everyone know she had tits. She wore a white dress blouse with all but the very top button done up tight. I figured normally she'd have them all buttoned, but tonight she was being daring.

Being in here proved it.

I glanced again at the guy beside her. His face rang bells in my head, but I'd be damned if I could exactly place him. Trying to made my stomach churn.

He was older than her by a good fifteen years and was within a combs length of not having a hair left on his head. He wore what I call the comfortable style: Open necked sweater, no shirt, and soft looking slacks. He looked just plain wrong standing beside the redhead.

Then, while I was looking directly at him, he did the weirdest damn thing. The old dude, just plain as could be, reached down and grabbed her ass.

The woman didn't even flinch and I shook my head.

The things you see in bars never ceased to amaze me. She laid two bucks on the bar mat and went back to searching through her purse for change. Women who looked for exact change in a bar were no-tippers. Guaranteed. Amazing how cheap some people could be.

Of course, with her I doubted if she knew any better. Yet she stood there letting some old guy grab her ass.

Go figure.

I was still waiting and she was still digging when the bald dude reached up and placed his hand on her left tit. He didn't squeeze or nothing. Just held it there.

Again she didn't seem to notice.

"Wait 'til you get outside, would you?" I said to the guy.

He looked up at me and smiled. "So I'm right," he said, taking his hand off her tit. "It's the time."

He looked at me real carefully. "But I almost didn't recognize—"

He stopped as she found two quarters and laid them next to the bills.

"I don't know what you're right about," I said. "But don't do that kind of shit at my bar."

"Excuse me?" she said, looking up at me for the first time.

I noticed she had huge brown eyes. Puppy eyes, too big for her thin face. She didn't strike me to be the type to let some jerk grab a quick feel in public.

"Just talking to your friend there." I nodded in the old guy's direction.

She took a quick glance his way, then looked up at me. Her eyes seemed even bigger, and her face had turned a sick white under the light layer of makeup. "You can see him?"

I glanced over at the guy. He was just looking at me, half smiling.

These two were beyond the college weirdos we got in here on a Friday night.

"Two-fifty," I said, counting the money out loud as I scooped it off the bar and put it in the cash drawer. "Thanks."

I started pretending to work at something in the well. Rule number one when it came to strange customers. Ignore them. After a while they usually went and bothered someone else.

"No," the woman said again, reaching across the bar and touching my shoulder. "Please tell me if you can see him."

"Come off it, lady. Of course I can see him. And don't make believe you couldn't feel his hand on your boob, either."

At that, she got real red and her face went from white to a bright pink that sort of blended right up into her dark red hair.

The guy laughed. "Now you've done it."

The woman whirled and shouted at the empty air about three feet to the guys left, "Keep your hands to yourself and leave me alone!"

She grabbed her drink, stalked over to a table and sat down with such force I thought the chair was going to give way.

Wow. One mad woman.

The older guy was laughing, leaning back with his hands tucked into pants pockets.

"I'm her dead husband," he said as if that would explain everything. "But she was fiery like that when I was alive."

Again he laughed as if he had said something funny. "By the way, my name is Dave."

Full moon. That was it. All the crazies hit the bars on a full moon. Documented fact. This Dave guy proved there must be a full moon out tonight, because he was as crazy as they came. I went back to wiping at the bottles in my well, hoping he'd just move away.

But he didn't. Instead, he moved over closer. "Don't believe me, do you?"

"Sure I do," I said.

Second rule when dealing with a nut case. Agree with them and they smile and go away.

"But you don't," he said. "I can tell. And I seem to remember I didn't either. Which means you didn't. Which..." He waved at the air. "Oh, never mind. Here. Touch my arm and I'll prove it to you."

I glanced up. He had his arm stuck straight out over the bar and was holding it there waiting for me to touch it.

Third rule. Humor them. I reached up to touch his arm just above the jacket sleeve.

My hand went right through.

"Christ," I said, yanking my hand back.

"See. Ghost all the way."

I reached out to touch his shoulder.

He let me.

My hand went right though his chest and I couldn't feel a thing. Nothing. Just like I was sticking my hand out in the air.

I pulled my hand back and glanced at it. Nothing wrong. Hell, now I needed a drink. These idiots were starting to make me see things. Not a good sign.

Especially so early in the night.

"Bet you can't touch my leg, either," the guy said.

"No thanks," I said. Then I purposefully laughed. It probably sounded strained. "Tell me how you did it. You really had me going there."

"It's easy," he said. "First you die. Then you find someone who can see you."

"Cute," I said. "Real cute. You want something to drink?"

"Yes, but no thanks," he said. "I'm afraid I couldn't pick it up if you made it for me."

To prove his point, he reached out and stuck his hand through the fruit tray sitting on the bar. Then, for a final show, he put his hand right through a bottle of limejuice sitting beside the tray. I could see his sleeve inside the bottle, tinted green.

He pulled his hand out and held it up. "Believe me now?"

I didn't know what to think. Part of me wanted to turn and run for the back room as fast as my little shoes could hit the floor. But another part of me was real curious. The part that kills cats won over the part that wanted to take a coffee break.

"I'm not sure," I said. "What exactly do you want me to believe?"

"That I'm a ghost."

"Then the answer is no," I said. "What else would you like me to believe?"

"How do you explain that you can't touch me?"

I shrugged real obviously. "I don't do explanations. I make drinks. Besides, there are a lot of people in here I can't touch. Your wife, for instance."

I pointed in her general direction. She was staring at me. I waved. She looked flustered and turned back to watch the jukebox and the one lone couple dancing in front of it.

"Hell, go ahead," the guy said. "She's single. I've been dead a year now. She's starting to forget me. Soon she won't even remember that I exist."

Rule number four with crazy customers. If the first three rules don't work, be rude to them. That always does it.

"Is she good in bed?" I asked. "Wouldn't want to go wasting my time with some skirt who won't even get on top. Know what I mean?"

But the old guy didn't flinch. He gazed over at his wife and got this faraway look, like he was remembering the first time he got to first base at the old drive in. Then his eyes sort of misted over and I had a twinge of guilt. But only a twinge.

"She used to be real good," he said, after a moment. "When she wanted to be. No one better. You'll like that."

"I'll what?" I shook my head. This guy had gone way beyond crazy and he was towing me along as if I were a damn trailer. No more.

"Look, if you don't want a drink, why don't you move along. All right?"

"God, I've forgotten," he said, "just how—"

"Can you really see him?" The wife had gotten up and stormed back over to the bar. "I can't believe he followed me here."

"Lady, I really don't know what you're talking about."

"Tell her I still love her," the old guy said. "But that I'm leaving now."

The red head was staring at me as if she hadn't heard a thing the old man said, waiting for me to say something.

"He said he's leaving now," I told her, playing along with their stupid game.

"Is he gone?" she asked, looking around.

"No," I said, glancing at him.

The old guy shrugged. "I can't leave. I'm sort of tied to her. Got to stay close. But I guess I could go outside."

She looked in the direction I had glanced, then back at me. "Tell him I'm leaving. And tell him thanks for spoiling my evening."

She slammed her drink down on the bar in front of me and headed for the door with short, quick steps.

"Looks like we're leaving," he said. "Next time she'll be alone."

"Sure she—"

Right in the middle of my snappy answer, he faded and disappeared faster than a puff of smoke on a windy day.

"Shit," I said and leaned over the bar to check out the floor where he had been standing. Nothing but stains and cigarette burns in the carpet. That did it.

I grabbed a highball glass and poured myself a good solid double shot of well bourbon. I added two ice cubes and a splash of soda, then headed for the back room. I needed a break. It was going to be one damn long night.

Two

Two nights later, during the slow time between the business drunks from happy hour and the regular night drinkers, she dropped back into the bar. The ghost guy had been right. She was alone.

I was cutting lime wedges, getting ready for what promised to be a steady night. She came through the door, paused a moment to let her eyes adjust to the dim light, then came over to the bar and sat down on the end stool.

"Hi," she said, almost too softly for me to hear over the song on the jukebox. "Remember me?"

"Sure do," I said, sliding a bar napkin in front of her. "Figure out your problem with that guy?"

I glanced quickly around the bar. He wasn't anywhere to be seen.

She slowly moved the napkin back and forth in front of her real self-conscious like, as if she almost didn't remember. Finally she said, "I'd rather not talk about him."

"Can't say as I blame you," I said, making my voice sound as cheery as I could. "He was a strange bird, that one. What can I get for you to drink?"

She looked up at me with those huge eyes of hers and smiled a soft thank you smile. "I'll try a Fuzzy Navel. I heard they were good."

I don't know if it was right at that moment that I fell for her, or if it was sometime over the next few hours as she sat at the bar and laughed at my stupid jokes. But I know that it was right at that moment that I started noticing how really pretty she was.

About halfway though the evening I finally got around to asking her name.

"Alice," she said. "Alice Rule? What's yours?"

I didn't want to tell her, on account my name was the same as the strange dude who called himself her dead husband. So instead of Dave, I said David. She didn't even flinch. She said she liked that name. Said it was strong and showed character. Maybe it was at that moment that I fell in love.

Hell, I don't know.

Before she left, I asked her out for lunch the next day and she said yes without even a moment's hesitation. She said she worked as a buyer for a local department store and I could pick her up there.

We had lunch together the next few days and every night she came into the bar to sit and talk. After a while the place started to seem empty without her sitting on that end stool.

After a week, the regulars were really starting to take a liking to her. That convinced me even more that she was really someone special.

I'd served some of those folks for years. I knew and trusted their judgment. When they liked a person, it meant something. They really liked Alice and made her feel welcome and safe.

On my night off, six nights after we met, she took me to her apartment to cook me dinner.

The place was a small, tidy, warm one bedroom, with pictures of parents and one sister on the wall, a white fluff-ball of a cat, and a couch that was so soft, you didn't want to get up.

A single woman's perfect apartment.

Dinner was the best chicken I had ever tasted and later she served a perfectly chilled white wine. I didn't have to come back for breakfast and I didn't get much sleep.

Thinking back now, it was odd that not once during that week did we talk about the guy she yelled at the first night. I don't remember, but

I suppose I figured it would come up sooner or later and was happy to have it later.

Hell, I had a few things in my past I didn't much like, including an ex wife I wasn't real excited about.

It wasn't until two full weeks from the day I first saw her that the strange guy appeared again. She was sitting on her normal stool, talking to Wilber, the retired truck driver who was one of the old time regulars. They were laughing about something and I was staring at her from the other end of the bar, thinking about how young and healthy she was looking, when I noticed out of the corner of my eye a slight movement.

I glanced around and there was the bald guy, Dave, sitting at the bar across from me.

He hadn't come in. I knew that. I had been facing that front door and no one had come through it since Wilber. So just how the hell had he gotten in?

I started to ask him, but he held up his hand and put his finger to his lips for me to be quiet.

"Don't let her know I'm here," he said. "I wanted to see how things were going. Got tired sitting out front all these nights."

"Siting out front?"

Little stabs of jealousy cut at my stomach.

He motioned for me to turn my back so Alice and Wilber wouldn't see me talking. "They can't see me," he said. "But they can see you talking."

"We going to start that shit again?"

But I said it so Alice couldn't see me. I stood with my back to her and pretended to be working on something in the well. She was far enough down the bar she couldn't hear me over the jukebox.

"Let me prove I'm a ghost once and for all," the bald guy said.

He stood up. "I'll show you. Then, when you believe me, maybe we can talk." He walked right through the bar, then through the back bar and disappeared into the mirrors behind the call liquors.

"David?" Alice called out as I stared at the mirrors. "Everything all right?"

"Sure is," I said, scooting quickly along the bar until I was in front of her and Wilber. "Just working on getting ready for the night."

I straightened her drink, then gave her hand a squeeze, proud of the fact that I kept my hand from shaking.

She smiled at me. I felt almost guilty for not telling her what was going on. But at the same time, I wasn't sure exactly what I was seeing. And I didn't want to go losing her, scaring her off by being a nut case.

The bald guy came walking out of the mirrors, back through the bar, and sat down on the end stool.

"Need another drink here?" I asked Alice and Wilber, forcing myself to not stare in the bald guy's direction.

Both said no, so I gave Alice's hand another little squeeze and went back to the ghost. He'd made a believer out of me with the walk through the bar routine.

But what the hell did he want?

"Looks like everything is progressing as I remembered it," he said as I moved back into position by the well with my back to Alice.

"You remembered it?" I asked. "You lost me. In fact, you being here has me damn confused, to say the least. Who the hell are you?"

I had a bunch more questions for him, but figured that would be enough to start.

He laughed. "My name is Dave. I'm Alice's dead husband. I told you that. Although, from how young she's starting to look, I doubt if she will remember me. I've been staying outside lately, away from her."

He glanced down the bar at her. She lives forever, you know. So do you, so do I, only in a different sort of way than her."

I shook my head and laughed. "Hold on one damn minute. Past you name, I didn't follow a word of that."

It was his turn to laugh. "I doubt if you'd believe much more. I know I wouldn't have. Just enjoy while you can."

"Enjoy what?"

"Alice," he said, softly. "The next ten years."

He gazed in her direction and sighed, then glanced back at me. "I only wanted to remind you I was here. You'll understand when your time comes. Maybe you can break the cycle."

"Wait—"

He was gone again. Not even a cloud of smoke. I glanced over the bar at the empty stool, then grabbed a glass and filled it with ice.

Time for me to have a drink.
A very large drink.

THREE

That night at my place I almost got up the nerve to ask Alice about the bald guy. But it had been a long night, I was tired, and Alice was in a "playful" mood, so the question never got asked.

The next day it just didn't seem as important somehow. Not that I forgot about it. I didn't. It was just never the right moment. And after the ghost didn't show up for a while, there seemed to be little point in asking.

Alice spent a lot of nights sitting on her end barstool and over the next month I found out a lot about her past. But not one word was ever said about being married. In fact, her history filled in solid all the way from high school to the night she came into the bar the first time. There didn't seem to be any time that she could have been married. But why would a ghost lie to me? Made no sense.

Two months after we met, we started talking about getting married. She liked the idea.

I liked the idea.

We'd do it and then she'd help me go back to school, finish the master's degree and get a real job.

Of course, by the time we started making those kind of plans I was head over heels in love and not questioning anything. The truth of the matter was, I wasn't thinking about it. I plain didn't want to.

Six months from the day we first met, we were married in the Methodist church downtown, the big one with the huge colored windows and the ten-step altar. We had to climb all ten of those suckers and I was so nervous, I almost didn't make it.

Alice held me up.

Before the service, while I was standing in the front of the church waiting for Alice to come flowing down the center aisle, I thought I saw the bald guy in the balcony above the entrance.

He was wearing the same clothes he had on in the bar. He waved, gave me the thumbs up sign, and then disappeared when the music started.

I didn't understand.

Four

Ten years and two days later, I died.

And then I understood.

The doctors told Alice it was a massive coronary arrest.

I was forty-one.

The moment I found myself sitting next to her in the hospital waiting room, listening to the news of my death, wanting to comfort her, hold her, I knew I was the bald guy.

As best I can let me explain what I think happened. If Alice had been the one to have died, I don't think I could have survived. We shared everything. We were more in love the last day then the day we were married.

Not that we didn't have our troubles. Turned out that Alice had one hell of a temper. There was no getting in her way when she was mad. I had a drinking problem that almost split us up three years into things. But she helped me though the drinking and I usually laughed at her temper.

Until I died, I didn't really realize how totally dedicated to me Alice was. Obsessed might be a better term. I figured that the first time around, her total dedication was why I got stuck here, couldn't move on into the next life until her attention was turned to someone else.

And that's why she went back.

Back into the past, her past, my past, dragging me with her until she again found me and married me. Her love held me near her like a dog on a leash.

And all those years I hadn't really noticed.

In fact, I'd enjoyed it.

But it isn't anywhere near as much fun now that I'm dead. And somehow, someway, I have to break the cycle.

After the funeral, she had holed up in our house and wouldn't go or do anything. She didn't eat and was losing weight really fast. I figured she was trying to kill herself so that she could join me. Even though I wanted to break the cycle, I couldn't take the thought of her doing that.

That's when I let her see me for the first time.

Scared her something awful.

I guess those first few times I still didn't have the hang of being a ghost. Making yourself visible is no easy task. You'll discover it takes a lot of real concentration and energy. I suppose I looked sort of watery and not all there.

I couldn't tell.

Like Vampires, mirrors don't work for ghosts.

Maybe it was my reappearing that started her returning to the past. At first, she wouldn't admit that I was even there. If I'd have stopped then, stayed invisible, I might have allowed her to get through her grief and on with her life.

But my showing up, trying to get her to eat kept her in our past. The more I was there, the more she regressed. I could feel the years drifting, coming unstuck.

She didn't like me only being a ghost. She wanted me to touch her, hold her or even talk to her for longer than a few minutes at a time.

She wanted me back, alive, the way I had been the day she met me.

That's you. You're me. Now do you understand why I've been telling you all this? Don't talk to her when she comes back into the bar in two days. I'm not strong enough to break the cycle on this end except by telling you this story.

After years of marriage, you'll understand.

But you can end it. Don't let the next cycle start.

At that moment Alice stood up from the table near the jukebox and stormed back over to the bar. "Can you really see him?" she demanded. "I can't believe he followed me here."

I glanced over at the old balding guy who claimed to be my ghost and who had told me the wildest bar story I had ever heard, then back into her huge brown eyes.

"See who?"

She looked puzzled for a moment, then smiled.

She took a long drink off her glass and set it empty on the bar. "What did you call that drink?"

"Fuzzy Navel," I said, sliding the empty over the bar and into the dish rack.

She walked down the bar and pulled out the end stool. "I think I'll have another. I always heard they were good."

The old guy sighed and then vanished without so much as a pop or a wisp of smoke. I saw him again sitting in the balcony of the church the day Alice and I were married.

And it was a wonderful ten years.

Kill for a Statistic

A Bryant Street Story

Dean Wesley Smith

Kill for a Statistic

Damon Felt worked in a bank, for heaven's sake. He wore bottle-sized glasses and a wool suit that seemed slightly too large for his tiny frame, and when he moved he seemed deathly afraid of bumping into anyone or even being noticed.

He was a walking, talking cliché of a meek human, more than likely too afraid to stand up and say anything at all, which chances are had kept him in his assistant to an assistant manager position for ten years. His actual title was Vault and New Accounts Manager.

Seriously, who made up this stuff?

Everything I had seen and found out about him painted him as exactly what he seemed in real life. A 125-pound man who just got by in life. His meager salary paid his expenses and utilities for his nondescript suburban home on Bryant Street to the south of Las Vegas in Henderson, and left him enough for food, television cable, and a nice meal out at a local restaurant every Thursday night promptly at six.

Of all the twisted psychos and subdivision nutjobs I had investigated on Bryant Street, Damon Felt was the most puzzling. Pathetically normal to fifty levels. I just knew there had to be something deep inside him that drove him to buy a house on Bryant Street.

No one just accidently bought a home on Bryant Street in any subdivision in any city. I know.

My name is Carson Range and I have been stalking the secret of this stupid street for a decade now. And without a doubt, because of my obsession with the street, I was going to be dead a lot sooner than I would have expected.

Bryant Street was that kind of place.

My entire journey to my death started with an assignment by an editor at a paper I used to work for in Oregon about a number of weird events on the same subdivision street. And the more I dug, the more I realized that the street was just a wasteland of screwed-up humans.

And it seemed that everyone who buys a home on the street is drawn to the street for a reason. And it's not some magic thing, I am sure, but a force that makes people think the standard suburban street is special.

Well, Bryant Street is special, just not in the way they all first think.

When I changed jobs to a paper in Denver, I learned that the Bryant Street there had just a screwed-up history as the one outside of Portland, Oregon.

By my best count, doing a ton of research, which as a reporter I am damn good at, there are over 400 miles of Bryant Streets in the suburbs of twelve major cities. Some of the streets are only a block or so long, a couple streets go on for miles.

Every last one of them has registered a number of strange events, deaths, murders, missing persons, and so on.

The newest Bryant Street appeared in a new subdivision of Las Vegas in the Henderson area in 2005. That one scared me because it actually wound through the hills for just under three miles.

That is a lot of screwed up, let me tell you.

And promises of even more screwed-up messes.

I moved to Vegas in 2010 and got myself a good deal on a small home in North Las Vegas, just about as far across the Vegas Valley as I could get from Bryant Street. I didn't need anything more than a small house since I was single at the age of thirty-eight and planned to remain that way.

Damon Felt, meek banker and cliché, had bought a home on Bryant

Street during the worst of the Las Vegas real estate recession of 2008. For what it is worth now in 2022, he made a killing.

Since I started to work for a local Vegas paper and kept an eye on Bryant Street, there had been a dozen deaths in eleven years on the street, seven people were hospitalized with mental health issues, four people went missing, and two of the houses burnt to the ground.

Five more houses along the three miles are sitting empty and in some sort of limbo because of missing owners, even in the hot real estate market.

I now have files on eighty people or couples or families who live on the street, and all of them had one issue or another.

Except for Damon Felt.

I had to try to figure out what drove him to live on that street.

So I did what any busy person would do when faced with a need and a little too much money. I set up surveillance cameras watching his home. Cost me a pretty penny, but was worth it.

I even managed to get one hidden on a garage behind his house.

The cameras were motion activated and I downloaded the server and reset everything remotely every two days.

Holy shit was Damon Felt boring.

In the months I watched him and his stupid schedule, one house on Bryant Street burned down and two of the other residents died in one fashion or another.

But good old Damon Felt did exactly the same thing every day, left for work and came home at exactly the same time, turned off his bedroom light at exactly the same time.

Day after day, month after month, always the same.

Right up until the point that it wasn't.

I had hired a computer hacker to dig into Damon Felt's finances and he got me one detail I didn't know about. Damon had a storage unit about four blocks from his home.

And I had a private detective teach me how to track Damon's new minivan. Always a gray one that he traded in every year for a new one that looked identical. He always paid cash. It seemed the newer the car, the easier it was to track. Who knew?

So I got all that set up, and waited for more months.

Boring months.

Damon Felt always kept to his exact schedule. He never went to his storage unit.

Until he did.

And every day after that first day, his storage unit became part of Damon Felt's schedule.

He didn't seem to be moving anything in the van, but he went there every day and stayed exactly thirty minutes and then went home.

Now, to say at this time that I was obsessed with Bryant Street and Damon Felt would be a very sad understatement.

Thankfully I was single, didn't drink much, loved my reporting job, and had enough money to live nice. I didn't much care for any form of gambling, considering my reporting job enough of a gamble.

But Bryant Street and Damon Felt had me hooked, like a smoker just wanting one more cigarette before promising to quit.

Well, my one more cigarette would kill me. I just didn't know it.

So when I realized Damon's routine had altered so that he spent time in his storage unit every day, I rented one right across the narrow, paved road from his.

I got a bunch of empty boxes from a stationary store and wrote on them in big black felt marker so they looked like there was something in them. Then I took my bike that I hadn't used in years and some other stuff and after three trips across town, I had the small unit looking like I was actually storing stuff in it.

Then parking my car away from my storage unit because I didn't want Damon recognizing it, I had the door open to my unit when he arrived.

It was a moderately warm spring afternoon, sunny as always, with almost no wind. I pretended to work arranging the boxes.

Damon arrived looking exactly like he looked in the bank. Wool suit, bland tie, thinning hair combed perfectly.

He got out of his van, locked it, and then unlocked his storage unit.

As the door went up, I could see he had hung a privacy curtain about two feet deep inside.

What the hell was that for? What was he doing in there?

He looked around, but I had timed that moment to have my back turned so he wouldn't think I was paying attention, then he pulled the curtain aside and ducked in, letting the curtain fall back into place.

But what I saw in that unit turned my blood cold.

For a second I thought what I saw was women's bodies.

You know, active imagination.

I took a breath and realized what I had seen were mannequins.

Naked women's mannequins.

And they had been smashed up something awful, at least the ones I caught a glimpse of.

Then, from the other side of the curtain I heard a shout.

"Take that!"

And there was a smash that echoed along the narrow road between rows of storage units.

Then a moment later another, "Take that!"

Followed by another smash.

I ran across the short distance to his storage unit, stopped just short of the curtain, and said, "You all right in there? I heard a crash."

"I am fine," Damon Felt said. "Please come in. But watch your step."

I pulled back the curtain and stepped inside.

The storage unit was a large one, a good twenty feet deep and twenty feet wide. Five or six bulbs hung from cords giving the place a very bright feel.

And it was full of female mannequins in different states of wholeness. Numbers of them had the empty painted eyes staring up at me from a head on the ground. There had to be a good fifty of them, the ones to the back less damaged. He clearly had been beating on the ones at the front.

"This is quite satisfying," Damon Felt said, actually smiling. "Would you like to try?"

He offered the bat in his hand to me.

I think I actually shuddered.

Not once in my life, with all my dates, girlfriends, and two fiancées, had I ever been angry enough at a woman to take a bat to her.

Not once, not even close.

Never crossed my mind, to be honest.

The entire scene just sickened me.

"My online therapist tells me this would be good for my pent-up aggressions."

I nodded, and Damon Felt looked at the different pieces of mannequins and smiled. "Surprisingly, it really does help."

Again I just nodded.

This guy was one sick human.

Damon smiled again, holding the aluminum bat. "After a few more days I might take some pieces of these home and see if I can build a brand new woman. That should be entertaining."

At that moment I knew that Damon Felt belonged completely on Bryant Street.

"It would be a lot more fun than spying on someone you don't know," he said. "Don't you think, Mr. Range?"

What he said took me a second to register that he knew what I had been doing. But by that point it was too late.

My obsession had caught up with me like that one last cigarette.

The bat caught me against the side of my head and sent me stumbling into the aluminum wall and down to the ground.

God that hurt.

I tried to climb back to my feet, but nothing seemed to want to work.

"Putting together mannequin parts should be a lot easier than real women," Damon Felt said. "I have tried that and I never seem to make it work."

I struggled to climb to my feet, but without luck. Why didn't I just trust that he lived on Bryant Street for a reason and leave it alone?

Too late now.

Damon Felt smiled. "Don't worry, I won't use any of your parts. I don't really like men."

The last thing I saw was Damon Felt's small smiling face an instant before the bat sent me spinning down into darkness to become just another statistic of Bryant Street.

The Woman in the Wall

A Mary Jo Assassin Story

Dean Wesley Smith

ONE

Assassins had a code. At least Mary Jo did.

Her code was simple. Don't kill anyone unless you know why you were hired to kill them. And the more difficult the task of killing, the better.

This fine July morning, the streets of New York were already hot and sticky and the smells were mixed breakfast smells and garbage left outside overnight. The traffic and the city seemed louder than normal, and more people were on edge. New Yorkers didn't smile much as it was, but on this hot morning, no one was smiling.

New Yorkers always wore black. Wearing black on a hot summer's day was never a good idea, yet most New Yorkers still wore black. Mary Jo doubted most of their closets had another color.

Mary Jo had on a pair of jeans, tennis shoes, and a white blouse with a floppy white hat to keep the sun off her face. Her outfit screamed tourist, which was exactly what she wanted.

New Yorkers ignored tourists more than they ignored being hot wearing black on a summer day.

The plan this morning was to kill her mark while passing him on the sidewalk. She would brush against him and stick him with a fast-acting poison that would vanish from the bloodstream in less than thirty minutes and make it seem like he had had a heart attack right there on the sidewalk.

A sweating, overweight guy in black dropping dead on a hot summer's sidewalk. Not going to make news or even draw the slightest bit of attention.

Of course, by the time he walked ten to twelve more steps before going down, she would have vanished into the crowd.

Her mark was an overweight white guy going bald and in his late thirties. He worked at a publishing company, one of the big ones, as an editor. He had a wife and teenaged kid and his wife worked as an accountant. They lived in Queens and between their two salaries they barely made enough to get by.

In other words, the guy was so plain no one but his family would notice if he died. He had left no mark on the world anywhere that she could find. None.

Sort of sad, actually. Not even the authors he edited much liked him.

The fantastically rich woman who had hired Mary Jo to kill him lived in Chicago in a two-story penthouse suite. She had family money from shipping and oil. At least her mark worked. Mary Jo doubted the Chicago woman had ever worked a day in her thirty-plus years on the planet.

Mary Jo's contract on this poor fool of an editor was six million. The Chicago woman had paid the two million up front and Mary Jo knew for a fact that Chicago rich woman had the other four million ready to transfer.

This guy as an editor made less than a hundred grand a year and had a small retirement account and life insurance of fifty thousand that wouldn't last his family long at all.

So why did Chicago rich lady want this guy dead?

Something just felt off. Way, way off.

There was no connection between Mary Jo's client and her mark. None at all that Mary Jo could find and she was damn good at finding things.

At first Mary Jo figured maybe balding editor guy had rejected something rich Chicago had written and she had taken the rejection personally. Mary Jo knew writers as a group could be a very nutty bunch, and if that was the reason, this guy would be dead, no problem.

Mary Jo had no issue with revenge for any reason. She considered that a valid reason to kill.

But Chicago rich woman wouldn't dare break a nail on a computer keyboard, so that hadn't been the case.

After weeks of searching and searching, Mary Jo had decided to just go ahead and do the job this morning, get it out of her mind, and then move on. After all, she was an assassin. It's what she did, what she had been hired to do now for thousands of years.

She just wished Jean, the love of her life, was still here. But two years ago Jean had left and Mary Jo missed her every day, especially with really strange jobs like this one.

Especially when it ran smack into Mary Jo's code. And that code was that she needed to know the why of the death. Revenge was fine, hatred was fine, old family debt was fine, double-crossed was fine.

Just about any human emotion was fine by Mary Jo and she had killed many over the centuries for all those reasons and more.

But here there was no reason. No connection. It was as if her client in Chicago had just picked this guy at random.

And that bothered Mary Jo.

Bothered her enough on this hot, sweaty morning to irritate her.

So she let her mark walk by on the crowded sidewalk on his way to his tiny, cluttered office on the sixteenth floor of a building just off Broadway. He would live another day.

For now, Mary Jo needed to go to Chicago.

She hated Chicago. Especially on a hot summer day.

And she hated the airport even worse.

But she had to find out why the guy she had just passed on the sidewalk needed to die.

Two

Mary Jo sat in a surprisingly comfortable over-stuffed chair in the bright living room of her Chicago client. Mary Jo was sipping on a bottle of water she had found in the massive fridge in the modern and massive kitchen that looked out over the Chicago River.

The living room she sat in now was surprisingly tastefully done in browns and tan colors, with expensive art on the back wall away from the floor-to-ceiling windows that looked out over the city and the lake beyond.

Mary Jo was surprised those windows didn't radiate heat, since it was so hot outside right now, but they seemed to be very special glass. She could be very comfortable here and that did not match at all with her research on this woman.

Mary Jo's research on the woman who lived here showed her as the classic rich bitch who stood five-six and always wore massive heels and often dressed in leopard patterns.

At that moment, the woman who lived in this surprisingly comfortable home unlocked her front door and came in. Mary Jo knew the woman would be alone, but Mary Jo had a pistol with noise suppressor in her hand on the arm of the chair, pointing at where the woman would enter the room.

Just in case.

Mary Jo had cleared the alarm and left no sign she had gotten in here, so the woman was going to be very surprised when she headed for the kitchen with her groceries.

As expected, the woman came around the corner with a bag of groceries in her hand, but she didn't even jerk when she saw Mary Jo sitting there.

Mary Jo was short, about five-two, with dark hair, a slim figure, and dark eyes. That was pretty standard build for assassins. They all seemed to be about the same height and shape and build.

This woman was also short, but with bright gold hair that was clearly fake. And green eyes that Mary Jo knew instantly. All the pictures and descriptions had this woman being five-six with brown eyes, not five-two with green eyes.

"Damn, you are as good as I remember," the woman said, not even missing a step as she headed toward the kitchen. "You want to help me put these away?"

Mary Jo could not believe any of this as she watched the woman walk past, then stood to follow her into the kitchen, leaving the gun on the arm of the chair.

"Great cover. Stunning computer work," Mary Jo said as she went into the kitchen, waited until the Chicago woman, aka Jean, put the groceries down, and then turned her around and kissed her long and hard.

And Jean kissed her back just as hard.

Damn, Mary Jo had missed Jean the last two years. More than she had wanted to admit.

Three

Mary Jo and Jean first ended up naked together in the huge master bedroom shower, then fifteen minutes later they were in Jean's massive bed. They didn't come up for air for a good hour.

And good was an understatement. Call it a great hour.

Then holding each other with the soft, cool sheets over them as they did for years in New York, they talked.

Two years before Jean had gone undercover to track down a mark that both of them were convinced somehow had connections in the Assassin's Guild. Whoever that was, they needed to clear that person out before he or she did real damage.

And they were too obvious together, becoming too well known with other assassins, so they split up and Jean vanished.

Mary Jo had kept on, living in their old place, doing jobs on her own. Missing Jean every day.

So the editor had been Jean's way of contacting Mary Jo, knowing that Mary Jo would never be able to kill the guy without first talking with the client and finding out the connection.

Mary Jo had made no progress finding the problem person in the Assassin's Guild, so that was her first question to Jean.

"Actually, yes, I found her," Jean said. "Two weeks ago. Would you like to meet her? Meet the person who caused us to be apart for two long years?"

Mary Jo just looked into the eyes of the love of her life and could see the humor, but also the seriousness there.

"I would love to," Mary Jo said.

"This way," Jean said, pulling Mary Jo out of bed and leading her back through the living room completely naked.

"This is getting me all hot," Mary Jo said, following Jean, "and not in a summer heat kind of way."

Jean laughed. "Down girl, lots of time for that."

Jean was moving down a fairly wide hallway toward what looked like a guest bedroom and suite when she stopped and touched a spot on the wall and a seamless, but very heavy and thick door recessed and silently moved to the side.

Behind the door was a thick floor-to-ceiling glass that looked bulletproof and behind the wall, naked on a concrete floor, was a woman who looked like another assassin.

Jean pointed to the walls. "Two-foot thick concrete that exists on no plan for this place or this building. Ten-inch bulletproof glass buried into the concrete on all four sides."

"How did you get her in there?"

"Glass lifts two feet into the concrete ceiling. When lowered, it seals."

The woman on the floor pushed herself to a sitting position when they came in and just sneered and shook her head. Mary Jo couldn't imagine how it smelled in that small room since there was no toilet and the woman had clearly over the time in there had used a corner as a restroom.

There was also no bed or any sign of anything else.

"Mary Jo and Jean together again," the woman said, clear contempt in her voice.

Mary Jo could tell this woman was starving and wouldn't last much longer.

"Meet Romalda," Jean said. "The Guild calls her the Black Card. They had suspected her of working against them for a century now, but it wasn't until I trapped her and spent a lot of time with truth drugs of one type or another that the Guild and I got the confirmation we needed."

Mary Jo stared at the sneering woman for a moment, then nodded.

"So this woman cost us two years apart?" Mary Jo asked.

"And we believe she worked alone," Jean said.

"Why would I work with anyone else?" Romalda asked, clearly insulted. "That shows weakness and your relationship is sick to anything normal and sanctioned by the church."

"She became a killer for the Catholic Church?" Mary Jo asked, looking at Jean. Over the centuries a number of assassins had gone that way, but not something Mary Jo had expected to hear in this modern world.

Jean just nodded.

Mary Jo put her arm around Jean and pulled her close. "Great work."

Then Mary Jo kissed Jean and she kissed back, long and hard, their naked bodies pressed together in a wonderful way.

The entire time, Romalda just sat on the concrete floor and stared at the display of love and emotion.

When Mary Jo came up for air, she smiled at Romalda and said, "You don't know what you are missing."

"You will burn in your own juices in hell," Romalda said.

"Got a hunch you are going to beat us there by a long ways," Jean said, smiling.

Then Jean turned to Mary Jo. "The Guild has given us permission to terminate her, but I have no desire to stoop to that and waste my time."

"I agree," Mary Jo said. "She seems perfectly fine in there."

"Say goodbye, Romalda," Jean said, taking Mary Jo's arm and turning her toward the door.

Mary Jo glanced over her shoulder at the panicked face of Romalda.

"Just remember," Mary Jo said, "the last image you are going to see in this world is our two naked butts."

Mary Jo and Jean both stopped, wiggled their butts at Romalda, then Jean shut off the light and the heavy door to the hallway slid closed behind them and vanished.

Mary Jo and Jean laughed all the way back to the huge bed.

Over a wonderful Chicago pizza, delivered so that they could eat it naked, Mary Jo decided that a beautiful penthouse was a great way to live through a hot summer in Chicago.

So they did, giving no thought to what was buried in the walls of the place.

Jean cancelled the contract on the poor editor, and he vanished back into obscurity.

And that fall, they moved back to their wonderful apartment in New York and the blond that Jean had been pretending to be also vanished as if she never existed.

They both loved being back in New York and together, they just fit in their apartment.

For two women in love, there was just nothing like living in the city.

A Lack of Tomorrow

A Bryant Street Story

Dean Wesley Smith

A Lack of Tomorrow

On the day the human race decided to start over, Rose Brackhahn spent until almost dark working in her vegetable garden in the backyard of her home on Bryant Street. The garden only took up about a quarter of the yard, but it felt huge to Rose's seventy-two years of a bad back and a tweaked knee. Yet she managed to keep it producing into the fall every year. She loved the fresh tomatoes, strawberries, and zucchini best of everything she grew.

It had been a warm day, but not hot. Rose wore what she called her "get dirty" clothes of jeans, a really old spaghetti-stained cotton blouse, and tennis shoes that had seen better days twenty years before. She had her regular "kick around the house" clothes waiting for her on her back porch to change into when she was done. Jeans, a cotton blouse, and nicer tennis shoes.

Rose hadn't worn a dress in maybe twenty years, since her husband Lenny had been killed in a work accident. Couldn't see much point to it. But her good ones still hung in her closet and every few years she sent them off to be cleaned just so they would always be ready if she had to wear one.

Lenny had been a handsome man in his own way. Broad shoulders from working construction and a smile that had melted her when they first met.

He was taller than her and she loved to tuck right in under his arm so he could hold her. She had brown hair like his and both of them had green eyes, which always got them comments when they went out.

He had been a gentle man and she missed him every day, talked to him at times with decisions, and dreamed about him at night, good dreams, with him smiling and them dancing.

Lenny would be proud of her garden this year, but now, her back was telling her she was done for the day, at least in the garden. She still needed to cook herself a nice dinner and there was *Jeopardy!* to watch before bed. She and Lenny loved that show and after he had died she had just continued watching it, sometimes pretending he was beside her.

She had just finished changing her clothes and washing her hands and arms when the first alert siren went off.

"Now what?" she asked out loud. The damn sirens went off far too often in this town. She remembered back when the emergency alert sirens only went off if something really serious was happening.

She went to the television and clicked it on, only to discover that something really, really serious was happening.

It seemed that Russia, about to collapse from all the sanctions imposed on it, decided the United States and Europe were to blame and managed to launch a lot of nuclear bombs. Basically Russia decided to kill itself and take the human race with it.

United States and European allies had launched a lot of rockets in return.

North Korea, taking advantage of the moment to kill itself as well, had launched a bunch of rockets at the United States. The United States and its allies were in the process of taking off the map the country formally known as North Korea.

Russia had also launched a bunch of rockets at China, so China was retaliating.

Everything seemed to be aimed at Russia or North Korea. Even China fired some big rockets at North Korea, their former alley.

Live feeds from around the world were coming in of big mushroom clouds.

"Lenny," Rose said to the room. "Looks like we have finally killed ourselves."

Rose had lived her entire life under the threat that this would happen someday. It seemed like a bad movie that it was happening now.

Rose left the television going and went into her kitchen and cooked herself a nice dinner, maybe one of the best she had had in a long time. A celebration-type dinner with a steak, potatoes, and some fresh asparagus from her garden.

Then she put it on a plate on her kitchen table and went into her bedroom and put on her best dress for the occasion.

If she had gone to a funeral, she would have worn the dress. It seemed appropriate for the funeral of the human race.

Then she poured herself and Lenny a glass of wine from a bottle she had opened for cooking a few days before.

She held her glass up in a toast. "Lenny dear, looks like I will be joining you fairly soon."

She sipped the wine and then turned the television so that she could watch the end of the modern world while she ate dinner at the kitchen table.

Things just kept going, but she still enjoyed the steak and the melted butter over the asparagus was wonderful.

She did the dishes as more and more of the world's cities just vanished right in front of cameras.

Now her home on Bryant Street was on the outskirts of Portland, Oregon, but she doubted anyone would waste a bomb on Portland unless one of the North Korean shots just got lucky.

After an hour more of watching the end of the world instead of *Jeopardy!*, she changed into night clothes and with one last look at the dying world, shut off the television and went to bed, using earplugs to block most of the sounds of the sirens.

The next morning, as usual, the sun through her bedroom window woke her up. She took out the earplugs to hear the morning birds chirping as if nothing had happened yesterday.

Maybe it hadn't, for all she knew. She was an older woman and sometimes just imagined things, like the time she imagined Lenny was beside her in bed and was comforting her.

Of course, that had been caused by a fever and she was doing fine as it was without Lenny, but not a day went by she didn't miss him.

She fixed herself her normal breakfast and then, while eating, turned the television back on.

It seemed she had not been imagining things.

All of Russia was gone, most of Europe, North Korea, and Japan. The East Coast of the United States was pretty much wiped out and there was no sign yet of any of the major leaders in Washington. All were either still in shelters or feared dead.

Southern California, San Francisco, Las Vegas, Phoenix, and Seattle were gone. As she had figured, Portland, Oregon, and a bunch of Midwest towns had been spared.

A lot of Canada and Mexico and most of the Southern Hemisphere had been spared as well except for cities in Australia and South Africa.

She watched for a bit, then decided before it got too late in the year, she needed to expand her garden. She was going to need it.

So she spent a long day in the garden, expanding it and planting potatoes and more tomatoes.

Then she went inside and spent the early evening doing an inventory of her pantry. Luckily she had many jars of peanut butter and many, many boxes of crackers, one of her favorite snacks. With the veggies from her garden, she could make it a while until things started to rebuild.

She watched the television again as the newscasters tried to make sense of everything that had happened. Rose knew there was no sense to be made of it, but it would have helped if Lenny had been there to talk her through some of it.

So she shut off the television and took her sore body to bed.

Every day she worked in her garden and planned for a winter without heat and things like that, whatever she could think of.

Then on the fifth day there was no sun, just a dark, black cloud and the people on the television warned everyone to stay inside.

So she did. She had all of her blinds down and her curtains drawn, so she turned on a light over her favorite reading chair and took a book that she had been wanting to read from the shelf of books in her living room and spent the afternoon resting her back and sore knee and just reading.

Turned out to be one of the most pleasant days she had had in a long time.

The next day, as was normal for Portland, Oregon, it rained and the gutters ran black with the soot from the sky. The television said it was dangerous stuff from all the bombs over Russia and China and North Korea.

It rained for two more days and everything outside Rose's windows turned black.

As did her treasured garden.

It was almost as if she could see the plants wither and just die when covered with the black soot from the sky.

It seemed from the television that all of Portland and the rest of the United States was covered in thick, deadly radiation. Unless they were underground, no one would survive.

"Not long now, Lenny," she said. "I'll be joining you."

Civilization and a lot of the human race would die. But the scientists said that there would be survivors and that the human race in a thousand years would rebuild.

Rose just shrugged.

She had, after her husband's sudden death, come to grips with both living alone and dying alone. It was just what she did. Bombs or cancer or a bad heart. She had always known something was going to take her on to the next world.

Too bad the rest of humanity had to go with her.

After two more weeks of keeping herself distracted by reading, Rose really missed the fresh vegetables from her garden, but even with more rain, the clouds never left and everything stayed black.

And it was getting colder at night, but so far the power was still on and newscasters were still at the television station, so she watched them some each day. She figured they were being brave and doing their jobs, so she owed them some of her time, even though they didn't have nice things to say about the future and at times broke down into tears themselves.

She hadn't cried. She was going to see Lenny again.

In another week she was down to eating peanut butter and crackers and not a lot of those. She had no idea why she wanted to stay alive longer, but she knew if she took the easy way out, Lenny would be disappointed in her.

She had opened her blinds during the gray days and had seen no one moving at all outside. Not even any tire tracks in the black mud on the streets.

Where would anyone go?

Covered in black mud and dust, the Bryant Street homes looked more Art Deco than anything. Weird and kind of pretty at the same time.

Two weeks later the black clouds had not lifted. Rose had run out of food two days before and just about the time she ran out of food, the power went out.

Her house, without heat, got amazingly cold very quickly, even though it was the middle of the summer. The people on the television before they quit called this a nuclear winter. Rose didn't remember it being this cold ever, even in the middle of the winter in Portland.

And Rose had developed a number of nasty sores on her arms and legs that the news people said everyone would get from the radiation poisoning.

Rose could feel herself slipping away on the second day without power. She was covered in blankets and shivering and the hunger pains had just about vanished since she had nothing to eat at all in days. Just water, but the glass of water on the table beside her had frozen while she slept.

"Well, it was a fun run," she said to her home, a home she had loved on a street she had loved. "Thanks!"

Then she just pulled the blankets and quilts up tight under her chin and closed her eyes. "Hey, Lenny. Here I come and you had damn well better be ready."

Matchbox Agenda

Dean Wesley Smith

Matchbox Agenda

THE SOUNDS of the crowded Denny's Restaurant faded around him as Ben Trager stared at the little red box with the black stripes on both sides. The cardboard box held his entire life.

One match his luck, another his loves, another his actions. Everything his future held, all bundled up in the dark in nice neat rows. Each match facing the same direction, each match having the same potential, each match promising the same opportunities.

This morning he had felt like one of the matches: Wooden, explosive, and ready to burn up at any moment. But unlike his real life before now, the matchbox was full, giving his life a newness, a freshness he could have only dreamed of a few minutes before.

This morning, when leaving his four-bedroom home in Stevens Heights, his life had basically been over. His future was clouded and meaningless. He had nowhere to go, no place to be, nothing he wanted to do.

He and his wife had argued again, he had hit her again. His two teen-aged children hated him for good reason, he hated his job, and he hated himself for hitting his wife and messing up his life so completely.

He had driven around, lost, directionless, until he saw a Denny's

Restaurant. He had pulled in and got out of his van, standing there staring at the newspapers in their dispensers trying to decide if he should go in and eat or not. It didn't seem to matter either way.

How could he, a man with a good college degree and wonderful potential fifteen years before, end up like this? Where had he gone wrong, what had he missed, how could he have been so stupid?

Then, as he stood there, staring at nothing but a blank future, a man coming out of the restaurant asked if Ben needed some matches.

Ben had only shrugged. He wasn't even thinking clear enough to tell the man he didn't smoke.

The guy tossed him the box of matches hitting Ben in the chest. "Decided to give up smoking while having breakfast," the guy said, shaking his head. "No smoking, no matches."

With that the man walked off leaving Ben standing there holding the box of unused matches from a man who had made a decent choice about life.

It wasn't until Ben sat down inside that he understood that his future had been given to him. He had been tossed the secret to putting his life in order.

He turned the box over and over in his hands, not even daring to set it down on the Formica-topped table. The sounds of the wooden matches inside were reminders of all the possibilities ahead. He could either start something fresh and growing, or sputter out useless and spent. It would be up to him.

The damn box held his life.

What was he going to do with it?

"You going to play with those things all mornin'?" the waitress asked, putting a large glass of water in front of him. "Or you want some breakfast?"

Ben placed the matchbox carefully down on the table and glanced up at her. She was early forties, about his age, with a wonderful, welcoming smile. She had on a blue uniform, a blue hat that sat slightly tipped on her blonde hair, and rings on every finger but the important one. The empty skin of that finger glared at him as she held her order pad and waited for him to move.

He smiled back at her and managed to not glance down at her chest any farther than her name badge. "Jenny," he said. "Nice name."

Her smile got even larger. "Thanks."

Today, with a new life in front of him laid out in the box, he knew that everything was possible again. Even good sex.

Of course, he had his future in the box, she had her life stretched out ahead in order tickets hung on a swirling ring that took her life into the kitchen and then sent it back, burnt and overcooked.

But who knew what might happen with a carefully chosen match.

"Bacon and eggs, eggs over easy, bacon crisp, wheat toast light."

"Drink?"

"Small orange juice," he said.

She raised an eyebrow as she wrote that, then gave him a large smile and turned away.

The orange juice had been the perfect touch. Had he given her the hint that her ringless finger needed? He doubted his marriage could be saved, not with his past actions, so it sure wouldn't hurt him to start thinking of other chances.

Wow, what a difference a box of matches and a future could make, and he hadn't even used up a match yet.

He took off his overcoat and adjusted his tie. If he was going to keep his job with the county auditors much longer he was going to have to shape up there as well. No doubt that would take a match or two.

Wait. Was that worth it? Or should he use a few of the matches to find a new job, one that he would like to do. Suddenly the possibilities were endless, and he loved that feeling. It felt young, healthy, vibrant.

He picked up the box and rattled it carefully, not wanting to damage any of his future chances. The morning felt brighter, some of the weight was lifting off his shoulders.

He took a deep breath and kept staring at the matches as the waitress placed his orange juice on the table, smiled at him again, and left.

Good contact, no wasted match.

He slowly opened the box and looked at the neat row of sticks there with their bulging ends. One match seemed to stand out more than any other, and he touched it with one finger, then picked it out of the box.

He slid the box closed and put it on the table, staring at the one match. Such a simple little thing to have such possibilities.

It could light a cigarette for a man who would die of cancer.

It could start a camp fire to keep a family warm on a camping trip.

It could light a gas stove to feed hungry children.

It could start a raging forest fire.

For him it could do so much more. This box held his plans for the future.

He held the match between his thumb and index finger of his left hand. The first thing he needed to do was settle the situation left over at home.

One match in one hand.

One problem to fix.

He pulled out his cell phone with his right hand and punched in the number for home.

The phone rang until the machine picked it up. He didn't blame Gloria for not answering, if she was even still there. More than likely she had already left, going who knew where.

When the message machine came on he said calmly, "I know you understand I am sorry for what happened this morning, but sorry is no longer enough. This afternoon I will find a counselor who will take me on an emergency basis, and I will check myself into a hotel until I can be sure I will never strike another woman again. If I have to check myself into a hospital, I will solve this problem. I know this will take time. I don't expect you to forgive me or even help me. I'll call you tonight to let you know where I am."

He clicked off the cell phone, surprised at the words that had come out of his mouth. He had always been adverse to counseling.

The last flame of the match burnt his finger slightly and went out.

He stared at it the burnt remains, shocked at those as well. He didn't remember lighting that match. Yet the burnt smell of sulfur mixed with the smell of coffee and bacon as a faint wisp of smoke vanished into the air.

"Hey, no smoking in here," the waitress said, sliding his plate of food in front of him, then almost dropping the smaller plate covered in toast.

"Not smoking," he said, smiling at her. "Sorry about that. Didn't mean to light it." He pushed the last of the burnt match away.

She smiled and winked. "No more accidents, honey," she said, putting her hand on his shoulder. She turned away, letting her hand linger a fraction of a second longer than it should.

He watched her walk, her ass moving in a very fine fashion under the tight uniform. There, in that blue uniform, was a future that might be fun exploring.

He stared at the matchbox. He had used a match, a possibility in his new future, and it felt good to be on the right road. No matter what happened at home, or with this waitress, or any other woman, he would never allow his temper to run loose again. He would find a way to control it. The match had made sure of that.

He dug into the eggs, hash browns, and crisp, perfectly cooked, bacon, staring at the box of matches in front of his plate while he ate. To have a future again felt so wonderful he wanted to just shout to the world.

About halfway through the eggs he opened the box so that he could stare at the pile of matches, and all the possibilities laid out there in neat rows.

His hopes.

His dreams.

A saved marriage, a better job, a new house, more money, respect for himself. All of those things were there, one match after another.

For the first time in years he felt less angry about everything.

He finished his eggs, crunched on the wonderful taste of the last piece of bacon, then washed it all down with the orange juice. Perfect breakfast for a day of major life changes.

"Done?" the waitress asked, appearing at his shoulder and reaching for his plate.

"Just beginning," he said, smiling up her. If she could only see all his dreams and hopes and roads to travel, she would screw his eyes out tonight.

She was smiling at him, not looking at the table, when he said "Just beginning."

She stopped suddenly, the plate halfway off the table, then went to put it back down, clearly thinking he meant that he wasn't done with breakfast.

But she wasn't looking at the plate, but instead into his eyes.

The edge of the plate hit the large glass of water and tipped it over, pouring the water into the open box of matches, washing away everything in a pool of ruin.

"Shit, shit, shit!" she said, tossing a dirty towel she had with her into the puddle of water. "Sorry, I'll get some more towels."

She turned to the counter as he just sat there, the water dripping coldly onto his suit pants and down into his crotch.

He didn't even shout, he didn't cry, he didn't even move.

He just sat there starting at his water-soaked, scattered future, ruined on the table.

The room grew dark as his anger flooded back.

Clumsy bitch had ruined everything.

The waitress grabbed a few towels behind the counter and headed back his way.

He wanted to hit her, break her damn neck.

He didn't dare let his anger come out at her. Not here, not now.

He stood, took out his wallet, and put twenty bucks into the puddle. Then he turned, leaving his future on the table, and walked out the door.

By the time he reached the sidewalk outside, he could barely move his feet. He felt as if he were walking in quicksand, the anger gone as quickly as it had come.

Nothing mattered anymore.

He had hit his wife.

His children hated him.

He was about to lose his job.

He hated himself.

There had been enough matches in that box to help him, but he had let those chances be wasted as well by flirting with a woman instead of paying attention to what mattered.

His entire life was a waste.

He climbed inside his van, put the keys in the ignition, but didn't start the car.

He couldn't think of any reason to start the car. He had nowhere to go.

So instead he just sat there, staring blankly ahead, a man with no future.

No hope.

No matches.

Dead Even

A Poker Boy Story

Dean Wesley Smith

Dead Even

Bob showed up in the poker room at Spirit Winds Casino on Christmas Eve. Bob, like his name, was a very short man. I guessed he came up to my shoulder at best, even with heels on his boots. It's always interesting to me how names fit people. Bob fit Bob perfectly.

His black hair was short, the nails on his fingers were trimmed short, and even his nose was short. He wore a golf shirt that seemed a size too small, and brown slacks that covered brown dress shoes. He did not have the appearance of having money, but over the years I have come to not trust appearances very much, since I look like a slob most of the time, yet I have money and am a super hero.

In looks, I am, for lack of a better way of putting it, the cliché white male. I'm six feet tall, have brown hair that's graying slightly at the temples, and green eyes. Bob was the cliché short man who walked quick, talked quick, and had a flaring temper that might go off with just a wrong remark, or more likely, a bad beat at the table.

Cliché meet cliché.

Bob took every turn of the cards as if it was more than just a bad beat. He seemed to take it as an affront to his height. A ten would hit the table to give someone else a pair of tens to beat his pocket nines, and he acted if someone had just called him a runt.

It was a guaranteed way to lose money at a poker table.

Bad beats at poker tables are when a person thinks they should win, but the cards at the end of the hand say otherwise. Every poker player I know tells bad beat stories about how his pocket aces were beaten by jack/ten suited. Bad beats are the nature of poker, and I put them on people as often as people put them on me, so I pay no attention. Someone starts into a bad beat story and I just nod and think about what I'm planning on having for dinner.

All night long Bob kept complaining, and then continuing to play. He wasn't a bad player, but he wasn't a good one either. He knew just enough to think he was the best, and just enough to think he knew what he was doing, and just enough to think he could beat me and the rest of the group at the table. Of course he was wrong on all three counts. And he complained about it bitterly.

Clearly short Bob was not a happy man, either in poker or in life.

The turning point of the evening came when Bob had aces beat twenty minutes before midnight on Christmas Eve. He stared at the aces, then at the winning flush a guy named Carl had drawn into, then at the dealer, and for a moment I thought he was going to punch the dealer.

Now understand, during the evening so far, he had lost upwards of three grand in just under five hours, with about half of it sitting safely in the stack of chips in front of me. However, it was not my flush that had just put the bad beat on his aces.

I'm Poker Boy, and Christmas Eve or not, I played fair, and if someone wanted to give me their money across a poker table, I took it. There is no Santa in a poker game, but good old short Bob sure wanted to give me his money, so I was thinking kindly of him at that moment, even with him yelling at the dealer and complaining all the time.

I'm not sure yelling describes what Bob was actually doing. He was ranting, screaming, shouting, and even foaming at the mouth a little. He had stood up and was even leaning over the table. For a tall man, this might have been threatening. For Bob, it made no difference.

The rake, a guy named Henry, watches over the dealers in a poker room. Henry came over and asked Bob to calm down. All the while the dealer named Scooter just sat there, staring ahead, ignoring Bob's ranting and shouting and carrying on.

"I'm not going to calm down!" Bob shouted.

At this point, Krissy, the room manager on duty showed up at the table. She was about Bob's height, with long blonde hair and a smile that could fill a room.

Scooter kept ignoring Bob, shuffled up, and got ready to deal the next hand.

"What's the problem?" Krissy asked Bob, as if she didn't know exactly what the problem was.

"Your dealer's cheatin' me!" Bob turned and shouted right into her face. Then he stepped toward her.

I just sat there watching. These situations were not the things that Poker Boy got involved with. My job was to save helpless people and dogs, not stop idiots from making fools of themselves.

Besides, Krissy was one tough broad who had many different colored belts from different martial arts disciplines. If Bob was stupid enough to take a swing at Krissy, he would be lucky to see it turn Christmas day.

"Our dealers do not cheat, sir," Krissy said, her voice low and level as she spoke right into Bob's face. "And we have cameras to make sure they don't."

"I don't care about no damned cameras!" Bob shouted. "For all I know, the dealer and the camera man are in this together."

I glanced around at the other seven players on the table. All of us had some of this idiot's money. Did he think we were all in on his great conspiracy as well? Of course, I didn't say that. Instead the rest of us just sat there as if nothing was happening, staring at either our hands, the felt tabletop, or the wall beyond the table. The number one rule when there's a problem at a poker table was to stay out of it.

"I think maybe a little walk might calm you down," Krissy said, moving to take Bob's elbow and turn him from the table.

"I don't need a walk!" Bob shouted, his face really red.

The next chain of events happened quickly.

Bob went to shove Krissy aside.

Krissy grabbed Bob's arm.

Bob tried to push Krissy.

Krissy moved a step out of the way, grabbing Bob in such a way that the man sort of lifted off the ground using his own forward motion, flew through the air with Krissy still holding on, and then came down flat, face first, on the empty table beside the one we were playing on.

Krissy now held Bob's arm behind his back with one hand and the back of his neck with the other, acting as if she had to do this every day.

Bob kicked for a moment trying to break free, but it looked like with each kick, he hurt himself, so he stopped.

Man, I was going to have to get to know Krissy better. She might come in handy as a sidekick on some of my adventures. Sure, I had super powers and all that, but sometimes a good hand-to-hand fighting master could beat a super power in the clinch.

"Deal this man out," Krissy said. She didn't seem excited or even winded. "And cash in his chips and give him his money."

Henry, the rake, moved to take what was left of Bob's chips. More than likely his anger had just saved him the last of his money.

A moment later, two large security men came in the poker room door, handcuffed Bob, and started to lead him away, with Henry carrying Bob's money right behind.

"Wait!" Bob shouted. "I have to stay. I have to win enough!"

Suddenly my Poker Boy alarm went off. I sometimes call this alarm my Ultra-Intuition Power. And right now that power was telling me in no uncertain terms that Bob needed my help, and not to escape the security guards.

I got up, leaving my chips on the table, and followed Bob, the guards, and Henry the rake. It felt as if we were having a little parade as the crowds parted to let us through.

The two large security men, with Bob walking between them like a small child being escorted to the principal's office, headed for the front door of the casino. When they had him safely out on the sidewalk and the handcuffs off, Henry gave Bob the remaining money and went back inside.

"Please don't return to this casino, sir," one big guard said.

"You're lucky Krissy's not going to press charges against you," the other said.

Bob just nodded, standing there in the cold evening air, the last of his money in his hand. He looked to be completely in shock and beaten, as if his world had just ended. Clearly he must have been playing poker with scared money, and the worst way to ever play poker is with scared money.

Scared money means the money you are using is not money you can afford to lose. You never gamble with rent or food or car payment money. Never. Ever. Only gamblers with problems do that.

"Where's your car, Bob?" I asked, stepping up between him and the guards and taking his arm. I turned him gently toward the closest parking lot.

"Around on the other side of the building," Bob said.

"I'll walk you," I said, glad I always wore my black leather coat and Fedora-like hat when playing, since we were going to have to go around the building and it was a cold Christmas Eve. It wasn't snowing or anything, but it felt cold enough to.

We walked in silence for a hundred yards or so, then finally Bob said softly, "I knew better."

"I know you did," I said. "How much did you need to win?"

"Six over the top of the four I had," he said, without looking at me.

We kept walking in silence, our breathing making frost waves ahead of us in the parking lot lights.

Now a couple times a year I have nights in live games where I win far over six thousand. And I've won numbers of tournaments with payouts a great distance over six thousand. But I doubted Bob had ever won that much in a casino, so whatever had made him try this stupidity on Christmas Eve had to be very important to him.

I clicked on my special Empathy Power.

To be honest, I just don't know what else to call the power. It makes people believe they can tell me anything, trust me with their very lives. And sometimes they do. But Empathy is the wrong name for it, but Trust Me Power just doesn't sound right. And neither does Make Them Talk Power. I'd figure it out some day.

With my Empathy Super Power on, I asked the next question. "Bob, what did you need the money for?"

Bob glanced at me. "What do you care?"

I notched up my Empathy Power. Little Bob needed a big dose. "Trust me, I care," I said, staring right at him to focus the strength.

He shrugged. "You wouldn't believe me if I told you."

I turned up the Empathy Power to the top of my capabilities and focused it at him like I was staring at a fly. Bob stood no chance. He was going to tell me.

"You would be surprised what I would *believe,*" I said.

He shrugged. "I wanted to die even."

Now, of all the reasons he could have told me why he wanted ten thousand dollars, that was not one I expected. I wouldn't have been surprised at his daughter needing an operation, or his needing to replace money he took from his wife to bet on the horses, or maybe even he needed to buy a girlfriend a new sports car.

"You're going to have to explain that one," I said, keeping my Empathy Power cranked up.

"Christmas morning at six-ten," Bob said, his voice level and matter-of-fact. "Not long from now, actually, I'm going to die."

"And how do you know that?" I asked, even more stunned.

"I told you that you wouldn't believe me."

"Oh, I believe you," I said. "I'm just wondering how you know, or are you planning this exit from the here-and-now."

I really didn't want to spend Christmas Eve babysitting a short guy who wanted to kill himself because his life sucked and he was a bad poker player. I would do it to save his life, but I didn't want to.

He laughed, the sound echoing over the frost-covered cars as we headed down a row, clearly getting closer to his car.

"Not planning a thing," he said. "In fact, I wish I could stay around long enough to learn how to play poker like you do."

"But, you're not?" I said, ignoring his compliment.

"Nope." He glanced at his watch. "About six hours from now I'll be as dead as they come. I just know it, like I know the sun is going to come up tomorrow, and the tide is going to change. Call it a special power of mine. Most people never understand that I get these feelings about things, so a long time ago I quit telling people."

I knew that feeling. I dropped my Empathy Power and focused another of my super powers on him to see if he was telling me the truth.

After a moment I realized he seemed to be.

"All right," I said, "I buy that you think you're going to die in about six hours. And you need the ten grand to pay off one last debt?"

"Naw," he said. "Actually I got a bunch of money in stocks, good equity in my house, and both cars paid off. But when I add up the worth of everything, now that the market is down, the balance owed on my house is ten thousand over what I got in assets. I wanted to leave this life even, just like I came in. It seems that's too much to ask, isn't it?"

Again he laughed and stopped beside a late model SUV. For such a little guy, he sure drove a big, expensive car.

"You got a wife and kids?" I asked, still not completely clear on why this guy wanted ten thousand.

"Sure do," Bob said, smiling. "She's back in Minnesota visiting family, and both my kids are grown and married. They are both with their spouse's families this year."

"They left you alone?"

"I wanted them to," he said. "I sort of set it up, and let me tell you, it took some convincing. But I figured why have them hanging around when this heart of mine lets go? It's going to be hard enough on them as it is."

I nodded, not knowing exactly what to say. Either they watched him die, or they got a phone call saying that he was dead. I honestly didn't know which was worse either. But Bob clearly knew for him and his family, and I gave him that.

"Well, it was good playing cards with you," Bob said. "A real pleasure to get beaten by one of the best."

He beeped his SUV unlocked and opened the big door, getting ready to climb inside. I couldn't just let him go off like this, especially since I knew he was telling the truth.

"Bob, wait," I said. "I'm a gambling man, I'll make you a wager. How much do you have left?"

He reached into his pocket and pulled out the bills Henry had given him, made a quick count. "About a grand."

"All right, I'll give you ten to one odds you don't die this morning. If you do, you have ten thousand from me and go out even, if you don't, I get your thousand."

He stared at me for the longest time. Then he asked, "Why would you do that?"

I shrugged. "I'm a gambler. It sounds like a safe way to get that last thousand of yours, since you won't give it to me at the table."

An aside. Actually, I'm not a gambler. In fact, I never play if I don't have what's called "the-best-of-it." I never bet slots, or any other house game where the odds are in favor of the house. I am a poker player, and in poker, skill is everything. And since I'm one of the best in the country, I usually get the best of other people.

But tonight, I placed a bet to help someone.

Again he sort of stared at me for a moment. Then he said, "You're not kidding, are you?"

"Nope," I said. I dug into my pocket and brought out a roll of bills and counted off ten big ones.

I usually carry about twenty thousand in cash on me when I'm headed into a poker room. Then, no matter the size of the game I find, I can handle the buy-in. It never occurs to me that most people would be scared to death walking around with that much cash. I'm a super hero, so I don't have a lot of worries about getting mugged.

"Give me your card," I said.

I figured him for a businessman, and every businessman I knew had a card, and he was no exception.

He dug it out of his wallet and handed it to me.

"Robert Day," I said. "Portland, Oregon. That's you and a current phone number?"

"It is," he said, nodding.

"And this is your car?" I asked.

"It is," he said.

I went around back and recorded the license plate number of the big SUV, then moved back to where he stood.

"Here's the deal," I said, talking quick so he didn't have a chance to say anything. "I give you the ten thousand right now. You go home, do what you had planned on doing tonight, and if you're dead in the morning, the money is yours. If your fear is wrong, and you live through the morning, you come back here tomorrow night at eight and give me my ten grand back, plus one thousand of your own money."

He sort of stood there, his mouth open.

I knew I was just giving him the money. This was the biggest sham bet ever come up with, and I was doing my best to sell it to him. But I knew I had lost the ten big ones if he took this, and I didn't care.

An aside. Bob was a real jerk, of that I had no doubt, but he was a jerk who needed my help, and just because someone was a jerk, that didn't mean I shouldn't help that jerk.

I held up the card and smiled. "I know where you live. And I figure I can trust you. Just don't go offing yourself to win this."

At that he laughed. "Are you kidding? I'd love to come back here tomorrow, give you your money and a thousand, and buy you a drink. If they let me back in the casino, that is."

"I'll set it up so they will," I said. "But I doubt they're going to let you play poker for a while."

"Not a problem there," he said, laughing. "I needed my head examined to go up against the likes of you and the others at that table."

"So do we have a bet?" I asked, still shoving my sham bet, which was the only way I knew how to help him.

He again looked at me for the longest time. I had long ago turned off my Empathy Power, and I can't read minds, so I had no idea why he just sort of stared at me.

Then he stuck out his hand. "We have a bet."

His handshake was firm and quick, as you would expect from someone who moved and acted like Bob.

I handed him the ten thousand.

He handed me back one thousand of it. "Nine-to-one odds," he said. "I only need ten thousand total to be even in life, and I have one thousand already."

"Even better," I said.

Did I mention I wasn't a gambler? I could figure the math of a poker hand to exact figures, but a sham bet like this one, I had no clue.

"Thanks," he said, staring at the money. "I don't know why this is so important to me. Seems silly, actually, now that I think about it. No one's going to care that I went out even except me, and I'll be dead."

"Just make sure you're back here tomorrow night with my money. My nine and your grand. I'm going to collect on that drink as well."

"If I'm alive, I'll be here," he said. "Thank you."

With that he got into his big SUV and started it up. He backed out, and with a blink of his lights, drove off.

I went back inside, got myself a large mug of hot chocolate to cut the chill, and went back to the table. I had just given a guy nine thousand dollars to make him feel better during the last few hours of his life. I had no doubt he was going to die, just as he said he would. I had the same power he had, only I called my power Precog-Power.

He was going to die at the exact moment he told me he was, from a massive heart attack. Not even being in a hospital would change the result, that much I was sure of. Otherwise I would have been working to get him to one.

No, the only thing I could do for him was help him make his goal of going out the same way he came into the world: Dead even.

It cost me nine thousand, but what the hell, it was Christmas.

I waited around the next night at eight, just in case we were both wrong. He didn't show, and by midnight, in a very good game, I had won most of my money back.

His death was reported in the paper the next day, exactly as we had both known it would be.

Two weeks later, a very short man came into the casino poker room asking for me. He looked like a younger and shorter version of Bob. He handed me an envelope with nine thousand in it.

The guy looked puzzled, then said simply, "My father willed this to you. Said it had to be cash and left instructions that I was to buy you a drink after I gave it to you. And never play poker with you."

I laughed and steered Bob Junior out of the poker room and toward the bar. On the way he asked, "How well did you know my father?"

"Not that well," I said. "Played some cards with him is all, but I liked him. An honest man."

"That he was," his son said, smiling. "That he was."

The Wait

Dean Wesley Smith

The Wait

The thick smell of urine mixed with antiseptic filled the air as the nurse led us into the famous Room 341 of Hilldale Nursing Home.

Since I had heard of this room so often for so many years, I expected it to be bigger. Maybe have signs or something. But it was simply a nursing home room with one bed, a small desk, and a television.

The home of the oldest human alive.

Dan, my boss and the reporter on this story, went in first. I followed with my camera and pack, wading into the smell as if into a deep lake. I was soon over my head and finding it hard to breathe.

"Henry," the nurse said clearly as she moved around behind the old man hunched in the wheelchair. She stood there, her too-pink hands on the handles of his chair.

"You have visitors."

Henry seemed not to care.

His thin gray hair barely covered his age-spotted scalp. His wrinkled, brown hands rested on the arms of the chair and a thin line of drool came from the corner of his mouth.

His pants were thick around his waist, as if he had a diaper on under them.

He looked like he might be 100 years old.

The records had him at 185 and tomorrow was his birthday. By sixty years, the oldest human.

No one could figure what kept him alive. Some said he had been a scientist and invented a cure for death. Others said his family had been naturally long-lived. I had heard a hundred theories and had seen his picture at least a thousand times in magazines.

In all the pictures he always wore a gray sweater and gray slacks. Maybe even the same sweater and pants he had on today. I had never seen a picture of him out of the wheelchair.

I credited some of those pictures of Henry with my desire to become a photographer. Sure, they were nothing more than pictures of an old man. And I knew, if given the chance, I could get a better picture, capture the true Henry.

Now, finally, the day before Henry's 186th birthday, after two years of fighting to get permission to visit, I was going to have my chance to photograph the man who refused to die.

Dan twisted around so I could see his face, then wrinkled his nose indicating the smell. "Let's make this quick."

I nodded.

"Well, Henry," Dan said, almost shouting as he leaned over beside the old man. "Tomorrow is your birthday. How are you feeling?"

In five years of working with Dan that was the stupidest question I had heard him ask.

Even as a gun-carrying redneck, Dan was usually all right. We argued all the time and I kidded him about his flat-top haircut as much as he ribbed me about my long hair. But all in all, we made a good team. I hoped today wasn't going to be an exception to that rule.

Henry didn't even blink an eye at Dan's stupid question.

I motioned for the nurse to step back so she wouldn't be in the picture, then I knelt and focused the camera in on Henry's face as Dan struggled to think of something else to ask the oldest man alive.

The wrinkles and sunken eyes sprang into sharp focus.

My hands were shaking with the excitement. This was my big chance. If I caught just one shot right, my work would be on the cover of every major magazine and newspaper in the country.

But something wasn't right.

The picture didn't feel as it should.

I moved in closer, trying for the exact right angle.

Then Henry blinked, turned his head slightly, and looked up directly into the lens with his huge, deer-like brown eyes.

The look froze me.

No one had ever taken that picture of Henry, with his eyes wide open, the clear intelligence still there.

No one.

Yet I had seen that look hundreds of times over my years of newspaper work.

In the eyes of mothers waiting for news of their lost child.

In the eyes of convicts on death row.

In the eyes of families waiting at airports for a plane that would never arrive.

Now I could capture that look in the eyes of the oldest human alive. All I had to do was move fast.

Yet I hesitated, continued to gaze into those eyes, into year after year of waiting, year after year of nothing but a single room, a single chair.

Suddenly I knew I was looking into the face of what it truly meant to live forever.

I lowered the camera and looked at Henry directly, without aid of the lens.

I no longer needed the picture. I had the image locked in my mind.

And my nightmares.

The world didn't need to see that picture.

Henry nodded slightly, as if saying, "I understand," and went back to staring off at a spot on the floor.

Waiting.

I stood, tapped Dan on the shoulder, and shook my head.

He looked around at me. "Why?"

"No good," was all I could say as I turned and waded out of the smell into the hall.

I kept moving until I hit the fresh air and the crisp bite of mowed grass on a soft wind. The sun felt great against my skin, as if I had been in a deep freeze for hours.

Henry was waiting to die. His birthday was not a celebration. It hadn't been for decades.

His body was a prison. No matter how much I had hoped for this chance, I would not take a picture of him waiting a wait that cannot be measured.

I would not hold him alive in a picture one moment longer than he was to live.

It was the very least I could do for him.

But I so wished I could do more.

I went out to Dan's van, climbed in and opened the glove box. Dan's revolver was there. Shells were in the box beside it.

It would be so easy.

I pulled the heavy weight of the gun out into my lap. For the first time in my life, the cold feel of a gun felt right.

I could do so much for Henry if I wanted.

I could do for Henry what Henry wanted, what he waited for every day.

I was still sitting in the passenger seat, holding the unloaded gun, when Dan got to the van.

He took the heavy gun out of my hands and put it back in the glove box. Then, without a word, he drove us away from there.

I never took another picture, never froze another person in time.

Over the years that followed, no one helped Henry.

And he just kept waiting.

In The Dreams Of Many Bodies

A Bryant Street Story

Dean Wesley Smith

In The Dreams Of Many Bodies

Harry Stentz couldn't be looking at the pictures in front of him on his computer.

Those pictures simply couldn't exist.

Cindy Wilson couldn't have kids and grandkids in pictures with her on the internet. She had died thirty-four years before.

He knew that for a fact.

He had killed her.

Yet there she was, smiling at the camera.

Not possible.

He stood up from the computer in his home office and walked into the hallway of his three-bedroom ranch, trying to catch his breath. His slippers shuffled along the hardwood floor as he headed for the kitchen.

He had made a mistake this morning going onto that social media site. He knew better. Now he didn't know what to do.

He had remodeled the kitchen just two years before, putting in state-of-the-art everything. It gleamed and he had kept it shining and clean, even after he cooked a really messy meal. He went to the sink and got a glass of cold water from the tap, then went and sat down at his ornate dining room table.

His kitchen and dining area always had a way of calming him on stressful days.

He had bought the table in case he ever had guests over, but in two years now he hadn't used it for anything but sitting and staring out at his own backyard.

He didn't mind. He loved doing that. The silence was wonderful. It helped him think and plan.

The day was going to be warm and the sprinklers had just shut off, leaving the lawn glistening in the morning sun. He loved green grass and didn't mind paying to keep it green.

He also had his front lawn kept perfectly and the shrubs and flowerbeds along the front of the house always trimmed and bright with colors. He liked to have his neighbors along Bryant Street know he cared for his home.

And that care cost him a pretty penny every month, but he thought it was worth it.

Besides he worked every day in his home. He wrote novels, detective novels to be exact, all with the same detective. Fifty-two so far and they had made him nice money for thirty-two years now.

So since he worked and lived in the home, why wouldn't he care for it more than anything he had ever cared for in his life. It was his safe place, his work place, where all his secrets lay.

He lived alone.

In fact, he had lived his entire life alone once his parents had died when he was seventeen. And he had lived alone for thirty-five years in this house. He had bought it with his grandmother's inheritance money and figured it would be a perfect home base for him.

Her money had also given him enough time to write his detective series of books.

This house was his entire life.

He finished off the glass of water and stood, moving to put the glass in the dishwasher. Then he reached in under the sink and flipped a small, hidden switch there under the front lip.

He heard a faint click.

He closed the cabinet door and turned and headed into the laundry room just off of the garage. To his right was the door leading into the garage, to his left were the washer and dryer and a shelf for supplies.

Under a storage shelf behind the door into the kitchen was another small hidden switch. He flipped it and heard another small click.

Then he went to the shelf unit beside the washer and dryer and moved one bottle on the top shelf over one inch and then slid the shelf unit forward and to one side.

Behind the shelf unit was a wooden door, the same one that had always been on the stairway down to the unfinished basement since he had moved into the house.

In the first year he had hidden the basement door.

The same year he had killed Cindy Wilson.

He went down the wooden steps carefully, letting the door behind him close and the lights in the basement come up bright.

The place had a damp, moldy smell to it, a smell that made his blood race. He had torn up the concrete floor of the basement years before, leaving only a small area of concrete at the foot of the stairs.

On that small patch of concrete was a large leather recliner, worn with use. He loved to just sit in that recliner and stare out over his life's work.

The rest of the basement was open and ran the entire length of the three-bedroom house.

He stopped and stood at the edge of the dirt, looking out over the entire field of beautiful mounds, carefully shaped.

Each mound was a woman he had killed. Fifteen across the far wall under his master bedroom and his second bedroom and master bath.

A second row of fifteen closer.

A third row of fifteen even closer.

He was working on the fourth row. Seven of the fifteen possible mounds had been built.

He also had room for a fifth row. He was still fairly young. He had time.

Each mound had an identical wooden box at the head of the mound and nothing more. But the boxes gave that added detail the space needed.

He stepped out onto a well-worn path on the hard dirt between the mounds and moved to the far row and then went to the left to the very first mound in the basement.

Cindy Wilson lay there. He had buried her there.

He picked up the box at the top of the mound and opened it, pulling out a picture of Cindy Wilson and a ring and a bracelet.

It was the same Cindy Wilson he had just seen on the computer. In fact, the very picture he had in his hands had been on her internet page as what she called a "blast from the past."

She had been a long-haired blonde with a bright smile and a biting sense of humor when he had met her. He had asked her out and she had said no.

She had been nice about it, saying she already had a boyfriend, but it was sweet of him to ask.

He killed her two nights later.

She had been beautiful. He tried to kill only beautiful woman, but a few times he had strayed.

He still kept to his routine. Every woman he killed he buried under a mound in his basement, small bits from her life and a picture or two in a wooden box at the head of the mound.

He put the picture of Cindy Wilson back in the wooden box and closed it, then went back to the staircase and upstairs.

What had been online must have been false. That would teach him to never look at a social media site again.

He had known better.

He went to his office and quickly deleted all references to his presence on that site. Then he backed up all his work files twice and stored them.

Then he shut off his computer completely and unplugged it.

Three hours later he was back from the store with a brand new computer. A computer that had not been contaminated with social media and false information.

He spent the entire afternoon setting up his new computer, then headed out to a late dinner.

At dinner in a fine Italian restaurant that smelled wonderfully of garlic bread and red meat sauce, he met a beautiful black-haired woman named Gina. She waited on him and smiled like she really cared.

He found out she was twenty-six, working on saving to open her own restaurant, and was single. She found out he was a writer and really opened up to him.

He remembered every detail, as he always did.

And he even got a picture of her to remind himself of the evening. She hadn't minded at all.

She would be perfect.

Four days later, in chapter three of his new Detective Harry Stentz novel, she died.

In the basement he dug another mound, with another wooden box.

And soon after his fifty-third novel came out to praise and rave reviews, talking about how realistic it all seemed.

Our Slaying Song Tonight

Dean Wesley Smith

One

The Garden Lounge functioned like a big family room for a lot of people. Comfortable described it. Earth-tone brown carpet, old-fashioned tables and booths, and no windows to let in the troubles of the outside world. The only way in and out for the people who came for friendship and relaxation was the wooden front door.

And, on Christmas Eve, the old Wurlitzer.

The jukebox sat against the wall beside the long oak bar like a king in a place of honor. Four special crystal drinking glasses with names etched on them over the Garden Lounge logo were in a handmade glass case above the old music machine. A large fern hung from the ceiling beside the jukebox, almost seeming to protect it from the stares of the customers.

The jukebox always sat unplugged and dark. The room's music came from a stereo hidden behind the oak bar. The jukebox was decoration only, except for Christmas Eve. And even on Christmas Eve I was the only one allowed to plug it in. It was just too dangerous any other way. On this particular Christmas Eve there were only four customers to witness the third annual playing of the jukebox.

"Well, Stout?" Carl said. "Is it time?"

I glanced over at Carl. At six-two, two hundred and fifty pounds,

Carl had more muscle than two other normal men. And his hands were so huge that his friends figured that women were afraid to get near him. He had never married, never had children. He spent his interest and his energy on a thriving construction business.

The other two there at the moment were David and his wife, Elaine. David was a pilot for a major airline and only allowed himself to drink on Christmas Eve. He had been my best friend before the jukebox had taken him away two years ago and changed his life. Since he came back with his wife, Elaine, we had again become close friends.

Elaine was a beautiful woman in her early forties, with long brown hair that streamed straight down her back and bright green eyes that caused everyone to ask if she wore contacts. She loved David with every part of her soul.

"All right," I said. I guess it's time."

I moved around the end of the bar and unlocked the glass case above the jukebox, then pulled out a glass with David's name on it and another one with Carl's name. I gazed at the other two glasses and the names of Jess and Fred before closing back up the case. Jess and Fred were old friends I missed seeing. I just hoped that when they left the Garden two years ago on Christmas Eve, they found good new homes. Every year I wished they would drop in to say hi. But they didn't know I was here, or remember the Garden and the time they spent here. So far only David and Carl had found their way back.

I moved around behind the bar, washed out the glasses, and filled them with their owner's regular drinks. Bourbon and water for Carl. Rum and eggnog for David. Vodka tonic in a normal glass for Elaine. And then for me I poured myself a mug of warm eggnog without any booze and held the mug up in a toast.

"To friends," I said, "both here and apart."

"I'll drink to that," Carl said and we all raised our glasses and drank.

"Now, I said, putting my mug down on the bar and pulling out a package from beside the cooler, "for the traditional playing of the jukebox this year I have something special."

Everyone laughed. I supposed that playing a time-traveling jukebox would be considered special enough for most. But I had a hunch that I had something even more special.

I unwrapped the package and held up the record.

"So what's so unique about this?" David asked as I handed the record to him and he turned it over to read the title. "It's just *Jingle Bells*." He shrugged and handed the record to Elaine.

"Before I tell you, I need to know if any of you have any strong memories tied to this song." I first glanced at Carl.

He shook his head. "Just feelings of being a kid and having fun. Nothing strong."

"Good. How about you, Elaine?"

"Same thing as Carl. For me this song has sort of always just been there."

I looked at David and he shook his head no.

"You sure?" I asked.

"Nothing that comes to mind," he said. "Which means we aren't going anywhere. Right?"

"That's what I was hoping for," I said. "This song has just always been there for me, too. With no distinct memories attached to it."

"So what makes it so special?" Carl asked, looking at the record and then handing it back across the bar to me.

"Well, with a jukebox that can physically take a person back in time to the memory that the song brings up, wouldn't you think that the *only* record in the jukebox when I found it was special?"

"You're kidding?" Elaine said.

I shook my head. "Not kidding. Remember I told you I found the old jukebox covered in a back hall of the first bar I tried to run. Well, when I went broke and took the old jukebox out just before the bank padlocked the doors on me, this was the only record in it at the time. It was hidden in a small folder inside the back door. The record and the insides of the jukebox were so covered with dust that when I started fixing the thing up, I missed seeing this record and instead put in one of my own. That was how I discovered that the jukebox sent people back to their memories. I ended up sitting staring at Jenny, my old girlfriend.

I held up the old record and looked at it. "I have never played this record."

"Which is why you asked us about our memories with this song. You're going to play it. Right?"

I raised my mug in another toast. "That's right. And tonight, unlike some Christmas Eves in the past, I'd like my best friends to walk out the front door at the end of the night, not through a memory and a jukebox."

Everyone laughed and drank to my toast. Then I went around, opened up the jukebox, and dropped in the record.

"Ready?" I asked as I shut the top and reached to plug in the jukebox.

"Fire away," Carl said.

"You're not really expecting anything, are you?" David asked.

I shrugged. "Not really sure what to expect. I have a feeling there is something special about this record. And combined with that jukebox, your guess is as good as mine. It is curious that this was the only record in there. I assume that the jukebox's previous owner knew what it could do. This may be nothing more than the song that had memories attached to it for him or her."

"And that owner went back, changed the past, and never got to the point where he owned the jukebox in his new future. Right?"

I shrugged. "One theory. Shall I punch it up and see?"

"Why not?" David said.

So I punched E-34, the slot I had put the record in, and stepped away from the jukebox and back around behind the bar.

What did happen was something I never would have guessed.

Two

As the song started, two men shimmered into being in front of the jukebox. The jukebox had never brought anyone *to* the Garden before. Only took them away, into their past memories.

One of men was an elderly gentleman wearing an apron and carrying a towel. He had thick silver hair and a worried expression on his face. I knew immediately from the way he was dressed that he was a bartender somewhere in the late fifties or early sixties.

The other man was almost a boy, with red hair, ragged overalls that hung loose on his thin frame, and a red plaid work shirt with stained elbows. With both hands he clutched a large revolver pointed at the old bartender.

We all instantly jumped and Elaine said something about the Holy Mother. Carl started toward the scene.

"No," I said. "I don't think they're really here."

Carl stopped and we all stared.

I was right. Our movements and the sound of our voices didn't alter the scene we were watching in the slightest. It was as if we were watching them through a one-way window.

"Money!" the boy demanded, waving the gun in the direction to the right of the bartender. His voice seemed distant, almost from down a long tunnel. Yet it was clear. "Just reach into that cash box and pull out a handful."

"Nope," the bartender said, wiping his hands on the towel. "You're going to have to take it yourself if you want it. That money is my money and I ain't giving it away to no child with a gun."

"I could shoot you," the kid said, poking the gun forward at the bartender's stomach.

"But you won't," the bartender said. "will you Billy? In fact, if you give me that gun right now I might not even..."

Just then the kid...Billy...seemed to be startled by something behind him that none of us could hear. He turned and as he did the old man reached out and took hold of the gun.

"It's my daddy's gun," Billy said, fighting to pull the gun back away from the bartender. "You can't..."

The explosion seemed almost too loud for one gun.

Too loud for a vision.

Way too loud for the song playing on the jukebox.

The explosion echoed around and around the bar as we watched the bartender grab his stomach and stagger back against the jukebox. His hitting it didn't disturb the record playing Jingle Bells.

Billy just stood there, holding the gun in both hands, staring as the old bartender slid down the jukebox into a sitting position on the floor, his back against the machine. Blood flooded out from the hole in his apron, turning the white cloth dark.

As the record ended, the old bartender took a deep breath and died.

Three

The last notes of Jingle Bells echoed around above the empty booths and tables as the two figures faded from the Garden Lounge.

After the sound of the struggle and the shot, the complete silence of the empty bar seemed the loudest of all.

"Holy shit," Carl said as he sat back down on his stool and took a long drink from his glass.

"I feel like I want to be sick," David said as he too sat down heavily on his stool. Elaine's face was pure white and she just stood there staring at the jukebox as if it might explode at any moment.

I knew how David felt. My stomach was clamped up into a tight knot and my hands were shaking as I tried to get my mug to my lips to get some of the eggnog to my completely dry mouth.

I had no idea what I had expected, but it certainly wasn't a murder.

"You sure know how to throw a Christmas Eve party," Carl said.

David tried to laugh and Elaine just hiccupped and climbed back up on her stool and put her head down on the bar.

"Christmas Eves tend to be that way around here," I said. "Maybe we'll just skip it next year."

"I'll drink to that," Carl said. And did.

David also took a long swallow from his glass and looked across the bar at me, then over at the jukebox. "So now what are we going to do?"

"I know what I'm going to do." I moved quickly around the bar, pulled the plug on the jukebox and then took the record out. It felt odd touching the record, as if I was holding some person's casket. Carefully I put the record back in the bag I had kept it in all these years. I stood the bag on the back bar and went back to my friends who had been watching.

"You think it was the murder that gave the jukebox its powers?" Elaine asked, sitting up and shaking her head slightly as if it might help put away what she had just seen.

I shrugged. "I don't think so, but I really have no idea. There are electronic parts in that thing that are not in any regular jukebox. I have always thought that what that thing could do was just mechanical. Besides that record hasn't been anywhere near that jukebox since I fixed it."

"So maybe," David said, "those two...ghosts, I guess you could call them, are attached to the song. Or more likely, that record." He pointed at the bag. "And obviously the jukebox."

"But why?" Carl asked. "And how? Makes no sense."

"Maybe we should play it again," Elaine said, "even though I don't want to. Maybe we could try to stop the murder."

"I doubt we could," I said. "It looks like it happened a long time ago. I think Carl is right. This makes no sense. But does a jukebox-time-machine make sense either? Yet there it sits. I think the best thing we can do is just let the record and the machine alone until we get more information."

"I'll drink to that," Carl said and raised his glass.

"That's what you said before the floor show started," David said. "Remember?"

Carl shuddered. "I got to stop saying that."

FOUR

It took me most of the next year to dig out all the information about what we had seen that night. The murder had occurred in 1959, in a bar called Danny's in a little town in the northern part of the state. The bartender was the owner of the place, Danny Kline, and his murderer was nineteen year-old Billy Webster. Two witnesses had come in just in time to see Billy grab some money from the cash box and run out the back. They found him two days later on a bus headed south, and the trial was quick and without much doubt as to the outcome.

Initially Billy was sentenced to the gas chamber, but after four years on death row, his sentence was commuted to life in prison. It wasn't until I was reading the account in the old newspaper file about his new sentence that I decided what I would do. Maybe Elaine had been right. Maybe we should try to stop it.

Christmas Eve this year was going to be interesting again.

FIVE

For a change, I had strung Christmas lights around the bar to make it feel more festive. And I had even put up a tree in one corner so that now the bar not only smelled of smoke and stale beer, but it had a faint pine scent. I sort of enjoyed that.

"So what's the big surprise you have been hinting at this year?" Carl asked as I opened the glass case above the jukebox and pulled down two of the special glasses. "Because if it's anything like last year, I think I'm going to just head for home."

"I'll go with Carl," Elaine said. "My stomach didn't settle down for a week last year. And I've got a turkey to cook tomorrow that I'd like to taste."

I laughed and moved back to the well to make everyone their drink. "Nothing to worry about, I hope."

"Sounds threatening to me," Carl said.

I just laughed, but I think David could tell by the way he looked at me that I really was worried. Not so much worried about what I had planned working. But more about the final results. What I was going to do might give away the Garden and everything else, including our lives.

I finished making the drinks and raised my mug of eggnog in a toast. "To friends – and doing the right thing."

"I'll drink to that," Carl said, and this year everyone laughed.

I took a drink and set my mug back on the bar. "We have a special guest this Christmas Eve. He's in my office right now waiting for us to finish our toast. You've all seen him before, but none of you have met him." I smiled at their puzzled frowns and went down the bar to my office door.

"Bill, come on out."

Elaine gasped at the name and Carl said, "I'll be a son-of-a-bitch." as the balding, gray-haired Billy Webster opened the office door and walked over to my side. Twenty-eight years in prison had been hard on him. He had obvious scars and he limped slightly off his left leg. He had a beer-gut stomach and deep, sad eyes. In the two years since his parole he had worked as a janitor for the Elk's Lodge. He nodded to everyone as I did introductions.

"Stout," David said, "are you thinking what I think you are thinking?"

I nodded. "Seemed like a good idea to me."

"But if it works," David said, "and the old bartender stays alive and keeps the jukebox, then you may not be here. Did you think about that?"

I just tried to smile.

"And did you think about the chance that we would be gone, and that would mean..." He turned to look at Elaine and she nodded that she understood. It was because of the jukebox three years earlier that David had been able to go back and save her from dying in a car wreck. If the jukebox wasn't in the Garden Lounge for me to send David back, Elaine would be dead.

"But there is a real good chance it won't work out that way," I said. "And Elaine will be as alive as she is now and all of us will be right here, drinking. Besides, if we hold onto the jukebox when the song ends and the world switches, we remember the old timeline. That's how I remembered you two when you didn't come back."

"But you don't know if Elaine will stay for sure, do you?"

My stomach felt cramped and my hands were sweating. "No, I don't."

Billy cleared his throat. "I came here because you said you might be able to help me. I'm just kind of wondering what this is all about."

"It's about taking one hell of a chance," David said.

"It is at that," I said. "But not for you, Bill. The chance is ours. What we need you to do is simple. There was a song playing on a jukebox when you shot old Danny. Remember?"

Bill nodded.

I picked up the sack from the back bar and pulled out the record. "And this was the song. Right?" I held the label and title up for him to see.

Bill again nodded, this time real slowly. There was a shocked look on his face as he stared at the old record. Then he looked up at me. "How did you know? There is no way that anyone could have..."

"Too long a story to explain right now. But if you would just trust me, I think you may have a miracle handed to you this Christmas evening."

"I don't believe much in miracles," he said, still staring at the record.

"Well," I said, glancing over at where David and Elaine sat with worried expressions. "I do. So you are just going to have to trust me."

God, if I said that one more time I wasn't going to believe it either. I just wished I felt as sure of what I was doing as I sounded.

I led Bill down the bar to the jukebox, opened up the lid and put the record in its place. Then I reached around back of the jukebox and plugged it in.

The colored lights flickered on and a slight hum and the smell of burning dust came from behind the jukebox. I reached into my pocket and pulled out a quarter and handed it to Bill. "Your miracle," I said.

He looked at the quarter and then at me. "You're nuts, you know. I knew I shouldn't have come here." He started toward the front door.

"Wait," I said. "Everyone wants a chance to go back and correct their mistakes. Don't you?"

Bill stopped and turned back to face me. "Of course I do. I wished it every day for twenty-eight long years. But I ain't no fool and damned if I will be taken for one. What is done is done. And that is the way it is and should be."

"Sometimes that is the truth and sometimes not." I said. "I'm just offering you a chance to make up your own mind. Nothing more. It is up to you to take it."

"Mr. Stout, I personally think you are as crazy as they come and I met some crazy ones behind the walls." He glanced down at the quarter in his hand. "But I suppose you have got me this far, I might as well finish your damn game and let you all get your laughs."

I only hoped we would be laughing when this was over.

He moved back to the jukebox and dropped the quarter in.

"All you have to do," I said. "is punch E-34 and think about the night you killed Danny. But give us just a second."

I quickly hurried around behind the bar and slipped industrial strength ear-plugs to everyone sitting there. "Put these on and think of playing golf or snow skiing or something different when the song starts. Otherwise you'll end up back last Christmas Eve."

"No chance," Elaine said and stuffed the earplugs hard into her ears. "But are we going to see that scene again this year?"

I shrugged. "Don't know. With Bill here anything is possible, I suppose." I nodded to Bill. "Go ahead."

He shook his head in disgust and turned to the jukebox. Carefully he punched up E-34 as I did everything I could do to think about the last round of golf I played.

It worked. The only one of us who disappeared out of the bar that Christmas Eve was Bill Webster. As the song started, he blinked twice and then, with a sad frown on his face, he was gone.

And the murder scene did not show up again.

For that I was grateful.

Six

I motioned for everyone to grab their drink and move over to the jukebox. I could barely hear the song through the plugs so I watched down through the glass until the record was almost over. Then I motioned for everyone to touch the jukebox. I knew without a doubt that Billy would not kill Danny if he had a second chance. But what I didn't know was how Danny being alive would change the history of the jukebox.

If the history of the jukebox did change and I never found it in the back hallway of my first bar, would we be here now, holding onto the jukebox or not?

I didn't really know.

I tried to smile at David beside me, but he was focused on Elaine, as if his pure mental energy would keep her there. I hoped beyond hope that it would.

Carl was standing near the back of the jukebox, with one hand on the chrome and the other on his drink. As the song ended he raised his glass in a toast motion.

The air around the jukebox shimmered.

And Bill appeared.

I thought for a moment I was going to faint.

He looked over at the bar where we had been sitting and then turned around and faced our stunned faces. He had come back. How the hell had he done that?

I pulled the earplugs out as fast as I could, but David had beat me to the question. “What happened?”

Bill smiled and then laughed a low, almost mean laugh. “I shot the son-of-a-bitch again.”

“What?” was all I could manage to say as both David and Elaine backed away from him.

Again Bill laughed, only this time I could tell he was thinking back to what had just happened. “You know, Mr. Stout, I just didn’t believe you until I found myself standing there with my daddy’s big heavy gun in my hand pointed at old Danny.”

“But why did you shoot him again?” I asked. “If you knew where it would take you?”

Bill shrugged. “At first I didn’t think I would. But I kept the gun pointed at him and just sort of stood there and listened to that damn song and looked at old Danny and thought. I thought about how I had killed him the first time and about how I had paid my debt. And I thought about the little apartment I have now and my job down at the Elks Club cleaning up.”

He faced me directly. “And you know something, I’m a hell of a lot happier now than I was then. My old man was beating me all the time. I was holding Danny up for enough money to get out of town and away from my daddy and his big fists. Well, killing Danny did that for me too. It got me away from that son-of-a-bitch and his fists. He never hit me once after that.”

Carl just shook his head and I moved over to a stool and sat down.

“So you shot Danny again?” Elaine asked.

“Yes ma’am,” Bill said. “As far as I am concerned, he was dead thirty years ago, so I really wasn’t shooting anyone new or alive. But, I did remember what Stout and David here were arguing about. I remember Stout said something about that if I didn’t shoot Danny, you might die and he might lose this bar. Now that would be killing somebody new and I just couldn’t do that.”

Both Elaine and David just stared at Bill with their mouths slightly open.

Bill stepped toward me. "I'd like to thank you for a real nice gift, even though it didn't work out. Not that I pretend to understand exactly how you did it. But as they say on the TV, it is the thought that counts."

He reached out and shook my hand. "Maybe I'll stop by sometime for a drink," he said and then laughed. "But only if you promise me one thing."

I felt more lost than I had in years, so all I could do was nod.

"Promise me you won't play that song while I'm here?"

Finally his words got through the shock I had felt when I saw him reappear. I started to laugh and he joined in and so did Carl and David and Elaine.

"I'll do one better than that," I said after a moment. I stood and leaned over the jukebox and unplugged it, Then I opened the top and took out the old record and with a quick flick of the wrist smashed the record over the edge of the planter beside the jukebox.

"How's that?" I asked.

Bill laughed. "Looks as if you got yourself a new customer."

Both Elaine and David applauded and Carl said, "I'll drink to that."

It took both David and me to stop Elaine from hitting him.

TEN STORIES

BY

KRISTINE KATHRYN RUSCH

Monuments to the Dead

Kristine Kathryn Rusch

The California Perspective: Reflections On Mt. Rushmore

by
L. Emilia Sunlake

> The union of these four presidents carved on the face of the everlasting hills of South Dakota will contribute a distinctly national monument. It will be decidedly American in its conception, in its magnitude, in its meaning, and altogether worthy of our country.
>
> —Calvin Coolidge at the dedication of Mt. Rushmore in 1927

Cars crawl along Highway 16. The hot summer sun reflects off shiny bumper stickers, most plastered with the mementos of tourist travel: Sitting Bull Crystal Cave, Wall Drug, and I (heart) anything from terriers to West Virginia. The windows are open, and children lean out, trying to see magic shimmering in the heat visions on the pavement. The locals say the traffic has never been like this, that even in the height of tourist season, the cars can at least go thirty miles an hour. Kenny, the photographer, and I have been sitting in this sticky heat for most of the afternoon, moving forward a foot at a time, sharing a Diet Coke, and hoping the story will be worth the aggravation.

I have never been to the Black Hills before. Until I started writing regularly for the slick magazines, I had never been out of California, and even then my outside assignments were rare. Usually I wrote about things close to home: the history of Simi Valley, for instance, or the relationships between the Watts riot and the Rodney King riot twenty-five years later. When *American Observer* sent me to South Dakota, they asked me to write from a California perspective. What they will get is a white, middle-class, female California perspective. Despite my articles on the cultural diversity of my home state, *American Observer*—published in New York—continues to think that all Californians share the same opinions, beliefs, and outlooks.

Of course, now, sitting in bumper-to-bumper traffic in the dense heat, I feel right at home.

Kenny has brought a lunch—tuna fish—which, in the oppressive air has a rancid two-days dead odor. He eats with apparent gusto, while I sip on soda and try to peer ahead. Kenny says nothing. He is a slender man with long black hair and wide dark eyes. I chose him because he is the best photographer I have ever met, a man who can capture the heart of a moment in a single image. He also rarely speaks, a trait I usually enjoy, but one I have found annoying on this long afternoon as we wait in the trail of cars.

He sees me lean out the window for the fifth time in the last minute. "Why don't you interview some of the tourists?"

I shake my head and he goes back to his sandwich. The tourists aren't the story. The story waits for us at the end of this road, at the end of time.

~

When I think of Mount Rushmore, I think of Cary Grant clutching the lip of a stone-faced Abraham Lincoln with Eva Saint-Marie beside him, looking over her shoulder at the drop below. The movie memory has the soft fake tones of early color or perhaps early colorization—the pale blues that don't exist in the natural world, the red lipstick that is five shades too red. As a child, I wanted to go to the monument and hang off a president myself. As an adult, I disdained tourist traps, and had avoided all of them with amazing ease.

Later, I tell my husband of this, and he corrects me: Cary Grant was hanging off George Washington's forehead. Kenny disagrees: he believes Grant crawled around Teddy Roosevelt's eyes. A viewing of *North by Northwest* would settle this disagreement, but I saw the movie later, as an adult, and found the special effects not so special, and the events contrived. If Cary Grant hadn't stupidly pulled the knife from a dead man's body, there would have been no movie. The dead man, the knife, were an obvious set-up, and Grant's character fell right into the trap.

Appropriate, I think, for a Californian to have a cinematic memory of Mount Rushmore. As I study the history, however, I find it much more compelling, and frighteningly complex.

The Black Hills are as old as any geological formation in North America. They rise out of the flat lands on the Wyoming and Dakota borders, mysterious shadowy hills that are cut out of the dust. The dark pine trees made the hills look black from a distance. The Paha Sapa, or the Black Hills, were the center of the world for the surrounding tribes. They used the streams and lakes hidden by the trees; they hunted game in the wooded areas; and in the summer, the young men went to the sacred points on a four-day vision quest that would shape and focus the rest of their lives.

According to Lakota tribal legend, the hills were a reclining female figure from whose breasts flowed life. The Lakota went to the hills as a child went to its mother's arms.

In 1868, the United States government signed a treaty with the Indians, granting them "absolute and undisturbed use of the Great Sioux Reservation," which included the Black Hills. Terms of the treaty included the line, "No white person or persons shall be permitted to settle upon or occupy any portion of the territory, or without the consent of the Indians to pass through the same."

White persons have been trespassing ever since.

~

Finally I can stand the smell of tuna no longer. I push the door open on the rental car and stand. My jeans and t-shirt cling to my body—I am not used to humid heat. I walk along the edge of the highway, peering into cars, seeing pale face after pale face. Most of the tourists ignore me, but a few watch hesitantly, as they fear that I am going to pull a gun and leap into their car beside them.

Everyone knows of the troubles in the Black Hills, and most people have brought their families despite the dangers. Miracles only happen once in a lifetime.

I see no one I want to speak to until I pass a red pick-up truck. Its paint is chipped, and the frame is pocked with rust. A Native American woman sits inside, a black braid running down her back. She is dressed as I am, except that sweat does not stain her white t-shirt, and she wears heavy turquoise rings on all of her fingers.

"Excuse me," I say. "Are you heading to Mount Rushmore?"

She looks at me, her eyes hooded and dark. Two little boys sleep in the cab, their bodies propped against each other like puppies. A full jug of bottled water sits at her feet, and on the boys' side of the cab, empty pop cans line up like soldiers. "Yes," she says. Her voice is soft.

I introduce myself and explain my assignment. She does not respond, staring at me as if I am speaking in a foreign tongue. "May I talk with you for a little while?"

"No." Again, she speaks softly, but with a finality that brooks no disagreement.

I thank her for her time, shove my hands in my pockets and walk back to the car. Kenny is standing outside of it, the passenger door open. His camera is draped around his neck, reflecting sunlight, and he holds a plastic garbage bag in his hand. He is picking up litter from the roadside—smashed Pepsi cups and dirt-covered MacDonald's bags.

"Lack of respect," he says, when he sees me watching him, "shows itself in little ways."

~

Lack of respect shows itself in larger ways too: In great stone faces carved on a mother's breast; in broken treaties; in broken bodies bleeding on the snow. The indignities continue into our lifetimes—children ripped from their parents and put into schools that force them to renounce old ways; mysterious killings and harassment arrests; and enforced poverty unheard of even in our inner cities. The stories are frightening and hard to comprehend, partly because they are true. I grasp them only through books—from Dee Brown to Peter Matthiessen, from Charles A. Eastman (Ohiyesa) to Vine Deloria Jr.—and through film—from documentary to documentary (usually produced by P.C. white men), ending with *Incident at Ogala*, and from fictional accounts (starring non-natives, of course) from *Little Big Man* to *Thunderheart*.

Some so-called wise person once wrote that women have the capacity to understand all of American society: we have lived in a society dominated by white men, and so had to understand their perspective to survive; we were abused and treated as property within our own homes, having no rights and no recourse under the law, so we understand blacks, Hispanics, and Native Americans. But I stand on this road, outside a luxury car that I rented with my gold Mastercard, and I do not understand what it is like to be a defeated people, living among the victors, watching them despoil all that I value and all that I believe in.

Instead of empathy, I have white liberal guilt. When I stared across the road into the darkness of that truck cab, I felt the Native American woman's eyes assessing me. My sons sleep in beds with Ninja Turtles decorating the sheets; they wear Nikes and tear holes in their shirts on purpose. They fight over the Nintendo and the remote controls. I buy dolphin-safe tuna, and pay attention to food boycotts, but I shop in a grocery store filled with light and choices. And while I understand that the fruits of my life were purchased with the lives of people I have never met, I tell myself there is nothing I can do to change that. What is past is past.

But the past determines who we are, and it has led to this startling future.

I remember the moment with the clarity my parents have about the Kennedy assassination, the clarity my generation associates with the destruction of the space shuttle Challenger. I was waiting in my husband's Ford Bronco outside the recreation center. The early June day was hot in a California desert sort of way—the dry heat of an oven, heat that prickles but does not invade the skin. My youngest son pulled open the door and crawled in beside me, bringing with him dampness and filling the air with the scents of chlorine and institutional soap. He tossed his wet suit and towel on the floor, fastened his seatbelt and said, "Didja hear? Mount Rushmore disappeared."

I smiled at him, thinking it amazing the way ten-year-old little boy minds worked—I hadn't even realized he knew what Mount Rushmore was—and he frowned at my response.

"No, really," he said, voice squeaking with sincerity. "It did. Turn on the news."

Without waiting for me, he flicked on the radio and scanned to the all news channel.

"...not an optical illusion," a female voice was saying. "The site now resembles those early photos, taken around the turn of the century, before the work on the monument began."

Through the hour-long drive home, we heard the story again and again. No evidence of a bomb, no sign of the remains of the great stone faces. No rubble, nothing. Hollywood experts spoke about the possibilities of an illusion this grand, but all agreed that the faces would be there, behind the illusion, at least available to the sense of touch.

My hands were shaking by the time we pulled into the driveway of our modified ranch home. My son, whose assessment had gone from "pretty neat" to "kinda scary" within the space of the drive (probably from my grim and silent reaction), got out of the car without taking his suit and disappeared into the backyard to consult with his older brother.

I took the suit, and went inside, cleaning up by rote as I made my way to the bedroom we used as a library.

The quote I wanted, the quote that had been running through my mind during the entire drive, was there on page 93 of the 1972 Simon and Schuster edition of Richard Erdos' *Lame Deer: Seeker of Visions*:

> One man's shrine is another man's cemetery, except that now a few white folks are also getting tired of having to look at this big paperweight curio [Mount Rushmore]. We can't get away from it. You could make a lovely mountain into a great paperweight, but can you make it into a wild, natural mountain again? I don't think you have the know-how for that.
>
> —John Fire Lame Deer

Lame Deer went on to say that white men, who had the ability to fly to the moon, should have the know-how to take the faces off the mountain.

But no one had the ability to take the faces off overnight.

No one.

We finally reach the site around 5 p.m. Kenny has snapped three rolls of film on our approach. He began shooting about 60 miles away, the place where, they tell me, the faces were first visible. I try to envision the shots as he sees them: the open mouths, the shocked expressions. I know Kenny will capture the moment, but I also know he will be unable to capture the thing which holds me.

The sound.

The rumble of low conversation over the soft roar of car engines. The shocked tones, rising and falling like a wave on the open sea.

I see nothing ahead of me except the broad expanse of a mountain outlined in the distance. I have not seen the faces up close and personal. I cannot tell the difference. But the others can. Pheromones fill the air, and I can almost taste the excitement. It grows as we pull into the overcrowded parking lot, as we walk to the visitors center that still shows its 1940s roots.

Kenny disappears into the crowd. I walk to the first view station, and stare at a mountain, at a granite surface smooth as water-washed stone. A chill runs along my back. At the base, uniformed people with cameras and surveying equipment check the site. Other uniformed people move along the top of the mount; it appears that they have just pulled someone up on the equivalent of a window-washers pull cart.

All the faces here are white, black or Asian—non-Native. We pass the Native woman as we drove into the parking lot. Two men, wearing army fatigues and carrying rifles had stopped the truck. She was leaning out of the cab, speaking wearily to them, and Kenny made me slow as we passed. He eavesdropped in his intense way, and then nodded once.

"She will be all right," he said, and nothing more.

The hair on my arms has prickled. T.V. crews film from the edge of the parking lot. A middle aged man, his stomach parting the buttons on his short-sleeved white shirt, aims a video camera at the site. I am not a nature lover. Within minutes, I am bored with the changed mountain. Miracle, yes, but now that my eyes have confirmed it, I want to get on with the story.

Inside the visitor's center is an ancient diorama on the building of Mt. Rushmore. The huge sculpted busts of George Washington, Abraham Lincoln, Thomas Jefferson, and Theodore Roosevelt took 14 years to complete. Gutzon Borglum (Bore-glum, how appropriate) designed the monument, which was established in 1925, during our great heedless prosperity, and finished in 1941, after the Crash, the Depression and at the crest of America's involvement in World War II. The diorama makes only passing mention—in a cheerful "aren't they cute?" 1950s way—to the importance of the Mount to the Native tribes. There is no acknowledgment of the fact that when the monument was being designed, the Lakota had filed a court claim asking for financial compensation for the theft of the Black Hills. A year after the completion of the monument, the courts denied the claim. No acknowledgment of the split between native peoples that occurred when the case was revived in the 1950s—the split over financial compensation and return of the land itself.

Nor is there any mention of the bloody history of the surrounding area that continued into the 1970s with the American Indian Movement, the death of two FBI agents and an Indian on the Pine Ridge Reservation, the resulting trials, the violence that marked the decade, and the attempted take-over of the Black Hills themselves.

In the true tradition of a conquering force, of an occupying army, all mention of the on-going war has been obliterated.

But not forgotten. The army, with their rifles, are out in force. Several young boys, their lean muscled frames outlined in their black t-shirts and fatigue pants, sit at the blond wood tables. Others sit outside, rifles leaning against their chairs. We were not stopped as we entered the parking lot—Kenny claims our trunk is too small to hold a human being—but several others were.

One of the soldiers is getting himself a drink from the overworked waitress behind the counter. I stop beside him. He is only a few years older than my oldest son, and the ferocity of the soldier's clothes make him look even younger. His skin is still pockmarked with acne, his teeth crooked and yellowed from lack of care. Things have not changed from my youth. It is still the children of the poor who receive the orders to die for patriotism, valor, and the American Way.

"A lot of tension here," I say.

He takes his ice tea from the waitress and pours half a cup of sugar into it. "It'd be easier if there weren't no tourists." Then he flushes. "Sorry, lady."

I reassure him that he hasn't offended me, and I explain my purpose.

"We ain't supposed to talk to the press." He shrugs.

"I won't use your name," I say. "And it's for a magazine that won't be published for a month, maybe two months from now."

"Two months anything can happen."

True enough, which is why I have been asked to capture this moment with the vision of an outsider. I know my editor has already asked a white Dakota correspondent to write as well, and she has received confirmation that at least one Native American author will contribute an essay. In this age of cynicism, a miracle is the most important event of our time.

The boy sits at an empty table and pulls out a chair for me. His arms are thick, tanned, and covered with fine white hairs. His fingers are long, slender and ringless, his nails clean. He doesn't look at me as he speaks.

"They sent us up here right when the whole thing started," he said, "and we was told not to let no Indians up here. Some of our guys, they been combing the woods for Indians, making sure that this ain't some kind of front for some special action. I don't like it. The guys are trigger happy, and with all these tourists, I'm afraid that someone's going to do something, and get shot. We ain't going to mean for it to happen. It'll be an accident, but it'll happen just the same."

He drinks his tea in several noisy slurps, tells me a bit about his family—his father, one of the few casualties of the Gulf War, his mother remarried to a foreman of a dying assembly plant in Michigan, his sister, newly married to a career army officer, and himself, his dreams for a real life without a hand-to-mouth income when he leaves the army. He never expected to search cars at the entrance to a National Park, and the miracle makes him nervous.

"I think it's some kind of Indian trick," he says. "You know, a decoy to get us all pumped up and focused here while they attack somewhere else."

This boy, who grew up poor hundreds of miles away, and who probably never gave Native Americans a second thought, is now speaking the language of conquerors, conquerors at the end of an empire, who feel the power slipping through their fingers.

He leaves to return to his post. I speak with a few tourists, but learn nothing interesting. It is as if the Virgin Mary has appeared at Lourdes—everyone wants to be one of the first to experience the miracle. I am half-surprised no one has set up a faith healing station—a bit of granite from the holy mountain, and all ailments will be cured.

The light is turning silver with approaching twilight. My stomach is rumbling, but I do not want one of the hot dogs that has been twirling in the little case all afternoon. The oversized salted pretzels are gone, and the grill is caked with grease. The waitress herself looks faded, her dishwater blond hair slipping from its bun, her uniform covered with sweat stains and ketchup. I go to find Kenny, but cannot see him in the crowds. Finally I see him, on a path just past the parking lot, sitting beneath a scraggly pine tree, talking with an elderly man.

The elderly man's hair is white and short, but his face has a photogenic cragginess that most WASP photographers find appealing in Native Americans. As I approach, he touches Kenny's arm, then slips down the path and disappears into the growing darkness.

"Who was that?" I ask as I stop in front of Kenny. I am standing over him, looming, and the question feels like an interrogation, as if I am asking for information I do not deserve. Kenny grabs his camera and takes a picture of me. When we view it later, we will see different things: he will see the formation of light and shadow into a tired irritable woman, made more irritable by an occurrence she cannot explain or understand, and I will see the teachers from my childhood enforcing some arbitrary rule on the playground.

When he is finished, he holds out his hand and I pull him to his feet. We walk back to the car in silence, and he never answers my question.

Speculation is rife in Rapid City. The woman at the Super Eight on the Interstate hands out her opinion with the old-fashioned room keys. "They're using some new-fangled technology and trying to scare us," she says, her voice roughened by her six-pack a day habit. Wisps of smoke curl around the Mt. Rushmore mugs and the tourist brochures that fill the dark wood lobby. "They know if that monument goes away there's really no reason for folks to stop here."

She never explains who she means by "they." In this room filled with white people, surrounded by mementoes of the "Old West," the meaning of "they" is immediately clear.

As it is downtown. The stately old Victorian homes and modified farm houses attest to this city's roots. Some older buildings still stand in the center of town, dwarfed by newer hotels built to swallow the tourist trade. Usually, the locals tell me, the clientele is mixed here. Some business people show for various conventions and must fraternize with the bikers who have a convention of their own in nearby Sturgis every summer. The tourists are the most visible: with their video cameras and tow-headed children, they visit every sight available from the Geology Museum to the Sioux Indian Museum. We all check our maps and make no comment over roads named after Indian fighters like Philip Sheridan.

In a dusky bar whose owner does not want named in this "or any" article, a group of elderly men share a drink before they toddle off to their respective homes. They too have theories, and they're willing to talk with a young female reporter from California.

"You don't remember the seventies," says Terry, a loud-voiced, balding man who lives in a nearby retirement home. "Lots of young reporters like you, honey, and them AIM people, stirring up trouble. There was more guards at Rushmore than before or since. We always thought they'd blow up that monument. They hate it, you know. Say we've defaced—" (and they all laugh at the pun) "—defaced their sacred hills."

"I say they lost the wars fair and square," says Rudy. He and his wife of 45 years live in a six-bedroom Victorian house on the corner of one of the tree-lined streets. "No sense whining about it. Time they start learning to live like the rest of us."

"Always thought they would bomb that monument." Max, a former lieutenant in the Army, fought "the Japs" at Guadalcanal, a year that marked the highlight of his life. "And now they have."

"There was no bomb," says Jack, a former college professor who still wears tweed blazers with patches on the elbows. "Did you hear any explosion? Did you?"

The others don't answer. It becomes clear they have had this conversation every day since the faces disappeared. We speak a bit more, then I leave in search of other opinions. As I reach the door, Jack catches my arm.

"Young lady," he says, ushering me out into the darkness of the quiet street. "We've been living the Indian wars all our lives. It's hard to ignore when you live beside a prison camp. I'm not apologizing for my friends—but it's hard to live here, to see all that poverty, to know that we—our government—causes that devastation because the Indians—the natives—want to live their own way. It's a strange prison we've built for them. They can escape if they want to renounce everything they are."

In his voice I hear the thrum of the professor giving a lecture. "What did you teach?" I ask.

He smiles, and in the reflected glare of the bar's neon sign, I see the unlined face of the man he once was. "History," he says. "And I tell you, living here, I have learned that history is not a deep dusty thing of the past, but part of the air we breathe each and every day."

His words send a shiver through me. I thank him for his time and return to my rented car. As I drive to my hotel, I pass the Rushmore Mall—a flat late 70s creation that has sprawled to encompass other stores. The mall is closing, and hundreds of cars pull away, oblivious to the strangeness that has happened only a few miles outside the city.

By morning, the police, working in cooperation with the FBI, have captured a suspect. But they will not let any of the reporters talk with him, nor will they release his name, his race or anything else about him. They don't even specify the charges.

"How can they?" asks the reporter for *The New York Times* over an overpriced breakfast of farm-fresh eggs, thick bacon and wheat toast at a local diner. "They don't know what happened to the monument. So they charge him with making the faces disappear? Unauthorized use of magic in an un-American fashion?"

"Who says it's magic?" the CNN correspondent asks.

"You explain it," says the man from the *Wall Street Journal*. "I touched the rock face yesterday. Nothing is carved there. It feels like nothing ever was."

The reporters are spooked, and the explanations they share among themselves have the ring of mysticism. That mysticism does not reach the American people, however. On the air, in the pages of the country's respected newspapers and magazines, the talk revolves around possible technical explanations for the disappearance of the faces. Any whisper of the unexplainable and the show, the interviewee, and the story are whisked off the air.

It is as if we are afraid of things beyond our ken.

In the afternoon, I complain to Kenny that, aside from the woman in the truck and the man he talked to near the monument, I have seen no natives. The local and national native organizations have been strangely silent. National spokespeople for the organizations have arrived in Rapid City—only to disappear behind some kind of protective walls. Even people who revel in the limelight have avoided it on this occasion.

"They have no explanations either," Kenny says with such surety that I glare at him. He has been talking with the natives while I have not.

Finally he shrugs. "They have found a place in the Black Hills that is *theirs*. They believe something wonderful is about to happen."

"Take me there," I say.

He shakes his head. "I cannot. But I can bring someone to you."

Kenny drives the rental car off the Interstate, down back roads so small as to not be on the map. Old faded signs for now-defunct cafes and secret routes to the Black Hills Caverns give the area a sense of Twilight Zone mystery. Out here, the towns have names that send chills down my back, names like Mystic and Custer. Kenny leaves me at a roadside cafe that looks as if it closed when Kennedy was president. The windows are boarded up, but the door swings open to reveal a dusty room filled with rat prints and broken furniture. Someone has removed the grill and the rest of the equipment, leaving gaping holes in the sideboards, but the counter remains, a testament to what might have been a once-thriving business.

There are tables near the gravel parking lot outside. They have been wiped clean, and one bears cup rings that look to be fairly recent. The cafe may be closed, but the tables are still in use. I wipe off a bench and sit down, a little unnerved that Kenny has left me in this desolate place alone—with only a cellular phone for comfort.

The sun is hot as it rises in the sky, and I am thankful for the bit of shade provided by the building's overhang. No cars pass on this road, and I am beginning to feel as if I have reached the edge of nowhere.

I have brought my laptop, and I spend an hour making notes from the day's conversations: trying to place them in a coherent order so that this essay will make sense. It has become clearer and clearer to me that—unless I have the luck of a fictional detective—I will find no answers before my Monday deadline. I will submit only a series of impressions and guesses based on my own observations of a fleeting moment. I suppose that is why the *American Observer* hired me instead of an investigative reporter, so that I can capture this moment of mystery in my white California way.

Finally I hear the moan of a car engine, and relief loosens the tension in my shoulders. I have not, until this moment, realized how tense the quiet has made me. Sunlight glares off the car's new paint job, and the springs squeak as the wheels catch the potholes that fill the road. Kenny's face is obscured by the windshield, but as the car turns in the parking lot, I recognize his passenger as the elderly man I had seen the day before.

The car stops and I stand. Kenny gets out and leads the elderly man to me. I introduce myself and thank the man for joining us. He nods in recognition but does not give me his name. "I am here as a favor to Little Hawk," he says, nodding at Kenny. "Otherwise I would not speak to you."

Kenny is fiddling with his camera. He looks no different, and yet my vision of him has suddenly changed. We never discussed his past or mine for that matter. In California, a person either proclaims his heritage loudly or receives his privacy. I am definitely not an investigator. I did not know that my cameraman has ties in part of the Dakotas.

I close my laptop as I sit. The old man sits beside me. Silver mixes with the black hair in his braid. I have seen his face before. Later I will look it up and discover what it looked like when it was young, when he was making the news in the 1970s for his association with AIM.

I open my mouth to ask a question and he raises his hand, shaking his head slightly. Behind us, a bird chirps. A drop of sweat runs down my back.

"I know what you will ask," he says. "You want me to give you the answers. You want to know what is happening, and how we caused it."

My questions are not as blunt as that, but he has the point. I have fallen into the same trap as the locals. I am blaming the natives because I see no other explanation.

"When he gave his farewell address to the Lakota," the old man said in a ringing voice accustomed to stories, "he said, 'As a child I was taught the Supernatural Powers were powerful and could do strange things.... This was taught me by the wise men and the shamans. They taught me that I could gain their favor by being kind to my people and brave before my enemies; by telling the truth and living straight; by fighting for my people and their hunting grounds...'

"All my life we have fought, Ms. Sunlake, and we have tried to live the old path. But I was taught as a child that we had been wicked, that we were living in sin, and that we must accept Christ as our Savior, for in Him is the way.

"In Him, my people found death over a hundred years ago, at Wounded Knee. In Him, we have watched our Mother ravaged and our hunting grounds ruined. And I wish I could say that by renouncing Him and His followers we have begun this change. But I cannot."

The bird has stopped chirping. His voice echoes in the silence. Kenny's camera whirs, once, twice, and I think of the old superstition that Crazy Horse and some of the others held, that a camera stole the soul. This old man does not have that fear.

He puts out a hand and touches my arm. His knuckles are large and swollen with age. A twisted white scar runs from his wrist to his elbow. "We have heard that there are many buffalo on the Great Plain, and that the water is receding from Lake Powell. We are together now in the Hills, waiting and following the old traditions. Little Hawk has been asked to join us, but he will not."

I glance at Kenny. He is holding his camera chest high and staring at the old man, tears in his eyes. I look away.

"In our search for answers, we have forgotten that Red Cloud is right," the old man said. "*Taku Wakan* are powerful and can do strange things."

He stands and I stand with him. "But why now?" I ask. "Why not a hundred years ago? Two hundred years ago?"

The look he gives me is sad. I am still asking questions, unwilling to accept.

"Perhaps," he said, "the *Taku Wakan* know that if they wait much longer the People will be gone, and the Earth will belong to madmen." Then he nods at Kenny and they walk to the car.

"I will be back soon," Kenny says. I sit back down and try to write this meeting down in my laptop. What I cannot convey is the sense of unease with which it left me, the feeling that I have missed more than I could ever see.

~

"Why don't you go with them?" I ask Kenny as we drive back to Rapid City.

For a long time, he does not answer me. He stares straight ahead at the narrow road, the fading white lines illuminated only by his headlights. He had come for me just before dark. The mosquitoes had risen in the twilight, and I had felt that the essay and I would die together.

"I cannot believe as they do," he says. "And they need purity of belief."

"I don't understand," I say.

He sighs and pushes a long strand of hair away from his face. "He said we were raised to be ashamed of who we are. I still am. I cringe when they go through the rituals."

"What do you believe is happening at Mount Rushmore?" I keep my voice quiet, so as not to break this, the first thread of confidence he has ever shown in me.

"I'm like you," he says. His hands clutch the top of the wheel, knuckles white. "I don't care what is happening, as long as it provides emotion for my art."

~

We leave the next morning on a six a.m. flight. The plane is nearly empty. The reporters and tourists remain, since no one has any answers yet. The first suspect has been released, and another brought into custody. Specialists in every area from virtual reality to sculpture have flooded the site. Experts on Native Americans posit everything from a bombing to Coyote paying one last, great trick.

I have written everything but this, the final section. My hands shook last night as I typed in my conversation with Kenny. I am paid to observe, paid to learn, paid to be detached—but he is right. So few stories tug my own heartstrings. I won't let this one. I refuse to believe in miracles. I too want to see the experts prove that some odd technology has caused the change in the mountainside.

Yet as I lean back and try to imagine what that moment will feel like —the moment when I learn that some clever person with a hidden camera has caused the entire mess—I feel a sinking in my stomach. I want to believe in the miracle, and since I cannot, I want to have the chance to believe. I don't want anyone to take that small thing away from me.

Yet the old man's words do not fill me with comfort either. For the future he sees, the future he hopes for, has no place for me or my kind in it. Whatever has happened to the natives has happened to them, and not to me. Please God, never to me.

The sunlight has a sharp, early morning clarity. As the plane lifts off, its shadow moves like a hawk over the earth. My gaze follows the shadow, watching it move over buildings and then over the hills. As we pull up into the cloud, I gasp.

For below me, the hills have transformed into a reclining woman, her head tilted back, her knees bent, her breasts firm and high. She watches us until we disappear.

Until we leave the center of the world.

At the Crossroads

An Abracadabra Inc. Story

Kristine Kathryn Rusch

At the Crossroads

An Abracadabra Inc. Story

Ninety-seven degrees, and so humid the air felt like a live thing—a wet, disgusting, heavy live thing. Kailani stood at the edge of the curved road, the asphalt pale and gray in the heat. Just behind her, the red air-conditioned Ford Something Or Other she'd rented with Abracadabra Inc.'s money. Just ahead of her, a parking lot covered in pale blond gravel, tire tracks suggesting most people turned around here, and headed back to Greenwood proper.

Not that this wasn't part of Greenwood; it was. The oldest African-American neighborhood in the entire town. The blue-and-gold Blues Trail sign not too far from here gave a thumbnail history on this neighborhood, called Baptist Town because—the sign said—one part of the town was anchored by McKinney Chapel M. B. Church, the other part by a former cotton compress, whatever that was.

She might look like she belonged in this neighborhood—and genetically, at least, part of her did, but she was Hawaiian born and raised. Part Native Hawaiian, actually, which was what people in Honolulu focused on. Or rather, haoles in Honolulu focused on that. Here, she was just another dark face in a town filled with dark faces.

A bead of sweat ran down the side of that dark—well, golden, really—face of hers. She'd dressed for the heat. She wore a headband around her unruly curls, keeping them off her skin. Her shirt—white to reflect the sun, very thin cotton to keep her cool—was short-sleeved, so she wouldn't offend someone by wearing something too skimpy. Cargo pants—not shorts, because she had no idea what she was going to run into, and she wanted to keep her legs protected.

The only concession she made to her mission, if she could call it that, were the thick-soled athletic shoes she wore with a pair of extra thick knee socks, which were making her much too hot right now.

She'd give anything to crawl back into that car, crank up the AC, and drive as far from here as she possibly could.

But, Abracadabra had told her this was her last assignment if she didn't step up, the last full month on her contract, the last pay period before she had to give up that outrageous salary they'd been paying her for the past two years.

Failure that she was.

Couldn't handle magic any more than she could handle music.

Problem was, if she walked away from the magic career like she'd walked from the music, she would have nothing left.

Twenty-seven, and nearly out of dreams. Was that how people became bitter? Because she was edging on bitter, real fast.

A heat mirage rippled at the far edge of the parking lot, near some overgrown trees, their limbs weighted down with leaves. Back in Hawaii, she would have known what kind of trees they were, and whether they had any magical component, but here, she knew absolutely nothing about the local vegetation.

She knew damn near nothing about anything here.

Except that this parking lot sometimes held a makeshift wooden stage, and on that stage, every blues musician from Robert Johnson to Howlin' Wolf to Amos Wetterly played. She could almost hear the echoes in the air, the fast picks, the dry-as-dust voices, the sadness lurking all around her.

Behind her, a train whistle sounded, but it seemed very far away. Which wasn't possible, considering the railroad tracks weren't more than a block from this parking lot.

Baptist Town was literally on the other side of the tracks from downtown Greenwood; the railroad and the rivers cut the town into sections, and like so many towns in the South, some sections were more desirable than others.

She would have expected a high-end magic shop to be in the high-end part of Greenwood, where the expensive hotel she had chosen just to spite Abracadabra was. Supposedly, the shop was here, on this bit of land, even though she couldn't see the store at all.

As an enforcer for Abracadabra Inc., she'd gone into a hundred stores, checked their magical bona fides, made sure they weren't (or were no longer) selling evil spells. The problem of stores selling bits of dark magic was worse in Europe than it was here, or so she was told. She'd never been there, but she knew that the European model had traveled to certain parts of the U.S.

Those European-style shops were recognizable by their layout. They had tiny harmless spells up front, from almost-ineffective potions that tourists could buy to a small harmless one-time wish that could be encased in a tchotchke. In a backroom only the magical could see, actual magical items glittered in cases, ready for use by someone who knew how to wield them. And in a secret part of the shop, a part that often was restricted to customers whose family had been on a list since the dawn of time, lurked spells that were vile, dark, evil, and strange. As well as items that could be used for nefarious purposes, items that had long-standing blood magic, or terrible crippling curses.

She had never encountered those stores in Seattle, where she had been before. Seattle and the Pacific Northwest didn't have a deeply bred European heritage. The historical influences in the Pacific Northwest were Native American, Asian, and Alaskan. There was some European influence, but filtered through the white Americans who had migrated to the Northwest in the 19th century—frontier culture, which had an entirely different vibe.

The American South was different, though. It took experienced investigators and enforcers to work here, usually people born and bred here, because the history was as tangled as the history in Europe. Some seemingly innocuous blocks, like the one which held her upscale hotel downtown, looked perfectly civilized, but shimmered with hatred and old conflicts buried just beneath the surface.

Here, in this parking lot, the things beneath were not the same old conflicts and hatreds—at least as far as she could tell. She wasn't a local, and the history she knew came from books or her Blues Trail map or the silly road signs that told her less than she wanted to know.

She felt deeply out of her depth here, more than she had ever felt in the Northwest. She had asked Judson Quartermein, her handler, why they were sending her on this job. She was worried Abracadabra was sending her because they perceived her as African-American, not because of her abilities. There were a lot of African-Americans working as enforcers for Abracadabra Inc., but most of them worked in Europe, where the evil side of the magic was less personal for them, less entwined with the blood of their ancestors.

Quartermein hadn't answered that question, probably knowing that Kailani would have pulled out of the assignment if the answer had been anything approaching yes. What Quartermein had said—in email, no less—had been a fake-confused response: *But I thought you've traveled all over the South.*

Kailani had traveled the modern Southern music circuit—going from Nashville, where she felt decidedly unwelcome, to Memphis, which wasn't as influential a music community as it used to be, to New Orleans, where she had really been out of her depth, and then over to the Gulf to work the casinos in Gulfport and Biloxi.

There, as she sang night after night for a bunch of drunks feeding slot machines and ignoring her, she saw her future—not magically saw it—just projected her life forward. If she stayed a working musician, traveling from bad bar job to bad casino job to the occasional cruise ship job, maybe backup singing for someone more famous than her, then singing to drunks at midnight was as good as it got. She'd be fifty-sixty-seventy like some of the musicians who worked earlier shifts, and she would never leave those smoke-filled environs, never play for people who actually cared about anything she was doing.

All she could hope for in that circumstance was that someone would raise their head away from their cards, or stop as they staggered away from the machine that had held them in thrall, maybe caught by a good riff, or by the somewhat unique throaty alto in her voice, or by the growl she would sometimes use just to remind herself she still had it.

The other future she might have had, the one she'd been striving for since she was six and realized that she could sing better than anyone else she ever knew, was the one she'd seen older musicians have—the famous musicians, who became less famous as time went on. Even they ended up singing to drunks at midnight, unless—of course—they'd handled their money well (most of them hadn't) or wrote some memorable song and still got royalties, or hadn't really fallen in love with touring.

The difference between those midnight concerts and hers was a matter of degree. The famous performed in larger rooms. They headlined. They never got the corner bar in the back of the casino—or no real stage at all.

And the truly famous had one other curse—or at least, that was how she thought of it. They were doomed to sing the same song sets at every concert for the rest of their natural lives.

Did Aretha ever get tired of singing "R-E-S-P-E-C-T"? Did Billy Joel hate "Piano Man" as much as Kailani had come to? Did Paul McCartney wish he'd never dreamed up "Yesterday"?

She had never got the chance to ask them, although she had asked several touring bands, the ones that were assembled by the lesser lights of some famous decades-old band (the brighter light, always either dead or moving on to a solo career that had or had not worked). The members who would talk to her, and there were few, usually gave her a blank smile and a *That's our bread and butter, hon.*

But she couldn't imagine singing bread-and-butter songs for forty, fifty, sixty years.

The very idea scared her. She was a *performer*, not a writer, someone who sang other people's songs, even when claiming them as her own.

Just like she was an enforcer for Abracadabra Inc., not a creator. She didn't own the shops she was investigating. She didn't create spells. She learned them, augmented them, made them her own—yes, but only so she could do her job.

And to hear Quartermein tell it, she wasn't even doing that very well.

That heat mirage seemed bigger than it had a moment earlier, almost like a heat wall that shimmered and shifted. She squinted at it, trying to bring it into focus. She had heard about shops that were invisible to all but a few, although she had never encountered one—at least, not that she knew of.

But this store might be one. No one had told her, but then, Quartermein hadn't told her much at all. Just sent her here to investigate.

Last chance, Akani, Quartermein had written, using her last name, like he always had. She had started using his in self-defense. *Do this right, you stay with us. Screw it up, you're gone.*

If she wanted to keep her job, she had to do this right. And she didn't believe she had the skills to do this right.

Why the hell didn't they just fire her? It would have been kinder.

Maybe they needed some direct cause. This case would probably give her that.

She gripped her white shirt and fanned it away from her body. She wasn't used to this kind of humidity. Even though the sunlight was filtered through the moisture in the air, the rays still felt potent on her skin, as if she were burning up.

I'll take the job, she had written to Quartermein, *but first, tell me. Why me? Delta magic isn't something I'm familiar with.*

And that was when he had mentioned her travels all over the South. It wasn't until she stood here, outside the safety of her air-conditioned car, that she realized what she had taken as a kind of answer hadn't even risen to the standard of a non-answer.

He had hated her from the start. She had come to Abracadabra from another profession, and that wasn't common. Most enforcers had actually gone to college with a magical career in mind; most of them had studied history—mundane history, history of the non-magical—about the area where they hoped to work.

She hadn't. She had been at a disadvantage from the moment she walked into Seattle headquarters three years ago.

The heat mirage shimmered silver and purple and white, with shots of blue, like veins. The mirage was now at least six feet tall and wide as the entire parking lot.

That had to be the store, and it was revealing itself to her. The only other place that had revealed itself to her had been Seattle Headquarters itself. At the time, she had been new to Seattle and had thought the building had always been there. It was only when she walked by it with some non-magical friends that she realized others couldn't see it at all.

She took a deep breath of the cloying air, and walked across the gravel. Sweat rolled down her side, and along her back. She didn't think that sweat was because she was too hot.

The silver and white overtook the purple, although it remained, like beads of rain on a window. Then the silver and white coalesced into a sun-bleached building, one that wouldn't have looked out of place in this neighborhood, with its ancient storefronts and the shotgun houses just down the road.

She was scared. She wasn't sure she had ever been scared going into a magic shop before, not even when she knew it was selling things so dangerous they could kill with a single touch.

The blue lines formed into faded musical notes. The purple formed the roof. The name appeared in a startling yellow above the shimmering whiteness, humming and crackling like 1960s neon. *Crossroads.*

A door appeared last, recessed, with a circular glass spyhole that resembled the porthole of a ship. But old bars used to have doors like that, giving the illusion of light and openness where there was none.

As she reached the door itself, words appeared on that glass. They looked like they had been scratched in with a razor blade.

Enter at Your Own Risk

The "s" in risk was backward, and looked more like a "z."

"Being a bit dramatic, aren't we?" she said to herself.

The letters shifted and rearranged themselves.

Would you rather we said Beware All Ye Who Enter Here?

The "s" remained backward.

She stopped, half admiring the moxie. She had never seen a spell do that before.

"Bravo," she said, then put her hand on the door, and pushed it open.

She let in a trail of sunlight. Dust motes floated across an empty wooden floor, as if the building had been abandoned decades ago. She'd seen that trick before; it was designed to discourage the slightly magical, the ones who would never use their talents except accidentally, spending their lives complaining about the strange events that always happened to them.

She stepped inside, letting that wedge of sun cover her like glowing armor. The interior smelled of sawdust, old beer, and even older cigarette smoke. Through the haze, she saw tables, chairs, a few neon signs that were not lit up, and maybe, a stage.

The door slowly creaked closed, making the sunlight wedge smaller and smaller until it vanished altogether. The door finally snicked shut, and as it did, something whirred, then clicked.

It took her a moment to realize she heard the sound of a jukebox engaging. She wouldn't even have recognized the sound if it weren't for old recordings she had heard. She actually had never seen a jukebox that worked with 45s—or rather, never heard one outside of old movies.

An acoustic guitar started up, the recording scratchy and old, tuned odd—probably a 78, not a 45—the melody almost shuffle-style, riveting in its seeming simplicity, although she knew what she was hearing was much more complex than it appeared. The bass line provided the rhythm, probably with some kind of pick, and the treble sounded hand-plucked, not strummed.

She ran her thumb over her forefingers, feeling for calluses that remained, even though she hadn't played a guitar in—what?—four years? Voices rose in the background, the din of conversation in a bar, as the guitarist added a slide to his introduction.

And then the voice she expected—old, mono, not quite faithfully reproduced, but the best the technology could do at the time. Reedy and full at the same time, filled with both fear and longing, lyrics describing a man at the crossroads, looking east and west, sun going down. The song had always chilled her. Not the Cream version, with Clapton on the guitar. The original 1938 recording, done in one take, Robert Johnson with his face to the wall, singing about a man at a dividing point in his life.

"Like any song," a deep, beautiful, musical male voice said out of the gloom, "it's about whatever you want it to be. But you really shouldn't listen to the lyrics out of context of the time. Black man at an intersection of a deserted road, far from anything, as the sun goes down. Of course, he falls to his knees and prays. Prays he'll be delivered from the hell that would be coming at him in a car—white boys, enforcing sundown curfew. Left alone there at the crossroads, poor Bob, as he calls himself, just might die there."

She blinked, eyes adjusting to the darkness. She couldn't see the owner of the voice—not yet—but she knew he would reveal himself soon enough.

She hated this kind of trickery. It existed only for tourists and gave real magic a bad name.

"I'm supposed to be scared?" she asked.

"Lots of blood mixed into this land," the voice said. "That blood gives rise to the decay you can smell wherever you go."

She'd had enough. "You scare people with that? I can't hardly believe it. It's as cheesy as an old ghost story."

A spotlight appeared on the makeshift stage, giving just enough ambient light to dispel a bit of the gloom. More dust motes rose, and made her wonder what they really were. Because this showmanship was beginning to annoy her.

"It *is* an old ghost story." The voice sounded amused.

She wasn't amused. "No, it's not. It's bullshit. Next you're going tell me that Robert Johnson met the devil at that crossroads, and traded his soul for his amazing ability on the guitar. I've tried playing 'Cross Road Blues,' every guitar player has, and replicating his sound is nearly impossible. But that doesn't make it magic."

The light came up even further, revealing a tall man seated in an old wooden chair, a slender guitar near him, a pick in his hand. He wore tattered jeans over muscular legs, a T-shirt that showed his flat stomach, and loafers with no socks at all.

The epitome of magazine cool, from another era. The kind of cool that whites from that era expected of powerful black men.

She hadn't come all the way into the room. She still couldn't see clearly enough to take a step forward, and sometimes, shops like this one had booby-traps for the unwary.

She was wary.

"You don't believe that he sold his soul?" the man asked, picking up the guitar.

She snorted. "It's an insulting story, concocted by white musicologists to explain why a black man became so very talented. It's not just insulting to African-Americans, it's insulting to all musicians."

"You don't believe in sundown towns either?" the man asked, resting his powerful hands on top of the guitar.

"Oh," she said, "I believe in sundown towns. Racism takes all forms, and I think I've experienced most of them. Add in a bit of misogyny and that describes my life in a nutshell."

His right hand now gripped the guitar just under the frets as if he were considering playing it, and stopped when she spoke. She caught the slight turn of his head, so slight she doubted most people would have seen it.

But she had seen it before. In fact, she had seen it in Mississippi, in strange light. Because in some circumstances, light made her golden skin seem paler than it was.

She couldn't have passed, in a long-ago era when people of color sometimes made that choice, but it wouldn't have been her skin color that revealed her. It would have been the Pacific Islander in her features. Nothing about her face looked Old-World European.

"You thought I was white," she said with a bit of amusement in her tone. "You want me to re-enter, so you can give me the spiel for the tourist of color?"

His head went back ever so slightly, as if she had struck him.

"Nice heat mirage trick," she said. "It makes anyone who believes in magic feel special when they enter the door. I should've realized it wasn't an invisibility spell from the start, but some kind of trickery. That stupidity on the glass window should have tipped me off."

He stood. The spotlight grew even brighter, revealing the entire stage. It was covered with instruments, and furniture from a long-forgotten era—cane-backed chairs, gigantic jugs, washing boards inside old wooden barrels. Makeshift musical instruments, the kind that musicians cobbled together when they had no money in an era with no money, were scattered against the back wall. In front of those makeshift instruments, on unpainted wooden shelves, were actual instruments—battered trumpets, hand-carved fiddles, bone flutes. A bass leaned against the shelf, with mother-of-pearl inlay and some carvings on the side that Kailani had never seen before.

"You are not of this place," he said, his beautiful voice reverberating throughout the room.

"You mean the Delta?" she asked. Then she didn't wait for his response, because she knew that was what he meant. "No, I'm not. You took a quick read, figured out I wasn't from here, and guessed wrong."

Her magic was stronger than his, which surprised her. She could actually read him, knew what cards he was going to play before he played them.

He was going to use that voice of his—that magical voice—to seduce her into calm. Not that it would work. Magical sound spells, usually based on charm, rarely worked on her. That was why she could assess musicians back in the day. She could've been a producer for some label, because she would have known automatically which voices would appeal in a recording and which would appeal only in person.

So, as he started to speak, she raised the lights. The interior wasn't an old juke joint or an old bar or anything like it pretended to be. It was one of those junky antique shops that covered this part of the country. Folding tables, covered with small items, stood like sentries in front of open boxes brimming with kitsch and old newspapers and the ugliest kewpie dolls she had ever seen.

Musical instruments were scattered around an old player piano that looked like it hadn't been touched since the mid-1930s. The jugs and cane-back chairs and wooden barrels remained, the barrels filled with kazoos and harmonicas and kid-sized banjos. Old 45s, still in their sleeves, leaned against a battered coffeepot that looked like it belonged in a John Wayne western. Clothing, heaped on top of open steamer trunks, gave off the scent of mothballs—and that was what tipped her off.

The building had smelled of old beer before.

She was inside another spell, and it annoyed her.

"I want to speak to the owner," she said.

The man tilted his head, and studied her through slitted eyes. "Why?"

"What business is it of yours?" she asked.

"I don't bother her for small reasons," he said.

"Trust me," Kailani said. "This is not a small reason."

He shook his head once, as if he couldn't believe what she was asking of him, and then he vanished, leaving dust motes to swirl in the air.

She didn't touch any of the items on any of the tables, not sure what they really were. She didn't try any spells of her own either, because the magic in this place was subtle, and it had caught her twice. It might be strong enough to capture her magic as well.

A beaded curtain that Kailani hadn't seen until now pushed back and a short round woman stepped through it. Her cheeks were as round as she was and delightfully red, her hair a brown and gray frizz that was thinning on the very top, much like Kailani's paternal grandmother's had...

Kailani blinked, willed the magic away. "Stop," she said. "Stop. Let me see this place as it truly is."

Someone laughed. Kailani couldn't tell if the laughter was male or female. The woman had vanished though, along with the beaded curtain. If Kailani hadn't known any better, she would have thought she was alone in the room.

"Normally, I would ask what do you mean by *truly*," the voice said. It sounded female, but it had the same rich timbre that the male voice had had, as if the voice itself were an instrument. "But you're from Abracadabra Inc., so you believe you already know."

Kailani's spine stiffened. She wasn't supposed to identify herself, not on an early mission like this one. If anything, she should have identified herself when she came back (if she came back). But she hadn't said a word, which meant that the people here had seen through her enough to understand who she was—what she was.

Which was, most of the time, a firing offense.

"At least have the courtesy of showing me who I'm really talking to," Kailani said. "True form. I won't ask for a name."

"Ah," the voice said, "Abracadabra and its European traditions. Names are not important to us here. I'll share mine willingly. But appearances—they're supposed to be deceiving."

Kailani crossed her arms, feeling nerves jump in her stomach. She had told Quartermein that she knew nothing about the Deep South, and this proved it. She was asking all the wrong questions, believing she was dealing with one kind of magic when, in truth, she was dealing with another.

"I'll note two things," Kailani said, keeping her own voice level and maybe even slightly bored. "The first is that you have yet to share your name with me, although you just bravely said that it wouldn't matter if you did. And the second is that I know I'm still dealing with the same person. Your voice gives you away. A hell of an instrument you have there, with amazing range."

The spotlight on the stage turned orange, and a woman in a tight 1940s housedress—blue with small dots—stepped on the stage. She grabbed a feather boa off a settee that hadn't been on the stage a moment before, and wrapped the boa around her neck. Her face looked battered, but those round cheeks remained, and so did the dark eyes, the ones that had narrowed at Kailani when she first arrived.

"You are a musician," the woman said, sounding just a bit surprised.

"No," Kailani said.

"Ah, but you are. Only musicians can hear the tonal similarities in my various voices. Why would a musician give up her career to work for Abracadabra Incorporated?"

Kailani almost said, *The order is wrong; I gave up my career, then went to work for Abracadabra Inc.*, but she didn't. She didn't say any of it. She wished she hadn't thought it.

She hadn't been able to actually see what was in this place, to know if there were magical items that would channel her thoughts to the woman on the stage, or if the woman was so magical that she could hear the thoughts herself.

The woman made Kailani feel defensive, and that had to be by design.

Which meant that either Kailani or Abracadabra itself was some kind of threat.

"You're stalling," Kailani said, keeping her tone level. "I need to see the owner."

"What makes you think you aren't?" the woman asked.

"The fact that you're playing games," Kailani said.

The spotlight shut off with an audible clunk. The light that Kailani had raised vanished as well.

Then, slowly, the lights came up over the stage. No spot. Dim lighting, replicating the same smoky bar that Kailani had thought she was in before. Women in short skirts, dancer's legs crossed at the ankles, sat on the cane chairs. Men in suits a little too baggy to be modern stood behind them, hands on the women's shoulders, fedoras tipped rakishly. Music swelled, and the lights started swirling.

Another damn set piece.

Kailani had had enough. She clapped her hands together. Dust exploded outward from them, dust she had brought with her, dust that destroyed glamour.

The entire stage vanished. The walls vanished.

Sunlight filtered through an old roof, half caved in. In the distance, the whistle of a train. The air was suddenly humid and much too hot. The building itself smelled of mildew, rot, and decay.

She edged slightly to one side, so that she could see the door she had entered in. Only there was no door. Posts stood on either side, holding up what remained of the roof.

She wasn't inside a building. She was in front of the old stage. It hadn't been makeshift at all. Someone had co-opted it for the magic shop.

She did not step outside, because that might activate the glamour again. Instead, she walked around the stage to the back, saw one wooden barrel filled with brackish water, some dented beer cans, and roach clips. Guitar picks were scattered across the floor like diamonds, and beyond them, a shattered upright bass, held together only by its strings.

The upright bass was the largest instrument she had ever seen. It was pear-shaped, but it had a gigantic hole that started right beneath the violin corners near the C-bouts. The F-holes were gone, but the bridge remained, clinging to broken shards of wood as if the instrument itself would cease to exist if the strings couldn't remain taut.

She walked across the guitar picks, crouched, and made a tiny illuminate spell with her fingers. She peered through that hole, and saw an actual shop inside, small and cramped and exactly what she had initially expected.

With her left hand, she took the strings, felt cat gut—sheep intestine, really, marking the bass older than she thought—and whispered a different anti-glamour spell.

Nothing changed.

The interior of the bass was a bottle world, made from the same spell that put actual sailing ships into wine bottles. Someone had taken the entire shop, miniaturized it, and placed it inside the bass.

This was the actual magic shop.

This was Crossroads.

At some point, someone—or something—had destroyed part of the bass to attempt to get to the store.

That someone—or something—had failed.

She took a deep breath, and placed an all-purpose protect spell around herself. The spell was a common one, one she had no worries about anyone stealing, even advertently.

Then she pulled the strings aside as best she could and bent over.

She was careful not to touch the edges of the bass, because if she did, she might get trapped. The edges of the bass could snap her protect spell. She stepped inside, gingerly, her body shrinking as she placed herself inside the magic that created the bottle world.

This shop smelled of shaved wood. In the back, someone tuned a fiddle, followed by some raucous bowing across the strings. It only lasted a second, but she recognized it as the test it was meant to be—a person trying an instrument that had powers it probably shouldn't have.

Instruments hung on the walls. Most of them she recognized. Saxophones, trumpets, fiddles, guitars, flutes, trombones, and basses lined one wall. Beneath them, upright pianos, the kind you'd find in a honky-tonk. To one side, drug paraphernalia—nothing major, just bongs and roach clips and thin papers for rolling your own. Jars held all kinds of leaves, most of them a form of marijuana, but some different kinds of tobacco products.

Another wall featured the entire string family, every woodwind ever invented, and a complete brass section. The percussion instruments sat on the floor beneath them, an entire orchestra's worth of drums.

One wall was half open, revealing more rooms, some with pipe organs, others with harpsichords, still others with every form of piano imaginable. Some of the other rooms contained kalimbas, balafons, and talking drums. She saw lutes and gagakus, pi-pas and ukuleles, and hundreds upon hundreds of instruments she could not identify.

Directly in front of her, on a thin wall that leaned against another half-open door were more basses and guitars and upright pianos, along with accordions, blues harps, and an old-fashioned Fender Bass Man amp. Empty beer bottles decorated a few shelves, along with some fat hand-rolled cigarettes hanging out of ashtrays as if they'd been forgotten.

Floating across the ceiling, black-and-white images of musicians, moving fast.

"So you're not a musician, huh?" asked a woman sprawled on two kettle drums as if they were some kind of settee. She was tiny, not even five feet tall, and so thin she looked like she could act as a mallet herself.

But she was the model for the women who had been on stage earlier, with long dancer's legs, and features that were as sharp as the keys on the pianos. Her eyes were a surprising blue, her skin ebony, and her black hair unusually straight and short as the fringe on her sequined blouse.

"Musicians," she said, "are the only ones who can enter here."

This was Crossroads' secret room. The question was whether or not it was Crossroads' secret room for musical mages or whether everything in here had some evil component.

"And you can see the faces on the ceiling, can't you?" the woman asked.

Kailani studiously did not look up.

"Don't even try to lie to me," the woman said. "I saw you glance at them after you stepped inside. You're a failed musician, with broken dreams."

The woman's voice was not musical. It scratched like the opening of an old record played on a crank-up turntable.

"I can help with those dreams," the woman said.

Kailani's heart leapt. She knew that there were some musical spells, not unlike the one the legend described for Robert Johnson. But those spells weren't Delta Blues spells. They were ancient European spells, designed with a kind of Faustian air. A deal with the devil, but not one that cost a soul. Sometimes it cost ever so much more.

"I'm sure you can help," Kailani said, "but I am not here for me."

The woman snorted, sat up, and crossed those long legs at the ankle, her hands caressing the animal skin pulled tight across the top of the drum.

"Of course you're here for you," the woman said. "You wouldn't have gotten in this part of the store if you weren't here for you."

Kailani gave her a half-smile. "I'm with Abracadabra Inc., just as you surmised. Of course I got back here."

"You are the first," the woman said. "Your self-important conglomerate has tried to access our store for more than fifty years. They had to send someone with equal parts magical ability and musical ability, mixed with loss and broken dreams."

Then the woman leaned back, hands on the edge of the drum, the dress over her torso glittering with hundreds of black beads. They matched her fringed hair, making her look like she was about to leap off the drums, shimmy across a makeshift stage, and then dance with all the confidence of a Cyd Charisse.

The woman watched Kailani carefully, as if expecting a reaction.

But Kailani had learned how to keep her face impassive almost at the same time she learned to walk. The way that people (haoles) used to call her names, say horrid spiteful things, the way they believed she was worth ever so much less than their little pale-skinned children. She had experienced that from the moment she could breathe, and she had let it in.

It had trained her to watch first, respond later.

"It's the blues, honey," the woman said. "You need to have the blues to enter here."

"The blues are everywhere in this part of the Delta." Kailani knew that much. She had been here long enough to learn that. "Everyone gets the blues sometimes."

"But not everyone can channel those blues through their bones, and then give comfort to others who suffer." The woman sat up again, no longer in that near-seductive position. Now she was every school teacher Kailani had ever had.

And that made Kailani nervous.

"Our first instrument," the woman said, "is our voice. Our best instrument is our body. Everything channels through that. And you, my girl, can play the blues."

The dream Kailani had never tried. The blues were not Hawaiian. They sounded strange in a venue filled with sunlight and smelling of suntan lotion. There were other songs better suited to the islands, more powerful, with just a bit more hope.

She had never felt that hope, which was why she left. And she didn't learn blues there. She had learned jazz—nightclub jazz—which was as close as she could get.

Even traveling through the South on her first trip, she hadn't dared sing the blues. She felt like she was an outsider, trying to understand someone else's music.

Now, this woman was telling Kailani that she had the blues in her bones.

Catching her in a dream, a broken dream, a voice in her head said. *Break the glamour.*

"It's not a glamour," the woman said. "It is a gift. You are wasting yours."

Was this the kind of offer Robert Johnson had received at his crossroads? Had he actually gone to a crossroads? Met someone memorable and magical who had given him a gift of music?

"No," the woman said. "Of course not. Robert Johnson had a dogged tenacity. No one could stop him from learning and growing and becoming the best musician who ever lived. He would have too, if he hadn't had his own personal demons. He was, in many ways, the opposite of you."

Kailani started. The woman was listening to her thoughts, which meant that the room conducted thoughts the way that some of these instruments conducted sound.

"Excellent," the woman said. "Bring in science so that you step back from the magic. Try to distance yourself from what I'm offering you."

"You're not offering me anything," Kailani said, and then bit her lower lip. She shouldn't have said that out loud. She was clearly hooked. She knew it, and the woman knew it.

The woman had a small self-satisfied smile on her face. The smile vanished the moment Kailani noticed it.

Was the protect spell no longer working? Was that how the woman eased into her mind, made her want something she really didn't want?

"You are brilliant and magical and you know how spells work," the woman said. "You know that your spell is still intact. I am not touching your mind because the spell failed. I'm touching your mind because you want what we offer."

"You're not offering anything," Kailani said again, only this time, she said that deliberately.

"We offer apprenticeships with the best musicians in the world," the woman said. "Look at the images on the ceiling. If you could choose one, who would it be?"

Kailani didn't have to look; she had already seen the images. They were burned in her brain.

"Billie Holiday," Kailani said, deciding to play along and find out exactly what the offer was.

The woman's etched eyebrows rose. Kailani had surprised her.

"Her voice was nearly gone by the time she died," the woman said.

"But her power was not," Kailani said. "Her vocal techniques are as inscrutable as Robert Johnson's. They sound easy and straightforward and can't be copied."

The woman stood. The kettle drums receded to the back of the room, and a small stage appeared. An old-fashioned microphone on a long narrow stand stood to one side, a trio sat to one side, one member holding an upright bass, another an acoustic guitar, and the third a blues harp. An upright piano sat even farther back.

The woman walked to the microphone and caressed its length as if it were a lover. Her black-spangled outfit had morphed into a tight red dress with no fringe at all. She had a gardenia tucked behind one ear. Her hair was ironed and rolled into a bun, 1940s style.

She was probably trying to look like Billie Holiday, but she looked more like Diana Ross from *Lady Sings the Blues*.

The woman glanced at the piano, then gripped the microphone as if she were about to start singing. Instead, she said, "Billie Holiday. She had one thing you do not, the one thing that cannot be taught."

Kailani stood very still. She wanted to hear this, but she didn't want the woman to know how much.

"She had courage," the woman said.

Kailani felt a protest rise in her throat, and held it back.

"No, you can say it." The woman leaned into the microphone as if she was going to kiss it. "Go ahead."

"You're talking about 'Strange Fruit,'" Kailani said.

"Strange Fruit" was a haunting song about lynching. Holiday fought to have that song released in the 1930s.

"I am talking about her entire career," the woman said, her voice cold. "Holiday took her heart and bled every night on stage. You have never bled for your music. You don't bleed for your magic either. You are too afraid."

Kailani felt as if an opportunity was slipping through her fingers, an opportunity she hadn't even realized she wanted until now.

"If I could learn from her," she said. "I would—"

"Be no different than you are now." The stage vanished. Now, the woman stood alone under a spotlight.

Kailani had a strange sense of movement but she couldn't quite identify why. The darkness around her, the focus on the single spotlight, made her slightly dizzy.

The woman raised her chin. She no longer looked young, no longer reflected Diana Ross or Billie Holiday or some dancer that Kailani had not recognized but probably should have.

Instead, the woman's face had lines, the hair a springy silver. Only the blue eyes remained, startling in their clarity.

"Tell Abracadabra Incorporated that they don't need to send anyone here ever again," the woman said. "And tell them that the fact that blacks perform a type of magic they do not recognize as legitimate does not make it black magic."

And then the spotlight winked out.

Kailani stood in complete darkness. She let out a breath, then said, "I'm...still interested."

But her words fell flat, as if she had spoken in a room with sound dampeners, a room with no reverberation at all.

"Please...?" she asked, not quite sure what she was asking for.

She noted a smell first, humid and dank, with a touch of greenery.

Then sunlight, bright and powerful, hit her skin first with a blast of heat, and then poked at her eyes.

They watered, and she had to blink the tears away.

A hot wind played with her clothes, pulling the sweat off her body. Behind her, a train whistled.

It took another moment for her eyes to adjust, but they didn't need to. She knew where she was. The gravel parking lot on the edge of Baptist Town, in Greenwood, Mississippi.

It looked like no time had passed at all. Her car's engine was still ticking, adjusting to the fact that she had shut it all down.

The sun looked like it hadn't moved. The wind was new, but it was gone already—a single breeze that had caressed her almost mockingly.

She took that step forward she had denied herself earlier, hoping to activate the glamour again. But there was no heat mirage, just blond-brown gravel on a turnout in the middle of a road, at the edge of a neighborhood on the Blues Trail.

"I will do whatever you need," she said. "Please."

She wasn't sure if she was asking for herself or for Abracadabra. Or if she felt the loss because she had been placed under some kind of spell.

But her protect spell remained intact. Had she been someone without magic, she would have thought it all a dream.

It wasn't; she recognized the dislocation, the sense of movement, even that wind. She had been inside a bottle world, and then she had been expelled from it.

She wondered if the woman would have sent her away if Kailani had picked someone else to study from. The others on the ceiling—they included Etta James, Nina Simone and even Janis Joplin.

A wind batted at Kailani's hair. *They had courage too*, the woman said.

Kailani didn't see it, not the way she saw Holiday's battle for "Strange Fruit." The breeze died around her, as if disappointment had killed it.

Kailani wondered if that thought had taken away her very last chance to go back into Crossroads.

But she wasn't going to head back in. She knew that now. It was lost to her.

Quartermein had sent her because he thought she had a personal combination that would allow her to investigate Crossroads. She had managed to make it inside.

She wondered if that would be enough for her to keep her job.

She stood on that gravel lot, the road curving around her, and glanced at the sun. It was beginning to go down. It had become later than she thought.

Sundown. The dangerous time.

She walked around the parking lot, just once, knowing that the heat mirage was gone for her, the entry was closed.

She wanted to care more than she did.

But she also knew she was no longer at a crossroads. She had to put her dreams behind her. They were childish dreams, dreams she was not capable of fulfilling.

The air was still. It made her uncomfortable.

So she got in her car, and drove away.

Corpse Vision

A Faerie Justice Story

Kristine Kathryn Rusch

Corpse Vision

Joe Decker couldn't remember who poured him into the taxi that brought him to Le Café du Dôme. Either way, it had to be one of the Midwestern boys—gangly Jim Thurber or the new guy—whatsisname? William?—Shirer. Neither of them knew Decker had a room at the Hôtel de Lisbonne—him and everybody else at the *Trib* except that old stick Waverly Root. Of course, without that old stick, the paper wouldn't get out everyday for the ex-pats and tourists to read in their little Left Bank cafes. Some were saying—mostly the folks over at the *Paris Herald*—that an alcoholic wave was sweeping through the offices of the *Paris Tribune*, making it damned impossible to get anything out let alone a daily paper.

Like the deadbeats at the *Herald* could talk. What they said about the *Trib* applied to the *Herald* as well: Each and every day, a goodly proportion of the staff was insensate due to drink—half because it was there and half because it wasn't.

Joe Decker didn't drink when he worked. He drank after he worked, and then only because he didn't want to face his typewriter in that little room off Boulevard St. Michel. If anyone had told him he'd be writing hack in Paris while he was supposed to be writing his brilliant first novel, he would've laughed.

He'd come to Paris with $300, his typewriter, and a one tiny suitcase of clothes, figuring that, with the franc worth damn near nothing against the dollar, he could afford one year, one year of typing, one year of thinking, thinking, thinking. Six months later, he had 5,000 words of unadulterated horseshit and fifty dollars, barely enough to pay for the room which he was heartily sick of.

Besides, no one in Paris had heard of Prohibition or if they had, they thought it one of those crazy American ideas that would never work.

Oh yeah sure, it would never work. It had never worked him into a huge thirst, which he tried to slack on nights like this when he'd turned in his copy on some stupid tourist gala no one here gave a good goddamn about but which actually got sent home because the folks back at their parent paper, the *Chicago Tribune*, thought such things were the important goings-on in Paris.

He remembered heading down the twisty back stairs of the *Trib* building, the presses thudding, the air hot with fresh ink. Funny man Thurber had come along and Whatsisname Shirer, still all googly eyed because he hadn't seen anything like this back in Ioway or Illanoise or wherever the hell he was from, and they'd planned one drink, just one—and the next thing Decker knew he woke up in this taxi with a throbbing headache and a mouth that tasted of three-day old gin.

In his exceedingly bad French, he'd asked the cabby where they were going. The cabby just waved his hand imperiously and said, "Le Dôme, Le Dôme," and Decker wasn't sure they were heading to the Dôme because Thurber or Whatsisname had told the cabby to go there, or because the cabby, like every other French taxi driver, knew the Dôme was the place to take drunk Americans so that they could get home.

Decker's head was too fuzzy to conjure the words to get the taxi to the Hôtel de Lisbonne. Besides, he wasn't sure he had the scratch. The ride to the Dôme was gratis—or would be if he couldn't find a franc or two—because someone there would cover the fare, if not one of the patrons then one of the uniformed police officers who paced the beat near the taxi stand.

He would have to promise to pay them back. And he would pay them back. He had paid everyone back, which was about the only good thing he could say about himself at the moment.

Nothing he did was any damn good, not even the daily copy he wrote for the *Trib*. The words were fine, the prose was solid, the assignments stank. His friends were just as miserable as he was (although, as Wave Root said, miserable in Paris is like happy everywhere else), and there wasn't even a woman in the picture. Well, not a relationship woman. There'd been more than Decker's fare share of one-night women. He might have even had one tonight.

The thought made him search his pockets as the taxi pulled up on the Rue Delambre side of the Dôme. The café had been on this corner for nearly thirty years, but only since the War had it become a haven for Americans. Know-it-all Hemingway, the only one of Decker's acquaintances who had finished his novel after he arrived in Paris, called it one of the three principal cafes in the Quarter, and the only one filled with people who worked.

No one who worked was there now. The tables on the terrace were empty, the chairs pushed out expectantly. A glow fell across them from the café's open doors.

Decker staggered out of the taxi, handed the driver the lone franc he'd found in his front pocket, and had to grip the pole marking the taxi stand to keep from falling.

Not only did he have a throbbing headache, but wobbly legs as well. He had to stop drinking, that was all there was to it.

"Coffee?"

Decker still had one arm wrapped around the pole. He thought maybe the ubiquitous uniformed policeman had spoken to him, but he didn't see an ubiquitous uniformed policeman. Instead, he saw an elderly man sitting against the wall, beneath the awning that someone should have rolled up by now.

"Or are you one of those British gentlemen who prefer tea?"

The old man spoke the oddly clipped English that Parisians learned —not quite British upper-class, but not quite British lower class either. Continental English, Root called it. Incontinent English, Thurber always amended when Root had left the room.

"Water would probably help," Decker said, not sure he should let go of the pole.

"Water *will* help. Alcohol dehydrates the system. That is half of what causes the so-called hang over."

The old man put a deliberate space between "hang" and "over." It was those kinds of errors that Decker usually found funny. The French often mangled English idioms, like the time the editor at *Le Petit Journal* had introduced Decker to his assistant, calling the man "my left hand"—and not meaning it as any kind of joke.

"*Monsieur*," the old man said with a wave of a hand. "*Une bouteille d'eau*."

Decker was going to tell him that the waiters here never showed up when you wanted them, and certainly wouldn't show when there were only a few customers, but the waiter who appeared, happily prying the top off a bottle of water, contradicted his very thought.

Of course, the old man wasn't just French. He had to be a regular. French regulars were prized at places like this, places which the Americans had taken over, like they had taken over most of Montparnesse just south of the Luxembourg Gardens. It was essentially an extension of the Latin Quarter without being in the Latin Quarter at all. It had been that way since the 16th century when Catherine de Medici had expelled students from the university. They had set up shop here and called it Montparnesse.

Decker knew such things about Paris, indeed, he had become a font of Paris trivia in his two years at the *Tribune*, all learned with bad schoolboy French and only a modicum of charm.

"It would be nice if you joined me," the old man said to Decker as the waiter put down the empty bottle and a single, rather grimy glass.

"Easier said than done," Decker said, not certain he could let go of the pole and remain standing.

The old man had a croissant in front of him and, despite the hour, a cup of coffee. He wore a proper black suit but no hat, which looked odd in the thin light. His hair was a yellowish white, speaking of too many hours in cafes around cigarette smoke.

As Decker lurched closer, using tables and the occasional chair to maintain his balance, he realized that the old man's beard was yellowish brown around his mouth. His fingers were tobacco stained as well. But he held no pipe and no cigar or cigarette had burned to ash in the tray in the center of the table.

Decker made it to the table and sank into the chair the old man had pushed back for him. It groaned beneath his weight. He tugged his suit coat over his stained white shirt. He had to look as filthy as he felt.

The old man poured water into the glass. The water looked clear and fresh despite the fingerprints on the side of the glass.

"You are an American newspaper man, yes?" the old man asked.

"Yes," Decker said, not that it was a hard guess, given their location.

"Joseph Decker, the American newspaper man, yes?" the old man said.

It gave Decker a start that the old man knew his name. "Is there another Joe Decker in Paris?"

The old man ignored the question. " "I have a story for you, should you take it."

Everyone had a story for him. Usually it was the kind of thing tourist rumors were made of, like why there were no fish in the Seine. But the old man didn't look like someone who would give Decker a song and dance.

Of course, Decker wasn't yet sober, so he had to assume his judgment about all things—like the kind of man the old man was based on how he appeared—was probably flawed.

"It's two a.m.," Decker said, "and—"

"Three a.m.," the old man said.

"Three a.m.," Decker said with a flash of irritation, "and I'm drunk. If you're serious about this story thing, we'll meet here tomorrow when I've had a chance to sleep this off, and we can talk then."

"I do not go out in the daylight," the old man said.

Two years ago, Decker would have rolled his eyes. But by now, he'd seen and heard everything. There were guys on the copy desk who didn't go out in the daylight either, saying it hurt their precious eyes.

Decker went out too much in the daylight, seeing things that sometimes he wished he hadn't.

He flashed on her then, body crumpled beneath Pont Neuf, feet dangling over the edge of the walkway along the banks of the Seine, pointing toward the river.

He closed his eyes and willed the image away.

"And that is why I do not," the old man said. "You see them too."

Decker opened his eyes. The old man was staring at him. The old man's eyes were blue and clear, not rheumy like Decker had expected. Maybe the old man was younger than Decker thought. He'd met a number of those guys in Paris—men in their forties who could pass for someone in their eighties by their clothing, their white hair, and their gait.

"I don't see anything, old man," Decker said.

"Nonsense," the old man said. "It is why you drink."

"I drink because I'm lonely," Decker said. *Because he kept writing the beginning to that damn novel over and over while Know-it-all Hemingway sat in this very café with his stupid notebook and scribbled story after story, book after book. Decker drank because he hated writing puff pieces for the folks back home, puff pieces about touristy restaurants and American musicians and writers like Know-it-all Hemingway. Decker drank because the stories he wanted to cover "would discourage the tourist trade from coming here." He drank because Paris wasn't the answer after all.*

"You drink," the old man said, "because it closes your mind's eye. I have watched you. You see too much."

"You've *watched* me?" Decker was getting more and more sober by the minute. "You're following me?"

"If you recall," the old man said with the patience people reserve for drunks, fools, and children, "I arrived before you did. But I must confess that I have been waiting for you."

"Me and all the other American hacks," Decker said.

The old man smiled, revealing tobacco-stained teeth. The smile was friendlier than Decker expected. "Admittedly, you American hacks, as you say, are dozens of dimes—"

Decker winced.

"—but I, in truth, have been waiting for you."

Decker drank his water. It did clear his head, although he wasn't entirely sure he wanted his head cleared. "What's so special about me?"

"You see," the old man said again.

This time, Decker did roll his eyes. He drank the last of his water, and stood up. "Old man, I'm so damned drunk that this conversation isn't making sense. How about I meet you here tomorrow at midnight, and I promise to be sober. Then you can tell me your story."

"It is your story," the old man said.

"Whatever you say," Decker said, taking the bottle of water and heading north.

He had a hell of a walk—at least for an exhausted drunk. Normally he wouldn't have minded the jaunt up to the twisty little streets near the Sorbonne. The Hôtel de Lisbonne was on the corner of Rue Monsieur-le-Prince and Rue de Vaugirad. All he had to was walk the Boulevard St. Michel toward the Seine and he'd be in his bed in no time.

But he usually avoided the Boulevard St. Michel. He avoided a lot streets in Paris, at least on foot. The old man was right; Decker saw things. But he usually attributed those things to drink or to too much imagination.

The soldiers he always saw marching through the Arc de Triomphe wore no uniforms he recognized. They marched in lock-step, their heads turned side to side as if they were little tin soldiers with moving parts.

But he didn't always see the soldiers there. Sometimes he saw a flag that he didn't recognize with a Fylfot in the middle. The Fylfot, an ancient elaborate cross, was supposed to ward off evil. But he somehow got the sense that the Fylfot itself—at least as used here—was the evil.

On the Boulevard St. Michel, he saw students rioting in the streets. The students were grubby creatures, with long hair and carrying signs that he did not understand. Sunshine shone on them, although he only saw them when it was dark.

Because of these visions, he studied Paris history, and found nothing that resembled any of it. The soldiers were unfamiliar, just like the flag, and the students too filthy to belong to any modern generation. He could dismiss such things as figments of his imagination.

But the woman—she had been real.

He had touched her, her skin cold and clammy and gray from the elements. Her eyes had been open and cloudy, her lips parted ever so slightly.

He had found her six months into his trip to Paris. Shortly after, he had wandered into the offices of the *Trib*, such as they were, and offered up his services.

Novelist, eh, kid? The man at the copy desk had asked.

Yessir.

You know how many novelists we get here, hoping for a few bucks? At least two a day. Sorry.

I have experience...

Those fateful words. *I have experience*. And he did. From his college newspaper to the *Milwaukee Journal*—yes, he had been a good Midwestern boy, once too, a boy who didn't like near beer. A boy who actually had dreams for himself.

Five thousand words of horseshit later, stories about the tourists (*Mr. and Mrs. Gladwell arrived this afternoon on a trip that has taken them from their home in Lincoln, Nebraska, to New York City through London, and now here, in Paris, where they are staying at the Ritz...*), stories about everything except the woman, crumpled beneath Pont Neuf.

Somehow he made it to the Hôtel de Lisbonne without seeing anyone, real or imaginary. The front desk was empty, so he reached over it and grabbed his key.

As he climbed the dark narrow stairs to his room, he heard a typewriter rat-a-tat-tatting. Someone was working on something, maybe a short story, maybe a novel, maybe a freelance piece for *Town and Country*.

He unlocked his room and stepped inside, then stared at his own typewriter, gathering dust beneath the room's only window. A piece of paper had been rolled in the platen since sometime last month, with only a page number on the upper right hand corner (27), and a single lowercase word in the upper left.

...the...

As if it meant something. As if he knew what he was going to do with it.

The paper was probably ruined, forever curlicued, although it didn't matter. If he finished typing on that page, he could pile the other twenty-six pages on top of it, flattening it out.

If he sat down now, nearly sober, the old man's words still echoing in his head (*You see them too*), he would write:

The woman discarded at the foot of the bridge looked uncomfortably young. Her brown hair was falling out of Gibson Girl do, now horribly out of fashion, her lips painted a vivid red. Part of the lip rouge stained her front teeth. If she were alive, she would turn away from him, and surreptitiously rub at that stain with her index finger.

He looked away from the typewriter, from that little accusatory "the." The description of the woman did not fit with the bucolic piece he had been writing, a memoir of Germantown Wisconsin in the days before the war, when he had been a young boy, and his father was still alive, tinkering with his new Model T, his mother tutting the dangers in the new-fangled machinery, the bicycle he himself had built from a kit, with the help of the man who lived next door.

Those were the kind of books people read now, memories of times past, not bloody, dark stories about dead women on Paris streets.

Decker took off his suit and hung it up, although he didn't brush it out, like he should have. He lacked the energy. As he pulled off his shirt, he realized the stains were worse than he had thought. Long, brown stains up front, looking like blood.

He was thinking of blood, though. He wasn't going to let his imagination win.

Besides, he still had one clean shirt. He needed to take the bundle to the laundry, along with his suit, so that he could look pressed and sharp again, instead of rumpled and disreputable.

He left his undershirt, boxers, and socks on, and tumbled onto the bed, the saggy mattress groaning beneath his weight. The bed hadn't even stopped bouncing by the time he had fallen asleep.

She was there in his dreams, her rich brown hair piled on top of her head, with a few curls cascading around her face. She sat on the edge of the bridge, feet dangling over the Seine, leaning back toward the road. Her eyes smiled, her lips—a perfect cupid's bow, just like the drawings she mimicked—rouged darker than her cheeks. The makeup softened her living face, making her seem as unreal as the women in the advertisements.

While her hair was old-fashioned, her clothing was not. No buttoned down shirtwaist for her with a long skirt that fell to her ankles. She wore a black skirt that grazed her knees, silk stockings with a perfect line up the back, and a blouse so soft that it seemed almost indecent. Around her neck, a simple St. Christopher's medal, and a delicate gold cross with a tiny diamond in the center. A gold band on her right hand, a band she twisted when she saw him approach, a frown creasing her lovely forehead.

He stopped beside her. She was American—he knew that without asking—and he held his reporter's notebook in his left hand, a pen in his right.

Her face shut down when he asked her name. And then her eyes clouded over, and her mouth opened ever so slightly.

The St. Christopher's medal disappeared and the gold ring too. But the expensive necklace, the gold cross with a diamond in the center, remained, as if it were her calling card.

He woke up thinking about it, twisted to one side, the bottom of the cross bent slightly as if she had fallen on it against the stone walkway.

She had worn no stockings when he found her body, and the sensible shoes, made for walking in a strange city (he knew that as clearly as if she had told him) had been replaced by thin heels, the kind flappers wore with their knee-length dresses and opera-length pearls.

He woke up thinking of the difference between the smiling girl in his dreams and the dead woman on the walkway, her skin cold against his fingertips.

He stared at his typewriter, his fingers itching to finish that sentence.

...the...

The.

The woman discarded...

Discarded.

He got dressed, and stumbled out of his room, ostensibly searching for breakfast, but really on his way to get another drink.

~

Still, that day, he made it to midnight without taking a nip from the bottle he kept at the bottom of his desk drawer. He didn't take the glass of wine offered with dinner, nor did he drink the shot of vodka offered to him by the White Russian he'd met while waiting for the American tourists he was supposed to interview in Le Procope.

He arrived at the Dôme exactly at midnight, sober as a judge. Decker had pressed his suit and worn his last clean shirt, mostly as an apology for the way he had looked the night before.

He hadn't examined himself in the mirror until this morning, but even then he had looked a fright—his hair standing on end, his nose bulbous, the capillaries in his cheeks bursting from too much drink. His eyes were red rimmed and he knew his breath was bad enough to kill any small rodent unfortunate enough to cross his path.

So he cleaned up, although no one at the *Trib* noticed, except Whatsisname Shirer, the kid from Ioway or Illanoise. Whatsisname Shirer had raised his eyebrows, but hadn't made a single remark, smart ass or otherwise, and so no one else seemed to notice.

Thurber was busy making up the news. Root was working, trying to get someone at the copy desk to expand the notes his so-called reporters had turned in. Most everyone else was so bleary-eyed that they would think they were imagining Decker in his spiffed up clothes and slicked-back hair.

Alcoholic wave indeed. It had become an alcoholic ocean, and he was seeing it for the very first time.

The Dôme had customers this night, at least a dozen sitting on the terrace, with more inside. The interior was grayish blue from all the cigarette smoke—it looked like a fog had blown through Paris and gotten stuck only inside the Dôme.

Outside, a group of men crowded around one of the tables. Decker recognized some of them from the *transatlantic review*. They spoke earnestly to each other, one of them shaking the stem of his pipe at a bespectacled man in an American felt hat.

Decker avoided them, just like he'd taken to avoiding Know-it-all Hemingway. Instead he circled to the other side of the terrace, near the taxi stand. This evening, one of the ubiquitous uniformed policemen paced, hands clasped behind his back.

The Dôme seemed normal, not like something out of a painting, the way it had the night before.

Because Decker was concentrating on its normality, he almost missed the old man, sitting at the same table, his back against the café's glass windows. Another man sat with him, younger, sharply French with his narrow face, black hair, and up-to-the-minute gabardine suit.

Decker wandered over toward them, as if they weren't his destination at all. When he reached the table, he pulled out the only other chair and sat.

"You're lucky I remembered," he said.

"I knew you would." The old man wore the same suit. His eyes were as clear as Decker had thought. "You have not had a drink."

Damn that incontinent English. Decker couldn't tell if the old man had asked a question or made a statement. "I told you I'd be sober. You told me you had story."

The younger man stared at Decker as if he thought he was rude. Maybe he was.

"I said, I had a story *for you*." The old man emphasized the last two words.

Decker looked at the younger man. "Maybe some introductions would be a good place to start."

"Maybe not," the old man said. "We shall perform the—how do you say?—niceties after we have determined what disturbs you the most."

"What disturbs me the most," Decker said, "are people who waste my time."

He shoved the chair back, about to stand, when the old man touched his arm. The old man's skin was cold. In spite of himself, Decker shivered.

"Americans are impulsive," the old man said to his companion.

"And somehow they have come to embrace a lack of politeness as if it is a virtue."

"Look," Decker said, almost adding "old man" like he had done last night when he was drunk. That had been rude, but not intentionally rude. "I deal in hard, cold facts. The first hard cold fact you learn about damn near anybody is his name, which you're not willing to tell me. So I'm not willing to stick around. See ya, pal."

This time he did stand. He was going to repeat the same walk he'd made the night before, up the Boulevard St. Michel. Maybe he should walk around the Luxembourg Gardens instead, meander instead of go directly.

He was nearly to the group of *transatlantic review* writers when the old man said, "The students, they will be in the street tonight. And tomorrow, the flag will fly over the Arc de Triomphe."

Decker stopped in spite of himself. A shiver ran down his spine. He hadn't told anyone about those waking dreams. Not even when he was drunk. Probably not even when he was black-out drunk, since he got quieter and quieter—a man who knew how to keep secrets, Root used to say, when he was the one who poured Decker into a taxi.

Decker pivoted. He walked back to the table, as the old man had known he would. But the old man did not smile like a man who had won an argument. Instead, he remained grimly serious. The younger man continued to stare.

"The soldiers leaning out of the Hôtel de Ville, do you not notice how blond they are?" The old man's voice was soft.

The other man watched Decker avidly, as if everything depended on his response.

The Hôtel de Ville was Paris's city hall. And he'd only seen soldiers there once, in the middle of a summer afternoon, as heat shimmered on the boulevards and he sat outside, trying to find a bit of air in a city not used to extreme warmth.

"They wore helmets," Decker said, knowing that was an admission.

"But they were fair-skinned, no?"

"Stocky," he said, wishing he hadn't responded. But that was what he had noticed, how stocky and square they were, as if the uniforms they wore with their unrecognizable helmets made them as solid as a boxer in the beer halls near Milwaukee.

"And they wore this symbol on their arms." The old man pushed a piece of paper forward with a Fylfot drawn on it.

In spite of himself, Decker sat back down. "Who are they?"

"A nightmare," the old man said. "One we pray we will not have. But our prayers will be for nothing. Because only strong nightmares leach backwards."

"Backwards?" Decker asked, thinking of the woman. Was that a backwards nightmare? He had seen her six months after he arrived—years ago now—and he dreamt of her every night, awakening from those dreams unsettled.

"The soldiers," the old man said. "They are little boys now, playing with battered tin soldiers from before the War. If, indeed, they are healthy enough to play. Most are hungry. Some are starving."

Decker frowned. Even when he was sober, Decker didn't understand the old man. The old man spoke nonsense. But a nonsense that Decker found enticing, in spite of himself.

"Starving?" Decker said. "Then why don't you do something?"

"Why don't you?" the old man asked. "Your country pushed for reparations. Your President Wilson. Somehow he knew how to cure the world. He made it sicker."

"Congress never ratified that treaty," Decker said, wondering why they were talking about the Treaty of Versailles conference from six years ago, from before he even arrived in the City of Light.

"And that makes it all better, no?" the old man said. "Leadership provided by your president here in Paris failed at home, so the fact that the other countries—"

"*Grand-pére*," the young man said, touching the old man's arm. "That is enough. He is not responsible for his country's follies."

"They are all responsible," the old man said.

Decker was frowning now.

"You were telling me about soldiers and little boys," Decker said, trying to get past this confusion. "Soldiers, little boys, and backwards nightmares."

"They are not nightmares," the younger man said. "They are visions. The future, haunting us here and now."

Decker frowned. "The future?"

The young man nodded. "Events so powerful they reach backwards to us. We have seen the soldiers for generations now. We have not understood them until—what is it you call it?—the Peace of Paris."

"You understand it now?" Decker asked.

"We understand that they are Germans."

"Marching into Paris." Decker snorted. "Are you hoping for this?"

Three men from nearby tables stared. Most everyone here served in the War or had lost someone who had.

"No," the younger man said, holding up his hands. "It is the worst kind of tragedy. But we do know, from the students who are also a vision leaching backwards, that Paris herself will stand."

"The students." Decker wasn't going to ask any more and he wasn't going to reveal what he had seen. He was assuming the younger man meant the grubby students he had seen some nights as he walked up the Boulevard St. Michel.

"St. Sulpice stands. Notre Dame stands. Le Tour Eiffel stands. In the distance, away from the shouting, you can see Sacré Coeur. The bridges remain. If the Germans were to destroy Paris, they would bomb the bridges so that no army could follow. Then they would destroy the monuments to destroy our souls."

Decker couldn't resist any longer. "How do you know the students appear later?"

"They are less solid."

"You can't touch them?" Decker asked.

"No," the younger man said. "You have not tried?"

He had avoided everything. He had avoided the students and the soldiers and the flags. He heard the whispery voices, and figured they had come from his own drunkenness.

"Can you touch current nightmares?" Decker asked.

"Only reality," the old man said.

Her skin, cold against Decker's fingers. So she *had* been real. Had he spoken to her once? Holding his notebook? Wanting to know who she was?

Why would he have spoken to her? He wasn't yet working for the *Trib*. He was playing at being a famous writer, the American James Joyce, yet to publish his *Portrait of the Artist As a Young Man*.

"Ah," the old man said, peering into Decker's face. "Something precipitated your visions. You did not see them when you first came to Paris."

Decker looked at him. The old man's skin was papery thin, his eyebrows so bushy they seemed to grow toward his scalp.

Paris had been clean. Paris had been pure. Truly the City of Light, all beauty and glistening stone, history calling to him.

Not like Milwaukee. Milwaukee had turned dark, especially near the lakefront. He had seen corpses of sailors, washed against the rocks, their uniforms still sodden with the waters of Lake Michigan. He had screamed the first time, and people had run to him, not to them, not even when he pointed....

He shook his head. He did not want to think of this. He did not want to remember it, how each street had something, someone, who sprawled along a road or had been shot on apartment steps or had been squashed flat by a new-fangled motorcar.

Sometimes two, sometimes three per block. He had walked with his eyes closed, and his mother—his beautiful tiny mother—whispering that he had to do something else, something that took him away from death.

Write your novel, she had said. *I will tell people of my son, the famous writer.*

And she had given him all of her pin money, money he knew she relied upon to get away from his father.

His father, who drank.

"What was that precipitated these visions?" the old man asked. "A drink, perhaps. You like your drink."

Decker stared at him, feeling his gaze go flat with anger.

"No, it could not be drink," the younger man said. "Or he wouldn't continue drinking. It's got to be hereditary. Let me see your hands."

Decker closed his hands into fists. He didn't want these people to touch him. He looked at the old man.

"You said you had a story for me."

"I have a city of stories, if you're willing to listen," the old man said. "But first, we must see the root of your vision."

Decker stared at him, then slowly, reluctantly, extended his right hand.

He had first seen her on the Champs Elysées, a vision in white. She looked like the old world blending with the new, her Gibson Girl hairdo, the wide-brimmed hat (with ribbons trailing it) that she carried in her left hand. Her dress was narrow, with a flip just near the knees, her stockings perfect, her shoes solid, old-fashioned, buttoned-up leather.

He had seen no Parisians woman dressed like that—mixing styles. Parisian women had their own style, a lot more fluid, a lot more suggestive, and all of them wore cloche hats (if they wore hats at all). She smiled when she saw him, a broad, wide American smile, the kind that held nothing back.

He tipped his hat to her. She laughed and continued onward as if she had known they would see each other again.

Of course they had. She had been looking at the sights, such a tourist, and he had been moving from park bench to park bench, staring at the monuments.

He had talked with her on Pont Neuf, more than once. She had laughed and flirted and never once told him her name. No one seemed to want to tell him names.

The thought disconcerted him for a moment, and the image of her laughing face wavered. He heard voices all around him, male voices mostly, and the air filled with tobacco smoke. An old man was peering at the palm of his hand as if it held the secrets of the universe.

And then she was back, looking at him sideways. She was holding his hand, palm up, as if she could see his future in it. She was young, enjoying Paris. He hadn't enjoyed Paris until her. Not like this—climbing the Eiffel Tower and going to Versailles to see the gardens, wandering through the Louvre, and eating bread and cheese for lunch in the Tuileries.

And he wrote. How he wrote. The novel, abandoned, he didn't care about Lincoln. He wrote instead about—

...the woman, discarded, like abandoned laundry at the base of the bridge. Her killer, dark, darker than anything Edgar Allan Poe could imagine in his darkest Rue Morgue dreams. The man carried her from the bridge itself, down the side, preparing to dump her in the Seine when someone called out...

He looked up, saw the younger man staring at him with something like horror, the old man with eyes full of compassion.

"Corpse Vision," the young man said. "You have Corpse Vision."

~

Decker wasn't sure he wanted them to tell him what Corpse Vision was, although he had a hunch he knew.

The memories scrolled backwards—like the nightmares the old man had mentioned—the first homicide call on the police beat, near one of the speakeasies by the lakefront. The dead man wore spats and a snazzy hat that blew toward Decker in the wind. He caught the hat, knew enough to carry it back to the detective, and as he did, his foot brushed the corpse, his ankle actually hitting the dead man's elbow.

A little bit of nothing—a bit of a shiver, a bit of a chill—but not much more until he returned to the *Journal's* city room. He found a typewriter and banged out his recollections, handing the paper to the copy desk for expansion. He went back to the desk to type a few impressions, like he used to do, for the novels he would someday write. But first, he rested his cheek on his fist and closed his eyes.

Spats rose from the sand, backwards, like a Charlie Chaplin film being rewound, shaking his fist at someone near on the docks. A flash of a knife, a dropped bottle of gin, some money clanging against the wood, and Decker opened his eyes, terrified of his waking dream.

The next morning, he went to the lakefront as follow-up, at least that was what he told himself, and instead, he saw the sailors, washed up on the rocks, the air cold off Lake Michigan, and two little boys, standing in the middle of the corpses, fishing.

That was when Decker screamed. The last time he screamed when he saw a corpse.

But not the first time.

The first time—Lord, he'd been ten. On his grandfather's farm. His father had come back from the stream, looking grim, the female barn cat following him, crying plaintively. Decker should have followed his father, but he was already afraid of the man. So he went to the stream, saw the tiny kitten corpse on one of the rocks, touched it—the cold damp fur—and turned.

The man behind him had no eyes. He was tied to a tree, his skin filled with holes, birds sitting on his shoulders and pecking at his face.

Decker had screamed and screamed. His father had come first, pulled him away, told him he was a baby—he knew it was spring and every spring, his grandfather took the pick of the litter for barn cats and drowned the rest so the farm didn't get overrun with cats.

Someday, his dad had said grimly, *this'll be your job.*

But Decker only dimly heard the words. Instead, he stared at the dead man tied to the tree, the birds taking chunks out of his face as if he were a particularly delectable roast. Decker wanted to bury his own face in his dad's chest, but he knew better.

He also knew he needed to gather himself, to stop being so upset, but he couldn't. He couldn't. He sobbed and sobbed and finally his dad picked him up like a sack of potatoes and slung him over his shoulder, carrying him back, Decker hiccoughing, his father whacking his butt with every single hitched breath.

His mother came into his room that night when he screamed again, the dead man alive in his room as a vision, running from men Decker dimly recognized. They would catch the dead man, carve him up, tie him to the tree, and laugh when they told him the birds would get him. They laughed. And Decker recognized the laughs.

But that wasn't why he screamed. He screamed at the sunlight afternoon invading his dark room, the trees no longer there leading down to the stream, the bank where he'd happily played just a few years before.

His mother had come and shushed him. She had cradled him as if he were still a baby, and rocked him, but she said nothing.

Except when she thought he was asleep, she went back to the room she shared with his father—*You promised,* she said.

I did not send him down there, his father said. *He went on his own.*

You should have watched him.

You coddle him.

He doesn't need to see.

At his age, I was drowning kittens. I had killed chickens and butchered pigs. I fished. You deny him childhood.

That isn't childhood, she said. *See what it has done to you.*

You used to love me, his father said.

Before the darkness ate you, she said. *Before it ate you alive.*

"You could spend your whole life in escape," the old man said, again misusing idioms. It was the odd choice of words that brought Decker back to the Dôme, not the fact that he wanted to be back.

The men from the *transatlantic review* had left. In their place, a group from the *Herald*. One of the reporters tipped his hat to Decker, who nodded. He couldn't for the life of him think of the man's name.

"Each place will be new and fresh until death," the old man said. "Then you will see—and in Europe, there is much death to see."

"I'm not seeing corpses," Decker said before he could stop himself. Not that he admitted anyway. He drank too much to remember what he saw. And what he did remember the old man called backwards nightmares.

"You are not looking," the old man said. "You have deliberately blinded your most important eye."

Decker was getting a headache, and he was starting to wish for a drink. This had been a mistake. He didn't like being sober, not any more.

"You lied," Decker said. "You said you had a story for me. This whole meeting has been nothing but gibberish."

He stood, conscious of how odd he felt. He didn't want to be near these men. He didn't want to be at the Dôme. He wanted to talk to his mother, and she was thousands of miles away, probably worrying about him, like she did. She worried.

She thought he could outrun the family curse. The old man just said he couldn't.

Decker didn't want to think about any of it.

"We will be here tomorrow night," the old man said.

"I won't," Decker said.

"Unless you finish the story," said the younger man.

"We would love to read it," the old man said.

"Sure," Decker said. And he would love to start over, that fresh bright attitude he had brought to Paris so far gone that he couldn't even remember how it felt.

Maybe he could recapture it somewhere else. He had heard nice things about Vienna. There was another sister paper in Geneva—or maybe that was a sister to the *Herald*. United Press operated out of most countries.

He could leave in the morning. He didn't need the language skills. He hadn't had all that many in France. Besides, French was the language of diplomacy. He spoke it just badly enough for people to take pity on him.

He was going to go speak it badly now at the nearest bar he could find. He would speak it until he couldn't talk any more, until he didn't think about all the things the old man had brought back into his mind. He would be so bleary-eyed drunk that maybe he wouldn't even dream.

But he made the mistake of stopping in his room first. He wanted more cash, which he found rolled up in his socks in the bottom drawer of the shabby bureau. Anyone would know to look in the sock drawer for money. It was a testament to how honest the staff was at the Hôtel de Lisbonne that no one had stolen his stash.

How honest or how lax. He couldn't remember the last time they cleaned his room.

He wiped a finger over the typewriter, removing dust. His eye caught the edge of that paper.

...the...

He sat down, xxed out the "the," and typed:

Sophie Nance Brown, daughter of Mr. and Mrs. Harcourt Brown lately of Newport, Rhode Island, in what the police initially reported as a bungled suicide attempt.

(Although, he thought, how could it have been bungled if she did indeed die?)

The body, discovered by an American tourist, fell on the walkway beneath the Pont Neuf. A witness claimed she had jumped off the bridge's wide stone railing, laughing as she fell.

But the American tourist contradicted these things, saying no one could have seen her fall. He found her at 7 a.m. Any witnesses would have had to been on the bridge in the middle of the night.

The American also pointed to her missing stockings and mismatched shoes. Her traveling companion, one Eleanor Rose Stockdale of Battle Creek, Michigan, said Miss Brown had never traveled anywhere without her St. Christopher's medal and her grandmother's solid gold wedding ring, both missing.

Police now believe Sophie Nance Brown is the third victim of a killer who play tricks on investigating officers. The witness who claimed she had fallen matched the description of a man seen carrying an unconscious woman to the base of the bridge around midnight.

Anyone with information about this most interesting case should contact the Prefect of Police.

Decker stared at the words. The paper did indeed come out of the platen curled, but he didn't care. The story was good enough for the *Trib*, if it published crime news like that (which it did not, afraid it would scare the tourists). But the story wasn't really good, just good enough.

He had written the facts as he had been trained. But that wasn't what he *knew*.

What he knew was this:

The woman discarded at the foot of the bridge looked uncomfortably young. Her brown hair was falling out of Gibson Girl do, now horribly out of fashion, her lips painted a vivid red. Part of the lip rouge stained her front teeth. If she were alive, she would turn away from him, and surreptitiously rub at that stain with her index finger.

She *had* turned away from him and wiped at the stain, the very first time she had seen him. Sophie Nance Brown, of Newport and Westchester and points south. Sophie Nance Brown with the laughing eyes, who said she had come to Paris for the *adventure*.

But her index finger was broken, bent backwards at an angle painful to look at, even now, when he knew she could feel nothing.

She had felt something. She had felt too much something when she went to the bridge after a long dinner on the Right Bank with friends. She wanted to feel the breeze in her hair, look at the moonlight over the Seine. She asked her traveling companion, Eleanor Rose Stockdale of Battle Creek, Michigan, to accompany her, but Eleanor Rose, a sensible girl, had heard that nice people did not stand on the bridges at night and had declined.

Later, Miss Stockdale would say she thought saying such things would discourage Miss Brown, but other friends said nothing discouraged Miss Brown when she set her mind to something.

Miss Brown had met a young man who had captured her fancy. Her interest in him was what she wanted to discuss with her friends at dinner. Knowing him had caused an ethical dilemma for her, especially since she was so far from home. He lived alone in a solitary room in one of the more disreputable hotels near the Sorbonne.

Miss Brown worried that she was too old-fashioned for the new morality, but too young to press the young man into something less exciting, something more permanent.

Instead of listening to her, Miss Brown's friends teased her "mercilessly." They laughed their way through dinner, interrupting her, until she grew angry, threw down her napkin along with a few francs and left the restaurant, heading for the Pont Neuf.

The Pont Neuf was suggestive, Miss Stockdale said, because Miss Brown found it romantic.

Miss Brown stood in the center of the bridge, peer out over the Seine at the famed lights of Paris, thinking that no woman should stand in such a spot alone. The light played with her old-fashioned hairstyle and her modern clothing, her ankles nicely turned out, the skirt accenting her shapely legs.

He had noticed that. He had noticed the contradiction from the start.

Decker paused, his wrists aching. He had them bent at an odd angle. His headache had cleared for the first time since he started drinking in Paris.

He wasn't writing news any longer—or at least, he wasn't writing news that he recognized. He was writing something else, *seeing* something else, something he didn't want to think about.

The pages had piled up on the small desk beside his typewriter. The voice was odd. It wasn't his, and it wasn't exactly the voice of impartial journalist. He was edging into something else, something his editors would disapprove of—"worried" and "thinking" and "noticing"—actual viewpoints, which were not allowed in the dispassionate prose of journalism.

Decker rolled another sheet of paper in the platen, ready to type that damning "the" again, ready to leave it, and count all of this as an aberration.

Instead, he continued:

He had watched her since she got off the boat. She wore a wide brimmed hat with a red ribbon, fanciful and old-fashioned. Her clothing hinted at a girl who wanted to break out of the old ways, but her hair spoke of a girl who cherished what had come before.

Almost Parisian. Modern, yet grounded in the past. He loved his city, and he wished others would as well. But he did not love the tourists, particularly the American ones, with their loud braying laughter and their lack of manners.

Although they grew their women tall and beautiful in America. Solid women, with high cheekbones and flashing eyes.

He followed her to her hotel, then watched her, meeting her first on the

Champs Elysées, then finding her in the Tuileries, regaling her with stories of his novel—every young man in Paris these days had a novel—his notebook clutched in his hand....

Decker stopped. Those memories, the things he saw, they weren't his? He frowned, trying to see something else, trying to remember when he had first met her. The date—

He dreamed of her. He dreamed of her, *after* he had found her. Six months into his stay in Paris.

Six months.

But he had never seen her, touched her, laughed with her. He hadn't really encountered her until he saw her half-naked foot hanging off the walkway, her shoe dangling over the sparkling waters of the Seine.

Only it wasn't her shoe. The killer changed the shoes. That was his little joke. He tossed her sensible shoes in the water and gave her little Parisian heels, delicate shoes that he had bought just for this purpose....

Not Decker. *Him,*

Etienne Netter, whose apartment in the Seventh Arrondissement had been in his family for six decades. His parents long dead, his mother distressed when he came home from the War with "haunted eyes."

"But at least I am home, Mother," he said plaintively, when so many young men had not come home. She had not seen what he had seen, how the blood turned French fields into mud, all for the sake of a few meters of advancement that would probably be lost the following day.

They said the Americans changed it all, with their energy and their numbers and their willingness to get killed. The Americans, big and hearty, like their women, who were stupid but lucky and somehow managed to end the war.

They liked him, these American women. They thought him their pet Frenchman. They thought his accent "quaint," his smile "romantic," his desire to write novels "almost American," even though the French had been writing novels before America was a country.

He charmed them, relaxed them, promised them he would show them the sights—and he did. He did. He showed them their own venal faces in the Seine before he raised their skirts, ripped off their stockings, and proved to them that French men hadn't lost all of their dignity in the trenches.

His mother, before she died, said he had lost his soul on the battlefield, that he had come home a shell, not a man at all, filled with dark compulsions not French. She tried to take him to church, but he would not go, not even to her funeral, after she had died, stepping in front of one of the automobiles that she so despised for ruining the lovely streets of Paris.

Stepping—that is what he told the police. She had lost track of where she was in the conversation, and she had stepped—

But she had not stepped. She had stumbled, after a shove, after she called him a monster, and said she wished he had died on the battlefield along with his soul.

Sometimes he thought she was right. He had seen the darkness coming for him those early days in the woods, lurking beyond the tanks and the flying machines, past the machine guns with their rat-a-tat-tats and their spray of bullets, the bodies falling, falling, falling in the mud. Beyond that, the darkness rose over the fields and extended across Europe, and he saw it coming toward him, then filling him, until there was no room for anything else.

He could pass on the darkness—he had done so with that beautiful American—but as he watched the hope die in her eyes, he remembered how that felt, and he could not, he would not, let her live with that. So he took the life from her, knowing (although she did not know) that it was no longer worth living.

He had taken her St. Christopher's medal because it should not touch darkness. He had left the medal and the ring she wore in the poor box at Notre Dame. He did such things, venturing into churches only for that, then escaping before the darkness polluted them as well.

Sometimes he thought he should have stumbled in front of that automobile instead of sending his mother there. Sometimes he thought he should have died, just as she said, in the mud-and-blood soaked fields, along with his friends. Sometimes he thought.

And sometimes, he did not.

. . .

Decker could not look at what he had written. He stacked the paper inside one of his folders and tied it shut with a ribbon, just like he used to tie the pages of his novel inside the folder, proud of his day's work.

This day—this night—he was not proud. He was spent.

He had seen things he had hoped to never see again.

Corpse Vision, the old man's grandson had called it.

Whatever it was, Decker despised it, much as the man he had written about, this Etienne, had despised the darkness in himself.

As Decker walked to the Dôme the following night, the folder under his arm, he saw the darkness lurking. It hid in the shadows, wearing uniforms he did not recognize—that symbol the grandson had drawn—marching in lock-step.

Nightmares seeping backwards.

But Etienne had been a nightmare seeping forward.

Decker winced. He did not want to think about it.

He hadn't had a drink in three days. His alcoholic wave was over.

He also hadn't been to the *Tribune* in three days. He wondered what Root would think, what Thurber would say. Maybe they were already searching for him, although no one had come to his room at the Hôtel de Lisbonne—or if they had, he had been too absorbed to hear their knock.

This time, Decker arrived before the old man. Decker sat at the old man's table, sipping coffee and eating ham, cheese, and bread, much to the disapproval of his waiter, who wanted to serve the coffee long after the meal was done.

Know-it-all Hemingway sat in a corner, scribbling in his journal. He did not look up as Decker came onto the terrace, and Decker did not call attention to himself.

But as he looked at Hemingway now, he saw something that startled him—an insecurity, a fear, so deep that Hemingway might not have known it existed. Superimposed over Hemingway—like a ghost in a Dadaist painting—was an old man with a white beard and haunted eyes. He hefted a shotgun and rubbed its barrel against his mouth.

Decker looked away.

The old man—his old man, not the spirit surrounding Hemingway—sat at the table, his grandson beside him.

Decker didn't ask where they came from. He didn't remark on their silent entrance. Instead, he handed the folder to the old man.

The old man untied the folder, opened it, and scanned the pages, handing them one by one to his grandson.

Decker read upside down, embarrassed by the words, their lack of cohesion, their meandering viewpoint. When the grandson saw the name Etienne Netter, he stood.

"My thanks," he said and bowed to Decker. Then he walked away, leaving the pages beside Decker's plate.

Decker did not touch them. The old man picked them up and put them back in the folder, which he tied shut, making a careful bow.

"It is more than I could have hoped for," he said. "You have saved lives."

Decker shook his head. "I didn't do anything."

"This man, this Netter, he is a new breed. You have heard of Jack the Red, no? Saucy Jack?"

"The Ripper," Decker said. "Decades ago. In London."

"The first of his kind, we think," the old man said. "If there had been one such as you, perhaps he would have been stopped."

"He was stopped," Decker said. "He only killed five."

"That we know of," the old man said.

He set the papers under his own plate, then extended his hand. "I am Pierre LeBeau. I run *Noir*, the central newspaper in the City of Dark."

Decker couldn't take the misstatements any more. "City of Light," he said. "We call Paris the City of Light."

LeBeau nodded. "Light has its opposite. You have seen the dark. You write of it. You know what is coming."

"Only because you tell me that it is," Decker said. He sipped his coffee, pleased that his hand remained steady. "How come I've never seen your paper?"

"As I have said, you kept your most important eye deliberately closed." LeBeau put his hand on top of the folder. "The paper has grown since the War. Before, we were a single sheet. During, we ran four. After, we grew to five, then ten, now eighteen. We need an English language edition. We will start with four pages on the expatriate community."

"More meeting the boat," Decker said. "More puff pieces."

"No puff, as you say," LeBeau said. "Warnings, perhaps. Stories that do not run in your *Tribune* or the *Herald*, things only hinted at in the fictions your friends write for the *transatlantic review*."

"Who would read it?" Decker asked, surprising himself. Normally he would ask about pay before readership.

"People like my grandson," LeBeau said.

"Where did he go?"

"He will take Etienne Netter and extinguish his darkness. Then he would help the police find justice."

"He'll kill him?"

"No," LeBeau said. "But this Netter might wish he were dead when my grandson has finished with this. For Netter will realize what he has done and why, and with the revival of his soul, he will feel remorse so painful that death will be the only way out. Yet death will be impossible for decades. It is our smallest but best measure of revenge."

Decker felt a chill run down his back. The conversations with LeBeau, as circular as they were, were beginning to make sense.

"We will pay triple what you earn at the *Tribune* for the first six months," LeBeau said. "Raises every quarter thereafter if you continue to perform."

"Perform?" Decker asked.

"You must follow the darkness," LeBeau said. "See where it will lead."

"And if I don't?"

LeBeau smiled. "I shall buy you your next drink. You will become one of the—what do they call it?—casualties of the licentiousness of Paris. There will be no novel, no more hack work as you call it, no more typing. Only drinks, until one day not even the drinks will work. You will go to a sanatorium, and they will try to help you, but you will be one of the hopeless ones, the ones who has rotted his mind and his body, but has not managed to destroy the vision that has haunted you since you touched that kitten decades ago."

It no longer surprised Decker that LeBeau knew so much about him. Nor did LeBeau's description of his future surprise him. Decker had seen it already, as his father drank more and more, until finally his grandfather drove his father away to "a hospital" where they would "help" him. No one had ever seen him again.

His mother would not speak of him. She had lived too close to his darkness. She feared it for her son.

But running from it hadn't worked. He had simply become a drunk in Paris instead of in Milwaukee. Even if he had no magic vision, he had a future like the one LeBeau had described.

And the writing had taken away the urge to drink.

Even if the things he wrote had chilled him deeper than anything else.

"I never met her, did I?" Decker asked the old man. "Sophie. I never did meet her."

LeBeau looked at him. "You met her. Her spirit, after she had died. She wished she had been with you instead of this Etienne. She used your similarities to pull you in. She wanted him stopped. She did not want him to harm anyone else."

It sounded good. Decker wasn't sure he believed it, but he wanted to. Just like he wanted to believe that *Noir* existed, that he would be paid three times his *Tribune* salary, that his Corpse Vision actually had a purpose.

"I suppose I can't tell anyone what I'm doing," he said.

LeBeau shrugged. "You can tell," he said. "They will not believe. Or worse, they will not care, any more than you care for them."

LeBeau glanced at Hemingway, still scribbling in his notebook. Decker looked too. Hemingway raised his head. For one moment, their eyes met. But Hemingway's were glazed, and Decker realized that Hemingway had not seen him, so lost was he in the world he was creating.

They were all creating their worlds. The expatriate reporters with their chummy newspapers in English, hiding in a French city that did not care about their small world. The novelists, sitting in Parisian cafes, writing about their families back home.

And the old man, with his darkness and nightmares looming backwards.

Decker already existed in darkness. He could no longer push it away. He might as well shine a light on it and see what he found underneath.

"I'll take four times the salary," he said, "and a raise every two months."

The old man smiled. "It is, as you say, a deal."

He extended his hand. Decker took it. It was dry and warm. They shook, and Decker felt remarkably calm.

Calmer than he had felt in months.

Maybe than he had felt in years.

He did not know how long *Noir* would be in his future. But he did know that his tenure there would be better than anything he had done in the past.

Anything he had seen in the past.

He opened his most important eye, and finally, went to work.

Death Stopped for Miss Dickinson

Kristine Kathryn Rusch

Death Stopped for Miss Dickinson

January 26, 1863
Near Township Landing, Florida

The air smelled of pine trees, a scent Colonel Thomas Wentworth Higginson associated with home. Here, in Florida, where dark, spindly trees rose around him like ghosts, Higginson never imagined he'd be thinking of Massachusetts, with its stately settled forests and its magnificent tamed land.

Nothing was tamed here. His boots had been damp for days, the earth mushy, even though his regiment, the First South Carolina Volunteer Infantry, had somehow found solid ground. He could hear the tramp, tramp, tramp of hundreds of feet, but his soldiers were quiet, well trained, alert.

Everything Washington D.C. thought they would not be.

Even in the dark, after days of river travel, Higginson was proud of these men, the most disciplined he had ever worked with. He said so in his dispatches, although he doubted Union Command believed him. They had taken a risk creating an entire regiment of colored troops, mostly freed slaves, all of whom had been in a martial mood much of the month, ever since word of President Lincoln's Emancipation Proclamation reached them.

A strange clip-clop, then the whinny of a horse, and a shushing. Higginson's breath caught. His men had no horses. They traveled mostly on steamers, and hence had no need of horses, even if the Union Army had deemed such soldiers worthy of steeds—which they did not.

He whispered a command: It was all he needed to stop his troops. They halted immediately and slapped their rifles into position.

He had a fleeting thought which made him smile—a Confederate soldier's worst nightmare; to meet a black man with a gun—and then waited.

The silence was thick, the kind of silence that came only when men listened, trying to hear someone else move. Breathing hushed, each movement monitored. No one wanted to move first.

Then Higginson saw him, rising out of the trees as if made of smoke —a black-robed figure, face hidden by a hood, carrying a scythe.

Higginson's breath caught. What kind of madness was this? Some kind of farmer lurking in the woods, killing soldiers?

The figure turned toward him. In the darkness, the hood looked empty. Higginson saw no face, just a great, gaping beyond.

His heart pounded. He was forty years old, tired, overworked and overwrought; hallucinations should not have surprised him.

But they did, *this* did.

And then the hallucination dissolved as if it had never been. One of his men cried out, and a volley of shots lit up the night, revealing nothing where the hooded figure had stood.

All around it, however, horses, men, Confederates—white faces in the strange gunlight, looking frightened and surprised. They surrounded his men, but could not believe what they saw—for a moment anyway.

Then their weapons came out, and they returned fire, and Higginson forgot the hooded figure, forgot that moment of silence, and plunged deep into the battle, his own rifle raised, bayonet out as, around him, the air filled with the stink of gunpowder, the screams of horses, the wild cries of men.

The battle raged late into the night, and when it was done, rifle smoke hung in the sky, the trees nearly invisible, the wounded crying around him. Thirteen bodies—twelve of theirs, one of his—gathered nearer each other than he would have liked.

Near the spot where he had seen the hooded figure, where he had imagined smoke, in that moment of silence, before the first shot was fired and the first smoke appeared.

Forty years old and he had never been frightened—not when he attacked Boston's courthouse trying to rescue escaped slave Anthony Burns, not when he fought with the Free-Staters in Kansas, not when he met John Brown with an offer to fund the raid on Harper's Ferry.

No, Thomas Wentworth Higginson had never been frightened, not until he saw those bodies, scattered in a discernable pattern in the ghostly wood where a spectral figure had stood not an hour before, and wielded a scythe, creating a clearing where Higginson would have sworn there had not been one before.

He reassured himself: Every man was allowed one moment of terror in a war. Then he resolved that he would never be frightened again.

And he was not. In the war, anyway.

But he would be frightened again, and much worse than this, in a small town in Massachusetts, seventeen years later.

~

May 23, 1886
The Homestead
Amherst, Massachusetts

Lavinia Dickinson stood in the doorway to her sister's bedroom. It still smelled faintly of Emily—liniment and homemade lavender soap, dried leaves from the many plants she'd preserved, and of course, the sharp odor of India ink that seemed embedded in the walls.

The bed was bare, the coverings washed and to be washed again. Dr. Bigelow had initially said Emily died of apoplexy, but he had written on her death certificate that she had been a victim of Bright's disease, which he swore had no contagion.

Vinnie had learned, in her fifty-three years, that doctors knew less than most about death and disease, but she trusted Dr. Bigelow enough to keep the sheets and Emily's favorite quilt, although she would launder them repeatedly before putting them away.

Vinnie had thought to burn them, but their mother had made that quilt, and it held precious memories. Still, Vinnie had time to change her mind. She would have a bonfire soon, before the summer dryness set in.

Emily had made her swear—had asked a solemn oath—that Vinnie would destroy her papers, *all* her papers, should Emily die first.

Vinnie had not expected Emily to die first. That bright flame seemed impossible to distinguish, even as she lay unconscious on her bed for two days, her breath coming in deep unnatural rasps.

No one expected Emily to die—least of all, Emily.

And Vinnie was uncertain how to proceed, without her stronger, smarter, older sister to guide her.

~

May 15, 1847
The West Street House
Amherst, Massachusetts

The moon cast an eerie silver light through Emily's bedroom window. She set down her pen and blew out the candle on her desk. The light seemed stronger than before.

She slid her chair back, the legs scraping against the polished wood floor, and paused for a moment, hoping she had not awakened Father. He would tell her she should sleep more, but of late, sleep eluded her. She felt on the cusp of something—what, she could not tell. Something life-changing, though.

Something soul-altering.

She dared not speak these thoughts aloud. When she had uttered less controversial thoughts, her mother chided her and urged her to pull out her Bible when blasphemy threatened to overtake her. Emily's father did not censure her thoughts, but he looked concerned, worrying that the books he bought her had weakened her girlish mind.

All except her father and her brother Austin recommended church, hoping the Lord would speak to her and she would become saved. She saw no difference between those who had become saved and those who had not, except, perhaps, a certain smugness. She was smug enough, she liked to tell her sister Lavinia. Vinnie would smile reluctantly, at both the truth of the statement and the sheer daring of it.

Everyone they knew waited to be saved; that her brother and father had not yet achieved this was seen as a failing in their family, not as something to be emulated. If she was not saved, she would not reunite with her family in Heaven. Indeed, she might not go to Heaven.

And, at times, such an idea did not terrify her. In fact, it often filled her with relief.

Eternity, she had once said to Vinnie, *appears dreadful to me*.

Vinnie did not understand, nor did Austin. And Emily couldn't quite convey how often she wished Eternity did not exist. The idea of living forever, in any way—*to never cease to be*, as she had said to Vinnie—disturbed her in her most quiet moments.

Like now. That silver light made her think of Eternity, perhaps because the silver made the light seem unnatural somehow.

She crept to the window, crouching before it, her hand on the sill, and peered out.

Behind their home lay Amherst's burial ground. The poor, and the unshriven slept here, alongside the colored and those not raised within the confines of a Christian household. Ofttimes she sat in her window and watched as families mourned or as a sexton dug a grave for a lonesome and already forgotten soul.

On this night, the graves were bathed in unnatural light. The world below looked silver, except for the darkness lurking at the edges. Something had leached all of the color from the ground, the stones, and the trees behind—yet the bleakness had a breathtaking beauty.

In the midst of it all, a young man walked, hands clasped behind him as if he were deep in thought. Although he assumed the posture of a scholar, his muscular arms and shoulders spoke of a more physical toil—farmer, perhaps, or laborer. Oddly the light did not make his shirt flare white. Instead, its well-tailored form looked as black as the darkness at the edges of the cemetery. His trousers too, although she was accustomed to black trousers. All the men in her life wore them.

He paced among the graves as if measuring the distance between them, pausing at some, and staring at the others as if he knew the soul inside.

Emily leaned forward, captivated. She had seen this man before, but in the churchyard in the midst of a funeral. He had leaned against an ornate headstone, resting on one of the cherubim encircling the stone's center.

She had expected someone to chase him off—after all, one did not lean against gravestones, particularly as the entire congregation beseeched the Lord to send a soul to its rest.

But he had for just a brief moment. Then, perhaps realizing he had been seen, he moved—vanished, she thought that day, because she did not see him among the mourners.

Although she saw him now.

As if he overheard the thought, he raised his head. He had a magnificently fine face, strong cheekbones, narrow lips, dramatic brows curving over dark eyes. Those eyes met hers, and her breath caught. She had been found out.

He smiled and extended a hand.

For a moment, she wanted nothing more than to clasp it.

But she sat until the feeling passed.

She ran to no one. She did no one's bidding, not even her father's. While she tried to be a dutiful daughter, she was not one.

And she would not run to a stranger in the burial ground, no matter how beautiful the evening.

No matter how lovely the man.

~

May 23, 1886
The Homestead
Amherst, Massachusetts

Piles of papers everywhere. Vinnie sat cross-legged on the rag rug no one had pulled out during spring cleaning—Emily had been too sick to have her room properly aired—and stared at the sewn booklets she had found hidden in Emily's bureau.

Once their mother had thought the bureau would house Emily's trousseau, back when the Dickinsons believed even their strange oldest daughter would marry well and bring forth children, as God commanded. But she had not, and neither had Vinnie. Austin had married well, or so it seemed at first, although he and Sue were now estranged, a condition made worse by the untimely death of their youngest child, Gib.

Vinnie wished Emily had given Austin this task. Emily lived in her words. She had better friends on paper than she had in person. She wrote letters by the bucketful, and scribbled alone late into the night. To destroy Emily's correspondence, Vinnie thought, would be like losing her sister all over again.

And yet Vinnie had been prepared to do it, until she discovered the booklets. Hand sewn bundles of papers, with individual covers. Inside, the papers were familiar: Emily's poems. But oh, so many more than Vinnie had ever imagined.

Emily gifted family and friends with her poems, sometimes in letters, sometimes folded into a whimsical package. Her tiny careful lettering at times made the poem difficult to discern, but there, upon the page, were little moments of Emily's thoughts. Anyone who knew her could hear her voice resound off the pages:

I'm nobody, she said in her wispy childlike voice. *Who are you? Are you nobody, too?*

Vinnie could almost see her, crouching beside her window, watching the children play below. More than once, she had sent them a basket of toys from above, but had not played with them.

Instead, she preferred to watch or participate at a great distance.

But once she had been a child, with Vinnie.

Then there's a pair of us, Emily said. *Don't tell! They'd banish us, you know.*

The poems had no date, and Emily's handwriting looked the same as always. Her cautious, formal handwriting, not the scrawl of her early drafts.

These poems had meant something to her. She had sought to preserve them.

Vinnie closed the booklet, and clutched it to her bosom.

Emily lived inside these books. However, then, could Vinnie destroy them?

~

May 19, 1847
The West Street House
Amherst, Massachusetts

The silver light returned four nights later. It was not tied to the moon as Emily had thought because, as she headed up the stairs to her room, she noted clouds forming on the horizon.

The night had been dark until the light appeared.

Instead of peering out her window, she slipped on her shoes and hurried down the stairs. Her father read in the library. Her mother cleaned up the kitchen from the evening meal. Her older brother Austin, home from school, sat at the desk in the front parlor, composing a letter. He did not look up as she passed.

She let herself out the front, simply so that her mother would not see her.

Cicadas sang. The air smelled of spring—green leaves and fresh grass and damp ground. All familiar scents, familiar sounds. The music of her life.

The strange silver light did not touch the front of the house. Perhaps the light came from some kind of powerful lantern, one she had not seen that night.

She stole around the house, her heart pounding. She never went out at night, except when accompanied, and only when it was required. A concert, a meeting, a request to witness one of her father's legal documents.

Unmarried girls did not roam the grounds of their home, even if they were sixteen and worldly wise. She was not worldly wise, although she was cautious.

And now what she was doing felt forbidden, deliciously daring, and exciting.

She rounded the corner into the back yard. The silver light flowed over the burial ground, but did not touch the Dickinson property. The darkness began at the property line, which she found passing strange.

But as she stepped onto the grass behind her house, the silver light caught her white dress, making it flare like a beacon.

She froze, heart pounding. Revealed. Her hands shook, and she willed them to stop.

She had nothing to be afraid of, she told herself. The burial ground was empty except for the light.

She tiptoed forward, trying not to rustle the grass. She kept her breathing even and soft. She had seen deer move this way, silently through thick foliage. The grass was not thick here. The yard man kept it trim for the Dickinsons, the sexton for the burial ground.

Yet she felt as if she were being watched. The hair rose on the back of her neck, and in spite of her best efforts, her heart rate increased.

It took all of her concentration to keep her breathing steady.

To walk in a graveyard at night. What kind of ghost or demon was she trying to summon?

All of Amherst already thought her strange. Would they think her even stranger if they saw her wandering through the graves, her white dress making her seem ghostly and ethereal?

Something moved beside her. She looked over her shoulder, half expecting Austin, arms crossed, a frown on his face. *What are you doing*? he'd ask in a voice that mimicked Father's.

Only Austin wasn't there.

No one was there.

She wanted to run back to the house, but she made herself walk forward, to that small patch of ground where she had seen the man four nights before. The graves there were not fresh. One had sunken slightly. Another had flattened against the earth. A third had a stone so old that the carvings had worn off.

The light seemed stranger here than it had from the window,

leaching the color from her skin. She seemed fanciful, a phantom herself. If someone saw her, they might not think they were seeing young Miss Dickinson, but a specter instead.

Something rose behind one of the ancient tilting headstones—a column of smoke, no!, a man dressed all in black, a cowl over his head, a scythe in his hand.

Emily fled across the grass, careful to avoid sinking graves, her breath coming in great gasps. She was halfway to the house before she caught herself.

It was, she thought, a trick of the light, and nothing more. She had expected to see a phantom in the graveyard and so she had—the worst of all phantoms, that old imperator Death.

She made herself turn. She was not frightened of anything, and she would not flee like a common schoolgirl from phantoms in the darkness.

Behind her, the sky was clear, the silver light still filling the burial ground. But there was no column of smoke, no cowled figure, no scythe.

There was, however, that handsome young man, leaning on a gravestone that looked like it might topple at any moment.

He smiled at her again, and her traitorous heart leapt in anticipation. But she knew better than to approach him—not because she was afraid of him; she wasn't—but because she knew once she spoke, this illusion of interest and attraction would fade, and he would see her as all the others had, as intense and odd and unlikable.

"Emily Elizabeth Dickinson," he said, his voice a rich baritone. "Look at you. 'She walks in beauty, like the night.'"

His use of her name startled her. That he so easily quoted Lord Byron startled her all the more. A literate man, and one not afraid of showing his knowledge of the more scandalous poets.

She straightened her shoulders so that she stood at her full height, which wasn't much at all. She knew some often mistook her for a child; she was so slight and small.

"You have me at a disadvantage, sir," she said. "You know of me, but I do not know of you."

His smile was small. "I know of many people who do not know me," he said. "In fact, I am astounded that you can see me at all."

"'Tis the strange light, sir," she said. "It illuminates everything."

"That it does," he said. "You should not be able to see it, either."

He was strange, from his word choice to his conversation to his decision to lean against a gravestone. Was this how others saw her? Strange, unpredictable, something they had never encountered before?

"If by that you mean I should not be out here among the graves, you are probably right," she said. "But it is a beautiful evening, and I fancied a walk."

He laughed. "You fancied me."

She raised her chin ever so slightly. "I beg your pardon, sir."

"I did not mean that like it sounds," he said. "You saw me four nights ago, and you came to see what I was doing."

He had caught her again. "Perhaps I did, sir," she said. "What of it?"

"Aren't you going to ask me what I'm doing here?" he asked.

"Mourning, I would assume," she said. "I did not mean to intrude upon your grief."

"You're not," he said. "I am not grieving. I am just visiting my dead."

Blunt words, harsh words, but true words. He was a kindred soul. Her entire family constantly admonished her for her harsh speech. But, she said, she preferred truth to socially acceptable lies.

It seemed, however, that others did not.

She took a step toward him. His eyes twinkled, which surprised her. Before she had thought them dark and deep, unfathomable. The hint of light in them was unexpected.

"Why visit at night?" she asked. "Wouldn't it be better to come here during the day?"

"Yes, it would," he said. "But daylight is not available to me. So I bring my own."

His hand moved, as if he were indicating the silver light. But it seemed to have no obvious source. If he had command of the silver light, then he also had command of the moonlight, something no mortal could possibly have.

So she dismissed his talk as fanciful. But intriguing. Everything about him was intriguing.

He tilted his head as he looked at her. There was a power in his gaze she had never encountered before. It drew her, like it had drawn her that first night. But she was suspicious of power and charisma, much as it attracted her.

"The real question," he said, "is not why I'm here, but why you're here."

"We've already discussed that, sir. I came to investigate the light."

"Ah, yes," he said softly. "But how did you see this light?"

"Sir?" The question disturbed her, and she wasn't quite sure why. She certainly wasn't going to tell him that her bedroom overlooked the burial ground. The fact that he had seen her in her room was already an invasion of privacy no one she knew would approve of.

"This," he said, sweeping his hand again—indicating the graves instead of the light? Had she mistook the gesture? "should all be invisible to you for another forty years."

She laughed at his naiveté. Death surrounded them always, didn't he know that?

"Death, sir," she said primly, and saw him start at the word, "is all we know of heaven. And all we need of hell."

His smile faded, and so did the light in his eye. "True enough," he said. "So. Don't I frighten you?"

He attracted her; he did not frighten her.

"I suppose you should," she said. "But you do not."

"Amazing," he said softly. "You are truly amazing."

He stood, dusted off the back of his trousers, and nodded at her, his mouth in a determined line.

"This meeting is inappropriate," he said.

She shrugged, no longer uncomfortable. "I have found that most of what I do is inappropriate," she said, wondering if she should admit such a thing to a man she had just met. "I did not mean to compromise you."

He laughed. The sound boomed across the stones. "Compromise me." He bowed slightly, honoring her. "You are a treasure, Miss Dickinson."

"And you are a mystery, sir," she said.

He nodded. "The original mystery in fact," he said. "And I think that for tonight, we shall leave it that way. Good night, Miss Dickinson."

Dismissed, then. Well, she was used to that. People could not stomach her presence long.

"Good night, sir," she said, and slowly, reluctantly, made her way back to the house.

~

August 16, 1870
The Homestead
Amherst, Massachusetts

Thomas Wentworth Higginson called her his partially cracked poetess. He knew, long before he traveled to the Dickinson home in Amherst, that the woman who wrote to him was different. He had many words for her—wayward, difficult, fascinating.

But none of them prepared him for what he found.

He arrived on a hot August afternoon, expecting conversation about literature and publication and poetry. He preferred literary conversation; he tried not to think about the war, although it haunted him. He dreamed of boots tramping on damp ground, of neighing horses, and startled men.

But he woke, panicked, whenever he saw the hooded figure approach, shrouded in darkness, carrying a scythe.

The Dickinson house itself was beautiful, easily the finest house in Amherst. Two vast stories, built in the Federal style, with an added cupola and a conservatory. Higginson had not expected such finery, including the extensive white fence, the broad expanse of grounds, and the steps leading up to the gate.

He felt, for the first time in years, as if he had not dressed finely enough, as if his usual suit coat and trousers, light worsted to accommodate the summer heat, was too casual for a family that could afford a house like this.

But he had known some of the greatest people in the country, and he had learned that finery did not always equal snobbery. So he rapped on the door with confidence, removing his hat as the door swung open.

A woman no longer young opened the door. Her eyes were bright, her chestnut hair pulled away from her round cheeks. She smiled welcomingly, and said, "You must be Colonel Higginson."

"At your service, ma'am," he said, bowing slightly.

She giggled, which surprised him, and said, "We do not stand on ceremony here, sir. I am Lavinia Dickinson. I'll fetch my sister for you."

She beckoned him to step inside, and so he did with a bit of relief that this clear-eyed, normal girl was not his poetess. He would have been disappointed if she had been wrapped in a predictable façade.

The entry was a wood-paneled room, dark and oppressive after the bright summer light. Lavinia Dickinson delivered him to the formal parlor dotted with lamps marking it as a house filled with readers. He sat on the edge of the settee as Lavinia Dickinson disappeared behind a door, leaving him, hat in hand, to await instruction. He felt like a suitor rather than an accomplished man who had come to visit one of his correspondents.

Eight years of letters with Emily, as she bid him to call her. Eight years of poems and criticisms and comments. Eight years, spanning his war service and his homecoming, two moves, and changes he had never been able to imagine.

Still, her letters arrived with their tiny handwriting and their startling poems. He had looked forward to this meeting for months now, had tried to stage it for a few years. But the poetess herself rarely left Amherst and he rarely traveled there.

His hands ached slightly, and he unclenched his fingers so that he did not crush his hat.

The house unsettled him; at least, that was what he thought at first. But as the moments wore on, he realized his unease came from the whispers around him, and then something stirring in the air, like a strong rain-scented wind arriving before a storm.

The door banged open, and the storm arrived. She was tiny, with her red hair pulled into two smooth bands. Her plain white dress made her seem young—it was a girl's dress—but the blue net worsted shawl over it was an older woman's affectation. She clutched two day lilies in one fist.

He would have thought her childlike if not for her eyes. They glowed. His breath caught, and he stood a half second too late. He had seen eyes like that before, although not nearly as manic, when he sat across from the militant abolitionist John Brown, whose raid on Harper's Ferry had helped start the war.

Higginson, along with five friends, had funded that raid. He would not have done so if he hadn't believed in Brown and his extreme methods. Most people had been frightened of the man, but Higginson hadn't been. He had thought then that Brown, whom some later called crazy, had the light of God in his eyes.

Higginson did not think God existed in Emily Dickinson's eyes. An odd silver light looked through him, and even though she smiled, she did not seem warm.

She thrust the flowers at him and said, "Forgive me if I'm frightened—"

She didn't seem frightened to him. She seemed excited, like a child about to receive a treat for good behavior. She held part of herself in check, but the excitement overpowered her control, making her jitter.

"—but I hardly see strangers and I don't know what to say."

That didn't stop her. She started talking, but he had trouble listening; all he could do was focus on those eyes. Killer eyes. He had seen eyes like that in some Rebel soldiers as they bayoneted his men. He made himself breathe, made himself listen, made himself converse, but he scarcely remembered what he said.

She introduced him to her father—a colorless old man, without much humor—and invited her sister to join them, but her sister demurred.

Instead, Higginson was stuck with Emily. He felt something drain from him as she talked, a bit of his life essence, as if being around her took something from him. It took all of his considerable strength just to hold his own against her.

The comparison to a storm wasn't even apt. She wasn't a summer storm, filled with rain and thunder. She was a tornado, sweeping in and seizing all around her. Only his encounter with her did not last an instant; it lasted hours.

And when it was finally finished, he staggered out of that strange house, relieved to be gone, and thrilled that she had not touched him. It took all of his strength to hold the day lilies she had given him. The day lilies and the photograph of Elizabeth Barrett Browning's grave.

Emily had smiled at him, a strange, sad, pathetic little smile, and said she was grateful because he had saved her life.

He hadn't saved her life. He hadn't done anything except read her poetry. He had even told her not to publish it because he thought it undisciplined, like her. Or so he had initially thought.

But that evening, as he sat alone in his rented room, trying to find words to express to his wife the strangeness of the experience, he realized that Miss Emily Dickinson hadn't been undisciplined. She hadn't been undisciplined at all.

In fact, it seemed to him, she was one of the most disciplined people he had ever met, as though explosions constantly erupted inside her and she had to keep them contained.

I never was with anyone who drained my nerve power so much, he finally wrote to his wife. *Without touching her, she drew from me. I am glad not to live near her.*

He couldn't write any more. He didn't dare tell Mary that he felt Emily Dickinson had taken something vital from him, that talking to her had made him feel as if he were one step closer to death.

~

December 18, 1854
The West Street House
Amherst, Massachusetts

Emily woke up in his arms, cradled against his chest. This man, who seemed so otherworldly, was warm and passionate. His breathing was even, regular, but try as she might, she could not hear his heart beat.

She tried not to think of that, just like she tried not to think about what she was letting him do, sneaking into her room, lying naked in her bed. Her father had never caught him here, and she used to be afraid of what her father would do.

But now she didn't have that fear. Now she was afraid of what this man would do, this man who carried silver light with him as if he held a lantern.

The light did come when he summoned it, just like he had said to her. And it fled when he asked it to leave. The darkness around him without the light was absolute. She felt safe with him, in that darkness, but when he left, terror came.

And he always left before dawn.

He could not handle the light—real light. Daylight.

Her time with him would lessen as summer came, just like it always had. They lived best in winter, together.

She knew what he was. She watched him, after he left her, fading as his light faded, disappearing into the absolute darkness he created. Over time, some of his silver light spilled into her and she could see in the dark better than a cat could.

She could see him don his cowl, and pick up his scythe.

The nights he left early, the nights he arrived late, changed Amherst as well. The days after those nights she heard stories of breathing ceased, and hearts stopped, and sometimes she saw the funerals in the graveyard beneath her window, and she knew they happened because he had been there. He had touched someone.

Not like he touched her.

She was different, or so he said, had been different from the day they met. She should not have been able to see him, not until she was nearly dead herself.

But she was beginning to think she was not alive, not really, that something inside her had died long before she had found him, that her spirit had vanished, that she had no soul.

Surely, she did not feel the stirrings her family felt at revivals, and she did not feel the call of God. She understood He existed, but at a distance, not as someone who could live within her heart.

In earlier times, less enlightened times, here in Massachusetts, they would have called her a witch.

She knew this, and this man, this man who held her, he confirmed it, declaring himself lucky to have found her.

"Love," he said, "does not come to us often."

And by "us," he did not mean her and him. He meant himself and others like him, those whom everyone else called Death. She was not sure who he worked for—the Devil? Or some unnatural demon? Or Heaven itself? For as she had said to him in their first conversation, Heaven would not exist without him.

Death had to occur before it could be overcome. And she could not die.

Or so she believed.

She pressed herself against his warm skin, losing herself in his familiarity.

To remain alive forever—to live for Eternity—to be Immortal: those things terrified her. She did not discuss them with him, because he thought them good, and she did not want to hurt him.

But he wanted her at his side forever.

And forever, to her, was much too long.

There are, he said to her once—just once—, *a thousand ways to live forever. The soul must be preserved.*

Caught like a butterfly in a jar? she asked.

He shook his head, and smiled his beautiful smile at her fancy. *Recorded,* he said. *The soul must find permanence somewhere. Memory fades and eventually souls do as well. Except for a select few, kept alive in word or deed or a powerful magic.*

Have you that magic? she asked.

Sometimes, he said. *I could preserve you.*

No, she said too quickly. Then calmer, as if it didn't frighten her, *No. I prefer to sleep. I don't want Eternity.*

You are the only one then, he said.

Do you have it? she asked.

Yes, he said. *And I would like to share it with you.*

She shuddered. *Promise me you won't. When the time comes. Promise me.*

But he wouldn't promise. And that silence lay like ashes inside her heart.

~

May 24, 1886
The Homestead
Amherst, Massachusetts

The room had become a pile of papers. Vinnie covered every bare surface with poetry, all written by her sister. Vinnie had finally counted the sheets—counted and recounted and counted again.

Each time, she got a different number, but each time, the number staggered her. At least a thousand.

At least.

And such poems! About things Emily should not have known. Secret things. Intimate things.

Things that made Vinnie blush as she read them, hearing—despite her best intentions—Emily's voice:

You left me, sweet—Emily never called anyone sweet, and yet here it was, an endearment, casual as if she spoke it often—*two legacies. A legacy of love a Heavenly Father would content had He had the offer of...*

Emily, writing of love, the kind of love that men and women had, not love that friends or family had. Vinnie knew that, not because of the word love, but because of the other legacy, the one she could hear clearest in Emily's voice, the one that made her sound bitter and frightened and just a little lost:

You left me boundaries of pain, Emily said, *capacious as the sea. Between eternity and time, your consciousness and me.*

Emily was so afraid of eternity, so averse to time that she did not learn how to read a clock until she was fifteen. Time scarcely touched her, not even near the end. She always looked like a girl. Others aged, but Emily remained as youthful as she had been when they moved from the West Street house to the Homestead. She had been perhaps twenty-five or so, a young woman surely, but one trapped in amber.

Vinnie aged, going from a plump young woman to a matronly old maid. Austin had become serious, his face falling into lines that aged him prematurely.

But Emily, in her white dresses, remained the same—at least on the outside.

And who knew what had gone on inside? Clearly Vinnie hadn't. And Vinnie thought she had known her sister as a maid, not as someone who could write, *Wild nights! Wild nights! Were I with thee, wild nights should be our luxury!*

What had Vinnie missed all those years? Were the townspeople of Amherst right and Vinnie wrong? Had Emily locked herself in the house because she pined for a man who left her? Had she truly been one of those women who, like Miss Haversham of *Great Expectations*, had lost herself because of a man?

How could Vinnie have not known that? How could Vinnie have not known about the man?

She sat among her sister's papers, and tried to remember. But the poems were undated and gave her no clue—except that her sister, whom Vinnie thought she knew well, had become a mystery, one Vinnie was beginning to think she would never understand.

~

October 30, 1855
The West Street House
Amherst, Massachusetts

He sat on the edge of her bed, splendid in his nakedness. Was he splendid because he was immortal? Or had he been splendid in life?

Emily was afraid to ask him. She had learned that direct questions made him glare at her with those empty death-filled eyes.

Some questions she left unasked. Others she danced around, got answers to. Sometimes he just told her unbidden, told her of his extreme loneliness, and how pleased he was to have found a kindred soul.

That was what he called her. A kindred soul.

And of late, Vinnie told her that in certain light, her eyes turned silver.

Emily shuddered and pulled the blanket around her before leaning against his naked back. He bent at the waist, his hands in his thick black hair.

"You have to stop it," he said in desperation. She had never heard this tone in his voice before.

"I can't," she said. "We're moving. Father has decreed it."

He shook his head. "You have to change your father's mind."

"It's not possible," Emily said. "My grandfather built that house. He lost it. My father has waited his entire life to buy it back."

His tone frightened her; his whole demeanor frightened her. She had never been frightened of him before.

But she continued to lean against him, trying to draw strength from his warm skin.

"I can't visit you there," he said, his voice shaking. "Not until..."

"Until?" she asked.

"Not for a very long time," he said. "Unless..."

She didn't like the sound of "unless." But the idea made him sit up, and turn toward her, taking her face in his hands. He often did that before he kissed her, but he didn't kiss her now.

Instead, he peered into her eyes.

"I could take you now. We'd be together. We could work together," he said.

And she felt something—a pulling, a change.

She wrenched her face from his grasp and looked away from him.

"No," she said.

"No?" he asked.

"No," she said. "I don't want to live like you do. I've told you that."

"But you are already half in my world," he said. "Come the rest of the way."

"No," she said.

"Then tell your father to stay here," he said.

She shook her head, resisting the urge to scramble off the bed. As long as he didn't peer at her like that again, he wouldn't be able to pull her life from her.

"You made that impossible," she said.

"Me?"

She nodded. "I am an unmarried woman. I am subject to my father's commands. I cannot influence him. So I will move with him."

And she felt—triumphant? Relieved? She wasn't sure. But not unhappy, like she might have expected. Part of her had always hoped this would end.

"You could come to the burial ground," he said.

She imagined it for a half moment—safe inside alabaster chambers, cradled in his arms—and then she shuddered. She would lose herself there. Lose herself, and lose track of time.

She didn't want to say no directly. He would get angry.

Instead, she said, "Is that why you can come here? The burial ground behind the house?"

He nodded. "I belong here."

"And I belong with my family," she said, wondering if that were indeed true. If it were true, why had she been able to see him? If it were true, why had he fallen in love with her?

"Emily, please," he said. "I won't be able to see you again, except fleeting glances at funerals."

"Or deathbeds," she said, wondering if, in some ways, that was what she sat on. A deathbed.

"Or deathbeds," he whispered.

She closed her eyes, not willing to see his anguish. And when she opened them, just a moment later, he was gone.

So was the strange silver light.

And something else—a part of her. A part she had not realized she'd had.

She went to the window and looked out. He was walking among the graves, like he had the first night she had seen him, his robe over his arm, his scythe carried casually in his left hand.

Walking away.

She wondered when she would see him again. How many years? How much time?

Would he again sit on her bed and tell her he loved her? Or would he be angry?

She wasn't sure she ever wanted to find out.

~

May 24, 1886
The Homestead
Amherst, Massachusetts

Vinnie clutched a pile of poems in one hand. So many about death. Perhaps those were even more shocking than those about love. And the death poems—they weren't typical reminiscences. They were odd, like Emily had been odd, and a bit unfathomable.

Vinnie had even heard Emily speak some of them aloud. Only Vinnie had not realized they were poems at the time.

Like this one, which Emily had spoken late one night, almost unbidden. She looked up from her scratching pen, and smiled sadly at Vinnie. Emily didn't speak the poem exactly as written. She added a bit to make it conversational. But Vinnie remembered it as if it had happened just a week before instead of decades ago.

"Sometimes I think a death-blow is a life-blow to some," Emily said, "who, until they died, did not become alive."

Vinnie had stopped walking by, looked at Emily oddly, and then shrugged, wondering what had provoked that outburst. She still did not know.

Had someone died recently? Had Emily been reacting to something? Or had she simply felt an inspiration?

Except that it felt true, as if something provoked it. Emily often broke into strangely structured speech when provoked, and now Vinnie knew why.

She had been reciting her own poems.

Vinnie wished she could go back, wished she could recapture memories of all of those recitations. Maybe she was; maybe that was why she heard Emily's voice whenever she read a poem. Maybe Emily had spoken them all.

Vinnie clutched the poems against her chest. How could she burn them? They had bits of her sister in them, clinging to them, as if she had not yet died.

~

March 8, 1860
The Homestead
Amherst, Massachusetts

They were calling her crazy and maybe she was, maybe she was. Certainly she felt wild-eyed and broken, her thoughts swirling in her head. Emily had taken to writing them down, capturing them in bits of paper, and then sewing them into bound booklets like she had done her herbs just a few years before.

At the West Street House, when she used to roam the garden, when she wandered the burial ground.

Emily buried her face in her hands. Her room here was larger than her room in the West Street house. She had a conservatory and a better kitchen. She should have liked it here, in the best house in Amherst.

She should have liked it.

But she didn't.

Her room here overlooked the street. The house was far enough back so that street sounds seemed faint, but through the trees, she could see the horses, watch the carriages, see the *life*.

She let her hands fall. Then she grabbed a sheet of paper, its smoothness soothing to her fingertips. She stared for a moment at the windows, then grabbed her pen and dipped it in ink.

She hadn't thought she would miss him.

I cannot live with you, she wrote. *It would be life, and life is over there behind the shelf the sexton keeps the key to…*

She paused, sighed, and held the pen away from the paper so it wouldn't blot.

She wasn't alive without him. He had taken something from her. Everyone noticed it. They had always thought her strange, but now they feared her, and she wasn't quite sure why.

She hid away from them, mostly because she didn't want to see the fear in their eyes.

She wrote, *I could not die with you.*

Was she writing him a letter? And if so, where would she leave it? Did she truly want him to find it, to know she missed him?

Nor could I rise with you, because your face would put out Jesus's...

Her hand trembled as she wrote.

They'd judge us—how? For you served Heaven, you know, or sought to. I could not.

No one dared see these. Not him, not anyone. Think of what they would say. Think of what they would do to her, even in this enlightened time.

She shuddered, feeling the temptation to go to him. But she could not. She dared not.

So we must keep apart, she wrote to him. She *was* writing to him now. She had known that, but she finally acknowledged it. *You there, I here, with just the door ajar....*

The door ajar. That was what the others felt. She straddled the world between, half her life there, half here. She hadn't fled him quickly enough.

She hadn't known what he would cost her, what she had chosen. Then, five years ago, she had tried to go back, not realizing it was too late.

So she lived in this strange half-world, neither here nor there, not willing to cross the threshold into his life—and Eternity, not able to fully live in hers.

She hadn't expected this, and she had no idea how to live with it.

Except to scrawl the maddening thoughts. Except to try to quell the feeling of panic, always rising inside.

Her pen, her paper. Her silence. She had nothing else left.

~

April 20, 1862
Worcester, Massachusetts

The envelope itself looked a bit odd, the handwriting tiny, the edges a bit too thick. That Higginson noticed it was odd too, considering the volume of mail he got lately. He had published an essay titled "A Letter to a Young Contributor" in the *Atlantic Monthly*, hoping to slow down the volume of unsolicited submissions the magazine got. Instead, his essay increased them. And worse, they were all addressed to him.

Only the most select made it to his study in Worcester. Later he would say he added the thick envelope because he had known it carried something marvelous, but at the time, he had taken it only because it struck him as unusual.

He sat in his leather-backed chair, a mound of manuscripts on one side, and his own writing paper on the other. Books surrounded him. He didn't keep newspapers in his study, preferring they remain in the parlor. The news since Lincoln's inaugural a year before had been ugly at best, and Higginson wanted to keep horror out of his study.

He had a hunch it would enter his life all too soon.

He slit the envelope with his letter opener, careful not to disturb the papers inside. A second envelope tumbled out, followed by five sheets of paper—four poems and an unsigned letter. He opened that envelope first, only to find a card inside with the name Emily Dickinson printed upon it in pencil. The five pages had been written in pen.

Intrigued, he started with the letter:

Mr Higginson,

Are you too deeply occupied to say if my Verse is alive?

The Mind is so near itself—it cannot see, distinctly—and I have none to ask—

Should you think it breathed—and had you the leisure to tell me, I should feel quick gratitude—

If I make the mistake—that you dared to tell me—would give me sincerer honor—toward you—

I enclose my name—asking you, if you please—Sir—to tell me what is true?

That you will not betray me—it is needless to ask—since Honor is it's own pawn—

The breathless style startled him and it carried over to the poems, all untitled. Of course the verse lived; he had never seen such life in poetry, and he had read a lot. An untamed life, that reflected the writer more than any other poems he had ever read, as if the writer put herself on the page without regard to convention, or even to a reader.

He reread all of the documents before answering Miss Dickinson. Her verse was alive, her words breathed. But the grammatical errors grated on him. He tapped the tip of his pen against his teeth. He had somehow to tell her that she wasn't yet ready for publication without destroying the spirit that crackled out of the poetry.

Finally he decided he would operate on the poems himself, and she would be able to learn from his surgery. He meticulously copied what she had done, then set about to repair it.

~

October 5, 1883
The Evergreens
Amherst, Massachusetts

It was a mistake, Emily knew it was a mistake, but she couldn't stop herself, she didn't dare stop herself, didn't dare *think* about any of it as she clung to Vinnie's arm and stepped outside the house. The fresh evening air seemed a mockery—next door, right next door, little Gilbert was dying, didn't the Gods know that?

Of course they did; they had ordered it, and because they had ordered it, she cursed them for reveling in the death of children.

She adored Gib, her brother's youngest child born late. Witty and funny and oh, so alive, he made her feel like a child again. Certainly she hadn't laughed so hard in the years before he learned to speak—maybe she hadn't laughed at all.

She loved him, her heart's child, and now typhoid was taking him, and she couldn't stay away, even though she knew she should, even though she tried.

She had picked the right moment to flee her own mother's bedside, and her father's too. Vinnie had to tend the dying, because Emily could not, frightened as she was of ever seeing *him* again.

But she could not flee Gib's bedside and forgive herself. Sometimes love made harsh demands, and this was one.

She walked across the yard into a house as outwardly familiar as her own. Huge, built in the style of an Italian villa, the Evergreens housed the other Dickinsons, the ones who ran her life—her brother Austin, his wife Sue, and their three beautiful children.

That Austin had all but abandoned Sue few knew except Emily. She didn't approve of Austin's mistress, Mabel Loomis Todd, but she didn't dare disapprove either, not after the way Emily had lost herself all those years ago. Austin was here tonight, but Miss Todd was not, and Emily was grateful for that. Even though she knew Miss Todd frequented Emily's home, Emily had not seen her and preferred to pretend that Miss Todd herself was little more than a ghost.

Vinnie put a hand over Emily's as they walked up the steps into the Evergreens. Emily had not been inside in fifteen years, seeing it only from the windows of the Homestead. Her heart pounded as if she had walked a thousand miles, and the smell—the smell nearly turned her stomach.

It was a sick house, reeking of camphor and vomit and despair.

But she continued forward, leaning on Vinnie a bit too much, walking up the stairs to Gib's bedchamber, the smells growing stronger, harsher, more insistent.

Vinnie, bless her, did not say a word. When they reached the door, Emily let out a sigh of relief. *He* was not there. Gib would not die this night.

The boy looked small in his bed, too thin for an eight-year-old, too frail to be the vital child Emily so adored. Sue—grown matronly in middle age—saw Emily and hugged her so tightly that Emily couldn't catch her breath. Austin peered at her from his post near the bureau.

"You're too frail," Austin said. "We don't need you ill as well."

Emily glared at him, and Austin looked away, as everyone did when she gave them her gimlet eye. Then she sat beside Gib and took his hand.

His eyes opened for a brief moment and he saw her. "Aunt Emily," he breathed, his voice raspy and congested.

"Gib," she said, unable to find words for the first time in her life.

His skin was too hot, his eyes glistened with fever. He turned away from her, but kept his hand clamped around hers. Sue placed wet cloths on his forehead, and Austin fretted about feeding the child.

But Emily simply held his dry little hand, hoping he would look at her again.

He did not.

Instead, there was an emptiness in the room. She looked up, the hair on the back of her neck rising. She and Gib were momentarily alone. Sue had gone for more cloths, Austin for water or perhaps just to escape, Vinnie to find camphor to ease Gib's increasingly labored breathing.

The light suddenly turned silver, and Emily inwardly cursed. She had not made her escape.

He had come, and he would see her, an old woman, losing a child of her heart.

She didn't look up. Instead she wrapped her free hand around Gib's.

"Don't take him," she said. "Please don't take him."

"You know I can't do that." His voice was as she remembered only more musical, deep and filled with warmth. "I have missed you, Emily, more than I could ever express."

"Don't." She brought her head up, and her gaze met his.

Damnation, he was still beautiful. His cowl was down, his scythe against the wall. He looked like he had moved in, and despite that, despite the horror of it, she felt his pull even now. He reached out to touch her and she leaned away.

"This is about Gib, not me," she said. "Don't take him."

"I must," he said. He didn't sound sorrowful. He didn't know Gib. She did.

"Take me instead," she said. "My life for his."

He shook his head. "You're already half mine, Emily," he said. "It's not a fair trade. Is there another life you would give for his?"

Her heart chilled. He would have her trade someone else's life for Gib's? What kind of bargain was that?

"Take me, *please,*" she said. "You have always wanted me."

He nodded. "And I still do. I love you, Emily."

She knew that; she also knew that she had loved him once, and feared him too. She didn't fear him now. All she feared was his power.

"So you have what you want," she said. "Leave Gib. Let him grow up."

He looked at his hands as if they were not his. Then he sighed. "I cannot, Emily. His soul is incandescent. Pure."

She knew his next words, but she didn't want to hear him say them. "And mine is not."

"I'm sorry," he whispered. "But you can come with us."

"No," she said. "*No.*"

He touched Gib, and Gib froze—froze!—the heat leaving his body.

"*No,*" she said again. "No!"

And then they were both gone—he and Gib, the scythe, everything—leaving only a frail shell behind.

Everyone came back into the room as if they had been summoned, Sue leading, tears on her dear familiar face, Austin looking ancient and horrible, and Vinnie, Vinnie, hands clasped to her chest.

They crowded the body and Emily staggered away, mouth tasting of paper, eyes dry, head aching.

"Take me home," she said to Vinnie. "Please."

Emily had to go home now, taking her fragile, ragged, worthless little soul. If she hadn't had a fruitless romance with *him*, if she hadn't wasted all of that time, she still would have seen him here, and she could have bargained with him, she could have given him her soul in place of Gib's and it would not have been worthless. Gib would have lived, and so would she.

But *he* had cheated her of that. He had known, and he had cheated her, because he claimed he loved her.

Could one such as that love?

She didn't know. She didn't want to think of it. Not now, and maybe not ever.

~

May 24, 1886
The Homestead
Amherst, Massachusetts

Twilight was falling as Vinnie picked up the last pile of poems. She had just lit Emily's favorite lamp, giving the room a brief scent of kerosene and burned wick.

Vinnie's hands shook. She was exhausted, but unwilling to quit. The poems—ah, the poems—they were Emily, and more than Emily. They were about her life too.

There's been a death in the opposite house, began one, and Vinnie set it aside. She could not read that. It was about Gib. There were a number about Gib, some even calling him by name.

Gib's death had destroyed Emily. From that moment forward, she had been ill, although most did not know it. She continued her letters and, clearly, her poetry, but little else, her eyes hollow, her expression always a little lost.

Not with a club the heart is broken, Emily whispered, *nor with a stone. A whip so small you could not see it...*

Like a poem, Vinnie thought. Like a poem.

"I can't do it, Em," she whispered as if her sister were still here. For all she knew, her sister was alive in the poetry, haunting the room like a restless ghost. "I can't do it."

Burning the poems would be like losing Emily all over again. And storing them would be wrong too, because Austin or his daughter Mattie might burn them, following Emily's wishes.

Vinnie would burn the papers, burn the letters. She would do that much. But the poems were alive, like her sister had been, and she could not destroy them.

Finally, Emily had to step out of her room and let the world see her as Vinnie had seen her, all those years ago—vibrant and witty and filled with an astonishing love.

~

May 15, 1886
The Homestead
Amherst, Massachusetts

He came like she knew he would, his face filled with triumph. Emily was too weak to fight him. She couldn't get out of bed, she couldn't even open her eyes, yet she could see him, sitting on the edge of the bed, his hand gripping hers.

"Are you ready to join me, Emily?" he asked, not trying to disguise the joy in his voice.

"No," she said. "I will never join you."

"You have no choice," he said. "I take everyone."

"But you do not keep them," she said. "You taught me all those years ago how to defeat you. When the memory is gone, the soul goes too. After Vinnie, after Austin, after Mattie, no one will remember me."

"Except me," he said.

"And you do not count," she said, "because you remember everyone you touched."

His eyes widened just a little. "You hate me, Em?"

"For Gib," she said. "I'll never forgive you for Gib."

"Never is a long time," he said.

"But do not fear," she said. "I have escaped Eternity."

"Would it be so bad, Emily, spending forever with me?" he asked.

"Yes," she said. "It would."

"You do not mean it," he said as he took what was left of her soul. She felt a momentary relief, a respite from pain she hadn't realized she had, and then a brief incandescent sense of joy.

Only a few more years and they would go quickly. Vinnie would see to it. Nothing of Emily would remain, nothing except a name carved into a stone above an old and sunken grave—and someday, not even that.

She had won. God help her, she had finally won.

~

May 15, 1892
Cambridge, Massachusetts

Higginson had the dream again. He used to dream of that clearing in Florida, filled with bodies laid out symmetrically. But ever since he turned in his edited version of *The Poems of Emily Dickinson* to the publisher, this dream had supplanted the other.

Emily, as he had first seen her, red hair parted, white dress, beseeching him not to betray her. *Honor me*, she would say, her eyes silver and terrifying. *Honor me.*

And he would say, *I am. I am making your work known.*

Then she would raise her arms, like a banshee from Irish lore, and screech, and as she screeched, the hooded figure would rise behind her and clasp his arms around her, dragging her to the clearing and all those dead men...

And Higginson would wake, heart pounding, breath coming in rapid gasps.

This morning, after the dream, he threw on his dressing gown and made his way to his study. He knew why he had had the dream this time. Another volume of *The Poems by Emily Dickinson* had arrived with a note that this was the seventh edition.

Seven. And more to come. He and Mabel Loomis Todd had barely touched the thousand manuscripts Miss Dickinson had left. He admitted to no one how surprised he was; he had thought her words too strange for the reading public, her gift too rare.

But they adored it, some, he thought, in part to the surgery he had felt it necessary to perform, ridding it of her excessive dashes and her breathless punctuation. But still, the essence of her lived.

Are you too deeply occupied to say if my Verse is alive? she had written him in that very first letter.

And now he could answer her truthfully: her verse was more alive than ever. *She* was more alive than ever.

So why had the first sight of the seventh edition filled him with such horror?

He picked it up and thumbed through it—stopping suddenly at unfamiliar words. He did not recall editing this poem.

He eased into his favorite chair, book in hand, and read:

Because I could not stop for Death,
He kindly stopped for me;
The carriage held but just ourselves

And Immortality.

There was no despair mentioned in the poem, and yet he felt it, like he felt that banshee scream.

What had she written to him once, when she mentioned his books about the War?

My wars are laid away in books.

Yes. Yes they were.

He closed the volume, determined to never open it again.

Waltzing on a Dancer's Grave

Kristine Kathryn Rusch

One

Greta held the railing tightly and peered over the edge. Twenty years ago, he had fallen from here, fallen, fallen, spiraling slowly until he landed five stories below with a thud that echoed through the yard. She had clutched her hands together, squeezing them, trying to erase the feel of his silk shirt against her palms, thinking that for someone as graceful as Karl, falling should have seemed like flying.

At least he hadn't screamed.

"Greta!"

She jumped, her breath caught in her throat. Timothy pulled open the glass doors and crossed the balcony.

"You shouldn't be out here," he said. "You'll catch your death." Then he flushed in the deep, almost purplish way that seemed exclusive to redheads. "I mean that—"

"I know what you mean," Greta said. She ran her hands over the goose bumps on her bare shoulders. "It's cold out here."

He put his arm around her back, warming her as he led her inside. The mansion still had a musty, unused air. Half of the company stretched out in the sunken living room. Long, graceful bodies reclined on the white sofas. Too many bare feet, with their corns, bunions, and bandages, rested on footstools. She always saw the bodies first. Her dancers were less human and more instruments to her.

Timothy closed the glass door. Sebastian glanced up from his place in the corner, his arm around the new brunette. Amanda Thigopolos. He was trying to get Greta's attention by playing at jealousy. She concentrated instead on the brunette. The girl was perhaps eighteen, just out of high school, and could dance as if she had been born in toe shoes. Amanda was fine. Thigopolos had to go—too long and too Greek. She could shorten it when she had her own name on the program. Thigopolos would be fine as long as she was part of the *corps de ballet.*

"I assume you're all settled," Greta said. The company turned to her as a unit. Faces—white, black, and brown, circles under most eyes and skin gray with pain—stared at her. Pain was part of being a dancer. She had learned that from Karl. *Ballet is impossible,* he would say. *Pain is a small price for doing the impossible.* She ignored the evidence of the dancers' exhaustion and overwork, and glared at them. "This isn't Sunday. I didn't say we would have the day off. Class in two hours."

They groaned. Dale sewed a knot on his shoe, bit the thread, and gave the needle back to Katrina. Lisa rubbed her feet. Sebastian frowned at Greta. She ignored him. "Well?" she said. They stood, stretched, and left the room in a jumbled line caught at the door, looking like a company on the first day of rehearsal season instead of one that had been together nearly six months. She sighed and pushed back the scarf covering her graying black hair. No. The hair was silvering, not graying. She was growing old elegantly, as Karl predicted she would.

Karl. He filled the room. She could almost catch the scent of his cologne, rich and overpowering, like Karl himself. Sometimes she thought she saw him out of the corner of her eye. Six feet tall and too thin, his leg muscles nearly bulging out of his jeans, his hair silver, and his brown eyes blazing. She remembered those eyes mostly in anger, never in repose. Anger, and that deep fierce hunger he seemed to have for her, the hunger she had once thought would consume her.

"Sorry you came?"

Timothy. She had forgotten about him. He stood next to her, as he always had, protecting her and backing her, the silent partner who liked to remain silent.

"It's the fiftieth anniversary of the company," she said. "It's only fitting that we do the anniversary performance here."

The words were by rote. She had said them ever since she had decided to return to Grayson Place. Usually the answer satisfied Timothy, but this time, he touched her arm. "I was asking about you, Greta."

She nodded. She remembered calling Timothy on the phone by the fireplace, her hands shaking so that she could barely dial. *Karl's dead,* she had said. *Did you call the police?* Timothy asked. *I want you to,* she said. Always there, always beside her, from the trial to the fight to save the company and onward, always caring about her and never asking for himself.

"I think that if we are going to keep the place, we'll have to redecorate." She reached across the table beside her and touched the rounded lamp base. Its garish brown-and-orange glass was the height of the sixties tastelessness. "It feels as if time has stopped here."

"Maybe it has," Timothy said, and in his eyes she saw Karl, falling, falling, reaching out to her as he spun, his shirt fluttering in the wind, his gaze on her, strong as Karl himself, pulling part of her with him.

She shivered. That had been twenty years ago. She ran her hands along her upper arms. The goose bumps were still there. Timothy put his arms around her, but she ducked out of his grasp.

"Class in two hours," she said, smiling slightly. "And I want to eat."

Two

Timothy watched her leave. Greta still moved like a young girl. Up close, though, her body gave her away. Her skin was wrinkling, softly, adding an elegance to her features, but the elegance was one of age. She was old, for a dancer, especially one who still practiced the art, but she was strong.

Greta was strong.

Timothy turned toward the balcony. Even now, he could feel the chill from that night. It had been cold when Karl died. Near freezing, although it was spring. When Timothy arrived, he found Greta, her hands shaking, still hovering near the phone. He had walked through the open glass doors, past the plastic patio furniture with its fringed umbrellas, past the deck chairs, Karl's portable record player, and the small television set where they had watched *The Wizard of Oz* because Karl loved watching Ray Bolger dance. The concrete structure seemed almost a mile long and Timothy walked it inch by agonizing inch, knowing that when he reached the wrought-iron railing, he would have to look down.

The railing still seemed to vibrate, but the trembling was caused by the cold and his own fear. Timothy touched the iron gently.

The imitation gaslight on the courtyard four and a half stories below illuminated Karl's mangled, twisted body. Karl, who had never made an ungraceful motion in his life, looked like a young boy who had tried his first *tour en l'air,* tripped, fallen, and refused to try again. Timothy wanted to whisper, "Get up, Karl, it's all right," but knew that Karl would never get up and everything would not be all right. Karl had died, and, in the living room, Greta washed her hands together like Lady Macbeth.

Timothy shivered. He'd tried to argue with Greta when she wanted to return to Grayson Place, but she wouldn't listen. She wanted to do the anniversary event, wanted to do it here, and nothing he could say would change her mind.

She hadn't been back to Grayson Place since the night Karl died. Even though she had inherited the mansion with Karl's estate, she had let Timothy take care of it. He rented it out to friends and dancers, keeping it in constant use, but he hadn't returned either. Not since the night he had decided to lie for her, the night before he first spoke to Greta's attorney, two weeks after Karl died and almost a year before Timothy actually testified at the murder trial.

"Mr. Masson?"

The brunette, the new one, the one Sebastian was dallying with, stood at the door. Timothy frowned, but couldn't recall her name.

"My room is cold," she said.

The whole place is cold, Timothy thought, but said, "The thermostat is on the baseboard heaters. You'll have to turn it up."

"It's up all the way and the heaters are warm." She shrugged. "But the room itself is freezing."

Timothy sighed inwardly. More and more, managing this company meant playing nursemaid. If he were a little more trusting, he would hire someone to do this part of the job, the road work, and the day-by-day scheduling. He smiled. Trusting had nothing to do with it. He couldn't leave Greta.

"Where's your room?" he asked.

"Third floor, last one on the left."

Greta's old room. Timothy didn't know why his heart started knocking at his rib cage. He followed the girl up the stairs, remaining one step behind her. Her long hair smelled of floral shampoo and he could see the muscles that had already developed into hardened lumps along her legs and arms.

The third floor was filled with light conversation, some laughter. A few doors were open, dance bags sprawled in the hall, leotards hanging over doorknobs.

As he passed one room, he heard a woman gasp. The door swung closed before he could look. He hadn't really wanted to look anyway. He had seen it all before—twenty-five years of before.

"Hey, Amanda's doing the casting couch school of dance," someone called from a half-open doorway.

The girl in front of him blushed a little, but kept walking. Timothy admired that. She had guts. She. Amanda. Timothy repeated the name in his head so that he would remember. Amanda. Amanda the Greek, the one whose last name Greta hated.

"Right here," the girl said. She stood to the side of the door in the last room, the one under the eaves.

Timothy stepped inside. The room was cold. Ice cold. Or perhaps the chill from the living room had returned. He hadn't been in this room in over twenty years. Not since the night (*he and Greta had made love in the big double bed under the slanting ceiling. He had scraped his back against the drywall and hadn't cared because he was with Greta. Everything was fine with Greta)* Karl had called Greta from the room. Timothy didn't know until the next morning that she had gone to Karl's bed, although he should have guessed, should have known. Karl, the great dancer who had become an even greater choreographer. Greta used to breathe his name when she spoke it: *Karl says . . . Karl wants . . . Karl believes . . .*

"I'm being silly, right?" the girl asked.

Timothy spun, half expecting to see Greta at the door. Amanda looked like Greta—tall, slim with long, dark hair. But there the resemblance ended. Greta hadn't looked that young, that innocent, for twenty years. "No," he said. "There's a definite draft. We'll have to move you to another part of the wing."

"That's okay," Amanda said. "I kind of like the room and it's only for a couple of days. I don't mind staying here."

I mind, Timothy thought. He crouched, touching the baseboard heaters. They were hot and the air coming through the outduct was warm. The chill seemed to be something that the heat couldn't dissipate, like an iceberg with its own refrigerator unit. "The heat's on. I could call someone—"

"No." The girl shrugged. "I'm not going to be in here much anyway. All I need is a few extra blankets."

"All right." Timothy left the room. The hallway felt like a sauna. Tension rippled off his back. He had been wrong coming to Grayson. There were as many memories here for him as there were for Greta. Perhaps more. "I'll see to it that the house staff brings up some blankets."

If the house staff was fully together. Timothy sighed. He had too much work to do. He wouldn't even get to watch class. Sometimes he wished that he hadn't stopped dancing. The pain and the constant physical exhaustion seemed easier to deal with than the myriad of tiny details that commanded his attention all day.

He walked down the hall, wondering how badly it would hurt the anniversary performance if he simply flew home.

Three

Greta felt as if she were twenty years old as she walked these stairs. They hadn't changed much. The white carpet had been pressed by too many feet, its nap matted and turned downward. The wooden railing had a newly polished feel. If she closed her eyes, she could imagine Karl waiting for her in the practice room.

She used to love to be near him, couldn't wait to touch him. The scent of his cologne used to send shivers down her back. But that had been in the early days, the first days. He continued to demand things of her, twist her to fit his shape, and she realized that nothing she ever did would be right for Karl.

Bend, Greta, arch—no, no, no, with finesse. Goddammit, girl, you could be a real dancer if you used that body of yours. Now, bend. No, like this . . .

It had grown worse after she had become his prima ballerina, the star of his company, and had moved in with him here at Grayson. Sometimes he would get her up in the middle of the night to try a new movement or run through a variation that had come to him in a dream. She had been always tired, aching, dancing with a constant pain in her left ankle, but that hadn't been the worst of it. The worst of it had been the choreography.

She took a deep breath to ease the tension from herself and then rounded the corner. The dance wing of Grayson Place had been hidden back in the trees. When Karl built Grayson, he had been afraid that rival choreographers would send spies, that dance critics would try to see his works before the premiere. So the dance wing had no windows. Pines and overgrowth protected the outside. No one could get to the auditorium and practice rooms without coming through the center of the mansion.

This wing had stayed closed after Karl died, but someone had cleaned it, polished it. Greta could remember when the white walls held dozens of sweaty fingerprints and long black slashes from brushes with dirty dance bags. Down here, she felt at home.

She walked into the practice room. Dancers were already parading in front of the mirror on the far wall. Mike, the rehearsal pianist, played random chords, checking to see if the piano was tuned. The floor glistened. Several dancers warmed up along the barre. Some stretched along the floor, while still others sat on the sides, sewing shoes and wrapping ankles. The room smelled of sweat and medicated lotion.

Greta didn't announce her presence. She went up behind Amanda and held the girl's waist to straighten her. No wonder Sebastian flirted with her. Her skin was smooth and supple, and she moved easily. Greta grabbed Amanda's right arm and bent it above the girl's head. "Your movements have to be softer," Greta said.

Sebastian was watching her. She couldn't read his dark eyes. She was growing tired of him. She was growing tired of all the young men. She hadn't had a lover older than twenty-four in nearly two decades. It was time to stop hiding behind their responsive skin and quicksilver moods, time to take a real risk in a relationship again.

She knew that Timothy was waiting for that.

"As usual," she said. "*Battement tendu.*"

Mike began the *battement tendu* music. Dancers slid into fifth position, feet touching and the heel of the right foot in front of the left toe. Then they extended one leg, moving the toe forward until it touched the floor directly in front of the body. Greta watched, seeing the differences in movement, the variations in style. The dancers slid their right foot back and then to the side, slid the foot back and behind. The movements seemed to take only a fraction of a second, but Greta saw each one.

"Sebastian," she said. "You're sloppy. Head up."

He didn't look at her, but continued watching the mirror as she instructed them through the *battement tendu jeté.* Small thuds echoed as feet slapped against the floor. Greta walked over to Sebastian, and kicked his left foot into place. "Don't look down," she said. He frowned.

They moved to the *battement frappé, battement fondu, rond de jambe.* The smell of sweat grew. Greta watched them, adjusted an arm here, a leg there. Finally she clapped her hands and the music stopped.

"Sebastian only. *Grand battement,"* she said. The dancers near Sebastian moved away. Under Greta's command, he brought his foot forward into a high extension. "Stay," she said.

He held the position, leg at a hundred-and-thirty-degree angle in front of him. His entire body started to tremble and his mouth opened into a small "o."

"Go on," Greta said. He moved down into a deep *plié* with one leg, the other in front. "Stay." She stopped beside him. "Messy, Sebastian. Your line isn't clean."

"What are you doing?" he whispered. Sweat rolled down the bridge of his nose and dropped to the floor. His body was still trembling.

She didn't answer. "Finish," she said. He slipped his legs back into fifth position. Then he stood, bent over, and clutched the back of his knees, stretching and taking deep breaths. Greta put her hand on his back. She could feel the ridges of his spine beneath her palms. "You're breathing too hard. Your posture's bad and you look as if you are thinking about your feet. You're lazy, Sebastian."

"Why are you singling me out?" he whispered. "What are you doing, Greta?"

A thread of anger traced its way through her stomach. If she hadn't slept with him, he would never have asked the question. She was Madame, the head of the company, and no one was supposed to question her.

"I am conducting class." She clapped her hands. "Whole group."

The dancers returned to the barre. She started again: *battement tendu, tendu jeté, frappé, fondu, rond de jambe.* But she wasn't watching the dancers. In her mind, she could see Karl moving among the dancers, yanking an arm out, extending a leg. One of the dancers exclaimed as if in pain, but Greta kept them moving.

"How much longer you want to repeat this pattern?" Mike asked. His voice had an edge to it, as if he had asked the question more than once.

Greta's heart was pounding. She didn't want to stay in the practice room any longer. If she did, the ghost of Karl's memory would have her out there, moving through her paces like she had moved Sebastian. Like she had moved Sebastian. Singling out one dancer had been Karl's trick. Karl had always done that to her as his way of proving that she was not his favorite.

Her stomach twisted and for a moment, she thought she was going to be sick. She clapped her hands and the dancers stopped. "Lead class, Katrina," Greta said and walked out of the room.

FOUR

Sebastian stood under the shower, letting the hot water caress his tired muscles, soothe his aching legs. He opened his mouth and listened to the droplets tap against his throat. The water tasted slightly of rust, but he didn't care. He frowned, remembering the odd note of command in Greta's voice. *Stay . . . Go on . . . Stay . . .*

A bar of soap hit him in the back and skated across the tile. Sebastian spit the water out of his mouth and then turned. Dale hung a fluffy blue towel he had stolen from the Hyatt on the peg beside his shower. "Get this," he said. "A shower room in a house."

"This isn't a house," Sebastian said. His back muscles twitched where the soap had hit him. "It's a goddamn fortress."

"No shit. Not even the American Ballet Theatre has facilities this good."

"The American Ballet Theatre didn't have several hundred million dollars *and* Karl Grayson." Sebastian picked the soap off the floor, rubbed the bar between his hands until it lathered and then began scrubbing his chest.

"I wonder why we don't use this place more."

Sebastian's hands had moved to his belly. The last three nights before they had come to Grayson, Greta had screamed *Nooooo!* in her sleep and then had said, a few minutes later, in a very flat voice, *Karl is dead, Timothy.* Her entire body would shake and when Sebastian tried to ease her into wakefulness, she would scream again. "Grayson died here," he said.

"So? Someone afraid it's haunted?" Dale ducked his head under the nozzle, spraying water in several directions.

Maybe for Greta it is, Sebastian thought, but said nothing. He finished soaping his legs, then moved to his feet. He had a new pain, almost like a bruise, between the first and second toes of his right foot.

"Madame was sure a bitch today, wasn't she?" Dale shook the water from his hair. "You gonna share that soap?"

Sebastian stood up. He tossed the bar as hard as he could, hitting Dale in the stomach. The soap bounced off and skittered away, as it had after it hit him. "I don't think Greta likes it here."

"Greta, Greta, Greta," Dale mimicked as he went for the soap. "I don't think she's too happy with you either."

"Yeah." Sebastian frowned. Greta's voice seeped back up to him. *Stay . . . Go on . . . Finish . . .*

"I think maybe you should keep your hands off that little girl for a couple of days and maybe Madame will let you dance like the rest of us."

"Yeah," Sebastian said, but he wasn't really listening. Amanda wasn't the problem. Greta didn't get jealous, not in the normal way. She knew that no one compared with her, knew that Sebastian needed a little adulation too.

She only got angry when his dalliances became disrespectful and this one wasn't even close yet. No. Something else was bothering her. Something she hadn't told him about.

Sebastian shut off the shower. He wrapped a towel around his waist, sloshed across the tile, and tiptoed onto the icy concrete floor lining the dressing room. He would ignore Amanda tonight and he would talk with Greta. Maybe then he would know what was really going on.

Five

Greta looked at the long, polished wood table in the dining room. Four white tapered candles flickered along its length. Twenty places, set with bone china, ran along the sides. One place had been set at the head. Greta stared at it. Her place now. She was head of this company. She sat in Karl's chair.

She had never really realized it before. She had been sitting in Karl's chair since the trial and since Timothy had found an attorney good enough to settle the estate. But she had never before let herself think about what sitting in Karl's place actually meant.

Bowls and empty wineglasses sat on the serving board behind the table. The dark red curtains were closed, blocking the view of the lake. Karl would have left the curtains open to watch the moonlight reflected on the waters.

She shook her head. That was wrong. He used to do that when they were alone. When the company was in residence here, the curtains remained closed so that no one would be distracted from Karl's petty games and speeches.

The smell of roast beef dominated the food scents coming from the kitchen. Greta's mouth watered. As she aged, she let herself eat things like red meat again, but she knew most of the company wouldn't touch the stuff.

Dancers were vegetarians, usually, trying to keep the calories down so that the body remained thin. She was thin and almost always cold—especially here, in this place. Thin, but strong. The muscles in her arms and legs were as powerful as they had been when she was twenty-four. When Karl had died.

Laughter echoed in the hallway. Greta started and turned away from the empty table. She didn't want to be down here when the company arrived. She wanted to make an entrance, to command their attention. That too was like Karl, but she couldn't care. Many things she would do here would remind her of Karl. They had to. She had gotten her start in Karl's company. He had been her first choreographer and the head of her first dance troupe. She had been in others, during and after the trial, but none were as well run as Karl's. She had adopted many of his techniques in her own. It was no wonder that here, in his home, she would remember that.

She went into the kitchen. A man dressed in a white chef's uniform placed broccoli florets on a bed of rice. A woman opened the long oven and pulled out the beef. On the other oven, over to the side, another woman set stuffed mushroom caps on a serving plate.

Once before, Greta had come through the kitchen to escape the dining room. Only that night, she had been escaping Karl and Timothy arguing over her. Timothy had been young then, and very hotheaded. The perfect male dancer, Karl used to say, temperamental, passionate, and very precise. It had been her relationship with Karl that had driven Timothy from the dance. And it had been Karl's death that brought Timothy back into that world.

She pushed open the other door and went up the back stairs to her room. Timothy had placed her in the guest bedroom suite, thoughtfully keeping her away from Karl's old room. She checked her appearance in the mirror.

Her skin was too pale and the shadows beneath her eyes were too deep. The long burgundy shirtdress that she wore open over her black silk camisole gave her additional height. The matching burgundy pants creased over the arch of her foot. If no one looked at her face, she appeared important, expensive, and powerful.

Then why was it that she felt like a trapped little girl again? The mansion brought back all of her helplessness, all of her rage. She clenched her fists together. Her fingertips were cold.

A sharp rap on the door startled her and she nearly cried out. She whirled around, staring at the door's mahogany surface.

"Greta?"

It was Sebastian.

"Can we talk?"

She glanced at the gold watch on her left wrist. "Dinner is in less than fifteen minutes, Sebastian."

"I know. This won't take long."

She sighed and pulled the door open. He looked wonderful. Sebastian, the company's star, in a black satin tuxedo that lengthened his shoulders and tapered his already thin hips into nearly nothing. She felt a heat on her cheeks as she stood away from the door. "Come on in."

He bent over to kiss her, and she turned her head so that his lips brushed her cheek. "You're stunning," he said.

"Thank you." She pulled away from him and walked to the table near the window. She put her hands on the leather armchair, indicating where he should sit. He ignored her.

"What happened this afternoon?" he asked.

The male animal in its youth. So proprietary. He let her lead him in the dance, but once the doors were closed, he seemed to think he was in charge. "You mean because I worked you harder in class than you've been worked in a long time? You're the headline star, the one who supposedly draws the crowds. If you can't dance at command, then the entire company is in trouble."

Sebastian ran a hand through his dark brown hair, leaving it slightly messy, making him look rakish and even more handsome than before. "It's not that," he said. "It's a lot of things. You don't seem like yourself."

So he had noticed that. He was more observant than she gave him credit for. She turned her back on him and looked out the window. Tall pine trees swished softly in the wind. She had been paying so much attention to the mansion itself that she had hardly noticed what was going on outside it.

"You don't know what *myself* is, little boy," she said and heard Karl in the words. He had been standing in the dining room, his hands tucked in the pockets of his jeans. *You don't understand me at all, Greta,* he'd said. *And why should you? To you, I am Oz, The Great and Terrible, and I am afraid that when you pull back that curtain and see that I am, in truth, a little old man without magic powers, but with the wisdom brought by age and experience, you will walk away, not realizing that wisdom is infinitely more valuable than illusion.*

"I know you well enough to know that you're on edge and upset."

She snorted and leaned on the chair she had been holding. Upset didn't describe how she was feeling. She hadn't been in the place since Karl died—Timothy had taken care of all the arrangements—and she was feeling frightened. "I don't like it here."

"Then why did we come back?"

"To do the anniversary performance." She looked down at her short, stubby fingernails. Even the burgundy nail polish couldn't hide the fact that, at forty-four, she still bit her nails.

Sebastian put a finger under her chin and lifted her face to his. He smelled faintly of cologne. "What's the real reason, Greta?"

She could see the brown flecks in his irises, the way his lashes turned upwards, and the tiny creases near the lids which narrowed his eyes and made his concern obvious.

The real reason. What was the real reason that she had returned to Grayson Place? The anniversary performance could have been held in New York. They would have had a less exclusive crowd, but a larger one. Something Karl had said. Something, the night before he died—

She shrugged to shake the memory away. "I don't really know," she said and to her surprise, tears lined her eyes. Sebastian slipped her in his arms. His body felt firm against hers, the satin warm against her skin.

"Stay with me tonight," she whispered. The words came from the little girl, the one who seemed a part of this place, the girl who was afraid to be alone.

Sebastian kissed the crown of her head. "I'll be here," he said.

Six

Amanda's mouth watered. The food smelled wonderful—roast beef, gravy, cheese-covered vegetables, and fresh bread. She hadn't eaten well since she had quit her waitressing job to join the company. An apple and scrambled eggs often served for all three meals. Dancers were supposed to be slim, but not anorexic. She watched the caterers carry the appetizers through the swinging doors. Amanda wondered how much she could eat without making herself sick.

Someone touched her shoulder. Amanda looked up. Katrina smiled at her. "Nice dress."

Amanda blushed. It wasn't a nice dress. Madame had insisted on formal attire for dinner, and all Amanda owned was her prom dress. She felt silly in a clingy, strapless gown that had seemed elegant in her high school gymnasium a year ago, but now seemed out of place and childish. Katrina, the petite principal dancer who had been with the company for six years, wore a bone ivory blouse over black silk pants. "You look beautiful," Amanda said.

Katrina handed Amanda a fluted glass filled with wine. "The secret to looking beautiful," Katrina whispered, "is to be comfortable. Everyone looks ridiculous in evening clothes. Look at Dale."

Amanda glanced across the room. Dale stood near the window, deep in conversation with Lisa. He constantly ran his finger around the neck of his shirt as if it were too tight, and when he leaned forward, she could see the cummerbund bunch around his narrow waist. She glanced back at Katrina, who smiled. "The imperfections are always there," Katrina said. "The secret is to pretend that no one will notice them. You really do look lovely."

She touched Amanda's arm and then walked away. Amanda took a deep breath. She looked lovely. Katrina's words gave her a sense of power.

Timothy took an appetizer off one of the trays as a signal that the food was available for consumption. Several other dancers picked items off the trays. Amanda walked over to the countertop. Stuffed mushroom caps, vegetables and dip, crackers and a dozen varieties of cheese—there was enough food here to last her for an entire week. She set down her wine, grabbed a napkin, and filled it. Her stomach rumbled.

"I love these things. I can always tell who starves themselves for art."

Amanda nearly dropped the napkin, but Timothy placed a hand beneath hers. "Careful," he said. "You can't let all that food go to waste."

His palm was warm and his eyes understanding. She smiled to hide the blush that was returning to her cheeks. "Thanks," she said.

"Is your room still so cold?"

She nodded. The goose bumps were just now beginning to recede. She had felt, as she slipped into her gown, as if she were changing clothes on a ski slope.

"I think maybe we should move you, then."

"No." The word escaped before she had a chance to think about it. Despite the chill, she liked the room. It reminded her of her bedroom back home, with the slanting ceilings and a view of the pines.

Timothy shrugged. "All right," he said.

She put a mushroom cap in her mouth. Her stomach grumbled appreciatively. The cap had been stuffed with spinach, cream cheese, onions, and various spices, the mushroom itself sautéed in garlic and butter. Food had never tasted so good.

Then Timothy stiffened beside her. She followed his gaze.

Sebastian stood in the doorway, his arm protectively around Greta.

Madame wore her hair in a topknot, strands framing her face, making her look younger and more vulnerable. Sebastian was watching her, and even from across the room, Amanda could see the love, admiration, and concern on his face.

She swallowed the mushroom cap. It felt like a lump in her throat. Suddenly she became conscious of the dress, her ragged haircut, and her inexpertly applied makeup. She started inching her way to the kitchen, but Timothy grabbed her elbow.

"Stay here," he said softly.

She looked up at him and saw her feelings reflected in his eyes. Only the feelings were deeper, older. She felt something flutter in her stomach, a sense of kinship, perhaps, and then she looked away.

Amanda watched as Sebastian led Madame through the room. What was there to love about that woman? She was beautiful, yes. Her thinness made her eyes wider and gave her a power that seemed to belong only to eastern European women. She moved with a grace and strength that all dancers had. But beneath that exquisite surface, Madame was cold. She had never said a kind word to Amanda in six months with the company, and the way she had treated Sebastian in class had bordered on nasty. When Amanda had gotten the job with the company, her roommates had warned her about Madame, saying that she was the cruelest choreographer in the business. She demanded perfection. But her company attracted crowds because she usually achieved it.

Madame made her way through the room, stopping to talk with an occasional dancer. Her movements seemed less fluid than usual, more brittle, and Sebastian's expression reflected a concern that Amanda had never seen. She shouldn't be feeling so out of place and jealous. She had known from the first that his main affection was for Madame. But Amanda had thought that the affection would die when he turned his attention to someone more reasonable. Once he had gotten to know her.

Being a professional dancer didn't stop childish daydreams. She took a deep breath. Timothy squeezed her arm. She nodded, as if to tell him that she would stay.

Madame took her place at the head of the table. Sebastian sat at her right. The rest of the company brought their drinks and picked seats.

Timothy kept his hold on Amanda's elbow. He led her to the chair beside his, to the left of Madame.

Sebastian nodded at her. His eyes held no apology. It was as if he didn't see her. Perhaps he never had. Amanda's stomach tightened. The servers placed a large plate of roast beef in the center of the table, two gravy bowls, potatoes, but the food had lost its appeal. She could feel Timothy watching her.

He leaned over, placed his hand on her bare back in a gesture of familiarity. "You have to eat," he whispered. "You have to smile and you have to enjoy yourself."

The words were kind and she knew their basic truth. If she had problems with Madame, Amanda would have to leave. A thousand dancers lived in New York, but the company had only one Madame.

Timothy took his hand from Amanda's back. Shivers ran up and down her spine. He handed her the platter of roast beef. The china was warm. She took two slices and passed the platter on.

"It's cold," Madame said.

Amanda looked at the other woman. Deep circles ran under Madame's eyes and, up close, her face seemed drawn and pale.

"I'll see if they can turn up the heat." Timothy put his napkin on the table.

Madame covered his hand with her own. "I don't think this has anything to do with the heat, Timothy."

Something seemed to pass between them, some knowledge that Amanda didn't catch. Timothy nodded. He grabbed a spoon and loaded his plate with broccoli and rice. Then he picked up Amanda's plate and did the same.

She turned her attention to the meal as, all around her, the room grew colder.

SEVEN

Karl sat on the balcony railings, one ankle resting on his knee, his hands on his thighs. He was talking to her, but Greta couldn't hear him. A chill, light breeze fluttered through her hair. Her ankle ached and her muscles were sore. She was exhausted, physically and mentally. Tired of fighting. Tired of Karl.

Behind him, the tall silhouettes of the pine trees were blue in the darkness. Through the trees, she could see the moon shimmering against the surface of the lake. Then she realized that it wasn't the moon. It was the northern lights.

Karl was still talking, gesturing now. She still couldn't hear him. She didn't feel like a twenty-four-year-old woman. She felt fifty and defeated, her life over before it had begun, trapped here in this place, under this sky, these stars, with this man.

"Karl," she said, her voice low, husky, seductive.

He stopped talking and watched her. She stepped forward, hitting the heels of her hands against his chest, hitting him with such force that he fell over the rail, clutching for her and missing. She thought, in a second of clarity, that if he had grabbed the railing, he wouldn't have fallen. But she had applied the right pressure to the right place and he fell, spinning, his shirt fluttering, his hands reaching for her, until he landed against the flagstones of the patio with a crack that echoed through the yard. She grabbed the railing and leaned over. His body was twisted, unnaturally even for a dancer, and a dark stain was seeping across the pavement.

For a minute, she thought he was fooling, waiting until she ran across the pavement to grab her wrist and wrench it behind her back, to hurt her as much as she had hurt him. But he didn't move. He didn't call to her. He was dead.

The realization brought her—freedom. Freedom. She had to call Timothy.

Suddenly he was there beside her, holding her in the darkness. Not Timothy, but Sebastian. How did Sebastian get in her room? And then she remembered letting him in because the mansion frightened her.

"You were talking about northern lights and calling for Timothy," he said. "Everything okay?"

She swept her hair out of her face. The hair fell to the center of her back, wrapping her in warmth. The soft, shining smoothness of it had seemed like her only comfort with Karl. "Nightmare," she said.

"You've been having them a lot since we decided to come back here."

"We didn't decide," she said. "*I* did."

And then she knew what was wrong. Karl had said to her in the dark, his lean body against hers, his hands caressing the insides of her thighs, *What I want most is to come back here in twenty years, at the fiftieth anniversary of the company—*

Thirty-fifth for you, Greta had said.

He shrugged, waving it away. *We'll have a gala here, at Grayson, showcasing the best of the company. You'll be a choreographer then, Greta. . . .*

If I live that long, she thought.

. . . And we will make a small fortune on memories.

He had been talking about that when she pushed him. The thought of another twenty years with Karl, under his thumb, losing the best of herself to his wishes—

She shivered. Sebastian drew the blanket up. "Must have been some nightmare," he said.

She nodded, remembering Karl, the feel of his hands on her skin. "You ever have those dreams that start out scary and you turn them into something freer, more pleasant, and then they start to get scary again, only worse—?"

Her voice shook. She wasn't sure if she was talking about her dream or her life. Sebastian still held her, but his grip had loosened. "Should we leave?" he asked.

She laughed, but the laugh sounded forced. "Because of nightmares? Don't be silly."

He eased her back down on the pillow, running his hand through her hair as if she were the child, and she clung to him, thinking about what she would have to do to cancel the fiftieth-anniversary gala. The ads were done, the promotion campaign had run for nearly two years. They were in the final stages. She couldn't pull the company away now without losing a fortune.

"We'll stay," she whispered against Sebastian's broad, furred chest. But, as she drifted off to sleep, she thought she heard Karl, laughing.

Eight

Timothy sat on the bed, his hands clasped tightly together and shoved between his thighs for warmth. He waited for Amanda to return from the bathroom. He wasn't supposed to be sitting on her bed. He was supposed to be investigating the room, seeing if he could find the source of the draft. But the room seemed warmer to him than it had before, and he wondered if perhaps the heaters had merely needed time to function properly. This entire wing had been closed off until a month ago. They should have expected more troubles than one room with poorly operating baseboard heaters.

He heard a movement in the hall and his heart started pounding again. He felt foolish, waiting here for a girl who could have been his daughter. It would be so easy to say that he had found nothing and leave her, pretending that the reason he had used to walk her to her room hadn't even existed. Easy, if it weren't for that expression she had worn when Greta entered the dining room with Sebastian. He knew that expression intimately; it was etched into the grooves of his face. Only he had let it eat at him, become part of him, as the betrayals were repeated over and over again. He wouldn't let that happen to this little girl.

Amanda. If he truly cared about her, he would use her name. Timothy stood up and tugged on the crease in his satin pants. He should go before he did more damage. He knew what it was like to be on the wrong end of a relationship. Amanda didn't need two men to teach her the same lesson.

Her door opened and he saw Greta there, the young Greta, the one he had fallen in love with. "Find anything?" she asked.

The voice was all Amanda, but it didn't entirely destroy the illusion. He saw two women, a ghostly one—the remembered one—superimposed on the real one.

"No," he said. He took her hand and brought her inside, closing the door behind her. Then he wrapped his arms around her, letting the light floral scent of her fill him. Her arms caressed his back, pulling him closer. He could feel the need in her grasp.

The room seemed warm, almost too warm, as he bent down to kiss her. Her hands found his hair, holding him, as their kissing grew more passionate. He slipped his fingers into her gown, unhooking the back, and it fell off her into a pile on the floor. She managed to unbutton him, free him, and he lifted her, her dark hair flowing over his arms, onto the bed.

He felt young again, a dancer again, strong and in love. As he entered her, his back scraped against the drywall, but the pain seemed worth it, worth this moment, Greta writhing beneath him, loving him as he loved her. Finally the pressure grew too much, the love too much, and he poured himself inside her, calling her name over and over, collapsing, sticky body against sticky body, his back aching and raw.

Something warm trickled against his ear. He pushed up onto his elbows. The girl's face looked back at him, mascara ringing her eyes and leaving black streaks down her cheeks.

"Jesus," he said. "Amanda." And his heart went out to her. He had made it worse. She had lost to Greta twice in one day. The chill returned, almost as if it left Amanda's body and seeped into the air around them.

"I'm sorry." Timothy buried his face into the hollow of her shoulder. Her skin was damp, but whether with tears or perspiration, he couldn't tell. "I'm so very sorry."

Nine

Greta wrapped the velour robe tightly around herself. She grabbed her hair, shook it a little, and let it cascade down her back. Sebastian grunted, sighed, and rolled over. She glanced at the bed. He had a fist pressed against his cheek. He looked like an exhausted child who had fallen asleep in the middle of a ballet. Poor boy. She had kept him awake half of the night.

The dreams were getting worse. She had thought that she had put them past her after the trial, but since she decided to return to Grayson, Karl had reentered her mind.

She opened the bedroom door and stepped into the hallway. It was dark, the thick grainy darkness that allowed her to see vague shapes. The carpet scratched her bare feet.

She had left her youth in this place. Karl wasn't the only thing that had died in the fall from the balcony. All of Greta's dreams had died with him. Funny that she had gone on to achieve them anyway. Here she was, a major choreographer, head of her own dance company, wealthy beyond what she had anticipated, and she felt empty.

Light filtered through the balcony doors, reflecting off the living room's white furniture. A too-full moon? Or the northern lights? She crossed the room stubbing her toe against a table leg and wincing with pain. When she reached the balcony doors, she touched the glass. It was cold.

This was the center of the mansion to her, the place she could not get out of her mind. At the trial, the experts had presented life in this room as verbally abusive, and her response as that of a classic victim pushed too far. All she remembered was the rage, the blind pure hatred. When Karl mentioned the anniversary performance again, she realized that he would never let her go, never let her be free to dance for anyone else. He would continue to borrow her choreographic suggestions and never let her work on her own. Forever, she would be his plaything, his woman, Karl's Greta, something he had molded in his Svengali-like wisdom.

Her feet were cold.

She was standing on the concrete balcony, looking over the edge. She had been acquitted of the crime. The best defense attorney in New York had planted a reasonable doubt in the jury's mind—there was no real proof that Greta had killed Karl—that, and Timothy's willingness to lie for her, to say he was with her the entire time. She had been acquitted, everywhere but in her own mind.

And in this place.

The hair on the back of her neck prickled. Someone was on the balcony with her. She turned and saw something white and see-through shimmering near the patio table. Goosebumps rippled up her arm. The shimmering shape had a vaguely human form.

"Karl?" she whispered. Her entire body was one large heartbeat. Her hands were shaking and she felt vulnerable pressed up against the railing. Would he get his revenge by killing her?

The shape gained solidity. Hands, splayed and flat, stretched out to her. Greta stifled a scream and moved away from the edge, tripping and nearly falling forward. Arms grew from the hands' wrists, slender, muscular arms. The hands grabbed at Greta, but slipped through her, dousing her in cold mist. She shivered, backed away, then remembered the railing. She would not trip and fall to her death. If she did that, she would be trapped here, with Karl, forever. But Karl couldn't grab her. Karl had no strength.

She circled around, away from the hands, until her back pressed against the glass. She groped for the metal door handle and yanked on it. The door stuck for a moment. The hands came for her, dripping mist, dripping cold. Greta tugged. The door slid open and she fell through it onto the thick carpet.

The hands hovered in the darkness. Greta was breathing heavily. She swallowed, then whispered, "I'm sorry, Karl. Really. If there had been some other way—"

"Karl forgives you." The voice was husky, female. "But *I* don't."

Greta stood up. Her legs were shaking as if she were about to perform. She grabbed the balcony door and swung it shut with a bang.

The hands faded. Greta turned and ran out of the living room, her robe flying behind her. The room was safe. Her room was safe. Sebastian was there and he would awaken her, comfort her, make her forget.

She so needed to forget.

Ten

Sebastian's eyes felt rough and gritty. His entire body ached. At least Greta was sleeping now. She had come back to bed ice-cold, shivering, and terrified. She wouldn't tell him what had scared her—perhaps that loud bang that had shaken him from sleep—and it took him the better part of an hour to calm her down. Then he slipped into a fitful doze, waking as sunlight spilled into the bedroom.

Food, some in trays hovering over Sterno, had been laid out across the table, and used plates were stacked on the buffet. It looked as if most of the company was already awake. They were probably walking or in the practice room stretching. The only person left in the dining room was Timothy. Sebastian grabbed a plate and heaped it with scrambled eggs, sausages, and fruit. He poured himself some orange juice and sat down next to Timothy.

Timothy looked old this morning. His hair was tousled and lines creased his face. He didn't look up to acknowledge Sebastian, but continued staring into his coffee.

"Greta hardly slept at all last night," Sebastian said.

Timothy looked up. His eyes focused on Sebastian for the first time, and Sebastian realized that the man hadn't even known he was there. "What?" Timothy asked.

"I said Greta hardly slept last night. Nightmares. And they seem to be getting worse. I think she was sleepwalking."

"Wonderful." Timothy got up, grabbed the silver coffeepot, and poured more coffee in his cup.

"I don't think she should stay here."

Timothy sat back down. "I don't think any of us should." He shrugged. "But we're committed."

"Can't we at least get Greta out of here? This place isn't very healthy for her." Sebastian's hands were trembling. He had never been this direct with Timothy before.

"It's never been healthy for her. No reason it should change now."

Sebastian swallowed, feeling the frustration build. "I don't think she should stay here, Timothy."

"If the company stays, she stays. You know that."

"Then let's cancel the performance."

Timothy smiled, but the smile was wan. "We've spent too much time and too much money on this performance. We couldn't cancel it if we wanted to. It'll all be over tomorrow. I think we can all make it until then." He took a final sip of his coffee and stood up. Sebastian watched the other man leave. Timothy had never been that curt with him before. Perhaps it was the mention of Greta's night. It was clear even to the half-observant how Timothy felt about Greta.

Sebastian sighed and picked up his fork. Water from his eggs had congealed on the side of his plate. He pushed the plate away, grabbed an orange from the fruit basket, and headed for the practice room.

ELEVEN

Greta awoke to the feeling of hands around her throat. She touched her neck, but found nothing. Then she reached for Sebastian. He too was gone.

She sat up, her heart racing. It was a dream, nothing but a dream. But she knew it wasn't. As she dressed, she noted a loose flap of skin on the toe she had stubbed. Her velour robe was streaked with dirt. She had been on the balcony during the night—and something had been there with her.

She tied her hair up in a kerchief and glanced at the clock. She was running late. Class in fifteen minutes. She decided not to eat—eating would simply get in the way. She would go down and warm up with her dancers. Exercise would remove the crawlies from her skin. And the memory of that voice.

Karl forgives you.

I don't.

She had heard that voice before, but she couldn't place it. It had sounded half-familiar, like the speaking voice of a famous singer. She took a deep breath to calm herself. It was daylight. Ghosts didn't emerge in the daylight. And the performance was tomorrow. She could last that long.

But as she walked down the stairs to the rehearsal wing, she wondered. It felt as if something were stalking her, following her. Twice she stopped on the stairs only to hear a stair creak behind her. She turned, but saw nothing.

An overactive imagination, she told herself. *If it wasn't the ghost of Karl, who could it be?* She was safe as long as she remembered that the thing which tracked her was intangible, trying to get her to make her own mistakes so that she would die.

Most of the company was already in the practice room. Greta stretched and then took a place at the barre. Her legs hurt—she hadn't been working out as she usually did—but she forced herself to work anyway, putting herself through paces that she hadn't done in years. The woman's face gazing back at her from the mirror was too old, and then she remembered. This was what she used to do when she had had too much of Karl, or when the trial got too rough. She would bend and twist her body beyond human measure and let her mind dwell on the physical aches instead of the mental and emotional pain.

Timothy used to accuse her of willing the emotions away.

A flash in the mirror caught her eye. Something white, not quite solid. She whirled, nearly lost her balance, and had to grip the thick wooden barre for support. Nothing. Nothing but dancers staring at themselves in the mirror, stretching their bodies as she had stretched hers. Sebastian wasn't even here, so no white Danskins appeared in the room.

Greta took a deep breath. She was tired and too tense. She always got this way at the end of the season. Add to that the stresses of the mansion and its memories, and it was no wonder she was spooked.

Spooked. She tucked herself into a *plié,* feeling the muscles in her legs tremble. She had killed Karl here, pushed him with all of her strength off the balcony. A *woman* should not be haunting her. The ghost in this place should have been Karl.

A cold hand touched her shoulder. Greta whirled. No one stood behind her.

"Are you all right, Madame?" Dale asked.

Greta nodded, feeling slightly foolish. "Are you cold?"

Dale smiled and wiped at his flushed face. "God, no. I think we could probably turn off the heat in this room."

She turned back and gripped the barre tightly, doing another *plié* and going down until her thighs were horizontal. She was the only one who felt the cold, the only one who saw the ghost. She had to handle this one all by herself.

Twelve

Amanda stood in the door of the practice room, watching Greta. The old woman moved with a perfection that Amanda's young body could not hope to achieve. Amanda rubbed her hands against her leotard. She was cold. She had been cold ever since she awakened, alone, Timothy gone. Timothy, with his cries of "Greta!" in what Amanda had hoped would be a moment of mutual comfort. Greta. Madame. The bitch.

Amanda dropped her dance bag beside all the others, taking in the familiar scents of sweat, leather, and lotion. She stretched, then rubbed powder on the inside of her shoes and took her place at the barre.

Madame whirled, her face pinched and frightened. She appeared to be looking for something, something she had seen. Amanda felt something touch her, cold hands running down her spine. For a minute she had the impression of a man falling, falling, spinning, his hands reaching out, and then she got dizzy as she followed him, clinging to him because he wouldn't let her go.

"You okay?" Katrina held her shoulders. Amanda blinked at the other dancer, still feeling off balance.

"I got dizzy for a minute."

"Sit down." Katrina led her to the side of the room. "You haven't been eating well, have you?"

Amanda started to deny it, but Katrina put up her hand. "I saw the way you ate last night. You can't cut out food. You need your strength for the dance."

Amanda nodded. Food wasn't what she needed. She needed to go somewhere warm. The cold had settled in the pit of her belly like a little iceberg fetus. She frowned, remembering the rush of chill air past her ears and the feeling of falling. "I'll be all right," she said.

"Okay." Katrina got up and walked to the barre. Amanda hugged herself and closed her eyes. She was lying on the flagstones, covered with blood—a man's blood. She looked up and saw herself leaning over the balcony. Then she reached up a hand and realized that it was etched in mist, that she had no substance.

Something was inside her. Those weren't her memories. That was Madame leaning over the balcony—a young Madame, looking vulnerable and frightened. "Get out," Amanda whispered, but the thing's icy fingers gripped her even tighter and she stood up, even though she didn't want to.

Thirteen

It was in the room. Greta couldn't ignore it any longer. She turned and looked at the dancers, keeping an eye on the mirror. She hadn't seen any more white flashes, no hands appearing mysteriously out of the air. If she stayed here, she *would* see that. It would reveal itself to her and she would look foolish in front of her dancers. She couldn't risk that.

If she left the practice room, it would follow. She adjusted her kerchief, stepped away from the barre and crossed the polished floor into the hallway.

Amanda followed.

Amanda. That little slip of a girl. Greta glanced over her shoulder. The girl's eyes held something strange. Fear? The girl glanced at her for a moment, Greta thought she was seeing herself. No. She was simply looking at a leggy, dark-haired teenager. All new dancers had that frightened expression, especially around their choreographer.

Greta hurried out into the hall, Amanda forgotten. The living room would be the place to go. No one would be there now. She hurried up the stairs. The bones in her ankles felt brittle, especially the left ankle, where she had had the old injury. She remembered this feeling in the pit of her stomach from those last days with Karl—a feeling of heaviness, oppression, coupled with the knowledge that if something didn't change, she would crack.

Sebastian nearly crashed into her as she rounded the top stair. He caught her arms. "Greta, are you okay?"

"Fine," she snapped. She didn't have time for Sebastian and his concerns. She was going to settle this. She could feel the shape at her heels, like a bad dream, hovering, threatening to reveal things that should remain secret. Greta opened the door to the living room.

Timothy sat in the overstuffed chair, staring at the silent phone. He glanced up at her, his eyes sunken and haunted. She couldn't stay here either. Timothy would try to handle it for her, and he couldn't. This was one that she had to handle herself.

Greta pulled open the balcony door, feeling cool air wash over her. Fear rose in her stomach, but she pushed it away. She thought she had ended things here once. She would try again. The ghosts lived on the balcony, not in the mansion. The memories centered around this concrete overhang with its molded iron railing.

She stepped onto the concrete, past the patio furniture, feeling the breeze whip at her kerchief. Behind her, the patio door closed. Amanda stood there, looking young, powerful, and angry.

"Leave me alone," Greta said.

"Like you left me all these years?"

The voice was not Amanda's. It was the voice Greta had heard the night before, in the darkness. A gauzy film completely obscured Amanda. Greta squinted, recognized the shape.

She should have recognized it. She had seen it enough in the mirror years back, dancing across from her, mimicking her moves. The dancer. The prima ballerina. The girl Karl had loved, used, and misused. The one who had approached Karl and hit him with the heels of her hand.

"You killed him," the voice said. "Then you *left* me here with him. And the only way I can get rid of him is to give him *you.*"

Amanda seemed diminished. Greta reached for her, and stopped when she felt coldness around the girl's body.

"Who are you?" Greta asked.

"So long that you don't even remember." There was pain in the voice. Amanda came closer.

Greta did not move.

"Let me show you," the voice said. Amanda touched Greta's arm. The chill slipped into her, filling her. Pain flooded in with the chill. Physical pain first, from the years of stretching an underdeveloped body into the dance. Then dreams of being a prima ballerina, adored by the crowd, by people, by those close to her. And then Karl, taking those dreams, shattering them, image by image. *You could be a dancer if you use that body of yours,* he had said at the height of her career. She had the adulation, but she couldn't enjoy it. She was talented, loved, but imperfect. Karl kept stretching her and stretching her until she thought that she would break, she *knew* that she would break, and she hit him with both hands and sent him flying—

The balcony door opened with a snap. Greta backed away. She didn't want Timothy and Sebastian to see her like this. Sebastian stopped at the doorway, but Timothy kept coming. Timothy, who had loved the girl, would recognize the girl who had possessed Amanda.

Suddenly the cold left Greta, separated from her, and she felt hands slap against her chest, Amanda's hands, chill hands. Greta's balance shifted, and she knew that she was going to fall. She grabbed for Amanda's wrists, but the cold was too thick. Greta's fingers slid off Amanda's skin. The iron railing dug into Greta's thighs and she fell, spinning, turning. Timothy leaned over the railing and she reached up to him—*Timothy!*—he had always saved her, always, but then there was nothing, nothing but flagstones, sharp, all-encompassing pain *(the last dance move, the final impossible twist)* and Karl's hands on her, lifting her.

Everything will be all right, he said, his voice kind and sad.

She looked up, saw herself—the other part of herself, the part made up of dreams and hopes, the part she used to think was the best part of herself—as mist engulfing Amanda. And as she watched, the mist disappeared.

Karl ran his hand along her hair. *Silver,* he said. *Just like I told you.* He put his arm around her. She looked down and saw her body twisted and bleeding on the flagstones. *You don't need it,* Karl said. *You will dance so much better without it. Come. There is much work for us to do.*

Work. With Karl. *Timothy!* she cried, but he turned away and she knew that he couldn't hear her, that he would never hear her or save her again.

You are mine, Greta, Karl said. He led her back inside, toward the auditorium. As they went through the open door, she thought she heard laughter, female laughter, following them.

FOURTEEN

The rusted iron cut into the palm of his hand. Timothy leaned over the railing. Greta lay there in a final, obscene curl, her body at last failing her. He sighed, having seen it before, from the same balcony, knowing that she, too, was dead. Only this time, it didn't come as a shock. Somehow he had always known that Greta would die, perhaps because she had never seemed completely alive—not since Karl's death.

Timothy turned. Sebastian stood against the glass doors, his eyes wide. Amanda clutched the railing, swaying. Her face was white, her features jutting out prominently against hollow cheekbones. He wondered how he'd ever thought that she looked like Greta. Amanda looked like herself.

Timothy closed his eyes, again seeing the young Greta push her older self off the balcony. Amanda was simply a tool, nothing more.

"Did you see it?" Timothy asked. He opened his eyes.

"Amanda pushed her," Sebastian whispered.

"No!" Amanda cried. Her voice was shaking. Timothy put a hand on hers. Her skin was damp, chill, as if she had been buried in snow.

"Madame fell," Timothy said. The second lie was easier than the first, perhaps because this time, it was not really a lie. "Greta slipped and fell."

Sebastian locked eyes with him for a moment, then looked away in tacit agreement.

Timothy took a deep breath. Time to go to the phone, to tell the police about another body at Grayson. And when that was over, he would have decisions to make, about the company, about the performance *(It wouldn't be an anniversary performance. It would be a memorial)*, about the publicity. Funny that he didn't feel tired. Or sad. Or even empty.

He felt free.

Handfast

Kristine Kathryn Rusch

HANDFAST

The most romantic gift anyone ever gave me? A gun.

Valentine's Day, ten years ago. Ryder. God, what a sweet man. Six-three, all tattooed muscle, black hair shorn off that year to accent his dark, dark skin.

We were on the roof of his place, trying to keep candles lit in the cold breeze blowing across the Hudson, eating take-out sushi with custom-made chopsticks clutched in our frozen fingers, sitting on lawn chairs wedged into the ice-covered snow.

Ry gave up on the candles midway through, decided to go to his apartment to get a lantern—he said—and did come back with one. Battery operated, large, already on. And in his other hand, a Tiffany's blue box big enough for a cake, tied with the ubiquitous white ribbon.

Despite the box, he couldn't afford Tiffany's. Not even something small, and certainly not something that large. Even if we could have afforded Tiffany's, we wouldn't have bought anything there.

We were militantly anti-ostentation back then. It went well with our lack of funds. But we *believed* it, acted on it, maybe even looked the other way when someone in a silk suit and shiny leather shoes ventured into the wrong alley, stepping in only when that rich bastard looked to be in trouble for his life—never stepping in to save his wallet.

I opened the box with trembling fingers, stuck the ribbon in my pocket and stared at a small lockbox that looked old and well used.

Ry nodded. He wanted me to open it.

So I did.

And saw the gun.

It wasn't any old gun.

It was custom-made, silver, and, I later learned, it glowed slightly when its owner touched it. It also designed its own bullets—silver for werewolves, holy-water-laced for vampires, and laser-lighty (filled with fire) for the unknown magical.

I long suspected—and never tested—that the miracle weapon could transform its bullets into whatever the owner imagined.

We handfasted me to the weapon. He claimed he had another one, but I never saw it.

Handfasting required the candlewax (he was planning ahead), a bit of mercury, a touch of burnt almond. And some other magical oil-based concoctions I'm not going to describe, just in case.

And yeah, handfasting—pagan term for wedding. But it also meant a bargain struck by joining hands. I thought then that applying hand to hand-grip was the same thing.

I had no idea where Ry had gotten the weapon or how he learned to control it. I didn't understand why he gave it to me.

I'd love to believe what he told me that night: He gave me the gun because he loved me.

But that couldn't have been entirely true, because who gave a gun out of love?

When I pushed the next day, asking the right way—*what made you think of me when you saw this?*—he said I was so much more talented than he was, I deserved the weapon, and the weapon deserved me. And then, the day after that, he admitted he had one too, and we'd go practice with them, just him and me, Upstate, the next time we had the dough.

There was no next time. There wasn't even a day after that. Not for Ry.

Someone caught him in our alley, shredded him, took the tattoos as souvenirs. I found him, still alive, barely. But not alive enough to tell me what happened. Or alive enough to let me know he heard me when, stupid me, I told him I loved him for the first and only time.

Fast-forward a decade to the winter that never died. Press coverage that year pegged it as the coldest in two decades, blaming arctic air that should've lived in Canada but, like any other snowbird, decided to move south.

I had my own place by then, two buildings over, tall enough to get the occasional sunset glinting off the nearby roofs. I liked that: the dying sunlight reached the kitchen of my glorious apartment, just about the time (in the winter at least) I was having whatever it was I scrounged for breakfast.

My apartment: three rooms, hard-fought. Actually purchased when the building went condo just before the damn housing crisis. Now I was —as the pundits so euphemistically call it—underwater, and for once, I gave a damn.

Then I'd come to my place, warded and spelled, with the most comfortable furniture I could find (mostly discards on garbage day, dragged up the elevator, refurbished and softened), and reveled in having a safe harbor, somewhere no one else ever breached. Not anyone, including the post-Ry lovers, the so-called friends, the clients and the hangers-on.

Just me and the silence I'd created, a place to refurbish myself after each day's hard knocks and scrapes.

Somehow I stopped being militantly anti-ostentation. I was still anti-ostentation—no one would mistake the interior of this place for anything fancy—but I'd grown up enough to have financial entanglements and to adopt some of the trappings of a good citizen.

Protective coloration, really.

I'd needed it.

Back in the day, me and Ry were a team, and he was the stronger. We'd partner up, go after the shadows, fight till dawn, screw till noon, sleep a little, and start over.

Then he died, and I went full-moon batshit crazy searching for his killers, never sleeping, the edges of the world growing jagged and dark, finding clues where none existed, missing clues that'd probably been there, going, going, going until I ended up face-down in an abandoned subway tunnel and no memory of how I got there.

I had to choose, with my face pressed against the oil and the decades-old piss, whether I'd keep going or whether I'd just let it all end.

And weirdly, it was Ry who saved me. Ry, with his crooked half-smile and his embrace of anything dangerous. Ry, who had a tattoo on his left bicep of a bright yellow smiley face holding a sword in one little gloved hand and a dripping scalp in the other, with the word *Onward* in gothic letters underneath.

That tattoo always made me grin, especially when he flexed it, making the sword move up and down as if the smiley face were marching at a parade.

I saw that tattoo as clearly as if it were in front of me and, instead of regretting the method of its theft, I let out a tiny laugh. That moved the dusty dirt in front of me, and almost made me gag on the stench. Which, for some reason, I also found funny.

I was exhausted and spent, and in some ways, ruined. Completely different than I had been before.

I sat up, then stood up, and staggered my way out of the tunnel, heading back into my life. Which I rebuilt—alone—bit by bit. In the places that had never functioned alone, I built—I trained, I learned, I *became.*

I stayed in the City. Because the City had taken Ry from me. I couldn't get him back: Magic didn't work that way—at least not any kind of magic I chose to participate in. But I could find the missing pieces.

I could find whoever or whatever had killed him.

I could have answers—

Or so I thought. At first. Before I realized that a girl's gotta eat. A girl's gotta live. A girl's gotta move forward.

So I did.

~

And then the winter of our discontent. Valentine's Day wasn't a bright spot for anyone. Yet another storm had arrived the day before, canceling flights, snarling traffic, and delaying the all-important flower deliveries to shops that relied on them. By the time the actual holiday rolled around, the City was enveloped in sleet on top of two feet of snow.

I rented an office near the alley where Ry got attacked. The office wasn't much—third-floor walk-up with a frosted door, frosted windows, and a radiator that clanged to its own tune but at least kept the place warm. I had an actual desk which I got from an office five doors down—a blond wood monstrosity that smelled like old cigarettes, giving the office a slightly musty air, something I actually liked. In keeping with the thirties motif, I kept an open bottle of Scotch in the bottom drawer, although I rarely touched liquor. Any more.

I cribbed an old leather sofa from that same abandoned office, and found two matching desk chairs in the garbage behind my apartment building. The only money I actually spent on furnishing the place was for my chair, which was the most high-tech thing I owned. It had more levers and dials and options than the first (and last) car I ever drove.

The office had no computer or phone or anything remotely resembling office equipment. I don't write reports. I collect funds up front, and don't give paper receipts. If I need more money from my clients, I ask them for more. If they refuse to pay, I refuse to work.

I'm not one of those private detectives who works *pro bono* because the case interests them. I work because I need the money—and if I didn't work, I'd go back down that crazy subway tunnel, and the overwhelming stench of decades-old piss.

It's not even fair to call me a private detective. I use the title sometimes because it's easier than explaining what I do. What Ry and I used to do. What I never stopped doing, after he was gone.

I shove the magic back where it belongs.

Sounds easy, but it's not. And there are only a few of us that can do it.

By now it should be clear: I wasn't sitting alone in my office on Valentine's Day because of the snow. I hated Valentine's Day with a bloody passion. I tried not to. It wasn't the fake holiday's fault I was always so miserable at this time of year.

I usually tried to tell myself that Valentine's Day had peaked for me that night on the roof, with the lantern and the Tiffany box. And sometimes that worked.

But not on the tenth anniversary. Not as I slogged my way through the snow and sleet, watching inane couples in their finery get out of cabs or stumble out of the subway, pretending the day (night) was perfect after all. Maybe it was the combination—wind, snow, Valentine's—that caught me.

Or maybe I was finally feeling my age for the first time.

Whatever it was, it convinced me to haul out that open bottle of Scotch the moment I collapsed into my high-tech desk chair. I had had the same open bottle of Scotch for months now, ever since a baby demon with a heart of gold (long story) had slept in my office for two weeks and nursed on the bottle like it was demon-mama's teat. No way was I ever drinking from that bottle again. So I got a new one—after I found baby demon's distraught mama and finally reunited the two of them.

Me, an open bottle of Scotch, sleet tapping the frosted glass like werewolf claws. I thought I had the night all planned—when the gun appeared out of nowhere.

The gun. You know, the one from the Tiffany's box.

Or so I thought at first.

Well, not entirely true, because you don't think about where a gun came from when it appears right in front of you, business end pointed at your face, trembling as if held by an unsteady hand.

And nothing else.

I set the bottle of Scotch down, then made myself calmly and deliberately screw the cap back on. I would have put the bottle back in the bottom drawer, but the gun's trembling got worse, and I really didn't want to get shot just because I was being a neat freak.

I wondered what kind of bullets were in that thing—silver, holy-water-dipped, flaming hot. Damn near any of them would kill me, since I'm just good old-fashioned flesh and blood. I stared at the wobbling muzzle of that gun, then realized I had some control.

We'd been handfasted after all. The weapon belonged to me and I to it, which was probably why it couldn't go through with the shooting.

I held up my right hand and said in my deepest, most powerful voice, *Come to me.*

The weapon's trembling increased, but it didn't move. My heart moved enough for both of us, trying to pound its way out of my chest.

I tried the command again, and again, the damn gun just shook more.

So, figuring the rule of three, I tried one final time. *Join your handfast partner.*

The gun stopped trembling. And then it whirled as if pursued, and floated away from me. I sat for a moment, stupidly, then realized that the damn gun didn't belong to me. It was a different weapon than the one locked in the lockbox I kept in the Tiffany's box.

I got up and stumbled after the gun. It floated down the hallway, then down the stairs, always staying at chest-height, just as if someone were holding it.

It reached the lobby, bumped out the door (I have no idea how it got open), and into the sleet. I followed, coatless, instantly chilled, and nearly slammed into a couple wearing less clothes than I was, giggling their drunk way out of a nearby bar. They didn't seem to see the gun, but I couldn't take my gaze off it.

Because it went into the alley, where Ry died. And then it started banging against the brick wall behind a Dumpster, as if it were trying to get into something.

I wished for gloves. And boots. And a coat. I was sliding on ice, and still the alley had the stench of weeks-old garbage. It didn't matter how cold or wet something got, the smells remained.

I tried not to look at the back corner, where Ry bled out. It was covered in a snow pile six feet high anyway. The gun kept banging and scraping, and I finally decided to violate one of the major rules of automated magic.

I got between the gun and the wall. The gun kept hitting the same brick, scraping it white. I grabbed the damn thing, surprised that my fingers fit where the mortar should have been.

So I pulled.

The brick slid out easily, and I slid backwards, nearly falling. I caught myself on the edge of the ice-cold Dumpster.

The gun turned itself sideways, shoving its grip into the open hole. It had stopped trembling.

It balanced on the edge of the brick below for just a moment, then toppled downward.

I jumped back, afraid it would go off by accident.

But it didn't.

It rested on top of the ice as if all the magic had leached out of it. Its color was different too. No longer silver, but a muddy brown instead. I tilted my head, blinked hard, my face wet with sleet.

I wiped my eyes with the back of my hand, smearing the cold rather than getting rid of it.

The gun still looked odd. I figured it actually looked odd—it wasn't my magical sight that had changed; the gun was different.

So I crouched. And looked closer.

And gasped.

Something had wrapped itself around the grip. Brown and mottled. It took a moment for my eyes to make sense of what I saw.

The word *Onward* in Gothic script.

Bile rose in my throat.

I nudged the gun with my foot, then managed to flip the weapon over. The image on this side was a distorted yellow, desiccated and faded.

I swallowed hard, my stomach churning.

Then I stood and made a small flare out of my right fingertip. I used the flare to illuminate the hole in the bricks.

Saw shreds, images. Messed on the top like someone had rifled a drawer, and laid flat below, like carefully folded linen napkins waiting for a fancy dinner.

I lost my not-fancy dinner. And breakfast. And every meal for the past week.

Some investigator.

I'd searched for those patches of skin from the very beginning—all six of Ry's tattoos—knowing his magic lurked in them.

Only, as I braced one hand on the wall, and used the other hand to wipe my mouth, I realized that there were a lot more than six scraps of skin in that wall.

A lot more.

I allowed myself to get sick one final time before hauling out my phone, and calling the only detective at the NYPD who would ever listen to me.

Ryder's older brother.

Dane.

~

He showed up ten minutes later, wearing a dress coat over an ill-fitting suit, and a this-better-be-worthwhile attitude. He wore his hair regulation cut, and he didn't have the muscles or the tattoos. Still, there was enough of a family resemblance to give me a start every time I saw him walk toward me. Same height, same build, same general energy.

"Three-hundred dollars up front for dinner," he said. "Includes five courses and champagne. We'd just finished appetizers."

"Special girl?" I asked.

"I'm hoping," he said. "We'll see if she's still there when I get back."

She might be waiting a long time, I thought but didn't say. I just showed him the open hole in the brick.

"What?" he asked impatiently.

"Just look," I said, my voice raspy, throat sore, my breath so foul I tried not to face him.

He grabbed his phone and used it like a flashlight, then backed away when he realized what he was looking at.

"What the hell?" he asked.

He peered into that obscene storage space, then looked at me, his handsome face half in shadow.

"How did you find this?" he asked, as if I had created the horror all on my own.

I poked the toe of my battered Nike against the gun.

He turned the phone's light toward it, saw the desiccated but still visible smiley face, and swallowed hard, then shook his head.

"You're out here without a coat or hat or mittens, and you're telling me you just stumbled on this gun?"

He didn't mention his brother's skin, wrapped around it, or the fact that there was more shredded skin in that opening.

"No, I'm not saying that."

Now that he mentioned how I was dressed, I realized just how cold I was. My teeth started chattering. I shoved my hands in the pocket of my jeans, not that it did much good.

"I asked you how you found this?" Dane snapped.

"And I showed you," I said.

"It means nothing." His voice went up, echoing between the buildings.

"Only because there are some things you refuse to let me tell you," I said, matching his tone.

He stared at me, breathing hard. I tried to stay calm, but it was difficult, considering how bad I was shivering.

"Magic?" he asked with a sneer he once reserved for Ry, but had transferred to me since Ry's death.

I nodded.

Dane rolled his eyes and shook his head. "You think this crap has been here all along?"

I shrugged one shoulder.

"You want to tell me, without talking about magic, how you came down here?"

I sighed. I could have said no, I supposed, but I didn't. "I followed the gun."

"And whoever was holding it," he said.

"I didn't see who was holding it," I said.

"Convenient," he said, "since it looks like Ry's gun."

It is *Ry's gun,* I wanted to say, but knew better. Because then Dane would ask me how I knew that, and I would point to the layer of skin wrapped around the grip.

"Ry told me he had one," I said. "I never saw it. How do you know it's his?"

Besides the skin, I mean, I added mentally. Of course, Dane didn't hear that.

"Pretty unusual thing, huh?" Dane said. "Ry called it magic. Me, I think it's some kind of toy, since it supposedly invents its own bullets."

I ignored that jibe. "He ever use it in front of you?"

"No, he wanted to take me to the range to practice with it, but he...." Dane let out a sigh. "He died before we could go."

"Who ended up with the gun?" I asked.

"I don't know," Dane said. "I never saw it again."

"So you remember it after *ten* years?" Lying on the ice, with Ry's skin wrapped around it, the gun didn't look *that* distinctive, at least not to me.

"I'd tell you I recognized it by that lovely silver barrel," Dane said, "but I didn't even notice that part at first."

I waited. I was going to make him say it, the bastard.

"I don't think we're going to have to test the DNA on that skin," Dane said quietly.

I nodded.

"But we might have to on the rest of this stuff in here." Dane peered at that hole. "Why would the gun turn up now?"

It had been exactly ten years since I got my gun. But I had no idea if Dane knew I had one too, and I wasn't about to tell him.

"The anniversary's coming up," I said.

"Yeah, like I can forget that," Dane said dryly. He sighed again. "I'm going to call this in. You need to go inside before you freeze solid."

"What about the gun?" I asked. "Do you think it should go into evidence?"

He looked at me. He knew what I was thinking. Hell, all of New York would have known what I was thinking. The city had seen a lot of news lately about weapons stolen out of the NYPD's evidence storage.

"You want to pick it up?" he asked.

Of course I didn't. Neither did he. But he had opened the door, and he was the magic-denier, not me. I reached around him, and with shaking fingers, sorted through the Dumpster until I found a box that wasn't too junked up. It was a shoebox with some stains along the bottom, but it didn't smell that bad, so I grabbed it.

I was going to scoop up the gun with the box lid, but I stopped half-way. I didn't want to mess up that grip. (That tattoo.) So I glanced at Dane. He was watching me closely.

I slid the lid underneath the box, then held the box in my left hand. I turned my right palm upward. Then I concentrated on the gun and hooked it mentally to my right hand. Slowly I raised my hand, and the gun rose too.

Once the gun was a foot off the ground, I crouched, slid the box underneath it, and turned my palm down. The gun bounced into the box, and I slapped the lid on it.

Dane watched me, face gray in the half light. His gaze met mine, but he didn't say anything. I knew, if asked, he would say only that I slid the box under the gun and scooped it up.

I offered him the box.

He shook his head. "You keep it."

"There could be evidence here," I said, taunting him.

He shook his head. "We'll have more than enough. Now, go inside."

He didn't have to tell me twice. I scurried to my building, feeling as if I would never get warm again.

So Ry had handfasted to the gun, just like I had.

I carried it up the stairs to my office, noting that the box did have an odor, but I wasn't sure if the odor came from the Dumpster or that tattooed slice of skin. I didn't want to think about that either.

Instead, I locked the entire box inside my office safe. Then I went to the ladies room down the hall ostensibly to run warm water on my hands but, in reality, to get whatever was on that box off my skin.

I shivered and shivered, even after I warmed up. The shivering didn't just come from the cold.

After I'd cleaned up, I grabbed my heavy down coat, my unattractive knit cap, and my gloves. I slipped everything on, locked the office, and headed home.

I needed to know if my own gun was still there.

When I reached the street, the cold returned with a vengeance. It was as if I hadn't gone inside to get warm at all.

A crime scene unit had the alley blocked off. Dane appeared to have left, and some unis guarded it all. They stared at me as if I were the bad guy. I pivoted, went the other way, and headed to my place.

At least the sleet had stopped, but the sidewalk was slippery.

The restaurants along the way—this place was so gentrified now—were filled with well-dressed couples pretending to be happy. And maybe they were over their—what had Dane said? $300 meals? I preferred the take-out sushi eaten with custom-made chopsticks on a roof so cold it made this evening seem like the Bahamas in summer.

I still missed Ry, the bastard. I liked to think I had moved on, but I hadn't. Not inside. Not where it counted.

I took an elevator to my apartment, and let myself in. The apartment was warm, homey, perfect, just like it had been since I bought it. I closed the door and locked it, then checked the wards just in case.

They were fine.

I peeled off my gloves and tossed them on an occasional table. Then I went into my bedroom and opened the closet.

There, on the top shelf, was the Tiffany's box. I pulled it down, and gingerly untied the ribbon. I tugged the lid off and looked inside. The lockbox was still there. I opened it too, and stared at the gun, gleaming in the light.

It looked no different than it had every other time I had looked at it. It was a shame I had never used it, a shame that it hid here in the dark, as if it were at fault for Ry's death.

I ran my fingers across its cool surface. It glowed faintly, in recognition. I wished I knew how to use it. I wished Ry had told me where he had gotten it, why he had chosen a Tiffany's box to keep it in, what it all meant.

I closed the lockbox, then closed the Tiffany's box, and retied the ribbon, like I'd done dozens of times over the years. I put the gun on the top shelf of my closet, then closed that door. If only it were that easy to put the gun out of my mind as well.

Something had caused the second gun to come to me. Something had powered it. Something—or someone.

I wouldn't know what until I knew more about the guns themselves.

I grabbed my cell to call Dane. Then decided I wasn't going to speak to him on the phone.

I would go to him, wherever that was.

I took my gloves off the occasional table and let myself out of the apartment, using the edges of my magic to track Dane.

It wasn't hard.

He was at the precinct, at his desk—which, I was certain—was not where he wanted to be.

~

The limestone façade of the three-story precinct building looked dirty against the sleet-shiny snow. Ry used to call it the Home of the Enemy, but he didn't really mean it. He was always mad at Dane for refusing to acknowledge the magic or the work Ry and I were doing.

The rivalry between them didn't mask the love they had for each other, though, and I knew Dane had been as torn up over Ry's death as I was.

I let myself inside, the smell of fear and sweat enveloping me. I took the steps up to the detective unit, and slipped inside.

Nighttime made little difference. There were always detectives poring over files, tapping on ancient computers, or talking tiredly into the phones.

Dane was sitting at his desk toward the back, hands pressed against his cheeks, staring down at some paperwork in front of him. His suit coat was hanging over the back of his chair, and his long dress coat was hanging on a peg on the wall.

I walked over to him and hovered, waiting for him to acknowledge me.

"At least fifteen different skin types," he said. "And they're just estimating. Who does that?"

He sounded tired. I guess the possibly special woman hadn't waited for him after all.

"Not who," I said. "*What* does that?"

"Yeah, some kinda animal," he said more to himself than to me. Because we both knew that he was deliberately misunderstanding me.

It was a good question, though. Demons shredded skin, but they used the unbelievable pain from the process to increase their own power. There were lots of creatures from all sides of the magical divide that consumed skin, mostly as food, and a handful that took the magic from tattoos.

But nothing native to New York. Because all of the native creatures destroyed the skin when they did what they did.

I knew of nothing that took tattoos like trophies.

"Was everything—" I couldn't bring myself to say skin fragments. "—tattooed?"

"Yeah," he said quietly. "Mean something to you?"

I shook my head, but he wasn't looking up. Maybe he took my silence as an acknowledgement.

"Do you know where Ry got the gun?" I asked.

Dane finally raised his head. He seemed to have aged years in the past few hours. He seemed surprised by the question.

"There were two," he said. "They belonged to my parents. I figured he had given one to you."

My cheeks heated. I had never told Dane about the gun. I hadn't told anyone.

Dane was frowning. "He was going to—you know—ask you to marry him. He was all goofy about it. He even found a Tiffany's box, because engagement rings come in Tiffany boxes. He thought you'd get it."

I thought we didn't believe in marriage. I thought marriage was so... middle class, so ostentatious.

I had missed the point.

Why me? I had asked Ry.

Because I love you, he had said, so sure, so certain.

And then, at my confusion, he had shrugged, said he was cold, and we'd better hurry. Still, we handfasted me to the gun. *My* gun. And his matched.

Like wedding rings.

Son of a bitch.

"Did your parents have wedding rings?" I asked.

"Oh, yeah," Dane said, "but my folks were pretty traditional. They wanted the guns to go to me and Ry, like we were supposed to split up the rings."

Dane leaned back, closed his eyes for a minute, shook his head, then added, "I was the only sane one. The only one who didn't see little sparklies in the universe or dark things crawling out of corners. My folks were so disappointed..."

Then he rocked forward and opened his eyes.

"I thought you knew," he said again, but I wasn't sure if he was talking about the guns or his parents or all of it.

I shrugged, pretending at a nonchalance I didn't feel. "What were the guns for?"

"Monster hunting," he said sarcastically.

I nodded, not going there.

"Thanks," I said, and threaded my way through the desks.

"Hey," he said. "You need help?"

Not your kind of help, I nearly said. Instead, I shook my head. "You guys are doing it all."

And as I walked out, I realized that was true. After I had come to my senses, I left the investigation in the hands of the police.

Even when I had known that whatever killed Ry hadn't been human—at least, by my definition. Maybe by Dane's.

But not by mine.

The guns had history, and I needed to find it. I could look in moldy books or try to find something accurate online. Or I could ask the guns themselves.

I didn't want to ask the one with Ry's tattoo wrapped around its grip. I wasn't sure who or what would answer me.

And I didn't want to find out.

So I walked back to my apartment, and got my gun down a second time.

Everyone describes silver as cold, but it's not. Especially when it's been indoors, and the endless winter continued outside. The gun was warm against my hand, the silver never needing polish.

I wrapped my hand around it, saw—

Ry, grinning as he watched me open the box...

I made that image disappear, saw—

Something huge and scaly, looming over a pair of sleeping boys, then a bright white light zinging out of the muzzle, and the huge, scaly thing exploding into a thousand little pieces...

I shook my head, smiled a little, saw —

Hands with two matching rings, clasped, each around the grip of a different gun. "With my heart, I hold you," a male voice so like Ry's said. "With my soul, I touch you..."

It was a handfasting ceremony, only of a kind I'd never heard of. With the guns in the middle.

Marriage, the old-fashioned way.

I rubbed my eyes with my thumb and forefinger. Then frowned, thought of an experiment, and decided to try it.

I set the gun on top of the box.

Then I went into my kitchen, and thought, *Join your handfast partner* at the gun itself.

After five minutes, it wobbled its way toward me, muzzle pointed at my heart, trembling like Ry's gun had.

Find your box, I thought, and the gun wobbled its way out the door. I followed it, as it returned to the very place it had started.

I picked the box up and wrapped my arms around it.

Anniversaries had power.

I had thought the gun came to me at the anniversary of Ry's death.

The gun had come to me at the anniversary of our love—the marriage he had tried to give me, ten long years ago.

With my gun in my shoulder holster, I went back to the office.

I doubted I would ever get warm, even though I was wearing my coat, thick gloves, and my hat. I was cradled in the heart of a long, cold winter, and I might as well embrace it.

Ry's gun was inside the safe, the remains of my favorite tattoo still attached to the grip.

First, I put my gun on the desk. Then, gingerly, I picked up Ry's.

He laughed.

I took my hand off the grip, shaking.

Then touched it again.

I don't care how dark things get, he said. *We'll always have each other.*

As if he hadn't left. As if he were still here.

I set the guns beside each other, and they started to glow. If they were real guns—real as in the way Dane defined guns—I would be fleeing now, expecting some kind of weird explosion.

But I was curiously unafraid.

The guns glowed and locked to each other. The tattoo grew into an entire man.

Ryder.

See-through, but there.

"I missed you," he said.

I didn't care if he was real or not. "I missed you too."

"I wasn't sure you'd understand," he said. "We never finished the ceremony."

"I know," I said.

He nodded, reached toward me, his hand going through my face. I felt nothing, not even a rush of wind.

And oh, how I wanted to.

"What happened?" I asked, because I had to, because I had a sense time was short.

"Demons," he said, and his image flickered.

He glanced at the guns. The glow was fading.

"No," I said.

"I love you," he said.

"I love you too," I said. "Stay."

"I wish." His voice was faint. "Balance the scales..."

And then he was gone.

Again.

The son of a bitch.

~

I felt it—the batshit crazy. It was coming back, or maybe it had never left. I could go after everything, clean up everything, fight everything—and be consumed.

Or I could stand up.

Fight.

Figure it out.

The guns didn't glow any more. The tattoo was gone.

I touched Ry's gun. It was cool. So was mine.

Balance the scales.

Demons—and skin.

I let out a breath, grabbed both guns, and headed to the alley below.

No crime scene tape. No footprints in the snow. No tire marks where the crime scene unit had parked their van.

The brick was back in place.

I walked to it, touched it, felt edges, still there. The hiding place, still there.

Son of a bitch.

"Finally," he said, his voice echoing between the buildings.

I turned. He looked bigger, eyes glowing ever so slightly red, Ry's face covering his imperfectly, five tattoos glowing on his scaly skin.

Saw—in my mind's eye—two boys, sleeping, a demon hovering over them, exploding in the dark, and scales raining down—on the oldest boy, the one closest to the door.

"Your parents took your magic away from you," I said.

"They thought they could," Dane said, his voice deeper, more echoey. "They took the wrong magic."

They took the good magic, leaving the scales.

Balance them, Ry had told me.

"You killed him," I said.

Dane didn't answer me, but the tattoos glowed. The death hadn't been intentional. I knew that, or Dane wouldn't have crumbled like he had. They had had a fight—over the guns?

"What do the guns have to do with it?" I asked.

"One of them is mine," he said.

"Why didn't you take Ry's after he died?" I asked.

"I couldn't find it. But you found it. Thank you," he said. "Now, give it to me."

I had no other weapons. I hadn't expected to fight demons tonight. I wasn't really in the fighting and slaying business any more. Just the investigating, resolving business.

I pulled Ry's gun out of my pocket. My hand trembled as I gave the gun to Dane.

He took it, looking surprised at the ease.

"I never realized you were this logical," he said.

"You never knew me," I said. Which was fair: I never knew him either.

And I had dismissed Ry. Ry, who had called Dane "The Enemy" right from the start.

Dane grinned. "I like you, you know."

I nodded, as if I cared. He looked down at the gun, and weighed it in his hand, as if it were something precious.

Which it was.

Join your handfast partner, I whispered.

The gun in Dane's hand trembled. He held it tightly. The tattoos on him—Ry's remaining tattoos—glowed.

Then peeled off, one by one, each fastening itself around the gun.

For a moment, there were two men before me, one thinner, less substantial, the other glowing red, the gun between them.

My gun had found my hand as well—and I didn't remember grabbing it. Then I realized it had heard the same command, thought the command was its.

I knew what kind of bullets demons took, but I wasn't sure I wanted to shoot Dane—not with Ry fighting him for the gun.

They struggled, the ice melting beneath their feet, the heat of Dane's evil warming the entire alley. The gun remained between them and then—

Something popped as if a bubble had burst.

Ry staggered backwards, substantial, bleeding (bleeding!!!), and falling, holding his gun.

Dane, dripping scales, reached for the gun and without thinking, I imagined white light—bullets—heading toward him.

They did, shooting out of my gun and hitting his torso.

I reached down, grabbed Ry, pulled him backwards with me, away from the white-and-red glowing demon-man in the center of that alley. We made it behind a stupid snowplow-created pile of snow when Dane exploded, bits raining everywhere.

Except on us.

Balance the scales.

Not just the scales of justice. The scales of a demon, returning where they belonged.

I wrapped my arms around a bleeding, warm, *living* man.

"Ry," I said.

"Took you long enough," he muttered.

"You didn't explain—"

"No excuses," he said, and then he passed out.

I had no story for the ambulance attendants. I had no story for the cops. I pled ignorance, lost memory, frostbite...I don't know. Those lies are gone, along with any trace of Dane.

Ry thinks Dane died that night ten years ago, and somehow his demon self managed to get to Ry, so that Ry's power would keep them alive.

But I think—the magic suggests it—that Dane died a lot longer ago than that. Maybe the night of the demon attack, the ones the gun stopped.

Because demons can create hallucinations, images, visions, like the crime scene. How easy for one boy to die and feed a dying demon, keeping it alive, just barely, waiting for the right opportunity to grow into something stronger.

From the moment I met him, Ry said he distrusted Dane. I thought that strange for brothers. But it wasn't. It was the man reacting to something he barely remembered from his own childhood.

Ry doesn't agree.

But it doesn't matter.

Because we've done purges. We've saged the entire alley. We've warded it and cleansed it. We invited old friends to do the same.

Dane's gone.

And Ry's here.

And it's no hallucination or vision.

The most romantic gift anyone's ever given me was a gun. And a handfast.

And a future.

Together.

At last.

Substitutions

Kristine Kathryn Rusch

Substitutions

Silas sat at the blackjack table, a plastic glass of whiskey in his left hand, and a small pile of hundred dollar chips in his right. His banjo rested against his boot, the embroidered strap wrapped around his calf. He had a pair of aces to the dealer's six, so he split them—a thousand dollars riding on each—and watched as she covered them with the expected tens.

He couldn't lose. He'd been trying to all night.

The casino was empty except for five gambling addicts hunkered over the blackjack table, one old woman playing slots with the rhythm of an assembly worker, and one young man in black leather who was getting drunk at the casino's sorry excuse for a bar. The employees showed no sign of holiday cheer: no happy holiday pins, no little Santa hats, only the stark black and white of their uniforms against the casino's fading glitter.

He had chosen the Paradise because it was one of the few remaining fifties-style casinos in Nevada, still thick with flocked wallpaper and cigarette smoke, craps tables worn by dice and elbows, and the roulette wheel creaking with age. It was also only a few hours from Reno, and in thirty hours, he would have to make the tortuous drive up there. Along the way, he would visit an old man who had a bad heart; a young girl who would cross the road at the wrong time and meet an on-coming semi; and a baby boy who was born with his lungs not yet fully formed. Silas also suspected a few surprises along the way; nothing was ever as it seemed any longer. Life was moving too fast, even for him.

But he had Christmas Eve and Christmas Day off, the two days he had chosen when he had been picked to work Nevada 150 years before. In those days, he would go home for Christmas, see his friends, spend time with his family. His parents welcomed him, even though they didn't see him for most of the year. He felt like a boy again, like someone cherished and loved, instead of the drifter he had become.

All of that stopped in 1878. December 26th, 1878. He wasn't yet sophisticated enough to know that the day was a holiday in England. Boxing Day. Not quite appropriate, but close.

He had to take his father that day. The old man had looked pale and tired throughout the holiday, but no one thought it serious. When he took to his bed Christmas night, everyone had simply thought him tired from the festivities.

It was only after midnight, when Silas got his orders, that he knew what was coming next. He begged off—something he had never tried before (he wasn't even sure who he had been begging with)—but had received the feeling (that was all he ever got: a firm feeling, so strong he couldn't avoid it) that if he didn't do it, death would come another way—from Idaho or California or New Mexico. It would come another way, his father would be in agony for days, and the end, when it came, would be uglier than it had to be.

Silas had taken his banjo to the old man's room. His mother slept on her side, like she always had, her back to his father. His father's eyes had opened, and he knew. Somehow he knew.

They always did.

Silas couldn't remember what he said. Something—a bit of an apology, maybe, or just an explanation: *You always wanted to know what I did*. And then, the moment. First he touched his father's forehead, clammy with the illness that would claim him, and then Silas said, "You wanted to know why I carry the banjo," and strummed.

But the sound did not soothe his father like it had so many before him. As his spirit rose, his body struggled to hold it, and he looked at

Silas with such a mix of fear and betrayal that Silas still saw it whenever he thought of his father.

The old man died, but not quickly and not easily, and Silas tried to resign, only to get sent to the place that passed for headquarters, a small shack that resembled an out-of-the-way railroad terminal. There, a man who looked no more than thirty but who had to be three hundred or more, told him the more that he complained, the longer his service would last.

Silas never complained again, and he had been on the job for 150 years. Almost 55,000 days spent in the service of Death, with only Christmas Eve and Christmas off, tainted holidays for a man in a tainted position.

He scooped up his winnings, piled them on his already-high stack of chips, and then placed his next bet. The dealer had just given him a queen and a jack when a boy sat down beside him.

"Boy" wasn't entirely accurate. He was old enough to get into the casino. But he had rain on his cheap jacket, and hair that hadn't been cut in a long time. IPod headphones stuck out of his breast pocket, and he had a cell phone against his hip the way that old sheriffs used to wear their guns.

His hands were callused and the nails had dirt beneath them. He looked tired, and a little frightened.

He watched as the dealer busted, then set chips in front of Silas and the four remaining players. Silas swept the chips into his stack, grabbed five of the hundred dollar chips, and placed the bet.

The dealer swept her hand along the semi-circle, silently asking the players to place their bets.

"You Silas?" the boy asked. He hadn't put any money on the table or placed any chips before him.

Silas sighed. Only once before had someone interrupted his Christmas festivities—if festivities was what the last century plus could be called.

The dealer peered at the boy. "You gonna play?"

The boy looked at her, startled. He didn't seem to know what to say.

"I got it." Silas put twenty dollars in chips in front of the boy.

"I don't know..."

"Just do what I tell you," Silas said.

The woman dealt, face-up. Silas got an ace. The boy, an eight. The woman dealt herself a ten. Then she went around again. Silas got his twenty-one—his weird holiday luck holding—but the boy got another eight.

"Split them," Silas said.

The boy looked at him, his fear almost palpable.

Silas sighed again, then grabbed another twenty in chips, and placed it next to the boy's first twenty.

"Jeez, mister, that's a lot of money," the boy whispered.

"Splitting," Silas said to the dealer.

She separated the cards and placed the bets behind them. Then she dealt the boy two cards—a ten and another eight.

The boy looked at Silas. Looked like the boy had peculiar luck as well.

"Split again," Silas said, more to the dealer than to the boy. He added the bet, let her separate the cards, and watched as she dealt the boy two more tens. Three eighteens. Not quite as good as Silas's twenties to twenty-ones, but just as statistically uncomfortable.

The dealer finished her round, then dealt herself a three, then a nine, busting again. She paid in order. When she reached the boy, she set sixty dollars in chips before him, each in its own twenty dollar pile.

"Take it," Silas said.

"It's yours," the boy said, barely speaking above a whisper.

"I gave it to you."

"I don't gamble," the boy said.

"Well, for someone who doesn't gamble, you did pretty well. Take your winnings."

The boy looked at them as if they'd bite him. "I..."

"Are you leaving them for the next round?" the dealer asked.

The boy's eyes widened. He was clearly horrified at the very thought. With shaking fingers, he collected the chips, then leaned into Silas. The boy smelled of sweat and wet wool.

"Can I talk to you?" he whispered.

Silas nodded, then cashed in his chips. He'd racked up ten thousand dollars in three hours. He wasn't even having fun at it any more. He liked losing, felt that it was appropriate—part of the game, part of his life—but the losses had become fewer and farther between the more he played.

The more he lived. A hundred years ago, there were women and a few adopted children. But watching them grow old, helping three of them die, had taken the desire out of that too.

"Mr. Silas," the boy whispered.

"If you're not going to bet," the dealer said, "please move so someone can have your seats."

People had gathered behind Silas, and he hadn't even noticed. He really didn't care tonight. Normally, he would have noticed anyone around him—noticed who they were, how and when they would die.

"Come on," he said, gathering the bills the dealer had given him. The boy's eyes went to the money like a hungry man's went to food. His one-hundred-and-twenty dollars remained on the table, and Silas had to remind him to pick it up.

The boy used a forefinger and a thumb to carry it, as if it would burn him.

"At least put it in your pocket," Silas snapped.

"But it's yours," the boy said.

"It's a damn gift. Appreciate it."

The boy blinked, then stuffed the money into the front of his unwashed jeans. Silas led him around banks and banks of slot machines, all pinging and ponging and making little musical come-ons, to the steakhouse in the back.

The steakhouse was the reason Silas came back year after year. The place opened at five, closed at three a.m., and served the best steaks in Vegas. They weren't arty or too small. One big slab of meat, expensive cut, charred on the outside and red as Christmas on the inside. Beside the steak they served french-fried onions, and sides that no self-respecting Strip restaurant would prepare—creamed corn, au gratin potatoes, popovers—the kind of stuff that Silas always associated with the modern Las Vegas—modern, to him, meaning 1950s-1960s Vegas. Sin city. A place for grown-ups to gamble and smoke and drink and have affairs. The Vegas of Sinatra and the mob, not the Vegas of Steve Wynn and his ilk, who prettified everything and made it all seem upscale and oh-so-right.

Silas still worked Vegas a lot more than any other Nevada city, which made sense, considering how many millions of people lived there now, but millions of people lived all over. Even sparsely populated Nevada, one of the least populated states in the Union, had ten full-time Death employees. They tried to unionize a few years ago, but Silas, with the most seniority, refused to join. Then they tried to limit the routes—one would get Reno, another Sparks, another Elko and that region, and a few would split Vegas—but Silas wouldn't agree to that either.

He loved the travel part of the job. It was the only part he still liked, the ability to go from place to place to place, see the changes, understand how time affected everything.

Everything except him.

The maitre d sat them in the back, probably because of the boy. Even in this modern era, where people wore blue jeans to funerals, this steakhouse preferred its customers in a suit and tie.

The booth was made of wood and rose so high that Silas couldn't see anything but the boy and the table across from them. A single lamp reflected against the wall, revealing cloth napkins and real silver utensils.

The boy stared at them with the same kind of fear he had shown at the blackjack table. "I can't—."

The maître d gave them leather-bound menus, said something about a special, and then handed Silas a wine list. Silas ordered a bottle of burgundy. He didn't know a lot about wines, just that the more expensive ones tasted a lot better than the rest of them. So he ordered the most expensive burgundy on the menu.

The maître d nodded crisply, almost militarily, and then left. The boy leaned forward.

"I can't stay. I'm your substitute."

Silas smiled. A waiter came by with a bread basket—hard rolls, still warm—and relish trays filled with sliced carrots, celery, and radishes, and candied beets, things people now would call old-fashioned.

Modern, to him. Just as modern as always.

The boy squirmed, his jeans squeaking on the leather booth.

"I know," Silas said. "You'll be fine."

"I got—

"A big one, probably," Silas said. "It's Christmas Eve. Traffic, right? A shooting in a church? Too many suicides?"

"No," the boy said, distressed. "Not like that."

"When's it scheduled for?" Silas asked. He really wanted his dinner, and he didn't mind sharing it. The boy looked like he needed a good meal.

"Tonight," the boy said. "No specific time. See?"

He put a crumpled piece of paper between them, but Silas didn't pick it up.

"Means you have until midnight," Silas said. "It's only seven. You can eat."

"They said at orientation—

Silas had forgotten; they all got orientation now. The expectations of generations. He'd been thrown into the pool feet first, fumbling his way for six months before someone told him that he could actually ask questions.

"—the longer you wait, the more they suffer."

Silas glanced at the paper. "If it's big, it's a surprise. They won't suffer. They'll just finish when you get there. That's all."

The boy bit his lip. "How do you know?"

Because he'd had big. He'd had grisly. He'd had disgusting. He'd overseen more deaths than the boy could imagine.

The head waiter arrived, took Silas's order, and then turned to the boy.

"I don't got money," the boy said.

"You have one-hundred-and-twenty dollars," Silas said. "But I'm buying, so don't worry."

The boy opened the menu, saw the prices, and closed it again. He shook his head.

The waiter started to leave when Silas stopped him. "Give him what I'm having. Medium well."

Since the kid didn't look like he ate many steaks, he wouldn't like his rare. Rare was an acquired taste, just like burgundy wine and the cigar that Silas wished he could light up. Not everything in the modern era was an improvement.

"You don't have to keep paying for me," the kid said.

Silas waved the waiter away, then leaned back. The back of the booth, made of wood, was rigid against his spine. "After a while in this business," he said, "money is all you have."

The kid bit his lower lip. "Look at the paper. Make sure I'm not screwing up. Please."

But Silas didn't look.

"You're supposed to handle all of this on your own," Silas said gently.

"I know," the boy said. "I know. But this one, he's scary. And I don't think anything I do will make it right."

After he finished his steak and had his first sip of coffee, about the time he would have lit up his cigar, Silas picked up the paper. The boy had devoured the steak like he hadn't eaten in weeks. He ate all the bread and everything from his relish tray.

He was very, very new.

Silas wondered how someone that young had gotten into the death business, but he was determined not to ask. It would be some variation on his own story. Silas had begged for the life of his wife who should have died in the delivery of their second child. Begged, and begged, and begged, and somehow, in his befogged state, he actually saw the woman whom he then called the Angel of Death.

Now he knew better—none of them were angels, just working stiffs waiting for retirement—but then, she had seemed perfect and terrifying, all at the same time.

He'd asked for his wife, saying he didn't want to raise his daughters alone.

The angel had tilted her head. "Would you die for her?"

"Of course," Silas said.

"Leaving her to raise the children alone?" the angel asked.

His breath caught. "Is that my only choice?"

She shrugged, as if she didn't care. Later, when he reflected, he realized she didn't know.

"Yes," he said into her silence. "She would raise better people than I will. She's good. I'm...not."

He wasn't bad, he later realized, just lost, as so many were. His wife had been a god-fearing woman with strict ideas about morality. She had raised two marvelous girls, who became two strong women, mothers of large broods who all went on to do good works.

In that, he hadn't been wrong.

But his wife hadn't remarried either, and she had cried for him for the rest of her days.

They had lived in Texas. He had made his bargain, got assigned Nevada, and had to swear never to head east, not while his wife and children lived. His parents saw him, but they couldn't tell anyone. They thought he ran out on his wife and children, and oddly, they had supported him in it.

Remnants of his family still lived. Great-grandchildren generations removed. He still couldn't head east, and he no longer wanted to.

Silas touched the paper and it burned his fingers. A sign, a warning, a remembrance that he wasn't supposed to work these two days.

Two days out of an entire year.

He slid the paper back to the boy. "I can't open it. I'm not allowed. You tell me."

So the boy did.

And Silas, in wonderment that they had sent a rookie into a situation a veteran might not be able to handle, settled his tab, took the boy by the arm, and led him into the night.

Every city has pockets of evil. Vegas had fewer than most, despite the things the television lied about. So many people worked in law enforcement or security, so many others were bonded so that they could work in casinos or high-end jewelry stores or banks that Vegas's serious crime was lower than most comparable cities of its size.

Silas appreciated that. Most of the time, it meant that the deaths he attended in Vegas were natural or easy or just plain silly. He got a lot of silly deaths in that city. Some he even found time to laugh over.

But not this one.

As they drove from the very edge of town, past the rows and rows of similar houses, past the stink and desperation of complete poverty, he finally asked, "How long've you been doing this?"

"Six months," the boy said softly, as if that were forever.

Silas looked at him, looked at the young face reflecting the Christmas lights that filled the neighborhood, and shook his head. "All substitutes?"

The boy shrugged. "They didn't have any open routes."

"What about the guy you replaced?"

"He'd been subbing, waiting to retire. They say you could retire too, but you show no signs of it. Working too hard, even for a younger man."

He wasn't older. He was the same age he had been when his wife struggled with her labor—a breach birth that would be no problem in 2006, but had been deadly if not handled right in 1856. The midwife's hands hadn't been clean—not that anyone knew better in those days—and the infection had started even before the baby got turned.

He shuddered, that night alive in him. The night he'd made his bargain.

"I don't work hard," he said. "I work less than I did when I started."

The boy looked at him, surprised. "Why don't you retire?"

"And do what?" Silas asked. He hadn't planned to speak up. He normally shrugged off that question.

"I dunno," the boy said. "Relax. Live off your savings. Have a family again."

They could all have families again when they retired. Families and a good, rich life, albeit short. Silas would age when he retired. He would age and have no special powers. He would watch a new wife die in childbirth and not be able to see his former colleague sitting beside the bed. He would watch his children squirm after a car accident, blood on their faces, knowing that they would live poorly if they lived at all, and not be able to find out the future from the death dealer hovering near the scene.

Better to continue. Better to keep this half-life, this half-future, time without end.

"Families are overrated," Silas said. They look at you with betrayal and loss when you do what was right.

But the boy didn't know that yet. He didn't know a lot.

"You ever get scared?" the boy asked.

"Of what?" Silas asked. Then gave the standard answer. "They can't kill you. They can't harm you. You just move from place to place, doing your job. There's nothing to be scared of."

The boy grunted, sighed, and looked out the window.

Silas knew what he had asked, and hadn't answered it. Of course he got scared. All the time. And not of dying—even though he still wasn't sure what happened to the souls he freed. He wasn't scared of that, or of the people he occasionally faced down, the drug addicts with their knives, the gangsters with their guns, the wannabe outlaws with blood all over their hands.

No, the boy had asked about the one thing to be afraid of, the one thing they couldn't change.

Was he scared of being alone? Of remaining alone, for the rest of his days? Was he scared of being unknown and nearly invisible, having no ties and no dreams?

It was too late to be scared of that.

He'd lived it. He lived it every single day.

The house was one of those square adobe things that filled Vegas. It was probably pink in the sunlight. In the half-light that passed for nighttime in this perpetually alive city, it looked gray and foreboding.

The bars on the windows—standard in this neighborhood—didn't help.

Places like this always astounded him. They seemed so normal, so incorruptible, just another building on another street, like all the other buildings on all the other streets. Sometimes he got to go into those buildings. Very few of them were different from what he expected. Oh, the art changed or the furniture. The smells differed—sometimes unwashed diapers, sometimes perfume, sometimes the heavy scent of meals eaten long ago—but the rest remained the same: the television in the main room, the kitchen with its square table (sometimes decorated with flowers, sometimes nothing but trash), the double bed in the second bedroom down the hall, the one with its own shower and toilet. The room across from the main bathroom was sometimes an office, sometimes a den, sometimes a child's bedroom. If it was a child's bedroom, there were pictures on the wall, studio portraits from the local mall, done up in cheap frames, showing the passing years. The pictures were never straight, and always dusty, except for the most recent, hung with pride in the only remaining empty space.

He had a hunch this house would have none of those things. If anything, it would have an overly neat interior. The television would be in the kitchen or the bedroom or both. The front room would have a sofa set designed for looks, not for comfort. And one of the rooms would be blocked off, maybe even marked private, and in it, he would find (if he looked) trophies of a kind that made even his cast-iron stomach turn.

These houses had no attic. Most didn't have a basement. So the scene would be the garage. The car would be parked outside of it, blocking the door, and the neighbors would assume that the garage was simply a workspace—not that far off, if the truth be told.

He'd been to places like this before. More times than he wanted to think about, especially in the smaller communities out in the desert, the communities that had no names, or once had a name and did no longer. The communities sometimes made up of cheap trailers and empty storefronts, with a whorehouse a few miles off the main highway, and a casino in the center of town, a casino so old it made the one that the boy found him in look like it had been built just the week before.

He hated these jobs. He wasn't sure what made him come with the boy. A moment of compassion? The prospect of yet another long Christmas Eve with nothing to punctuate it except the bong-bong of nearby slots?

He couldn't go to church any more. It didn't feel right, with as many lives as he had taken. He couldn't go to church or listen to the singing or look at the families and wonder which of them he'd be standing beside in thirty years.

Maybe he belonged here more than the boy did. Maybe he belonged here more than anyone else.

They parked a block away, not because anyone would see their car—if asked, hours later, the neighbors would deny seeing anything to do with Silas or the boy. Maybe they never saw, maybe their memories vanished. Silas had never been clear on that either.

As they got out, Silas asked, "What do you use?"

The boy reached into the breast pocket. For a moment, Silas thought he'd remove the iPod, and Silas wasn't sure how a device that used headphones would work. Then the boy removed a harmonica—expensive, the kind sold at high-end music stores.

"You play that before all this?" Silas asked.

The boy nodded. "They got me a better one, though."

Silas's banjo had been all his own. They'd let him take it, and nothing else. The banjo, the clothes he wore that night, his hat.

He had different clothes now. He never wore a hat. But his banjo was the same as it had always been—new and pure with a sound that he still loved.

It was in the trunk. He doubted it could get stolen, but he took precautions just in case.

He couldn't bring it on this job. This wasn't his job. He'd learned the hard way that the banjo didn't work except in assigned cases. When he'd wanted to help, to put someone out of their misery, to step in where another death dealer had failed, he couldn't. He could only watch, like normal people did, and hope that things got better, even though he knew it wouldn't.

The boy clutched the harmonica in his right hand. The dry desert air was cold. Silas could see his breath. The tourists down on the Strip, with their short skirts and short sleeves, probably felt betrayed by the normal winter chill. He wished he were there with them, instead of walking through this quiet neighborhood, filled with dark houses, dirt-ridden yards, and silence.

So much silence. You'd think there'd be at least one barking dog.

When they reached the house, the boy headed to the garage, just like Silas expected. A car was parked on the road—a 1980s sedan that looked like it had seen better days. In the driveway, a brand-new van with tinted windows, custom-made for bad deeds.

In spite of himself, Silas shuddered.

The boy stopped outside and steeled himself, then he looked at Silas with sadness in his eyes. Silas nodded. The boy extended a hand—Silas couldn't get in without the boy's momentary magic—and then they were inside, near the stench of old gasoline, urine, and fear.

The kids sat in a dimly lit corner, chained together like the slaves on ships in the 19th century. The windows were covered with dirty cardboard, the concrete floor was empty except for stains as old as time. It felt bad in here, a recognizable bad, one Silas had encountered before.

The boy was shaking. He wasn't out of place here, his old wool jacket and his dirty jeans making him a cousin to the kids on the floor. Silas had a momentary flash: they were homeless. Runaways, lost, children without borders, without someone looking for them.

"You've been here before," Silas whispered to the boy and the boy's eyes filled with tears.

Been here, negotiated here, moved on here—didn't quite die, but no longer quite lived—and for who? A group of kids like this one? A group that had somehow escaped, but hadn't reported what had happened?

Then he felt the chill grow worse. Of course they hadn't reported it. Who would believe them? A neat homeowner kidnaps a group of homeless kids for his own personal playthings, and the cops believe the kids? Kids who steal and sell drugs and themselves just for survival.

People like the one who owned this house were cautious. They were smart. They rarely got caught unless they went public with letters or phone calls or both.

They had to prepare for contingencies like losing a plaything now and then. They probably had all the answers planned.

A side door opened. It was attached to the house. The man who came in was everything Silas had expected—white, thin, balding, a bit too intense.

What surprised Silas was the look the man gave him. Measuring, calculating.

Pleased.

The man wasn't supposed to see Silas or the boy. Not until the last moment.

Not until the end.

Silas had heard that some of these creatures could see the death dealers. A few of Silas's colleagues speculated that these men continued to kill so that they could continue to see death in all its forms, collecting images the way they collected trophies.

After seeing the momentary victory in that man's eyes, Silas believed it.

The man picked up the kid at the end of the chain. Too weak to stand, the kid staggered a bit, then had to lean into the man.

"You have to beat me," the man said to Silas. "I slice her first, and you have to leave."

The boy was still shivering. The man hadn't noticed him. The man thought Silas was here for him, not the boy. Silas had no powers, except the ones that humans normally had—not on this night, and not in this way.

If he were here alone, he'd start playing, and praying he'd get the right one. If there was a right one. He couldn't tell. They all seemed to have the mark of death over them.

No wonder the boy needed him.

It was a fluid situation, one that could go in any direction.

"Start playing," Silas said under his breath.

But the man heard him, not the boy. The man pulled the kid's head back, exposing a smooth white throat with the heartbeat visible in a vein.

"Play!" Silas shouted, and ran forward, shoving the man aside, hoping that would be enough.

It saved the girl's neck, for a moment anyway. She fell, and landed on the other kid next to her. The kid moved away, as if proximity to her would cause the kid to die.

The boy started blowing on his harmonica. The notes were faint, barely notes, more like bleats of terror.

The man laughed. He saw the boy now. "So you're back to rob me again," he said.

The boy's playing grew wispier.

"Ignore him," Silas said to the boy.

"Who're you? His coach?" The man approached him. "I know your rules. I destroy you, I get to take your place."

The steak rolled in Silas's stomach. The man was half right. He destroyed Silas, and he would get a chance to take the job. He destroyed both of them, and he would get the job, by old magic not new. Silas had forgotten this danger. No wonder these creatures liked to see death—what better for them than to be the facilitator for the hundreds of people who died in Nevada every day.

The man brandished his knife. "Lessee," he said. "What do I do? Destroy the instrument, deface the man. Right? And send him to hell."

Get him fired, Silas fought. It wasn't really hell, although it seemed like it. He became a ghost, existing forever, but not allowed to interact with anything. He was fired. He lost the right to die.

The man reached for the harmonica. Silas shoved again.

"Play!" Silas shouted.

And miraculously, the boy played. "Home on the Range," a silly song for these circumstances, but probably the first tune the boy had ever learned. He played it with spirit as he backed away from the fight.

But the kids weren't rebelling. They sat on the cold concrete floor, already half dead, probably tortured into submission. If they didn't rise up and kill this monster, no one would.

Silas looked at the boy. Tears streamed down his face, and he nodded toward the kids. Souls hovered above them, as if they couldn't decide whether or not to leave.

Damn the ones in charge: they'd sent the kid here as his final test. Could he take the kind of lives he had given his life for? Was he that strong?

The man reached for the harmonica again, and this time Silas grabbed his knife. It was heavier than Silas expected. He had never wielded a real instrument of death. His banjo eased people into forever. It didn't force them out of their lives a moment too early.

The boy kept playing and the man—the creature—laughed. One of the kids looked up, and Silas thought the kid was staring straight at the boy.

Only a moment, then. Only a moment to decide.

Silas shoved the knife into the man's belly. It went in deep, and the man let out an oof of pain. He stumbled, reached for the knife, and then glared at Silas.

Silas hadn't killed him, maybe hadn't even mortally wounded him. No soul appeared above him, and even these creatures had souls—dark and tainted as they were.

The boy's playing broke in places as if he were trying to catch his breath. The kid at the end of the chain, the girl, managed to get up. She looked at the knife, then at the man, then around the room. She couldn't see Silas or the boy.

Which was good.

The man was pulling on the knife. He would get it free in a moment. He would use it, would destroy these children, the ones no one cared about except the boy who was here to take their souls.

The girl kicked the kid beside her. "Stand up," she said.

The kid looked at her, bleary. Silas couldn't tell if these kids were male or female. He wasn't sure it mattered.

"Stand up," the girl said again.

In a rattle of chains, the kid did. The man didn't notice. He was working the knife, grunting as he tried to dislodge it. Silas stepped back, wondering if he had already interfered too much.

The music got louder, more intense, almost violent. The girl stood beside the man and stared at him for a moment.

He raised his head, saw her, and grinned.

Then she reached down with that chain, wrapped it around his neck and pulled. "Help me," she said to the others. "Help me."

The music became a live thing, wrapping them all, filling the smelly garage, and reaching deep, deep into the darkness. The soul did rise up —half a soul, broken and burned. It looked at Silas, then flared at the boy, who—bless him—didn't stop playing.

Then the soul floated toward the growing darkness in the corner, a blackness Silas had seen only a handful of times before, a blackness that felt as cold and dark as any empty desert night, and somehow much more permanent.

The music faded. The girl kept pulling, until another kid, farther down the line, convinced her to let go.

"We have to find the key," the other kid—a boy—said.

"On the wall," a third kid said. "Behind the electric box."

They shuffled as a group toward the box. They walked through Silas, and he felt them, alive and vibrant. For a moment, he worried that he had been fired, but he knew he had too many years for that. Too many years of perfect service—and he hadn't killed the man. He had just injured him, took away the threat to the boy.

That was allowed, just barely.

No wonder the boy had brought him. No wonder the boy had asked him if he was scared. Not of being alone or being lonely. But of certain jobs, of the things now asked of them as the no-longer-quite-human beings that they were.

Silas turned to the boy. His face was shiny with tears, but his eyes were clear. He stuffed the harmonica back into his breast pocket.

"You knew he'd beat you without me," Silas said.

The boy nodded.

"You knew this wasn't a substitution. You would have had this job, even without me."

"It's not cheating to bring in help," the boy said.

"But it's nearly impossible to find it," Silas said. "How did you find me?"

"It's Christmas Eve," the boy said. "Everyone knows where you'd be."

Everyone. His colleagues. People on the job. The only folks who even knew his name any more.

Silas sighed. The boy reached out with his stubby dirty hand. Silas took it, and then, suddenly, they were out of that fetid garage. They stood next to the van and watched as the cardboard came off one of the windows, as glass shattered outward.

Kids, homeless kids, injured and alone, poured out of that window like water.

"Thanks," the boy said. "I can't tell you how much it means."

But Silas knew. The boy didn't yet, but Silas did. When he retired—no longer if. When—this boy would see him again. This boy would take him, gently and with some kind of majestic harmonica music, to a beyond Silas could not imagine.

The boy waved at him, and joined the kids, heading into the dark

Vegas night. Those kids couldn't see him, but they had to know he was there, like a guardian angel, saving them from horrors that would haunt their dreams for the rest of their lives.

Silas watched them go. Then he headed in the opposite direction, toward his car. What had those kids seen? The man—the creature—with his knife out, raving at nothing. Then stumbling backwards, once, twice, the second time with a knife in his belly. They'd think that he tripped, that he stabbed himself. None of them had seen Silas or the boy.

They wouldn't for another sixty years.

If they were lucky.

The neighborhood remained dark, although a dog barked in the distance. His car was cold. Cold and empty.

He let himself in, started it, warmed his fingers against the still-hot air blowing out of the vents. Only a few minutes gone. A few minutes to take away a nasty, horrible lifetime. He wondered what was in the rest of these houses, and hoped he'd never have to find out.

The clock on the dash read 10:45. As he drove out of the neighborhood, he passed a small adobe church. Outside, candles burned in candleholders made of baked sand. Almost like the churches of his childhood.

Almost, but not quite.

He watched the people thread inside. They wore fancy clothing—dresses on the women, suits on the men, the children dressing like their parents, faces alive with anticipation.

They believed in something.

They had hope.

He wondered if hope was something a man could recapture, if it came with time, relaxation, and the slow inevitable march toward death.

He wondered, if he retired, whether he could spend his Christmas Eves inside, smelling the mix of incense and candle wax, the evergreen boughs, and the light dusting of ladies' perfume.

He wondered...

Then shook his head.

And drove back to the casino, to spend the rest of his time off in peace.

Children of the Night

Kristine Kathryn Rusch

Children of the Night

Cammie pounded the stake into his heart. Whitney stood firmly beside her as Cammie brought the hammer down. The vampire roared once—arms flailing, long nails scratching the side of the coffin. Blood spurted onto the apartment walls and the freshly laid carpet. A rank, half-rotted smell filled the air. Still she pounded, until the thing in front of her had faded into nothing but wizened skin and bones. She let go of the stake, wiped her hands on her jeans and turned around.

The little girl in the doorway was no more than three. Her wide blue eyes dominated her cherubic face. She glanced at Cammie once, then scanned the room. "Daddy?"

Cammie scanned the room too, but saw no evidence of a human presence. Whitney stared at the child and bit his lower lip. The little girl crept across the carpet, her tiny tennis shoes leaving no mark on the shag. She knelt in front of the coffin, put her forehead against the wood and whispered, "Daddy." The airy, pain-filled sound was more plaintive than a wail.

~

Dr. Eliason took the little girl—she had never given Cammie her name —into the examination room. The little girl clutched her stuffed dog and didn't look back. Cammie slid down on the plush blue seat. The waiting room smelled of sickness, stale coffee, and antiseptic. She wondered how the receptionist could work here, day after day.

Whitney studied the magazine rack and finally grabbed an ancient *Time*. He sat down beside her, even though there were no other patients in the room.

"First kid, huh?"

The blood on Cammie's jeans had dried into a crusty brown handprint. "She called him 'Daddy.'"

"He probably was."

She picked at the handprint. Flakes of dried blood caught on her fingernails. "He shriveled up like he was centuries old. There's no way—"

"Cammie." Whitney's tone was gentle. "You've been doing this for what, a year? You should know that anything past five years would crumble that way. She's maybe three, so if he were five years, she was conceived just after, which is plausible, or she was his from a sperm back, also plausible. Or he kidnapped her when she was a baby, which is likely."

Cammie didn't answer. She brushed at the bloodstain, but it didn't come off.

Whitney grabbed her arm. His hand was warm. "I thought you knew all this."

"How the hell was I supposed to know this?" Cammie wrenched herself free and stood up. The receptionist glanced over the high, glassed-in desk, then looked away. "I spend six weeks in combat training, get my weapons certificate, learn how to avoid conversion or death, get my assignments and blam! I'm on the streets. No one told me about lifestyles, or children, or decay time."

"They wouldn't have recruited you if you didn't already know."

Cammie wrapped her arms around herself and wandered over to the magazine rack. She hadn't known. She had come straight from college with a major in psychology and a minor in history. She had spent all of two weeks on vampires in her senior psych seminar, finally dismissing them as the most alien and deadly of addicts. She had gone to work for the Westrina Center just like many of her friends had gone to intern at the alcohol rehabilitation center. Only the Westrina Center made it clear that there was no way to rehabilitate a vampire. They treated vampirism like a plague: eradicated only by isolation and death. The Center had tried rehabilitation twenty-five years earlier, but that had more than failed: it had doubled the vampire population in the city.

The door swung open, and Dr. Eliason came out, holding the little girl's hand. She clutched her stuffed dog to her left side, its fabric head crammed against her heart. Dr. Eliason spoke softly to her, wiped a strand of hair from her forehead and then smiled. He was a tall, broad-shouldered man who had the gentleness that Cammie always thought doctors should have. He had asked her out twice, but she had refused; she didn't want to learn that his gentleness was false, a pretense for patients and nothing more.

He left the girl by the door and came over to Cammie. "She's clean," he said. "Not a mark on her. Her blood is her own, and it's infection-free. She's well fed, well nourished, well cared for. She's also in shock. She might be one of the lucky ones. She hasn't said much, so maybe she'll forget all this. But I think you need to take her to the Center right away. They should be able to get her settled somewhere before the pain really starts. Those all her possessions?"

"She had a room full of stuff," Whitney said.

"Get that and bring it," Eliason said. He didn't look at Whitney. He was watching Cammie. "She needs as much of her home as you can salvage."

"Home?" Cammie choked the word out. A place that smelled of rotting blood, and filled with the presence of a man no longer human. Eliason was calling that home?

He put his palm against her face. She resisted the urge to lean into him, to let him comfort her like he had comforted the little girl. "Home, Camila," he said. "It's all she ever knew."

Whitney crouched and extended his hands. "Come on, hon," he said. "I'll take you someplace safe."

"Her name is Janie." Eliason's thumb traced Cammie's cheekbone.

"Janie," Whitney said, hand still outstretched, "come with me."

Janie wrapped both arms around her dog, rested her chin on the creature's head and shuffled forward. She brushed near Eliason, but when she saw Cammie she scooted to the far side of the room.

"It's okay," Whitney said.

Janie continued her walk, occasionally throwing Cammie a frightened glance. When she reached Whitney, she buried her face in his sleeve.

"I guess you've been elected to pick up her things," Whitney said. "I'll meet you back at the office."

Cammie nodded, pulled away from Eliason and bolted out of the room before either man could say anything else. She didn't want their sympathy—and she didn't know why she expected them to give it.

She had never returned to the scene of an eradication before. Her hands shook as she fumbled with the lock. She had always gone in, found the sleeping vampire and murdered it, before it had a chance to touch her or her partner. She never looked at the home; she never did the reports. She always went in, drove the stake, and left. One day's work in a month filled with paperwork, field-training seminars, and target practice. She had only killed five. Imagine finding a child on her sixth.

The door slid open easily, much more easily than she remembered. The smell—ancient blood and decay—slapped her, bringing up that familiar hatred which made the killing part of the job so simple. She squinted in the darkness. No sunlight filtered in from the blackout curtains, no light gained entry under doors. The little girl had lived like this—in putrid darkness—instead of playing in sunlight. Cammie suppressed a shudder and flicked on a light.

The artificial illumination revealed a room so normal that Cammie nearly stumbled. A television dominated the center, surrounded by a light brown sofa sectional. A doll rested her head against a pillow, and a child's blanket crumpled near the end. Books lined the walls, and in the dining room, Cammie could see an expensive stereo set and hundreds of CDs. She wondered where the money came from, and then decided that she didn't want to think about it.

She wandered into the kitchen. Child-sized dishes sat unwashed on the kitchen counter. She opened the dishwasher and found more child-proof bowls as well as an entire set of wine goblets. Cool water dripped off the rim. He had probably turned on the dishwasher just before he went to sleep.

She slammed the door with a metallic bang. She had come to get toys and clothes. Child things. She didn't have to snoop through the entire house.

Avoiding the room with the coffin and its remains, she went down the hall. The shades were up in the little girl's room. Sunlight flooded across a pink-canopied bed. Stuffed animals lined the floors and walls. A record player sat in the middle of the floor, the turntable still revolving. No wonder she hadn't heard them come. She had been playing records —and Cammie had been too preoccupied to register the noise.

If there had been any noise.

She grabbed a suitcase out of the closet and stuffed it with ruffly little-girl dresses, sweatshirts and blue jeans. She poured the contents of the underwear and sock drawers on top, then added two winter coats for warmth. The child had been well tended, physically.

The smell was making her nauseous. She went over to the window, pulled it open and sucked in the crisp outdoor air. She would never take another detail with a child involved. Never.

As if she had had a choice. No one had warned her about this one.

She took the suitcase and an armload of stuffed animals out to her car. She came back, grabbed the toy box and carried it down. Then she unplugged the record player, packed the records and stopped.

The little girl wouldn't want that toy. It would remind her of her father's death. Each time she put an album on the turntable and heard the scritch-scratch of a needle, she would see her father thrash as Cammie drove a stake in his heart.

Cammie doubled over and wrapped her arms around her head, as if the action would squeeze the thoughts out. She hadn't meant to kill a child's father. She hadn't meant to kill a person at all. She was killing an animal, something that preyed on human beings and lived off the blood like a wild thing. She hadn't known....

Slowly, ever so slowly, she stood up. She grabbed a garbage bag, filled it with the remaining stuffed animals and went into the kitchen. She took the child dishes from the dishwasher, dried them and placed them inside the bag. Then she went into the living room, grabbed the doll and her blanket off the sofa, and left the house for the final time.

The sunlight seemed brighter than it had moments before. She took several breaths to clear the stench from her nostrils. Her clothes had picked up the smell and the child's things also reeked. She would be glad when she got rid of them. She would be glad when this entire thing was over.

That night Cammie dreamed:

She was lying across her bed, reading. Forbidden sunlight warmed her feet, her back. She didn't dare make any noise. Daddy was sleeping. He hated to be disturbed while he slept, especially after a night out. In the other room, her brother thrashed in his crib. He hated to sleep in the daylight, just as she did, but Daddy insisted. That way he could spend more time with them. But what he called time was mostly watching television, sipping wine and waiting for him to go out on his nightly food run. He always came back with groceries and cooked them a large dinner which he never ate. Once she asked him why he didn't like food. He had smiled and said the wine was enough.

She sat bolt upright in her bed, arms wrapped around herself. Her heart was pounding as if she had awakened from a nightmare, but the dream itself had not been frightening. She even knew the dream's cause—the vampire and his little girl.

She got up and padded barefoot across the dusty hardwood floors of her apartment. She didn't get paid enough for the work she did, not when vampires had expensive homes, filled with expensive furniture, stereos and TVs. The digital clock read 3:45, so she didn't even bother to switch on her own small, black-and-white set. She didn't have cable, and at this time of night, nothing else was on.

She walked around her three rooms, touching the garlic and the crosses that the Westrina Center insisted fill her home. Protection, just like the security system they had installed protected her. She was safer than she had ever been in her entire life, and still her heart pounded with fear at being a vampire's child.

She went into the kitchen, pulled a mug off the rack, opened a tea bag and filled the kettle on the stove. Then she grabbed a book from the stack on the table. Something light and romantic, to tease her mind. Something different from her life. Something to occupy her until the sun rose—and she could sleep in the safety and warmth of the light.

~

The observation room was small and dark. Cammie clasped her hands behind her back and refused the chair Anita offered her. Anita settled her bulk into the armchair and leaned forward, placing her elbows on the windowsill. The elder woman looked comfortable and matronly; Cammie always thought her the perfect image of a mother—so perfect that, at times, Cammie wanted Anita to hold her and soothe away all her fears.

But they had never even touched. Their working relationship had been strictly professional, and a friendship had never developed.

"She's asked about a record player," Anita said, staring through the window at the brightly lit room below. "I assume you left it."

"She'd been listening to it when we got there. I thought it would hurt her."

"I'd sent Whitney for it, but they'd already sealed up the house." Anita leaned back, her face half in shadow. "You can't pre-guess another person's pain."

"But—"

"Don't but me. I've seen three generations of children through this place. We need to help whatever way we can."

"I'm sorry."

Anita nodded once. "That's better. I want you to get the court order and move through the red tape. The record player has to be here by this afternoon."

Cammie clenched her fists. "Is that why you brought me up here?"

"No." Anita waved at the chair. "Sit down."

Cammie didn't move.

"Sit down. You can't see from that height."

Cammie straightened her shoulders, and eased the tightness in her hands. She grabbed the edge of the chair and pulled it back, sitting in it, but not resting. "All right."

Anita leaned forward again. Down in the room, Janie piled her stuffed animals around herself like a protective wall. "Whitney tells me you know nothing about vampires and children."

"I know that female vampires prey mostly on infants and children under five."

"And male vampires?"

"Kill men, mostly, and occasionally create a female vampire."

"But what do male vampires do with children?"

"How the hell am I supposed to know?" Cammie kicked against the wall and pushed her chair back. Janie looked up, her expression startled.

"It's not completely soundproofed up here," Anita said. "She can hear when you pound the wall. I don't want her any more frightened than she is."

"Sorry," Cammie said, not feeling sorry at all. The little girl had lived with a vampire. Cammie had freed her, had saved her, and everyone in the center acted as if the child had suffered a tragedy.

"During the first thirty years of a male vampire's existence," Anita said as if Cammie hadn't interrupted them, "he still seeks companionship. He tries it first by creating female vampires, and when that fails, he adopts children. Sometimes, he can father them—especially if he tried in his first year. As his addiction grows, and his humanity breaks down, he abandons the children more and more, until finally, he either uses them as prey or he creates younger, more powerful vampires. Do you understand what I'm telling you?"

"You're telling me that I did the right thing."

"No." Anita put her hand on the glass, as if she were trying to touch the little girl. "I'm telling you that your actions yesterday ended a relationship. The vampire was still young enough to love this girl and treat her like a daughter. She lost her father—"

"Bullshit." Cammie whispered the word, then repeated it louder. "Bullshit. You people sent me over there. You told me to kill that vampire."

"Yes," Anita said. "And now I'm showing you the consequences of your action."

Cammie clenched her hands again, half wishing for a stake to drive through Anita's frozen heart. "Why?"

Anita reached out to her—first touch—and Cammie backed away. "Because you need to see it," Anita said. "And remember."

~

Stop him!

Cammie knew the voice belonged to her dream, but she couldn't wake up. She could see the faded night-gray of her bedroom, and over it, the forbidden sun-filled room of her dream. The voice came from down the hall: a man's voice, deep and angry.

Stop him!

She was holding a child, a little boy, clutching him to her shoulder, pressing his face against her skin to stifle his tears. She was lying alone in the safety of her own bed, knowing that what she was feeling wasn't real.

Stop him now!

"Shush, Ben, shush," she whispered in both worlds. "You don't want him to get up, do you? Please be quiet. Please."

The little boy snuffled once and then was silent. In the night-gray of her bed, she clutched the sheets and willed the fear to go away. The pressure of a little-boy body eased and then faded into nothing. She was completely alone. No dreams, no phantoms. Just her.

She got up and went into the kitchen. Without turning on a light, she made herself a cup of tea and sat at the table. The nights had grown longer. And each night, phantoms and dreams about vampire's children. She had had Whitney check for a boy-child in Janie's family. There was none. The little boy was an addition from her subconscious, another child to protect, a child who was not herself. But she wanted to protect no one. She wanted to go back to her job, to go to work without seeing the face of a little girl whose father she had murdered, or the nonexistent, frightened face of a dream boy who needed her strength.

~

Five children lived in the Child's Wing of the Center. She had always thought the wing housed children who had been bitten by a vampire or whose families had died at a vampire's hands. She had never realized that most of the children lost their fathers due to actions by the Westrina Center itself.

Cammie walked down the hallway, her rubber-soled shoes squeaking on the clean tile. A television blared from the game room. One child sat there, his arms wrapped around himself, eyes staring at nothing. Two other children sat in the sunroom, staring up at the light. But Janie was in her room, stuffed animals surrounding her like a small army.

Cammie took a chair and sat across from Janie. Janie's eyes grew wide, but she didn't move. Cammie slid closer. "Hi," she said. "I want—"

Janie screamed. She grabbed all of her animals against her and screamed as loud as she could. Cammie stood up. She could hear the sound of running feet in the hallway. "It's okay," she said, but the words sounded lame. "I . . ."

Janie's screams echoed in the wide hallway. Anita and two orderlies appeared at the door. "What are you doing?" Anita snapped.

Cammie said nothing. She stared at the terror on the child's face, at the little girl's arms protecting the last things of value in her world. "I'm sorry," Cammie whispered, and ran from the room.

She stopped at the empty reception desk in front and caught her breath. All she had wanted to do was talk to the child, apologize, and perhaps gain a little understanding. The understanding she had gained —but she hadn't expected the cost.

"What the hell were you doing?" Anita asked.

Cammie looked up. Anita stood beside her, arms crossed, the matronly look gone. "She okay?"

"I've got one of the orderlies with her now and I've got a call into Dr. Eliason because he's the only one she trusts." Anita's face was red. "Don't you understand? She hates women. Her father taught her that women are dangerous and you proved it by killing him. What were you trying to do?"

"I was trying to—" Cammie stopped. She couldn't explain, not the dreams, not the desire to get Janie out of her head. "—to talk to her."

"Well, don't," Anita said. "You've got another eradication tomorrow and I want you thinking about that, not some little girl whose life is no longer your concern. And I don't ever want to see you in this wing again. Do you understand that?"

Cammie nodded. She turned her back and walked out the door. The sunlight felt warm and soothing against her face. Dream image. She tried to shake it, but couldn't. She turned back for Anita in time to see Eliason go through the door. She clenched her fist and leaned against the small oak that they had built the sidewalk around. She could talk to Eliason. She would wait.

The sun had nearly set when he finally emerged from the building. Cammie stood, brushed off her jeans and called to him. He looked over. She braced herself for another round of accusations, like the ones she had received from Anita, but he said nothing as he walked over to her.

He took her hand. "You're cold," he said. "Let me get you some coffee."

She didn't argue.

They went to a small coffee shop near the Center. The shop was small and smelled of European coffee and fresh-baked pies. Eliason led Cammie to a table near the back.

"She better?" Cammie asked.

Eliason shrugged. "I don't know what better is in this case. Technically she was better when her father was alive."

"You too?" Cammie pushed against the table.

Elisaon caught her wrist. "He would have turned on her. They always do. This one's bothering you too much, Cammie."

"No one ever warned me about children."

"No one thought they had to."

She glared at him. The waitress set down two steaming mugs of coffee. Eliason took his, filled it with cream and sugar, and stirred as if nothing were wrong.

"You don't know the history of the Westrina Center, do you?" he asked.

"It's been here forever, and about fifteen years ago, it changed buildings, after this rehabilitation program started."

"Nice, encapsulated, short, and straight out of the manual. Ever wonder why they train so many people like you?"

"Because there's so many vampires."

Eliason smiled and sipped his coffee. "There's not that many vampires."

"They already told us when we started. High burnout. People last at most three years."

"And you've been here, what? Two?"

"One."

"When did the dreams start?"

Cammie jerked. Eliason stared at her. His eyes were dark brown. She had never noticed that before. "I'm the one with the psych degree," she said.

"But you never use it. Janie doesn't hold the answers for you. She's got to search for her own when she's ready. You, on the other hand, already know how to search."

Cammie felt a blush on her cheeks. She hadn't meant to disturb the child, but Eliason was right. She hadn't been thinking of anyone but herself. "Why did you ask me about the history of the Center?"

"Because," he said. "About twenty-five years ago, when the rehab program failed, a number of the counselors became vampires themselves. Too many vampires to stop in such a short period of time. The people left worked on keeping the threat from spreading, not at taking care of the vampires who already existed. They lived in an entire section of town, and no one went there, and no one left, not even the children who lived with a vampire, like Janie did. Do you understand me?"

"Not completely." The coffee churned in Cammie's stomach. "The children had to fend for themselves?"

Eliason nodded, then glanced at his watch. "I've got an appointment. Don't push yourself so hard, Cammie. And if you need me, I'll talk to you. I'll help you in any way that I can." He put some money on the table, got up and kissed her cheek. Cammie suppressed an urge to grab his hand and hold him. She felt as if they had been talking about something she almost understood. She took another sip of her coffee, and saw an old building rise unbidden in her mind. The Old Westrina Center. Perhaps the answers to questions she didn't even know awaited her there.

~

Cammie pulled up in front of the Westrina Center's former building. It had been abandoned nearly ten years before. Wire fences surrounded it, and garlic had been nailed to the door. All the windows were barred with small crosses, and none had been broken.

She had never stopped here, always preferring to avoid it—to look forward, not back. The new Westrina Center had modern facilities now and a new outlook. She was part of the best rehabilitation movement they had founded. She didn't need to look at the one that had failed.

Until now.

He's just a baby. I take care of him!

The little girl's voice was insistent. Cammie put her hands on the cold wire, but could see no one.

I need to see him. Nobody else knows how to take care of him...

She wandered around to the side of the building, saw the half-ruined remains of a playground. The swings were mere chains and the teeter-totter had rotted into the earth.

I don't want to play. I want to see him...

And then the scream, so long and shrill that she had to close her eyes. The sound ripped the pain from her belly, let it rise into her neck and mouth. She leaned her head into the wire, feeling the metal dig into her forehead.

She had clutched her little brother's hand tightly, as two people, smelling of blood, led her into the center. As they walked into reception, she was surprised to see how many people waited for her, how quiet they seemed. She said nothing. A slender man knelt beside her, pried her brother's hand from her own. She looked at her brother's face, the face she had protected all this time, and was startled at blood on it. Blood spattered all over his clothes. Tears built behind her eyes, but she didn't let them fall.

She hadn't wanted him to know, but there he was, blood-covered and frightened. She reached out to him, but the man picked him up and carried him away.

And she never saw him again. Too dangerous. Too unstable. Too frightened.

She pushed herself away from the fence. Her forehead ached and her entire body shook. She wiped her face with her sleeve, and then looked up. Eliason leaned against a tree, his arms crossed.

"You followed me," she said.

He nodded.

"And you knew."

"Yes," he said. "Current rehabilitation theory. You can't do anything for the parents, but you can save the children."

"I don't feel saved," she said and pushed past him.

"Cammie—"

His voice echoed behind her, one of many trailing into the growing twilight. Her father had called her Camila, her brother Cam-Cam. She had adopted Cammie because it brought no pain. Until now.

The Center looked cold in the early morning light. Cammie wrapped her old, ragged sweater around her shoulders as she got out of her car. She knew that she shouldn't be there. She wondered what had made her work for the Center at all. Some sort of post-hypnotic suggestion? Something from her past that forced her there?

She smiled without humor. She had spent the entire night worrying about just those things and had come to no conclusion. Except that this eradication would be her last.

She pulled the duffel with her gear out of the car. The duffel seemed heavier than usual. She pulled open the glass doors and found Whitney standing near reception.

"I thought you wouldn't come," he said.

"Been talking to Eliason, huh?"

He shook his head. "It's just happened to me before. I recognize the signs."

"What makes you stay here, year after year?"

"I guess I'm one of the ones who doesn't rehabilitate." He shrugged. "This is the only place that I've ever belonged."

Cammie shifted her duffel onto her shoulder. "Ready?"

Whitney studied her face for a moment. "Yeah." He picked up his gear and they walked back out the door. As they got into the Center's white van, he said, "You're not going to cop out on me, are you?"

"I'll stay," she said.

The van's plastic seat was cold. Cammie tugged on the sleeves of her sweater and closed her eyes. She knew what section of town they were going to; she didn't want to see the drive. Perhaps then, she would be able to concentrate on her work.

When the van stopped, Cammie grabbed her duffel and opened the door before she looked at the neighborhood. They had parked in front of a two-story brownstone, like the one she had grown up in. The apartments inside were long and narrow, and only the back bedroom—the one that had been hers—had windows at all. Perfect vampire country.

Whitney juggled his lock-picker's tools. "Last chance, Cammie."

"I'm going," she snapped.

He yanked his duffel up and climbed the crumbling concrete steps two at a time. Cammie followed, her nervousness like a stone in the center of her stomach. Perhaps she shouldn't have come. If she screwed up, made one single mistake, she would lose her life along with Whitney.

Perhaps that wouldn't be such a bad thing.

She shook the thought. She had to go in with an attitude of strength. In the daylight, she had more power than a vampire. In the daylight, she was the one who brought death.

Whitney scanned the outside wall for a security system. Seeing none, he tried the outside door. The knob turned easily, and the door swung open, revealing a narrow, badly lit hallway. A flight of stairs went up to the left, and to the right another door beckoned. Whitney went to it. Cammie pulled out her flashlight and illuminated the lock while Whitney picked at it.

The door opened before he could finish. Both Cammie and Whitney backed up. A little boy stood there, his face a mass of bruises, one eye swollen shut. "My daddy's asleep," he said, his voice tight with fear.

A rotted-blood smell seeped into the hallway like a bad dream. Cammie felt nausea return and stifled the urge to bolt.

"Take him to the van," Whitney said.

Cammie shook her head. "Either we both do or neither. That's procedure and you know it."

"Daddy says no one can come in. And I gotta stay." The boy barely spoke above a whisper. "He's asleep."

"And you're not supposed to wake him," Cammie said.

The boy nodded. A tear slipped out of his swollen eye.

"Go sit on the couch," she said. "We'll be out in a moment."

She slid the door open gently—quietly—and walked past the little boy. Whitney followed. Cammie knew this house. She had grown up in one so similar. Light seeped through the back bedroom door, but the other rooms were dark. She followed the smell to the vampire's room, paused for a moment to remove her mallet and stake, then eased the door open.

Dark. And smelling of rot. *Not supposed to go in there.* The little boy's voice or her brother Ben's? She didn't know. Her hands trembled, like they had before. It was the only way, the only solution. If she didn't, he would hit Ben again and maybe kill him, like he had killed that woman in the parking lot—like he had threatened to kill her.

Her eyes slowly adjusted. Pictures hung on the wall. An unused bed stood in the corner. The walk-in closet door was open and the smell seemed to beckon her.

"Wait, Cammie."

Cam-Cam, wait up.

But she couldn't wait. She held the stake and the mallet (dowel and hammer—too big for her small hands) before her like torches. The coffin stuck out a few inches into the room. She walked on one side, saw him sleeping there, so peacefully.

Hard to believe that face could bring such destruction. She knelt. A hand touched her shoulder. She didn't turn, didn't want to see Ben. She placed the dowel over the vampire's heart and brought the hammer down with all of her strength. He roared and sat up, foul breath covering her, stolen blood spattering the walls. She pounded again, ignoring the nails raking into her skin, the too-strong hands yanking at her wrists. She had to keep going. She had to. For Ben, if not herself.

He thrashed, kicked, his foot connecting with her shoulder, nearly knocking her off balance. But she clung to the dowel, kept pounding. Blood gushed from his mouth, through his fanged teeth and across her hands. Still she pounded, thinking it would never end. The stories were wrong. Vampires never died. They sucked life's blood forever.

And then he stopped. His hands slid down the coffin's side and shredded, the skin drying and flaking, the bones yellowing with age.

Behind her, a child cried. A little boy. *Ben*. But she ignored him, leaned her head on the dowel and took a deep breath.

"Daddy," she whispered. But he didn't answer. He would never answer. He had been dead a long time.

She rocked back on her heels, turned and saw Whitney staring at her, his skin white. He clutched the little boy against his chest.

"The child shouldn't have been here," Whitney said.

"He would have known anyway," Cammie said. She stood up and wiped the blood on her jeans. Her last vampire. Now, finally, she could move on. "Let's get his things, take him back to the Center. Anita will take care of him."

She restrained an urge to reach out to the child. She had done that once, with Ben a long time ago. It was one thing to see your father killed. It was another to be held by his killer.

"He'll survive," she said softly. "We did."

And then she left the bedroom, to wash the blood from her hands.

Sales. Force.

Kristine Kathryn Rusch

Sales. Force.

He said: *Our love is deep and powerful, epic.*

He said: *It will last for all time.*

He said: *Forever.*

He died on a Thursday afternoon in mid-winter, in Kaylee's arms, in a stupid hospital room with stupid white walls and a stupid brown blanket covering half of him, on a stupid hospital bed with stupid rails that dug into her back, and stupid machines that beep-beep-beeped, then beepbeepbeepbeeped before the stupid alarm sounded and the stupid doctors and nurses ran into the room with the stupid crash cart that did absolutely nothing.

Because, she knew, long before the doctors and nurses arrived, he had taken his last breath.

Never even opened his eyes, not after the damn car accident. Never smiled at her again, never said *I love you* one last time.

There was nothing pretty about the death, nothing pretty about him at the end.

Just her. Standing in the corner of the stupid hospital room, watching the pathetic doctors and nurses with their pathetic crash cart do everything they could to resuscitate a corpse.

~

"Fine," she'd say angrily to anyone who asked. "I'm *fine.*"

But of course, she wasn't fine. She'd never be fine again.

She told everyone she moved out of the apartment because she couldn't live there any more without him, and everyone took that to mean the memories were too much for her, when really it meant she had to move, as in legally.

She had to do a bunch of things that she didn't want to do because, as she learned the hard way, there was a difference between planning to get married and actually *being* married.

People even looked at her grief differently. *At least*, they'd say, *you still have a future.*

And she'd glare at them angrily, because what could she say, really? *It's a future I don't want?* Or *do you really know what the hell you're talking about?* Or *Do you* think *about the words that come out of your mouth or do you just let fly with whatever comes to mind?*

Yeah, she was angry, and yeah, she knew anger was step one of the grief wheel or whatever they called the dumb thing, but she also knew that she'd always been just a little angry. She suspected she'd been born angry, coming out of the womb with tiny fists clenched spoiling for a fight.

Dex had loved that about her. He'd said he loved everything about her.

He'd said he would never leave her.

She should have known better than to believe him.

Hell, she should have thought it through:

Every relationship ended. Sometimes it ended voluntarily with a breakup or an affair. Sometimes it ended with death.

Only the lucky ones died together.

Everyone else had to suffer through being a *survivor*.

And she hated that term most of all.

~

She went back to work after a week. Her boss, Nia, maybe the only person who understood how much Kaylee had loved Dex, told her to take more time.

But she didn't want more time. She'd moved back to the scruffy one-bedroom she'd had before Dex, which the landlord said he'd been holding for her, but they both knew the place was too tiny and too dark to rent to anyone else.

Her stuff fit in it just like it used to, the battered table, the mattress on the floor, the thrift shop dishes. The only things she'd taken from Dex's place—and yes, *taken* was the right word, since she had no legal right to anything—were his books. She left a few—the ones she'd read—but his family wouldn't know what he'd had and what he didn't have, and they weren't readers, so they wouldn't miss the books.

She'd slunk away, feeling like she was being evicted from the only home she'd ever had, and after she left, after she'd locked the keys inside, she regretted not taking at least one of his shirts, or his blanket or something, something that smelled like him.

Then she squared her shoulders and vowed to move forward. Memories of him would hold her back, not that she could get rid of them.

Not that she wanted to, deep down.

But the memories that kept coming up were the memories of his promises: *We're forever, blondie, just you and me. Forever.*

Forever was awfully damn short, and love was grand for an afternoon, and she was right back where she started, in a tiny little apartment with a great kitchen and no real light, and nothing to do but count the stains on the wall.

So why wouldn't she go back to work?

Work, at least, got rid of the aggression. Work gave her a purpose, made her feel alive. Okay, that last wasn't true. Work didn't make her feel alive.

It justified her numbness.

Because, really, who could kill something day in and day out, and remain one hundred percent in touch with her feelings?

Maybe, she thought as she drove to the dying wharf where the office was this week, it was good Dex was gone.

He'd been making her too sensitive, too touchy-feely.

Hell, the reason she hadn't married him yet was because she hadn't been able to figure out how to tell him what, exactly, she did for a living.

You see, Dex, there are magic creatures in the world, and most of them are pretty damn evil, just like in those books you read, and all of them, all *of them want a piece of someone's soul, so it takes someone without much of a soul to make them really and truly dead.*

I'm the person without much of a soul. So don't love me, Dex. Don't love me, don't marry me, don't stay with me.

She'd never said those words to him, but apparently, he'd heard them. He hadn't married her.

And he sure as hell hadn't stayed.

The office, in a dilapidated building near a rotting pier, was warded. It also smelled strongly of fish.

Kaylee made a face as she stepped inside. Nia stood near a long folding table that tilted to the left.

Nia was tiny, and would've been called cute by the folks who weren't paying attention, the folks who didn't see the daggers in her chocolate-brown eyes. Nia kept her black hair shaved close, she said, to control the curls, but Kaylee knew it was to make the work easier. Work took too much think-time, time that shouldn't be wasted on hair care or product or even a shampoo.

Maybe Kaylee would go for the shaved look too, although her skull wasn't as symmetrical as Nia's. Nor was Kaylee little or cute.

Kaylee had never been little or cute. Always big, always a bit of a bruiser, and over the years, she'd developed muscles on her muscles, as Dex used to say with admiration.

Nia held a clipboard. A dozen others hung on the wall from nails newly placed in the peeling paint. An ancient filing cabinet stood near a door that led to a small bathroom. The bathroom looked even more disreputable than the office did.

There was no computer equipment because Nia didn't play well with computers. Besides, computers left an electronic trail and Nia didn't like leaving trails. Not for this business.

She had one pencil behind her ear and a black pen in her hand.

"Last chance," she said by way of hello. "I'd beg off if I were you. Don't want be at home? Take a vacation, see the sites, find a grief counseling group, volunteer at a charity or something."

"Can you see me doing any of that?" Kaylee was a little offended that Nia had suggested any of it.

"I don't care what you do," Nia said. "I'm just warning you. You're perfect for this job, and that's a bad thing."

Kaylee stared at her. Nia was tough. She had a heart, although most people never saw it. Kaylee had. When Kaylee fell for Dex, Nia tried to talk Kaylee into leaving the business altogether.

Love and magic don't mix, Nia had said. *Pick one, K.*

Apparently Kaylee had picked one. She had picked magic.

"Who'm I supposed to kill?" she asked, keeping her voice level. She used to debate even asking that question, because often what she was sent to kill wasn't a "who." It was a "what." And "kill" might be a relative term. Sometimes "destroy" was better.

"You're not killing this time," Nia said.

"Just because I had to deal with Dex's death—"

"No," Nia said. "That's not why. You're investigating this time."

Kaylee let out a sigh. She hated investigating. She had given it up long ago. Others went into various parts of the city, investigated reports of dark magic or evil intent, and then reported back to Nia. Nia would assign someone to destroy the magic or the mage or both.

Kaylee had an affinity for destruction. She did not investigate well. Investigations required subtlety, and she was anything but subtle.

"I don't investigate," Kaylee said.

"You're the only one we got," Nia said.

"I'm not in the mood to investigate," Kaylee said.

"Tough shit," Nia said. "You stayed. You begged for work. You're doing this."

"I'm leaving," Kaylee said, feeling at loose ends. She had wanted the work, but not finesse work. She needed to crack some heads.

She went to the door, but it glowed red.

"You said I could choose," she said, without turning around.

"And then you asked who you were supposed to kill," Nia said. "That activated the wards. You're in now."

Kaylee felt a flash of irritation. It held back full-blown anger. But she knew, she *knew*, Nia was right. Once the agreement to take a job was made, it was binding.

Kaylee just couldn't believe Nia would give her the wrong kind of work.

Kaylee took a deep breath before turning around. Nia hadn't moved. Her pen remained poised over the clipboard.

"So what's the job?" Kaylee asked, letting her irritation flow through her voice.

"You're going in as a client."

"In where?"

"Armand's Potions on Fifth."

Kaylee sighed, pushing back even more irritation. "You investigated Armand's when it opened, or don't you remember? Legit white magic, no whiff of black—at least in the magical potions. Most everything else has too much alcohol and will simply make the client feel good."

"Yeah, I know," Nia said. "We're not investigating Armand. He's doing a potion sharing."

Kaylee felt her lips tighten. She hated potion sharings. They were the wine tastings of the magical world.

"Why would he do that?" she asked.

"Because I asked him to." Nia opened the clip on the clipboard and removed a piece of paper. It was a flyer, advertising a love potion. The flyer smelled like perfume, and made Kaylee a bit lightheaded just by being near it.

Nia smiled.

"Thought so," she said. "You're perfect."

"What does that mean?"

"Some of our regulars have been asked to invest in the love potion," Nia said.

"And you want to know if it's a scam," Kaylee said. "Send one of them in. Remove the spell if the potion works."

"Read the damn flyer," Nia said.

Kaylee didn't want to touch it. It glowed pink and made her feel happier than she wanted to feel.

The flyer claimed the potion didn't make someone fall in love. It took someone who had given up on love or who had lost too much in their life to ever try to love, and repaired their belief in love.

Kaylee had a slight headache now. "I'm perfect?" she asked.

"Yeah," Nia said and let the word hang. The reason she was sending Kaylee in was obvious to both of them.

"What's the catch?" Kaylee asked.

"That's what you're going to find out," Nia said.

The potion sharing wasn't being held at Armand's. Instead, it was in the back room of one of the swankiest restaurants in the city. Even the back room was swanky. Done in black and white with soft yellow lighting falling on the potion bottles scattered on various tables, the room looked elegant.

The clientele for this thing would be upscale, and even that made Kaylee nervous. She wasn't upscale. But Nia had dressed her that way. Kaylee had even had to go to a fitting. She wore some slinky glittery black thing that covered her muscular arms in soft material and made her look fat, not buff.

She liked buff. Buff made her intimidating. Buff got her in a room. Fat reminded her of high school, before she discovered her singular talents, back when she'd walk in a room and everyone would snicker.

At least cargo boots with dresses were in style, protecting her from heels.

Nia wouldn't magic her either, no protect spells, nothing. If Kaylee got hit with the wrong potion, well, then the magical medics on hand would have to handle it, and if somehow that goddamn love potion actually worked, Nia promised she'd unspell Kaylee and the victim of her love/lust.

Kaylee hoped that would happen before there was any damage.

Armand stood near the door. He was short, black-haired, and spray-tanned. He took her hand in his as she greeted him. Then he leaned forward and kissed her on each cheek, enveloping her in some kind of sandalwood cologne.

"We shall do this together, *oui?*" he said in her ear.

"If you say so, bub," she said, pulling back. Then she grinned at him, so that her words didn't seem so harsh.

His eyes twinkled for just a moment, and her heart fluttered. He was aware of the game they were playing. She hadn't forgotten that, but she hadn't realized he would be so deeply involved.

"I was so sorry to hear about your fiancée." He spoke louder and his accent was softer, weirdly enough. "When the heart hurts..."

He slipped her hand in his arm. Then he nodded at her courteously.

"For such hurt," he said, leading her toward one of the nearest tables. "We have remedies."

She looked at the bottles scattered along it. Genie bottles, Dex had called them once, when he visited the office in its temporary digs on 42nd Street. She had laughed and told him yes, genie bottles. Don't touch.

"For the pain," Armand said now.

Others stood near the table, some holding drinks, the bottom of their glasses wrapped in paper napkins. Waiters mingled with the guests, carrying silver trays with crudités. Kaylee wondered briefly if anyone had vetted the food: it wouldn't do to have a guest turn into a frog because they had a potion mixed with wine mixed with the wrong kind of pâté.

She had to bring herself back to the role. She wasn't watching the people; she was looking at the potions. She touched the descriptive cards on three bottles. Two cards remained unchanged, but the third released white smoke which then wrapped around her hand.

The smoke whispered, *I will help you forget.*

She drew back as if it bit her, and looked at Armand in very real alarm.

"I don't want to forget him," she said before she could think.

This, *this*, was why Nia said she was perfect. The pain, the grief, the loss, it took away a cautious part of her brain. It made her vulnerable to these very spells, the kind that preyed upon the weak.

"Forgive me, *mademoiselle*," Armand said. "Perhaps something a bit less...intrusive?"

She swallowed, wishing she hadn't accepted this assignment.

Beneath the play-acting, the anger was rising. She wanted to kill them all, just for having a good time.

She blinked, took a deep breath, said, "I just want a new future."

"*Mais oui*, *mademoiselle*, don't we all." Armand smiled at her, and squeezed her hand against his side. Weirdly, the movement was comforting.

She didn't want to be comforted. She wanted to hang onto the anger.

"Maybe, this will help you," he said, leading her to a table farther back. "A warning: it is expensive."

"Money is no object," she murmured, wishing that were true. But she wasn't buying. The company wasn't buying. They were *sampling*.

The table stood by itself. Extra lights poured down on it, soft lighting, the kind that theaters used on starlets, bathed a single bottle in warmth. The bottle, shaped like a flower about to bloom, glowed pinkly.

"Ah, it recognizes you, *mademoiselle*," he said. "It will work with you."

He snapped his fingers and a young man stepped out of the shadows. His features blurred. She wasn't sure if that was deliberate or if he wasn't really human.

It was not her job to find out. She was to taste the potion, and see if it was real.

The young man took a flower-shaped glass from a tray she hadn't seen, and poured just a bit of potion. A pink glow swirled out of it. She had a quick, panicky feeling that she shouldn't do this, that this was wrong, that she was betraying Dex, and then the glow swirled into her face, going up her nose.

She felt it, like an ice-cream headache, then it flowed into her, and she, and she—

Burst into tears.

Somewhere, in the back of her brain, her real self crossed its arms, and judged. She did not cry. Crying was weak. Crying was an indulgence. Crying was something no one should ever ever do.

Armand patted her back, clearly alarmed, and the young man—she had been wrong, he had sculptured features, almost vulpine, and dark intense eyes—enveloped her in his arms, comforting, holding, and she let him, dear God, she let him hold her because it felt right.

Not that she had fallen in love with him, or even that she was attracted to him. She had just needed someone to hold her since that car slammed into Dex, right in front of her, before she could even stop it, while she screamed for help, and then crouching with his broken body, wishing she had healing magic, not violent magic, although some of that leaked out too, because the car careened into a group of parked cars, and the damn driver died, just like he should have, careless son of a fucking bitch—

"Here, here," the young man said, handing her a tissue. She took it, but it was useless. He dabbed at her face, then wiped her tears with his thumbs, and she worried about him, capturing her essence, even though he had tears on his jacket, and she would have to report that to Nia, she would have to report it all—

Kaylee took a deep breath. And just that quickly, the tears were gone. But so was the ache she had felt since that goddamn hospital bed, on that bleak afternoon.

"What was that?" she asked, surprised that her voice did not shake.

"We call it a love potion," the young man said. "But that isn't quite true. It restores the heart, makes love possible again. You'll see."

"I didn't drink it," she said.

"No," he said. "You must buy the bottle to drink. And it is not a one-time potion. It is a treatment, really. It gets you past your grief and into your future. Isn't that what you wanted?"

Had he overheard her conversation with Armand? Or was this part of the sales pitch?

"So it won't make me fall in love?" she asked.

"It will *allow* you to love again," he said. "It is very delicate and very powerful."

"And very expensive, I'll bet." She sounded more like herself again, even though the anger was gone. She felt hollow without it. Hollow and a bit giddy, as if she were real-people drunk instead of Kaylee-drunk. Kaylee-drunk was usually bar-fight furious, and had gotten her arrested more than once.

"Ten thousand a bottle," he said, "but considering that it restores your heart, opening it to love, the price is low."

"How many bottles does it take to 'cure' someone?" she asked.

"Only one," he said. "We are not in the business of addicting someone. Only helping people."

It sounded so right, so smooth, so perfect. The real Kaylee, tucked in the back of her brain, arms crossed, knew that was a warning sign, but this Kaylee, still under the spell, nodded.

"I don't have ten thousand tonight," she said. "Can I get this at Armand's?"

"Only if you do so within the week," the young man said. "This batch, which seems to have an affinity for you, is nearly gone. If we do not sell the remaining ten bottles this evening, the rest will go to Armand's. But I must warn you, we do raise the price when there are fewer than five."

She nodded, almost without thinking. She wanted the bottle right now. Thank heavens Nia did not give her money. She would have spent it.

"I'll tell Armand to save me one," she said. Another tear leaked out of her eye. Dammit. She dabbed at it. "Thank you."

Then she staggered away from the young man. He had her tears, but she had some of his skin collected on the edges of her glittering dress. An even trade, or so her real self said. Her real self, which was still observing.

She passed Armand, and waved a hand at her eyes.

"I need to fix my face," she said.

"Yes," he said. Then, softer, "*Merci.*"

She almost asked *For what?* then remembered. Investigation, mission.

She staggered out of the back room into the restaurant, and toward the ladies room, which was near the back door. She pushed it open, and stepped into the alley.

The cool night air did not clear her head, although it made her chapped cheeks sting. She pivoted, almost went back inside—*she could find $10,000. If a whiff of the potion made her feel like this, imagine what the entire bottle would do*—but she managed to follow the plan.

She walked down the alley and turned left on the side street where Nia had parked her battered van. Kaylee climbed inside.

Her real self wanted to say, *Get it out of me. You don't know what it's doing to me*, but the rest of her looked at Nia, realized just how cute she was, wondered why they hadn't been closer friends—

"Tilt your head back," Nia said. "You drank, right?"

Kaylee shook her head. "Breathed it," she managed.

"Oh, sneaky," Nia said. She took a pipette, lit a match at the bottom of it, and then tapped the side, muttering a spell that Kaylee didn't recognize.

Pink glow streamed out of her nose and mouth, into the pipette. More hovered. Nia took another pipette, and then another, capping them as she trapped the glow inside.

In the end, six pipettes with vibrating glowing pink smoke stood in a little case, like an evil drug.

Nia continued the spell with four more pipettes, then did some kind of heal or reverse. Kaylee didn't know.

She was exhausted, battered, and empty.

And then deep down, she realized with bitter amusement, she finally felt angry.

She slept for almost two days, in a bed in the tiny backroom of the wharf office, with someone watching her 24/7. By the time she woke up—really woke up, not stirred enough to eat, roll over, and head back to dreamland—they'd finished testing the spell.

Nia accompanied Kaylee to her ratty apartment for a change of clothing, a shower, and a surprise pizza (paid for—even bigger surprise—by Nia). As they bonded over pepperoni and sausage in that kitchen too nice to fit into the rest of the apartment (and clean, because Kaylee had hardly been there since she moved back in), Nia proclaimed the spell elegant and powerful.

Kaylee knew about the powerful. The entire thing had left her shaken, and midway through her marathon sleep session she had demanded that Nia check to make certain no trace of the spell remained inside Kaylee.

It hadn't. The sleep, Nia had said, was probably overdue.

And now that Kaylee was awake, she figured Nia was right: Kaylee hadn't slept well since Dex died, and the exhaustion from the spell probably carried into the exhaustion from her grief.

What she didn't tell Nia was that the grief wasn't there any more, not like it had been. Not overwhelming and ever present. Kaylee didn't dare confess that it had altered because, in part, she was afraid she altered it.

She was a woman without much of a soul. Maybe she could only mourn so long. Maybe she could only love so deep. Maybe—hell, not maybe, actually—she wasn't like other people, and that probably extended to the way she grieved as well.

At least the pizza tasted good. Nia had also brought a six-pack of her favorite microbrew, and the dark beer seemed appropriate, both to the pizza and Kaylee's mood.

"So," she said, after three pieces. "The spell's legit. Expensive, but legit. What's wrong with that?"

"Nothing," Nia said. "Armand was happy. He makes a healthy commission off the sales."

"We weren't doing this for Armand, were we?" Kaylee tried to keep the question casual, but she didn't want to think she had (possibly) sacrificed her grief for Armand. She liked him, but she didn't like him that much.

"No," Nia said. "It's the investment angle. It still bothers me."

Kaylee had forgotten about the investments. They were what had interested Nia in the first place.

"It's an expensive commodity," Kaylee said. "There's clearly money to be made."

"Yeah." Nia took another piece of pizza. The cheese, still warm, clung to the rest of the pizza. She snapped the piece off with the edges of her fingers. "It's the method that bothers me. They're going for small investors. People who can put in a few thousand dollars and get some kind of stock. When you're selling a bottle for $10,000 that seems like tiny money."

Kaylee didn't pretend to understand investments. She barely had enough coin for this ratty apartment. She never asked for a raise because money hadn't meant much. Still didn't. What did she need besides food, a warm place to lay her head, and something to do every day?

"Maybe they're going to expand," she said.

Nia raised her head, frowning. "You said the potion was a one-time dose."

"That's not what he told me," Kaylee said. "You took it a bit at a time until you finished the bottle."

"And then, didn't he tell you, no more bottles?"

"Yes," Kaylee said.

"One-time use." Nia said that almost to herself. "So they're constantly in need of new customers. *That's* the flaw in the spell."

She got up from the table, leaving half of the last piece she took uneaten.

"You," she said to Kaylee, "are brilliant."

"Sometimes," Kaylee said. "Apparently."

Nia grinned at her, and then gathered her things. "I'll be in touch."

"I'll be here," Kaylee said, but she spoke to an empty room. Nia hadn't even used the door. She had simply disappeared.

Kaylee hated wasting magic like that. She only used her magic for big things. Well, the big things *she* could do. She couldn't make crash carts work or doctors arrive on time or men crushed by the front bumper of a car going 45 miles per hour in a 20 mile per hour zone come out of comas to say goodbye to their one and only love.

She shivered at the thought and felt the rag-end of loss. It was back. She just hadn't noticed.

Maybe because it had become part of her during her long sleep.

Maybe because it fueled her anger.

Or maybe, both.

The books she stole from Dex's apartment were stupid. They were about things she didn't give a rat's ass over. The history of baseball. The psychology of golf. Current political bestsellers. A few fantasy novels—heavy on the fantasy and short on the realism.

She read them anyway, and felt no closer to him. She was restless all over again, and thinking about doing more work. Nia hadn't called, but that didn't mean anything.

Sometimes Kaylee got work just by showing up.

She showered, then decided she needed something new to wear, something Dex hadn't commented on. She promised herself a latte and some incredibly rich dessert if she bought two pairs of pants and three shirts.

She ended up with two shirts and one pair of pants and called it good. The coffee shop three blocks from her place had closed in the last few weeks, so she went to the other place with excellent baked goods, across the street from Armand's.

He was there, getting enough coffee for his entire staff. When he saw her, he came over and bussed her cheeks, then put his hands on her shoulders and studied her face.

"Nia said it was hard for you," he said. "I am sorry."

Kaylee shrugged. "I suspect everything'll be hard for a while."

"I would hug you," he said, "but now that you are dressed as you, I feel I must ask permission."

She half-smiled. "The sentiment is enough, Armand, thank you."

"Let me pay for your order," he said. "In fact, let me pay for your next month's worth of orders."

"That's all right," she said.

"No, no, you do not understand, my friend. These potions, the commission is superb."

"Nia's worried that they're one-time and done," Kaylee said.

"That concerned me as well," Armand said. "But one person recommends to a friend who recommends to a friend. I have sold two separate lots since I last saw you."

"Lots?" Kaylee asked. "What do you mean?"

"Ten bottles per lot," Armand said. "I have sold twenty bottles, and I am halfway through the third lot."

Kaylee let out a small whistle. "That's a lot of people needing a love potion."

"A future potion, that is how I am selling it. One that heals the heart." Armand turned and gave the clerk his credit card. "You will set up an account for my friend, *de comprendre?*"

The clerk nodded, ran Armand's credit card, and then handed Kaylee a gift card.

"Hah," he said, shaking his head. "Accounts mean something different here."

She barely paid attention (although she did thank him). Instead, she was doing the math.

"It's been less than a week and you've sold 25 bottles?" Kaylee asked. "Doesn't that seem odd to you?"

"No," he said quietly, scooping up the cardboard container with the coffee drinks shoved into their respective holders. "My customers have had a rough spring. As have you."

He kissed her again, wished her well, and then left, before she could thank him a second time.

To be fair, she hadn't thought of thanking him, not for at least ten minutes after he left, when the cinnamon roll she'd ordered arrived, dripping frosting on the china plate, a latte steaming beside it.

She took a bite, then remembered that blurred face of the man selling the potion, and how he only became clear after she had breathed in the steam.

A rough spring.

The potion did give the person who used it hope for the future, a chance at rebirth, renewal.

But to have that, the person needed incentive. She needed a sense that the world did not work for her, that her past was too overwhelming to cope with alone.

She needed a great loss.

"Son of a bitch," Kaylee said, and nearly spilled her latte. "Son of a fucking bitch."

~

She didn't run to the wharf because, first of all, there was no running, not from this neighborhood. She would've called, except no one working for Nia had a cell phone—not that Nia had one either—and the landline probably wasn't installed yet (if it ever would be).

She could have taken a cab, but she didn't have enough cash. Besides, she wanted to get there faster than any traffic could take her. So, she had the clerk box the remains of the cinnamon roll and put it in a bag. Then she grabbed that, and her latte, and went outside.

And, for the first time since Dex died, she used her magic.

She transported herself from the sidewalk to the office.

Nia did not look surprised to see her, but then, Nia never looked surprised to see anyone.

"I want you to tell me I'm wrong," Kaylee said, her hand shaking. The magic use had made her lightheaded.

"Wrong about what?" Nia asked.

"Tell me they're not creating their own clients," Kaylee said.

"What do you mean?" Nia asked.

"The love potion makers," Kaylee said. "Tell me they're not doing anything wrong."

It took Kaylee almost a half an hour to explain the idea that had come to after talking with Armand. It wasn't what he said so much as what he implied.

His customers, their rough spring. Like hers.

Only "rough" was the wrong word.

Devastating. She had had a devastating spring.

Nia promised to investigate, and this time, she didn't assign Kaylee to the task.

Nia arrived at Kaylee's apartment one week later. Only this time, Nia brought a pizza and an address. It was in the West Fifties, a rehabbed brownstone that someone had poured a small fortune into.

"What am I looking at?" Kaylee asked, staring at the piece of paper.

"The sales force," Nia said.

"For the potion?" Kaylee asked.

"Yeah," Nia said.

"I'm not supposed to investigate this time?" Kaylee asked.

"That's a lot of questions for you," Nia said.

Kaylee shrugged. "It's been an odd case."

Nia nodded, one hand on the pizza box, as if she couldn't decide whether to eat or to leave.

"We investigated already," she said. "Think of the term. Sales. Force."

"They use what—magical means—"

"No magic," Nia said. "The potion is the only magic."

"But you tested it. There's no dark magic in the potion at all."

"It's pure and elegant," Nia said. "The company is not."

Kaylee felt cold. "What are they doing?"

"Creating customers," Nia said. "Just like you thought."

Kaylee felt a growing frustration. Her brain no longer worked as well as she wanted, since half of it was still processing the loss of Dex. Grief made her slow-witted; she hated that.

"How?" she asked.

"However they see fit," Nia said. "Drug overdoses, muggings gone wrong, car accidents. First they analyze the available money, then they look for a suitable victim, then they take away the most precious thing."

Kaylee had frozen when Nia said "car accident." Nia did not make statements like that without a reason. But Kaylee wouldn't put it past Nia to use the phrase to motivate Kaylee, without any evidence at all.

So, Kaylee asked, "Dex? Was he—?"

"Do you have money?" Nia asked.

Kaylee's cheeks heated. "No."

"Did you offer to invest in a love potion? Were you even contacted to do so?"

The heat grew worse. "No."

"Then, no, Kaylee." The words seemed unnecessarily harsh. But Nia's gaze wasn't harsh. It was soft with empathy, even though her statements made it clear that she had used the phrase "car accident" as a ham-handed attempt at manipulation.

"I only take care of the magical," Kaylee said, just because she was feeling ornery.

"Then I'll assign someone else," Nia said. "I thought maybe you wanted this one."

She headed for the door.

Principles, ethics. They belonged to Dex's world.

And Dex was dead.

"I want it," Kaylee said. "I want it even more than you know."

It wasn't quite shooting fish in a barrel. Shooting fish in a barrel wouldn't be quite as messy.

Kaylee could've just appeared in their brownstone, but she decided to do it the old-fashioned way. She walked up the stairs to the top of the stoop, knocked on the gigantic wood door, and waited until a man in a silk suit opened it.

"Yes?" he said politely.

"You're the sales team for the love potion Armand sells?"

"Yes," the man said, just as politely.

"I have a business proposition for you."

He looked at her, in her regular clothes—sleeveless T-shirt revealing her biceps, muscular legs straining at her jeans—and said, "Um—"

"Great," she said, and pushed past him. One hand, heart, hard push, and he was sliding down the wall.

The push was a little too hard, because bits of him remained on the wall as he slid down. Fresh blood is black. Heart blood is blackish red and viscous.

It'd be hell to clean up, but that wouldn't be her job.

"Stanley?" someone yelled from the main room. Woman's voice.

Kaylee walked into that room, saw six people, beautifully garbed, and two with actual weapons in holsters under their arms.

Kaylee smiled. "He's behind me," she said.

"And you are?" the woman asked, her shoulder-length brown hair swinging perfectly as she stood up.

"Totally pissed off," Kaylee said.

Three more pushes mostly to the people in front of her. They slammed backwards against the wall, leaving an even goopier trail than Stanley had. The two with the weapons—one man, one woman—unsnapped the holster, pulled out the guns, and didn't even get to the safeties before Kaylee knocked them back.

That left three people standing near the table where they'd all been looking over some plans. Three—two men, one woman. The men were sobbing, begging. She was watching Kaylee.

Kaylee shut the men up, left the woman.

She held Kaylee's gaze. The brains behind the operation, then.

"So," Kaylee said casually. "Close to any of them?"

"What do you mean?" she asked.

"Feeling their loss yet? Because I know a great potion that'll help you feel a hell of a lot better."

Then her lower lip trembled. She knew what Kaylee meant.

"Your idea?" Kaylee asked.

"Hell, no," she said a little too quickly. "Why would anyone do that? It's so heartless."

"It's not heartless," Kaylee said. "You just need to be a person without much of a soul. The killing doesn't impact you then."

"Like you," she said.

"Two peas in a pod, you and me," Kaylee said, and killed her. Maybe a little too slowly. Maybe enjoyed it a little too much.

Kaylee didn't have to try to hang onto the bits of herself any longer. There was no Dex any more, nothing really to strive for.

She was good at what she did.

And she never touched a goddamn thing.

She disappeared out of the room, ended up in her dingy shower. Peeled off the clothes, dumped them into the bucket of bleach she'd left for just that purpose (in case there was any viscous blood on her), and then tossed them, dripping, into a garbage bag.

She showered, poured the bleach down the drain when she was done, and felt absolutely no better.

But Kaylee felt like herself again.

No lingering effects from the damn potion, no desire for a better life.

And the anger, mitigated the right way, for the right reason.

It would build up again. Nia knew that. Hell, Kaylee knew that.

She preferred it that way.

She didn't want to meet anyone, not again. No potion, no nothing, would make her ever step into those forevers again.

She couldn't bear another hospital room, another goddamn broken promise.

He said: *Forever*.

She should've said: *Fuck you*.

But she hadn't. She never had.

And she knew she would regret that little decision from now on.

Until forever.

Amen.

Killing the Angel of Death

Kristine Kathryn Rusch

One

"I got another one." Rodrigo Jimenez sauntered through the uneven door into the tiny office.

Most people had to duck when they stepped inside. Rodrigo did not, and that always surprised Isadora. He looked like a much larger man—perfectly proportioned, almost square, with more muscles than she had ever seen on a human being before.

He stood just inside the canted doorway, his thumbs hooked on his back pockets and scanned the room as if seeing it for the first time.

She wished he wouldn't do that, because then she would see the room clearly too. Wax-coated paper coffee cups from the giant 1980s hot beverage machine in the shared hallway toppled out of the plastic garbage container near the door. The recycling bin was mostly empty, just a few circulars and advertising flyers that Rodrigo would toss in there whenever he came into the office first.

The pilled beige industrial carpet needed vacuuming (needed replacing, really), and an inch of dust covered the windowsill in front of the half-open window.

The dust wasn't Izzy's fault. The office was in a strip mall on a very busy road, and if the window was open, the entire place filled with road grit within fifteen minutes.

Still, the place was a sty. He knew it, and she knew it. He wanted it to be shipshape at all times; she didn't care. She figured the person who cared the most should be the person to do the work; he figured everyone should be cleanly.

That was only one of their many differences.

"We have enough people," she said, not moving from behind the faux wood oversized desk they had found at a warehouse that specialized in cleaning out old offices. At least she had a modern chair—her back didn't accommodate the green-and-steel concoction from the 1960s that Rodrigo had picked up at the same warehouse.

"We don't and you know it." Rodrigo flopped on the ratty brown couch—her furniture contribution—and folded his hands behind his head. "We need a sniper."

"I don't like guns," Izzy said for the five-thousandth time.

"Then leave the damn project," Rodrigo responded, as he had each time. It had become a ritual. They had to get through the *I don't like guns* routine before they could have a real discussion.

"You can shoot," she said.

"I'm not accurate at long distances." He tilted his head slightly. "That's a special skill."

She supposed she knew that. She supposed she knew lots of things. But most of that knowledge came from television. With Rodrigo, most of his knowledge came from life.

"You're stalling," he said. "You just don't want to go the Meeting."

She rolled her eyes. "God, the fucking Meeting." She hated the Meeting. Everyone there had eyeballed her weird the day she had given her "testimony," and the "facilitator" had had the balls to tell her that maybe she needed to find a meeting outside the city, in a place where people would understand her grief.

She had never even gotten to her grief. She had started wrong, started with the trigger—Bongo's death. She'd told them how losing her only friend had started a downward spiral, how she had actually stood in front of her medicine cabinet and stared at the contents inside, how the fact that he hadn't wound his furry feline way around her legs in that moment of crisis made the moment of crisis even worse.

She'd come back, though, because Rodrigo—whom she hadn't

known at the time—had touched her arm.

"These people," he said, "they don't get it. Some of us do."

And then he'd left. And because of that moment of compassion, she'd returned one more time, and had to endure some scrawny kid shaking his head and whispering loudly to the dumpy middle-aged man beside him, "Oh, God. The cat lady returns."

Rodrigo had saved her. He had shut the kid down with one steely look, then brought Izzy a coffee from the burned mess in the scratched gray urn at the back of the room.

She clutched the cup he'd brought her and listened to tales of grief clearly more harrowing than hers. The dumpy guy, watching his wife die by inches after she was burned in a fire; the scrawny kid, losing his best friend in a freak accident at a water theme park.

Most people didn't speak, though. They listened, picked at their clothing, watched the clock on the wall, and drank too much terrible coffee. The "facilitator," a thin nervous woman who seemed to prefer faded print dresses three sizes too big, mouthed the platitudes Izzy had expected: *Grief is a process. We all experience it differently. It's different with every death. Ride the waves and understand that this, too, will pass.*

If Izzy wanted platitudes, she would have gone to church. She had figured that something that billed itself as a Grief Support Group, held in a half-forgotten side room of City Memorial Hospital, would actually be run by someone with credentials, someone who understood grieving, someone who actually cared.

It seemed like the only person who had cared had been Rodrigo, and except for talking to her that first day, and bringing her the coffee on the second, he hadn't said a word. He just sat near the back wall, wooden chair tilted back, massive arms crossed, and watched the proceeding as if he were the body guard, not someone whose life had been upended by death.

She later discovered that *upended* wasn't even the right term. The last ten years of Rodrigo's life had been all about death, and he was trying to find a way to deal with it.

Or he had, before the shooting.

"It's not even the same Meeting," he said, as if to placate her.

"It's always the same Meeting," she said and made a face.

Two

The new Meeting was more of an offshoot, and could more accurately be described as a Survivors' Club. Yeah, they welcomed new members, but usually those people left when they realized the group was *that group.*

That group was the one that had—according to the media—failed so badly at providing support that one of the members hauled out an automatic rifle and slaughtered everyone in the room.

The truth was different, of course. No one had been in the room when Dugan had entered from a side door. The Meeting had ended. Half the group was standing on the sidewalk in front of the door. A few had already left, and two or three more were in the parking lot, on the way to their cars.

Rodrigo was close to the door, smoking a cigarette—illegally, since state law proclaimed that he had to be at least ten feet away. He saw Dugan barge out, swinging the rifle wildly, and Rodrigo said (not that anyone would listen) that Dugan wasn't in his eyes.

Rodrigo had seen PTSD, hell, Rodrigo *had* PTSD, and he knew when someone was flashing back, and he was convinced (not that he had any proof) that Dugan was back in whatever war zone his trauma had come from. Dugan had only described the events once—something about a group of guys arriving on a truck in a dusty village, swinging rifles, picking off everyone around them, and he had been sharing a meal with a friend, and he couldn't get his weapon out or didn't have the right weapon or something.

Anyway, Dugan walked with a limp, had a scar that ran up his entire left side, and more guilt than any man should have.

He had come out of the side door and picked off six people on the sidewalk before heading toward the parking lot, tripping on the curb, falling on his hands and knees, the rifle skittering away. He ran his fingers along the concrete, said something like, "Oh, Jesus, no," and that was when the first cop arriving on the scene had shot him.

Rodrigo hadn't had a weapon, or he'd have shot Dugan too, but not a shoot-to-kill. Something that would've let the man live long enough to explain himself, maybe long enough to feel regret.

Rodrigo had tried to stop Dugan. Rodrigo had been halfway to the parking lot when the cop wheeled up and fired out of the driver's side window. That was when Rodrigo—whose skin was darker than Dugan's—hit the deck.

Izzy knew this part of the story, because Rodrigo had told her. She had given up on the Meeting by then, given up on being called The Cat Lady, given up on the "facilitator," who had been shot in the shoulder and wrist, but who had survived. That "facilitator," whom Izzy couldn't stop thinking of as a job with air quotes, had never come back.

The hospital's insurance company paid for everyone's medical care, but refused to let any more grief meetings take place onsite without a trained psychiatrist running them. The hospital didn't have any trained psychiatrists it could "waste" on people who were "merely" grieving, so the Meeting moved to its current location, and the survivors acted as facilitators, rather like an Alcoholics Anonymous group.

Not optimal, but at least honest. And much as Izzy hated the Meeting, she still showed up sometimes and stood in the back, just because she kept hoping something would fill the hole inside her.

Or maybe she just wanted to see how everyone was faring. Grief piled on grief piled on grief led to breakdowns. She had no idea how much the trauma of a shooting added to the stress, but she figured it couldn't be considered minor.

She hadn't even been there, and she thought about it every single time she passed the old meeting site. She wouldn't even park in that wide-open parking lot, because there was a stain near the curb. Rodrigo said it was an oil stain, but she didn't think so. Three people had bled out there, and somehow that blood got absorbed into the cheap asphalt.

She firmly believed that places got haunted by the violent dead, and the hauntings always took a form that was recognizable by the survivors.

She counted herself a survivor, even though she hadn't liked most of the people who had died.

Now the Meeting was held about a half mile from the office, not near any hospital at all. The space was in the basement of an ancient Y. The Meeting shared the large room with AA, Adult Children of Alcoholics, Narcotics Anonymous, and Gamblers Anonymous. The weekly meeting schedule was posted in different colors for the different groups, plus there were flyers, and some poor kid who volunteered at the Y maintained the meeting schedule on the Y's creaky old website.

It was all too complicated for Izzy or, at least, that was what she told Rodrigo. He never missed a Meeting. He was more facilitator than the old "facilitator" had been, and he actually seemed to care about the others.

Which made his cooperation with Izzy all the more surprising.

He walked to the Meeting. She drove, because she wanted to be able to escape without waiting for him.

Her car was an ancient Mustang which had once been a new Mustang, her husband's pride and joy. Her husband was long gone—everywhere except in her guarded heart. His presence wasn't even part of this Mustang any longer.

He would have hated the way the leather bucket seats had tiny tears along the base, the garbage piled up behind the front passenger seat, and the fact that the Bose Sound System he'd lovingly put in by hand now couldn't play a cassette tape if she even owned one to play. The black exterior hadn't been washed in more than a year—the last time the day some kid had scrawled *Wash Your Fucking Car, Bitch, Or Lose It* in the dirt on the rear window.

She parked, like she always did, five rows down, where the parking lot had buckled and weeds as old as the Mustang had grown out of the cracks.

She had passed Rodrigo about three blocks away, charging forward because the man never walked slowly. She meandered across the parking lot in the mid-afternoon heat, wondering why she stayed in the city when the summers were torture and the winters were worse.

Then she stopped two doors down from the side entry to the Y, and watched people enter, trying to guess which one of them was the one that Rodrigo wanted her to see.

"You won't see her until you get inside."

As usual, Rodrigo had snuck up on Izzy. No matter how hard the man charged, he still moved like the Seal he had been a lifetime ago.

She didn't start, though, when he spoke to her, although her heart had sped up just a little. She had been prepared for him to come up behind her, and she had still been surprised when he spoke.

"A woman," Izzy said, glad she sounded calm. "I didn't expect that."

"You think women can't be snipers?" he asked, but didn't wait for her answer. Instead he walked to the door and pulled it open.

It was one of those heavy metal doors with a barred grill just above eye level—at least for her. The scents of sweat, chlorine, and fifty-year-old coffee wafted out at her.

The Meeting had been held here long enough now that she had begun to associate those smells with despair.

She stepped inside, blinking in the sudden darkness. It took a moment for her eyes to adjust.

This door opened into the old lobby. The new lobby was two floors up, and actually looked inviting. This one still had the Formica desk sticking out of the wall, the cubbyholes in the back that used to house mail and keys for the residents who lived upstairs, and a few chairs, crowded around the scratched window that opened over the pool.

The pool was also in the basement, but on a different side from the meeting rooms. The window didn't keep a lot of the sound out. Kids screamed and laughed. Something boomed and splashed, and a lifeguard yelled.

The pool was uncomfortably close to the meeting rooms in the basement. They were all damp and smelled of both mildew and chlorine.

There were no windows at all in any of the basement meeting rooms, single exits grandfathered in by virtue of the fact this building had stood in the same place since the 1930s.

The pool had been revamped in the 1970s, and at that point, someone had slapped cheap paneling all over the basement, but the paneling only made the rooms darker and the smell of mildew stronger.

She followed Rodrigo down the curving staircase behind the old desk, feet slapping against the metal stairs. The railing had rusted years ago, and hadn't been replaced. She always wondered if the damn thing would hold her up if she needed to catch it in a fall.

She doubted it.

But she doubted a lot of things.

At the base of the stairs, a confusing catchall area was the only place she ever saw anyone who swam. They'd come out of the locker room, hair wet, some kind of duffel over their shoulders, and gaze at her with bleary red eyes, wonder why an overweight woman with silver lining her hair was even anywhere near an athletic facility.

They never looked at Rodrigo that way. They looked at him like they expected him to order them back into the pool, then make them swim fifty laps before they thought of leaving again.

Doors veered off in five different directions, something she'd found very confusing the first few times she had come here. Now she knew they had to take Door Number Three (not marked that way—it wasn't marked at all. It was just the third door from the base of the stairs).

Above her, the florescent light buzzed and blinked, making her feel slightly dizzy. *Stay in this area too long,* her brain warned like it always did, *and we're going to give you the worst headache of your life.*

Rodrigo pushed Door Number Three open, and headed into the narrow hallway that contained three rather tiny bathrooms (of the male, female, and handicapped variety) and two different doors on opposite sides that led into the same damn meeting room.

It was the smallest room in the basement, and Izzy was convinced it had once been some kind of storeroom. Three florescent lights hid inside plastic panels on the ceiling, panels that lied and claimed there should have been six lights.

The ubiquitous back table held three of the Y's black beverage urns

—one for coffee, one for hot water and one, weirdly, for hot cocoa, even in the summer. Donuts from one of the morning meetings hardened on a platter near the cocoa urn. Clearly the morning meeting hadn't been Narcotics Anonymous because those folks always cleared out the sugar, even if it was crap sugar like those donuts.

Someone had put out the folding chairs in five rows of seven with an aisle in between, and a podium up front, causing Rodrigo to swear. Half the group, including the scrawny kid, were gathered near the coffee urn. Of course none of them could bother to set up the room properly.

Rodrigo slung the chairs into a circle like they'd been made of putty. It wasn't until Izzy start to help him that she realized one chair was occupied. A woman sat in the back corner, farthest from the door, out of view of the podium, and nowhere near the snacks table. She blended into the darkness as if she was made of it.

Izzy knew without Rodrigo saying a word that this was the woman he'd brought. Not because the woman had wrapped herself in darkness, not because she was good at remaining in the shadows, not even because she exuded an air of *fuck with me at your peril.*

It was because she was angry.

So furious in fact that the air around her felt like it had been charged with violence.

The last thing this group needed was another violent angry person who couldn't deal with whatever had happened to her. The group ostracized folks this obviously angry—had since Dugan decided his anger was more important than their lives.

Most angry grievers, they'd leave after the first meeting or two, but it was clear this woman had been here before. She didn't seem alarmed by Rodrigo, knew who to hide from, and actually had a question in her eyes when she saw Izzy.

The woman had been here enough to know that Izzy wasn't a regular. No five times per week whether she needed it or not for Izzy. More like once every five weeks whether Rodrigo could drag her here or not.

"Need the chair," Izzy said.

The woman didn't move. "Looks like you got more than enough."

That was true. Thirty-five chairs and only ten people near the coffee urn, twelve if you counted Izzy and Rodrigo. Thirty-five was the hopeful number they'd promised the Y when they took the space; thirty-five was the fiction they maintained even though the Meeting hadn't hosted more than twenty since the massacre.

"Still," Izzy said, "you shouldn't sit in the back."

"And you shouldn't come once in a blue moon and think that entitles you to giving people orders," the woman said.

"Iz," Rodrigo said. "Sit."

As if she were a misbehaving puppy. As if she would respond to orders at all.

To prove her independence or her contrariness or her orneriness, Izzy went to the other table, the one with stick-on name tags and blue magic markers, scrawled *Isadora* on one that cheerfully proclaimed *Hi! I'm ____________!*

She was half-tempted to add a smiley face with sharp pointy teeth after the second exclamation point, but figured that would only show her age, not help anyone understand her attitude.

She slapped the nametag on her shirt, hoping she would remember to remove the damn thing before someone on the outside grinned and pointed and said, *Isadora, huh? That's an unusual name.*

She didn't even get coffee because she wasn't going to stay long enough. She had a hunch she'd bolt in the middle of the first story. She was feeling itchy already.

But she sat in the chair Rodrigo had indicated, which was—not coincidentally—directly across from Hidey Woman. Izzy couldn't even see the woman's face in the shadows, just her scuffed Nikes and her bare ankles peeking out from a pair of pristine blue jeans.

From the pool area, the life guard's whistle cut through the low murmur of conversation. Last warning or clear the pool or Ready Set Go. Izzy never knew which it was, but she always found it amusing that this version of the Meeting started with a prompt from a *life*guard.

The world was full of ironies and this was one of them.

The group took their chairs, balancing coffee, some cookies she hadn't seen, and next week's schedule, clutched in nervous fingers. She recognized all the faces—the dumpy guy, who'd lost half his body weight after the surgery to remove a bullet from his spleen; the fat lady, mother of five full-term stillborn babies, who, like Izzy, hadn't been at the Meeting that day of the shooting; and the scrawny kid, who gave Izzy the evil eye, as if everything bad that happened in the world was somehow her fault.

Rodrigo didn't start the meeting. He rarely did. That afternoon, the honor fell on Clarabell, a wizened seventy-something who claimed she'd been named for a stupid clown on a stupid kid's TV show.

That's how my childhood played out, she'd said bitterly one afternoon before the shooting. *Imagine what that was like, particularly when it was clear to everyone but me that the obnoxious clown was male.*

Back then, she'd gotten sympathy from the Meeting—before the scrawny kid and the dumpy guy and their judgmental attitudes had shown up. Now, she never mentioned it and, Izzy noted, she no longer wrote *Clarabell* on her nametag. Now it simply said *Clara,* as if that made everything better.

"It's been five months," Clarabell said. "How's everyone holding up?"

No hellos, no *let's introduce ourselves,* no discussion of where and what the meeting was. Not even a mention of what she was referring to. If there were any newcomers here—and Izzy didn't think there were except maybe Hidey Woman—they were on their own when it came to understanding just what the hell was going on here.

"Just a reminder," said a bearded man near the door. "The hospital's insurance only pays for six months. If you want to continue therapy after that, you'll need a referral."

"And insurance of your own," the dumpy guy murmured.

"Fat fucking chance of that," the scrawny kid said.

"We've got each other, anyway," Clarabell said, but she didn't sound too sure of that. What did they have, really? A shared room in the dank basement of an old Y, an experience that bound them together in group tragedy, after they'd come together for comfort from personal tragedy.

That was about all Izzy could take. She bounded out of her chair, only to have Rodrigo grab her right arm and pull her down again.

He leaned over to her. "You're listening this time," he whispered.

Her stomach knotted. "She talk at all?" Izzy asked, nodding at the woman.

"Not yet," he whispered. "Maybe not ever."

"Then I'm leaving." Izzy shook off his hand, and stood again, saw the scrawny kid glaring at her, and knew what he would say if he felt like he could—like he used to before the shoot.

What happened, Cat Lady? Need to get home to kitty-kitty-kitty?

Fuck you, she sent him, as if telepathy were real. *Fuck you and your superior fucking attitude.*

Yeah, she still had anger issues. One year in, and she was beginning to believe that the wheel of grief wasn't a wheel at all, but a gauge with her needle stuck at *Fuck You Forever You Fucking Asshole.*

Or as Rodrigo liked to delicately call it, *The anger phase.*

Izzy pushed her way out, back to the narrow hallway, the strange little room of doors, the buzzing florescent, and the scuffed staircase. The smell of chlorine made her sneeze.

She was really tired, the kind of tired you got when every day was a burden, and every hour seemed to last longer than the one before it.

She glanced up the stairs like they were her enemy. Rodrigo had said the woman wouldn't enter by conventional means, which meant she wouldn't leave by conventional means either, and Rodrigo wanted Izzy to meet her.

Izzy could go back to the office, and wait, only to have Rodrigo bawl her out, and then drag her to yet another Meeting on yet another too-hot afternoon.

Or she could sit on the stairs and brood until the Meeting ended. One hour, if the schedule was to be believed. Because a half hour after this meeting ended, the Wednesday AA group would saunter in for their discussions of twelve steps, compulsions, and higher powers.

No one ever talked about higher powers in the grief groups that Izzy had attended. Higher powers were there to help with addiction, not with loss.

All she knew was that any time someone murmured *It was God's will* at the Meeting before the shooting, someone else would snap something rude about God.

It was Rodrigo's response that Izzy had never been able to get out of her head.

If that was God's will, he'd said, referring to something he had never really told the Meeting in detail, *then God is a goddamn motherfucking son of a whore sadist, and I hope to Christ I never meet the motherfucker face to face.*

Rodrigo's outburst had silenced the room. No one had seen him lose it like that before, and maybe not since.

Izzy had, but Izzy talked to him outside of the Meeting. Izzy knew that her anger was nothing compared to his and there were days when he felt a kinship with Dugan. *Sometimes,* Rodrigo said more than once, *it'd be a lot easier to blame someone for the whole mess.*

Why? she'd asked only once.

Because then I'd take the motherfucker out, he said, his voice so cold and chill and flat that she had no doubt he'd do it.

No doubt he'd find a way.

And she had held onto that for the six months before the shooting and four months beyond. The month of the shooting, she'd half blamed Rodrigo. If he'd been that close to everything, how come he couldn't stop Dugan? Dugan had taken out the one person that Izzy had liked at the Meeting, a sixteen-year-old girl whose baby sister had died of leukemia.

What had those parents done to deserve that response from God? They lost both their children—one to a disease that had a 90% survival rate for most kids, and the other to something stupid and random that had happened because she'd been trying to take care of herself, trying to move forward with a life that should have extended eighty or more years ahead of her.

Izzy tried not to think of Alyssa because it only pissed her off. Alyssa —no tats, one piercing in each ear, and only a slight hint of pink over her dark brown hair, straight As, and the ability to cry without moving her face.

She was the only one of the group who haunted Izzy, maybe because she had been the only one who had ever touched Izzy's heart.

The door banged open, and conversation filled the hallway beyond Door Number Three. Izzy stood, brushed off the back of her jeans, and leaned against the rusted railing, trying to look cool rather than distraught—not that anyone would notice.

Just her luck that scrawny kid would come out first. His skin was clearing up. He'd also gotten taller in the past few months, but his eyes were still sad.

She leaned toward something like compassion for him when he reached her.

"You know," he said, "the Meeting actually works better when you sit through it."

He didn't wait for her response. He bounded up the stairs two at a time, and disappeared before anyone else came through the door.

Apparently, the Meeting had bothered him too.

Izzy moved away from the stairs after that, taking refuge near the door to the women's locker room. No one else noticed her. She counted bodies as they left...seven...eight...nine with scrawny kid. Which meant that Rodrigo was still inside the room with Clarabell.

He could handle himself, but sometimes it was polite to rescue a friend, even if that friend had dragged you unwillingly to a meeting you really never wanted to attend.

Izzy sighed and pushed off the wall, heading into Door Number Three, listening for conversation as she went. Nothing. Which meant that either the door was still closed or they weren't talking or something else was going on.

Her stomach clenched, because it always clenched when something out of the ordinary happened around the Meeting. But she made herself ignore the feeling.

She opened the door, and as she did, the snap and slam of metal folding chairs being flattened grated her. Rodrigo was gathering the chairs, closing them with one hand and then adding them to the pile he managed to carry with the other.

At first glance, he seemed to be alone in the room. No Clarabell, no stragglers hanging out by the coffee.

Then Izzy saw the Hidey Woman stacking another set of chairs in the corner. That surprised Izzy. She figured Hidey Woman for someone who dwelt in the darkness and never helped anyone in the light.

"Isadora," Rodrigo said, as he added one more chair to his impossible arm pile. "Thought we'd lost you."

She wasn't sure if she should let Hidey Woman know just how vulnerable Izzy really was.

"Waited outside," she said. "Meeting go okay?"

"The Meeting never goes 'okay.'" Rodrigo was very good at spoken air quotes. "But we got through it."

That, she wanted to say to him, *was not a recommendation.* But she bit the words back because she also didn't want to discourage Hidey Woman from attending.

Izzy believed that if someone found the Meeting valuable, they should not be discouraged from attending.

Rodrigo took his impossible pile of chairs over to the Hidey Woman. Apparently his strong arms had reached their limit. He handed her the chairs as if they'd been at this routine for a while.

"We've got about ten minutes, Iz," Rodrigo said.

It wasn't so much a statement as a command. *Get your ass over here. If we're going to talk to her, we're doing it now.*

Izzy nodded, then walked across the room, almost stopping for coffee just so she would have something to do with her hands.

She reached Rodrigo and the Hidey Woman as they put the last two chairs into the pile. The room looked so much bigger when it was empty.

"Isadora, meet Lana." Rodrigo said.

Lana. The name didn't quite fit her. Too mundane, too short, too bland. The Hidey Woman—Lana—didn't move, seeming to wait to see what Izzy would do.

Izzy held out her hand. "Izzy. I prefer Izzy. Rodrigo likes the formal name."

Lana didn't nod. For a brief second, Izzy thought Lana wasn't even going to extend her hand for a shake, and then she did, slowly and languidly, resulting in one of those rich lady handshakes: *I'm too wealthy and pampered to bother to squeeze her hand. In another life, I would have hand you courtesy and kiss my ring.*

The attitude, the thought, and the shake that inspired it surprised Izzy. She'd expected a firm, masculine grip, something tough as tough could be. Rodrigo had said *sniper,* after all.

But Lana was tiny, and didn't seem to be any kind of sniper at all. She barely came up to Izzy's shoulder, but stood with the perfect posture that spoke of early (and intense) ballerina training. There was a set to her head, the way her feet seemed to prefer a modified version of second position, the precision in her movements.

Her hair was long and pulled into a bun, her dark eyes dominating her small face, and her chin was narrow, giving her face a startled foxlike appearance.

Not threatening at all.

But, then, people thought that about Izzy too.

"I thought we could talk to Lana about what we do," Rodrigo said.

Izzy looked at him. His chocolate brown eyes peered down at her with the full expectation that *she* would talk to Lana about what they were *planning* to do, since as of yet, they hadn't done anything.

There was no good way to start this conversation. Start with an apology, and Izzy would be at a disadvantage. Start with a question, and she gave Lana a chance to back out. Start in the middle of it, and Izzy would sound like a crazy person.

She chose a fourth option.

"You ever hear of the Angel of Death?" she asked. "We're going to take him out."

Three

The reactions were always predictable. Some people backed away. Others laughed nervously. A couple said, *Wouldn't that be nice.* And one or two—the ones that stuck—didn't say a word.

They simply waited for more information.

Lana's gaze never left Izzy's. Waiting. Withholding judgment until the very end.

"We're building a team," Izzy said. "Rodrigo believes you could be part of it."

Izzy deliberately left herself out of that statement. She didn't know enough about this woman, didn't know enough about what this woman could do. Wasn't even sure Lana was as billed.

Until Izzy remembered that air of violence, the one that had accompanied Lana in those shadows, making her seem bigger than she actually was.

"The Angel of Death," Lana said quietly. "You believe that is a real being?"

There it was: the loss of control of the conversation. And to make things worse, she answered a question with a question.

Izzy gave Rodrigo a sideways glance. He nodded, almost imperceptibly.

"You know there is," Izzy said, deciding to be somewhat aggressive. "If you didn't, Rodrigo wouldn't have brought me here."

Lana looked at him, as if seeing him for the first time. Then she brought that measuring gaze to Izzy.

"If there were such a creature," Lana said, "then it would be immortal and untouchable. Going after it would be a fool's errand. Even if you could kill it, something would replace it, and death would simply continue."

"You don't use death to stop death," Izzy said. "You use death to get revenge."

"'Vengeance is mine, saith the Lord,'" Lana said.

"If that were true," Rodrigo said, "all of human history would be very, very different."

Lana's eyes narrowed, and she smiled, tilting her head to the right as if conceding a point.

Her entire body relaxed just enough to be noticeable.

"You want to send a message," she said.

"I do," Rodrigo said. "I absolutely fucking do."

Four

They didn't ask her if she believed in the Angel of Death. She had asked them. Lana had done her best not to seem incredulous. She had tested them with the Biblical quote, because religious nuts often went off the deep end about the angel of death or the destroying angel or whatever Christianity called it.

Every religion had a personification of death, maybe to make it real. And each personification was different.

Just like each experience with the so-called Angel of Death was different. She firmly believed in those beings in the light people who had been brought back from the dead had seen. They hadn't been benign actors, beloved people from a former life. They had been death angels, deciding which fish to keep and which ones to throw back.

The death angels never really had a plan, she thought. More like a desire to see what would happen this time if they screwed with a particular person.

"I'm in," Lana said quietly. "I'm definitely in."

FIVE

The first time she had seen what they were calling the Angel of Death, she'd been six. She had been eating dinner at the kitchen table with her sisters, her parents, and her baby brother, still in his high chair. The room smelled of mushy peas and beef gravy, a radio played Madonna's "Vogue" in the background, and the grownups were talking about something Lana didn't understand. Then, the light in the room dimmed.

She looked up, saw a person, indistinct and shadowy, with his fingers wrapped around her father's throat.

Therapists later asked why she thought the person was male. She couldn't articulate it then; she could now. Male hands looked different from female hands. Just slightly: a little broader. A little flatter.

Or maybe, she sometimes thought, the hands had been familiar. Hands she had seen a lot as a young child, hands of a person she no longer remembered.

But she remembered that moment. Those hands, squeezing her father's throat. He continued talking, as if nothing was wrong, as if the knuckles on those hands around his throat weren't turning white with effort, as if the life wasn't being choked out of him, bit by bit.

"Mommy," she had said, terrified. "Someone's hurting Daddy."

Her mother had looked sideways, her own face indistinct in the memory, as if Lana had no words, no reference for the expression on her mother's face.

"I'm fine, honey," her father had said to her, his voice as calm as ever. "I'm just fine."

And then he had stood, put his fingers on the kitchen table for balance, and toppled sideways—someone—and she never knew who—catching him and easing him to the ground.

Of course, at that moment, he had already been dead.

Family lore said that Lana claimed someone had hurt her father after he had already fallen. But her mother always watched her with a bit of speculation, as if worried that Lana might tell *her* that someone was hurting her, and then her mother would die.

Her mother hadn't died yet, at least that Lana knew about. She hadn't seen or spoken with her mother in more than a decade.

There simply was no point.

They had nothing in common. The Bible that Lana could quote with ease was her mother's beloved book, not hers. Lana didn't have a religion. She wasn't an atheist. She believed there were things in the world that she did not understand.

But she also believed that they were unknowable, and that religions simply guessed, trying to make people feel better about their miserable little lives.

She had never thought of her life as miserable or little, not until recently. She couldn't shake the images, the fear, the guilt.

The anger.

And she had come to believe that people didn't die of old age; they died of an accumulation of death—dead parents, dead children, dead friends. At some point the accumulation defeated them, and they succumbed.

She could feel her accumulation pressing on her. Some people—they had low death tolerance. Others had a higher one, like a high pain tolerance. They could handle so much more than most people could

She was one of those, she had thought. But lately, she hadn't been.

It was the accumulation. Friends, colleagues, enemies. Victims, too, since she had killed her share, always at the direction of her government, for something she had once believed in, something she was beginning to think had been perverted, if it had ever truly existed at all.

Six

They took her to a dumpy office in a dying strip mall. Rodrigo and Izzy seemed at home here, with the 1970s wood paneling, the beige carpet that probably hadn't been cleaned since 1990, the couch that looked older than Lana.

She had expected something sparkly, something that spoke of magic, not something that looked as defeated as she felt.

They promised her pizza while they waited for the rest of the team. The pizza arrived first, which was probably good, considering that the team was much larger than she expected. The ham and pineapple pizza was mostly demolished when the first of more than a dozen people came through the hollow-core fake wood door.

She missed most of the names, mostly because the people pouring in weren't what she expected.

She expected more soldiers like her and Rodrigo. Or police. Or mercenaries. People with skills she knew and understood.

And there were maybe some of those—maybe seven, if she could judge by posture alone. But those weren't the folks who caught her eye. They passed by her as if they were partially invisible.

She was watching the gorgeous drag queen in a flowing pink pantsuit and glittery heels who had clearly dressed down for the afternoon. Then Lana noticed the young person who wore black jeans, a black shirt, had dyed his (her?) hair shoe-polish black like Joan Jett used to wear hers, wore black lipstick and black eyeliner, and had painted her (his?) fingernails black.

He (She?) was followed by another person whose gender was deliberately ambiguous, a slouchy thin person who wore a knitted hat despite the heat, a hoodie with a picture of kittens and chainsaws across the front, and jeans that had more holes than material.

Two twenty-somethings came in next. The twenty-somethings looked like teens, until Lana saw their faces full on. Prematurely lined, even though neither young man had reached his full growth. Their dark faces had the texture of hard leather, the kind of faces people who suffered from too much sun exposure usually got in their forties.

They barely acknowledged her as they flopped on the filthy carpet.

Behind them came a rotund woman who looked like she should have fronted a cable baking program from the 1980s, a scrawny elderly man with hollow eyes, and an ethereal girl who appeared to be no more than twelve.

The girl's eyes were dark, and, at this distance appeared to be without pupils. When Lana turned away, movement caught Lana's eye again, and for a half second, she thought she saw wings.

But when she looked at the girl directly once again, the girl looked like a normal twelve-year-old, long-limbs and flat torso, with the promise of beauty to come.

Not everyone came from the Meeting, as Rodrigo called it. Some Izzy had found; the others Rodrigo brought. The drag queen invited herself, after her gender-neutral friends had found the place—by accident, they claimed, although Lana was beginning to think there were no accidents here. The drag queen, in turn, had invited two thin, sad-faced men who sat in the back with their arms wrapped around each other, almost for protection.

There appeared to be more men than women which surprised Lana, and the women were less athletic than she would have expected. Three of them looked like teachers or librarians or some other cliché of middle age.

Several African-Americans, and one Asian-American woman who

looked tougher than everyone else put together. Everyone younger than thirty appeared to be mixed race, although with the makeup on the kid wearing all black, she couldn't really tell.

Lana took a can of Diet Pepsi, and retreated to a corner, leaning against the wall, the handgun she had a concealed carry permit for pressing against the small of her back. She always wore loose shirts to cover it, not that anyone ever noticed the gun or her. Although here, everyone saw her anyway, which was a brand-new experience for her.

She had spent so many years practicing the art of invisibility that she had no idea what to do when she was actually being seen.

"They're here to vet you," Rodrigo said, but didn't explain how they would accomplish that.

People found their places on the floor, leaning against the walls, and sitting on the handful of chairs. Some folks had brought coffee, others drank bottles of water they had brought with them. The two twenty-somethings each took a piece of pizza, then waved them at the others, as if asking permission to eat.

No one complained, not even Lana whose appetite had left her.

Izzy sat behind the desk, half hidden behind a slender PC that appeared to be the newest thing in the place. Rodrigo rested one thigh on the desk, bracing himself with his other foot.

Just like he was at the Meeting, he was the leader here without saying a word. He waited until everyone settled, and silence grew—except for the rattling of an air conditioner that had been old when this place was built.

Rodrigo studied the faces around him, then glanced at Lana.

"I think we might've found our sniper," he said.

She started. She had never told him what she had done. She had left it all behind, the shootings, the kill orders, even the rifles. She hadn't held a weapon in three years.

Correction: she hadn't *actually* held a *real* weapon in three years. Every time she fell asleep, she woke up to find her left hand braced underneath her rifle, her eyes pressed against the scope, her trigger finger at the ready.

That there was no rifle didn't really matter. There had been one. And, apparently, it would always be with her.

And, apparently, it would always be visible to sensitive folks.

Or folks who had done a boatload of research.

Although she wasn't sure how he could have researched her. Lana wasn't the name she had been given by her religious mother. Lana was the name she had chosen, picking that name only because it was easy to spell, easy to remember, and unusual enough in this day and age to make it feel like hers.

Rodrigo was watching her watch everyone else, which made her nervous. After the group had settled, she did an actual count.

Fifteen, not counting herself, Izzy, and Rodrigo.

Fifteen people who had somehow, for some reason, decided they needed to take out the Angel of Death.

Lana let out a small snort at the thought, felt a half-smile start, and made it stop before it became a full smile.

No one besides Rodrigo was looking at her now, and then she realized that wasn't true. One of the semi-invisible librarian women was staring at her, and so was the drag queen.

The drag queen, clearly over six feet tall, made taller by the heels in her glittery sandals, walked over to Lana, extended a manicured hand, and said, "Starina."

Lana raised her eyebrows, and said, "Really? You took on the name that Nathan Lane's Albert used for *his* drag queen in *The Birdcage?* Really?"

The drag queen let her hand fall. "Sarcastic and all-seeing. What did you find for us, Rodrigo?"

"Snipers are great observers," he said quietly. "And we don't need names. This is not the Meeting."

"I'd say welcome, honey," the drag queen said, emphasizing *honey,* "but I'm not sure about you yet."

Lana wasn't sure about any of them. She sipped her Diet Pepsi, trying not to wince at the fake-sugar aftertaste, and then watched them watch her.

"If we're going to stare silently at each other," Izzy said from behind the computer, "I'm going to go insane. So, one word or one sentence, name your last straw. We'll end with you."

She didn't say Lana's name, just glanced at her so that Lana knew who *you* meant.

"I'll start," Izzy said. "Cat."

She said it defiantly, as if challenging anyone to laugh at her. Lana wasn't sure she understood what Izzy was even asking for, given the cryptic nature of the one word and the command.

"Nephew," said one of the women sitting on the floor.

"Roadside bomb," said the military man next to her.

"Traffic stop," said the man beside him.

"Judy's," said the thin man with his arm around the other man. The other man nodded, and said, "Judy's."

That, at least, Lana recognized. Judy's nightclub shooting, October of 2016, in the middle of the presidential campaign from hell, everyone thinking that maybe the rhetoric from the Republican nominee (and the local candidates) inspired three shooters to kill twenty people and wound sixteen more, just one town over.

Lana had loved Judy's. Big-hearted, with a beautiful painting of Judy Garland in all of her incarnations adorning the wall that the police eventually shattered with big rescue vehicles they'd gotten because of 9/11 funding.

She expected the gender-neutral kid in all black to say Judy's too, but he (she?) said, "Faghole," and a teenage girl near him nodded. Lana knew the insult too. Instead of "asshole," "faghole" was something mean homophobic kids had started shouting at kids whom they found different. But she didn't know it was a place or a thing or something that would cause a vision of the Angel of Death.

The rounds continued.

"Best friend."

"Fucking cancer."

"Emergency room," said one of the librarian women. "Night after goddamn night."

So not a librarian. A nurse.

"Judy's."

"Fifteen-car pile-up."

"Traffic stop." Again. She didn't quite see who had spoken.

"The neighborhood, man," said one of the men on the other side of the room. "Just the freakin' neighborhood."

"Judy's."

The ethereal girl shook her head, waving her hand, as if she still couldn't speak about whatever it had been.

"Hot truck abandoned in the desert," said one of the leathery young men. The man next to him nodded.

The nearest desert was two thousand miles. But deserts, Lana got deserts. Deserts. They were deadly.

"My son," said one of the muscular men, whom Lana had pegged as a cop.

"Portage Elementary," said the man next to him.

The school shooting—the worst kind of school shooting (as if there were any good ones)—two states over. First-graders. Who the fuck killed first-graders?

At least two assholes in the United States had done so.

Two.

Spurred on by the Angel of Death.

Lana set down her Diet Pepsi, brought her knees to her chest, and hugged them.

The voices around her were dry, matter-of-fact, listing more family members, more friends, more circumstances.

The litany got to the drag queen, and Lana braced herself for another *Judy's.* Instead, the drag queen said, "Pepperbeans," and the beefy man next to her patted her hand, and gave her a sympathetic smile before he said, "The best grandmother in the entire world."

It took less than five minutes for the litany to reach Lana. She glanced at Rodrigo, who was staring at her. He hadn't said anything, just like the ethereal girl and one of the librarian women.

But no one mentioned that. No one urged them on.

Yet everyone stared at Lana as if she could give them her entire life story in one word. Last straw. They thought there was a last straw.

"You assume there's just one," she said quietly. Her voice wasn't as flat as she wanted it to be. She wanted to sound as matter-of-fact as they all had, and she couldn't.

She just couldn't.

She didn't belong here.

She pushed against the wall, then made herself stand. They all watched her.

"It's silly anyway, right?" she asked, "talking about death as if it's something we can attack, something we can stop."

The woman who hadn't spoken, the one who hadn't given a reason for being there, stepped in front of two of the other librarian-looking women. This woman was about fifty pounds overweight, but she carried it well. Her face had been sharp and angular once, but now there was extra flesh under her chin, a slight puffiness to her eyes.

Her hair was iron-lady gray, and she didn't wear any makeup at all. But she was wearing a dress, and not a sundress either. Something that pretended to be businesslike—or would have been forty years ago, when they didn't make suits for women.

"You were hoping for something magical," the woman said, her voice soft. She had a slight Southern accent, but from what state, Lana couldn't tell.

Lana wanted to deny the accusation, but she remembered her disappointment when she had seen the office, how she had wanted something sparkly, something that didn't look defeated.

But everything seemed defeated here—and she knew, they *all* had to know—there was no magic in defeat.

"Something...Disney," the woman continued. "Something...over the top."

Tears pricked at Lana's eyes. So what if she wanted that? So what if she had hoped for a little magic in her life? So what if she had thought maybe she would find it here?

"You make the mistake everyone makes when they think of magic," the woman said. "You think it's easy. It's not. We don't do easy here."

"What do you do?" Lana let the defensiveness out. "Sit around and plan revenge on something that doesn't even exist?"

The woman looked at Rodrigo, who shrugged one shoulder.

"You deny that death exists?" the woman asked Lana.

Lana let out a bitter laugh. "If only."

"Then stay. Listen. Assess when we're done."

"Let her go," one of the men said. He was one of the men she had taken for a cop, although his last straw had been something like the death of a parent or something. "We got enough shooters."

"Not long-range precision shooters," Rodrigo said. Then he looked at Lana, as if he was disappointed in her.

She stood even straighter, and measured the distance between her spot on the far wall, and the door.

"Snipers," he said, "usually don't join something like this."

"We're not joiners," she said.

"No," he said. "That's not it. Snipers usually think of themselves as the Angel of Death. They don't need someone to remind them that there is another mechanism in place, something that can kill without a scope and ammunition."

Her cheeks heated. "I'm not that arrogant."

"Oh, but you are," he said. "Or you would not have taken the job of sniper."

"I tested into it," she said. "Best shot in Basic. Best shot in every single unit I joined. They finally recruited me."

"And you let yourself be recruited," Rodrigo said.

The blood left her cheeks, taking the heat with it. "I don't 'let' myself do anything," she said. "I took the job."

"Why?" he asked.

They were all staring at her. Had she taken it because she was arrogant? Because she liked killing?

"Because there was no one better," she said, her fingers clenching into fists. "Because, there was *no one* better."

Seven

Jubilee had had enough. She watched the sniper woman step into the center of the room, small and powerful, her body in perfect shape, each motion made with great confidence. Jubilee had not been that confident at that age. In fact, she had only become confident when she had become her true self, a process that had taken forever.

Half the people in the room caught Jubilee's movement, and waited quietly. Her friends from Judy's, they knew that Jubilee could be tough when she needed to.

But she hadn't needed to in this group. She had let Rodrigo run everything, let Izzy handle all the details, figuring they were the organizing type.

Jubilee had other things to do, other things to think about.

But she didn't feel that way now. This group was much more important to her than she realized.

For one of the few times in her recent life, she wished she had worn something less dramatic, something less pink. She had seen that little sniper woman dismiss her, simply because she was wearing clothes that made her comfortable, clothes that made her feel stronger, and for some reason, she wanted the little sniper woman to respect her.

Jubilee would never learn.

That very thought had gone through her head when she introduced herself to the sniper woman as Starina. Jubilee had been poking, figuring a military woman with a tough background wouldn't respect her from the start.

Jubilee had been surprised that the sniper woman had known the reference, and had been even more surprised when the sniper woman had called her out about it.

Jubilee had just been developing a little trust in the sniper woman when she went all *This is a bunch of hooey* on them.

Jubilee stood. Tru clutched at Jubilee's arm, trying to stop her. Tru and their good friend Mica usually had a finger on the temperature of the room. But Jubilee didn't want a temperature. Jubilee wanted to make a point.

"Let her go," Jubilee said, nodding at the sniper woman. "She's made it clear that she doesn't want to participate. We don't need to convince anyone to be part of our group. People need to convince us that they belong."

She raised her chin ever so slightly, her voice shaking more than she expected. She hadn't thought she would be so passionate about who was on the team.

But she was.

Because this was important.

No matter what the sniper woman thought.

EIGHT

It had taken Jubilee years to find someone who had seen the same things she had. Not in the world—God knew anyone who was grew up queer or different experienced the same hatreds, the same prejudices.

It was those little fleeting glimpses of something else, something on the edges. Not just when someone died. But when someone hated. When someone harmed. When someone lied.

The first time she'd seen it, she hadn't even known Jubilee was inside her. Then she'd been Dennis, the kid who hunched over and hid most of the time. Dennis had been too tall, too "effeminate" in the words of her gym teacher, who had literally tried to knock "some sense" into her three weeks into the fall semester.

High school in Wyoming, where men were men, and Matthew Shepard had been beaten, tied to a fencepost, and left to die like a tiny 5'2" human scarecrow only two years before. Jubilee had met a lot of great people, compassionate people, in Wyoming, but none of them had understood the cost of growing up different in a small Western town unless they had experienced the same things.

Coach had tried to make Jubilee a basketball star. Anyone that tall needed to be playing basketball, that was Coach's thinking—ignoring Jubilee's lack of interest as well as a lack of physical coordination that came from a 10-inch growth spurt that had happened over the space of one short summer.

The tauntings, the beatings, the way some of the boys tried to catch her alone, to show her exactly what was waiting for her if she didn't toughen up, a reality all of her life, until she'd discovered some like-minded folk in (ironically) Laramie, who actually showed her how to deflect, how to avoid, how to protect herself.

Still didn't stop her from getting stomped that night in March, beaten within an inch of her life. She had been laying on the slushy concrete, her right cheek half-frozen against the ice, hot blood dripping down her face from her shattered nose, eyes half open, staring at Andrew as he died just across the parking lot from her—Andrew, the only person who had ever been kind to her. Andrew, who was not gay, was not trans, was not anything except the nicest human being in the entire world, killed because he had dared—*dared*—to befriend the wrong person.

That night, something had flashed underneath the streetlight, just before Andrew had died. Wings, maybe. A face, rather like Oz's big see-through head floating above the flames in the movie *The Wizard of Oz.* (Maybe that was one reason Jubilee idolized Judy. That moment when she faced down the Wizard. It was not just everything Judy had done, everything she stood for—but her courage, her desire to defend everyone, including a scarecrow who was smarter than anyone and more vulnerable than everyone knew.)

That night, on the ice, bleeding out, Jubilee (Dennis then) had stared at the wings under the street light. The wings got smaller, the face faded, and then there was the smell of vanilla, almost overpowering, and a touch of snow. She had the sense that the creature had just come from Andrew, that it had been (feeding?) on Andrew, and now that Andrew was no more—eyes empty, body unmoving—the thing had flown to her.

She hadn't been sure that was bad, not at that moment, with her whole life ahead of her filled with, as far as she could tell (as far as Dennis could tell) more beatings, more hatred, more loss.

Then something caressed Jubilee's face, feathers—or so it seemed—soft and soothing. And the smell of vanilla had grown a lot stronger. At least she liked vanilla. Vanilla suggested warmth to her, maybe even love.

Then, suddenly, she heard voices across the parking lot, voices that made her shiver or maybe just made her realize how helpless she was, broken against the pavement. She waggled her fingers, tried to move her feet—why, she'd never know, because she had no idea if those voices belonged to the boys who had beaten her and killed Andrew, or if the voices belonged to someone who might consider rescuing her.

One of the voices said, *There's another one,* and came closer, and she cringed. The smell of vanilla had disappeared, the feeling of warmth, the feathers on her face, replaced only by the crusty edges of blood around her nose, the throbbing in her shattered left cheek, her left eye, slowly swelling shut.

The voices belonged to people who had no idea who she was (what she was), thought she was just some boy who'd gotten beat up, and then they found Andrew too, and they thought mugging gone wrong, so they called the police, called an ambulance, and somehow, some way, Dennis survived.

Andrew was dead, but Dennis hung on for a few more years. Hung on to what Jubilee never knew, because the depression after that, the waves of despair, they grew and grew and grew.

And Dennis almost faded away.

Somehow she got out of Wyoming. Scholarships—at least education saved her, more or less. When you hid and studied you actually got somewhere.

For her, somewhere was NYU, New York, with all its variety, and she found like-minded people, she found people who saw *her,* not Dennis, and brought out *her,* brought Jubilee into the world, and showed her how to be herself. She entered a community that meant so much more to her than any other community ever had, graduated from college with a degree and a real job, where people didn't care who she was as long as she met the unisex dress code (she could do that), and for a moment—just a moment—she thought the world would treat her well.

Then she watched, watched, watched as friend after friend died. Some old timers, finally succumbing to the opportunistic diseases that took advantage of someone HIV-positive, others dying the same way Andrew had—from fists and bigotry and too fucking much hate.

By the time Jubilee had transferred here for work, she was strong. She was Jubilee. She was numb.

She knew the back passages of Judy's, and she knew how to recognize the Angel of Death. The Angel didn't have wings this time—sometimes the Angel had wings and sometimes it didn't. Sometimes it looked like a man, and sometimes it looked like a woman—rather like Jubilee at one point in her life. Sometimes it looked human and sometimes it looked like a clichéd demon. And sometimes, sometimes, it took the form of a lover or a loved one or souls who had passed and—she thought (they all thought)—would never return.

Only once had the Angel tried to impersonate Andrew. Only once. He had come toward her in the midst of her despair—one of those dark nights of the soul that not everyone climbed out of. She'd been beaten—again—in a parking lot—again—by assholes—again. But she'd learned those details much much later.

What she remembered, what had been real to her, was that feeling, that *Why the fuck am I bothering? Nothing ever changes.* She was twenty-five, out of college, still in New York, but in the wrong part of the city for a concert, and she'd dressed like Jubilee. Her mistake, even though they said that the victim should never consider their clothing a mistake, but she did, she had, and she felt—oh, God, she felt like *what was the goddamn point?*

The Fake-Andrew-Angel had reached for her just as she had thought *Maybe I'll let go this time,* and the Fake-Andrew-Angel had smiled at her. It extended its hands—which looked like Andrew's hands—and for a moment, she was fooled, thinking maybe it was Andrew, maybe there were good people where she was going, a different kind of life there, one that wasn't so painful.

Then the Angel's fingers brushed her face, like feathers, and it said, *Jubilee, Jubilee, it's been too long. Love, I've missed you*—and the words were so wrong, the sentiment so far off, that she knew, *she knew,* this wasn't Andrew. Not her Andrew, not the only person who had gotten her through that hellish high school. Not the person who had died defending her.

Had died defending Dennis.

So as the Angel put its Fake-Andrew fingers on her face, Jubilee slapped them away. Then she had punched it in the jaw.

The thing was, she had never punched anyone before. Not once, in her entire battered life. She'd been the punched. She'd never been the puncher. She usually curled into a fetal ball. She had stopped begging that night in high school, in that frozen parking lot where Andrew had died, because she'd learned then that begging only made things worse.

Her punch, though. Her punch had been involuntary, filled with a rage she had never before acknowledged that she had. Fake-Andrew-Angel had staggered backwards, surprised, hand on its cheek, its eyes black and all pupil for just a moment, wings flaring around it as if it planned to fly off.

Then it dropped its hands, and said in Andrew's plaintive voice, *I thought we were friends.*

Andrew and I were friends, Jubilee had said. *You pollute his memory. Get away from me.*

And the Angel left. Just left, as if it had been a vampire in a movie and she had thrown holy water on it.

Everything around her cleared. She wasn't in some magical realm. She wasn't even somewhere warm. She was in another parking lot, one she had not ever seen before.

Her torso underneath a dumpster that stank even though it was nearly zero degrees outside. Her knees and toes were numb—exposed to the cold because she was wearing the open-toed shoes she preferred at her favorite club—and her entire body ached.

The dumpster—it was a sign. Someone (smaller, not as strong) had tried to toss her in it. That someone had failed.

She never remembered the fight—not that it was a fight. It wasn't fair to call a beat-down a fight, and she never knew who attacked her, although she could guess why.

She couldn't remember anything from the evening leading up to the dumpster. The only thing she could remember was Andrew-Fake-Andrew the not-so-fake angel, and knew, at that moment, that she had tangled with something bigger than herself.

The ambulance that had arrived just as she had woken up out of that trance (was that why she had awakened? Because an ambulance had arrived? Because someone had tried to save her?) managed to get her on a gurney before she even knew what was happening. And then one of the attendants said that phrase that she had heard only once before in her life: *Wow,* one of the attendants said, *you'd think someone who had been through all that would be dead.*

Then he saw her looking at him through a rapidly swelling eye, and he winked at her. Not a sexy wink, but the wink of someone who knew and understood.

You're lucky, honey. You made it out this time, he had said. And that *honey* had been a gift, not an insult. Just a bit of understanding on a horrid horrid night, a night that should have ended everything.

The next morning, every part of her ached, except the bruised and battered knuckles on her right hand. Those bruises, the doctor said, looked more like electrical burns, but they didn't act like burns. They were clearly bruises that resembled the kind of burns Jubilee would have gotten if she had stuck her hand in an electrical socket and the socket had exploded.

That was how she had known the punch had been real, the surprise had been real, the Fake-Andrew-Angel had been real.

A therapist told her, later, that she had seen things, but they hadn't been real. They had simply been the electrical impulses of an oxygen-starved brain.

Science, the therapist had intoned, *has shown that most of these near-death visions are simply synapses firing in unusual ways because of the stresses on the body.*

But the knuckles? The bruising? The black streaks, which had remained for the better part of a year?

No one had answers for that. No one except Jubilee who, at that moment, decided to believe.

She'd even asked the therapist, taunted the therapist really, in the last hour they ever spent together, the last hour Jubilee ever paid for.

What caused these marks, then? Jubilee had asked.

The therapist shrugged. The person who was supposed to have all the answers *shrugged,* and said, *Your body simply chose to express the trauma in that way. Bodies do that.*

Jubilee hadn't believed that at all, although she found it curious that the therapist, who was part of the community, had seen marks like that before, had thought those marks somehow normal. Now, Jubilee would want to ask the therapist about it, but then Jubilee had simply felt rage.

The therapist had gotten a concerned look, folded her hands together, and intoned to Jubilee: *Respect the trauma, and you will eventually heal from it.*

Respect the trauma. Jubilee actually heard that part. Respect the trauma. Realize that something had happened to you. Something big, something profound. Something difficult.

Respect the trauma had become her mantra. And it got her through.

It got her through breakups and the deaths of friends. It got her through the loss of her soul-mother, the woman who made it possible for her to become Jubilee in the first place.

It got her through that night at Judy's.

She had been in her dressing room, getting ready to go onstage. She'd been performing at Judy's three nights per week. She'd been bartending on three other nights. The job that had brought her here was long gone.

That night, she'd heard gunfire, and it sounded close. She never know why she had grabbed three feather boas, and some extra-large panty hose at that moment, but she had. She burst out of her dressing room, pointed at the scared young stagehand, and told him in her most commanding voice to call 911. Which he did as she went to the doors that separated backstage from the gunfire, and she had locked them, tying the feather boas in place for added strength, protecting her backstage crew while they tried to escape out the exit doors.

At that point no one—not the shooters, not Jubilee—had thought about the stage as a way to get backstage. All she had done was think about the doors, barricading the doors.

There'd been three shooters that night, not one. The media couldn't decide if the deaths at Judy's had been an act of terrorism, an act of hatred, or an act of some local deranged minds, rather like the attack on Jubilee and Andrew all those years ago.

Jubilee knew it had been all three—she hated that term *domestic terrorism*—but that's what it was. Bigotry mixed with deranged minds, mixed with easy availability to weapons, and some sick reason to attack people who were only out to have a good time.

She'd gotten twenty people out, before one of the shooters broke through the doors she had locked. She kicked off her heels—not sure why she hadn't kicked them off before, but adrenalin, panic, had caused her to make some strange choices—and then she had climbed the catwalk as quietly as a 6'2" person could. Fortunately, she hadn't put on her costume. She was wearing her bra and Spanks, her real hair which she kept short so she wouldn't get too hot under her wigs, and her feet were bare now. Bare, making climbing easier, if painful.

She'd reached the top of the catwalk, and she'd dumped one of the lights downward, narrowly missing another one of the shooters, the one standing on stage, firing into the audience huddled on the floor. Later, she found out, he had been hit with shards of broken metal and glass. At least she had caused the motherfucker some pain.

He whirled, pointed his rifle upward, and shot God knows how many repeating rounds. Missing her as if she were Tom Cruise in every single movie he'd been in. The shooter ran as he shot, shouting at his compatriots that she was here, there was someone above them, someone else who had to die.

She'd seen the wings again that night, but not the Fake-Andrew-Angel. Instead, he had come to her—*it* had come to her—as her beloved soul-mother, sitting on the edge of the catwalk.

You know it would be less painful if you fell, her fake soul-mother had said, so far off target again, that Jubilee's breath caught. Whoever this so-called angel was, it was bad at its job. Or maybe it hadn't done its research or maybe it was simply supposed to confuse.

Instead, it had goaded her, just like it had the first time. Only this time, Jubilee jostled the catwalk, then kicked out with her bare feet, catching the fake soul-mother angel-asshole off guard, and it toppled headfirst toward the stage.

Its wings unfurled at the last second, but not soon enough to do anything except ease the fall. It landed with an ungainly thud and a cry of pain that everyone in the club seemed to hear, including the cops, who were, at that moment, shooting their way in.

Adding to the casualties of course. Because police in minority communities always added to casualties.

That was something she'd tried to impress on the four police officers on the team Rodrigo had put together, but those police officers still didn't understand it, not even the African-American one. They talked about triage and the need to save some if you couldn't save all, and she always argued that you had to save all, until she realized that arguing was futile. There were simply some things even reasonable people, even reasonable people with something in common, simply could not agree on.

No one shot her that night at Judy's. Somehow, she got out. She managed to find friends, reunite lovers, get phones to those who needed to call family *right now.* Someone gave her a coat, and someone found her some shoes, and still she worked, tirelessly, calmly, making sure everyone in her community was A-Okay.

The local papers started calling her the Angel of Judy's until she made them stop. Because she'd seen the angel at Judy's and it hadn't been one she wanted to emulate.

She'd been fine after that—no need for therapy, not her, not this time. She had finally (she thought) found her calling, the ability to hold friends, friend-family, and acquaintances together, to keep a damaged and grieving community alive. To be the rock in the center of chaos, the one everyone went to when they needed a shoulder, when they needed a hug or a good meal or just someone to sit quietly in the same room, listening to each other breathe.

And then Pepperbeans died.

Pepperbeans, her little long-haired white mutt of a dog. Pepperbeans hadn't been at the club that night, although Pepperbeans usually went everywhere with her.

But Jubilee had received a few death threats, ones she believed (she didn't always believe the threats), and when she believed a threat, she knew it was better to leave Pepperbeans at home, because sickos who targeted the LGBTQ community targeted animals too. Bigots always saw dogs as easy prey and Jubilee hadn't wanted to lose hers because Pepperbeans had had the misfortune to be at the wrong place at the wrong time.

Pepperbeans, fourteen years old, getting a little creaky, but not anything else. The dog loved her treats. She loved playing with Jubilee, and she loved cuddling at night—a warm little snuggle that had become reassurance after all the darkness.

Until the snuggle ceased to be warm.

Pepperbeans had died three weeks after Judy's. Perfect death, really. The kind that Jubilee would want if she got a vote in how she passed away. In her sleep, at home, snuggled against her favorite person in the whole wide world.

The vet said it had been quick and it had been natural causes, and no, Pepperbeans hadn't suffered at all. *If you have to pick a way to go,* the vet said, echoing Jubilee's thoughts, *then this is absolutely the best way.*

Not that it helped Jubilee. She beat herself up internally worse than any of the beatings she had gotten for being different. What had she missed? How could she have saved her dog? Why couldn't she save her dog?

And why—oh, God, why—did Pepperbeans have to leave now?

The despair threatened to eat her alive. Jubilee knew the despair wasn't all Pepperbeans. It wasn't even close to Pepperbeans. Izzy's words "the last straw" were accurate, if a bit minimizing. Pepperbeans simply stood for all the loses, all the deaths, the one last factor that nearly tipped Jubilee over the edge.

Until she remembered that she had punched one version of the Angel of Death, and shoved another version off a catwalk. What would she have done if she had seen the one that had come for Pepperbeans?

Would Jubilee have recognized it? Was there a dog version of the Angel of Death? Was it something she could have stopped?

And those thoughts brought the recriminations back all over again.

She clung to the recriminations even as she tried to find a way to make them stop. She played with them in her mind, over and over and over again, as she rebuilt Judy's, as she held friends, as she still provided comfort.

She even looked at other dogs, but couldn't—just couldn't face loving another one, loving something good and small and innocent. Not when she was surrounded by so much death.

And it had been that thought, that very thought, which had come to her in, of all places, a no-kill shelter, that she was surrounded by death, even in places like this, which had banned it.

She could see the Angel of Death. And if she could see that mother-fucker, she could hurt it. She could hurt it bad.

Once she did that, once she scared it like she had scared that one near the dumpster, she could demand that it change its ways. It could still do its job. People who got horribly ill, with no hope of recovery ever, just misery forever, they needed some kind of respite. And, if she were honest with herself, she didn't mind if the angel killed a few homophobes, a couple of terrorists, and a mass murderer or two.

But Pepperbeans, who had simply loved her? Andrew, the best person in the whole world? Her soul-mother, who taught Jubilee that we all had someone special inside us; we simply had to find her?

The Angel of Death shouldn't get to take the good ones. No one should take the good ones. No one at all.

Stalking sounded easier than it was. Jubilee probably could've staked out nursing homes or the ICU at the hospital, maybe followed some hospice nurse on her daily rounds, but that didn't just seem fair. That seemed wrong.

If she went to visit the dying, she should actually give them her time and her full attention, not scout around to see if some stupid "angel" approached on little death wings.

She had been sitting in a park—a dog park, honestly, because she missed having a dog. She watched other people's dogs frolic on the somewhat matted and stinky grass, and thought about stalking (and fucking destroying) the Angel of Death.

Only she didn't know how to go about it.

Then Rodrigo sat down beside her.

Nine

She hadn't known him then, hadn't known he was a good and kind person, hadn't known he gave as much (if not more) of himself than she gave of herself. All she saw was a squat muscular man glancing at her from the corner of his eye.

She was taller than he was, but obviously not tougher. She knew a man like him could take her down with two quick moves—had taken her down like that more than once.

Her heart started beating rapidly, and she gathered her purse, her book bag, and her coat.

"Stay," he'd said.

She gave him one of those dismissive smiles, the kind she'd learned from the woman who'd been her soul-mother. So many deflecting things Jubilee had learned, the way women blew off men without ever really confronting them.

She nearly dropped her purse, that was what kept her on that bench a half-second longer, grabbing the purse strap, mentally cursing, thinking about everything she could have done but wasn't doing and—to be honest—wondering why the hell she couldn't even get a moment of peace, when he spoke again.

"I want to kill him too."

She looked at Rodrigo in complete horror. He wasn't looking at her. Instead, he was staring at a little brown shih tzu that stood in front of him, tail wagging happily, and for a moment, Jubilee thought he had been talking about the dog.

"You see him," Rodrigo said. "I know you do."

She froze in place. Surely, he wasn't there. Surely, he wasn't talking to her. She had been leaning forward just a bit to gather her things, and she leaned just a bit more and, in a not-as-surreptitious-as-she-would-like kinda way—she looked to see if he was on his cell, if he was talking to someone else.

Of course he wasn't. He was talking to her.

He had meant it all for her.

Then he looked at her head-on. His eyes were brown, and they seemed kind. She hated it when the people who attacked her initially seemed kind. Things like that made her already-fragile belief in humanity become even thinner.

"Every time," Rodrigo said, "I see a man. He looks like a soldier out of uniform. Straight back, khakis, sleeves rolled up to reveal powerful arms. His face is wrong, though—not quite human, an approximation of human—or maybe we're all that kind of approximation when we're killing."

That phrase, that sentence, it made her shiver. Was he threatening her? She pulled her purse up by its strap, hugged it to her. The shih tzu barked playfully, and leapt back and forth, trying to get Rodrigo's attention again. Instead, another dog showed up, a bigger dog—some kind of mutt—and they ran off together, playing and barking with great joy, exactly the way the park should work.

Rodrigo must have seen her expression (how could he miss it, after all?) and he smiled ever so faintly. "I didn't mean to alarm you."

Talk of killing, talk of *death,* with a stranger, and he hadn't meant to *alarm* her?

Her coat was caught between her left thigh and the rusted metal armrest. She couldn't quite get free.

"Five tours," he said. "I kept reupping. I don't know why. Guess I thought I could make it better."

She froze again, heart still pounding, but somehow willing to listen.

How did he continue to find that sweet spot, the one that kept her just barely in place, unwillingly hanging on his every word?

"You see him," Rodrigo said again. "I *know* you see him."

And this time, he sounded just a little desperate, as if he didn't want to believe he had made a mistake sitting next to her, a mistake engaging in conversation with her, a mistake revealing so much about himself.

Revealing what, though? That he was just a little crazy? Or maybe not a little crazy. Maybe a lotta crazy.

She'd learned long ago not to engage with crazy. She managed to free her coat. She slung her purse over her arm, and stood up in one single movement.

But she couldn't help herself. She had to say something. She was going to say that she didn't think he should talk like that to strangers.

Instead, she told him something she'd learned in the community damn near her very first week in New York.

"Pronouns are important," she said. "It's not a 'him.' It's an 'it,' no matter how it presents itself. It's an it."

He rocked backwards as if she had pushed him against the bench. Then he tilted his head just a little, nodded, and smiled, as if her words had clarified something for him.

"What do you see?" he asked quietly.

"People I knew," she said bitterly. "Misappropriated images of people I knew. And wings. And it smells like vanilla. Put me off ice cream and vanilla lattes for the rest of my life, let me tell you."

He gave her a second smile, but it looked perfunctory, as if he knew her comment required one.

Then he patted the bench.

"Sit back down," he said. "Let's talk."

She didn't sit. She was never going to sit because some muscular man told her to.

He glanced at the bench, then shrugged just a little, as if to say that it didn't matter if she sat. It would be her loss to continue standing.

"There are people like you," he said, "like me. People who see him—it. Who see it."

In spite of herself, she appreciated the correction. He was trying. She wasn't sure she wanted him to try, but he was.

"It..." he seemed to be searching for the word. "It changes us."

"Death changes us," she said, shifting her purse on her shoulder. Dogs barked behind her, and a tall Doberman entered the park as if he and his person owned it.

Rodrigo inclined his head, giving her that point. Then he said, "I mean, when we see him...it. When we see it, we become different. We think of it as something..."

Again, he seemed to cast about for the word. But this time, he couldn't seem to find it.

"Something we can fight," she said.

His gaze flattened for a moment, as if that hadn't been the word he had been searching for. Then he sighed, and shook his head once.

"I was going to say we want to fight it, but that is wrong," he said. "Except for the deeply ill and those who die in an instant, we always fight death."

"And suicides," she said softly.

"Deeply ill," he repeated, and she bristled. She did not believe suicide was an illness. Sometimes, it was a choice in the face of great physical pain. Or in the face of a world gone mad.

Or maybe she simply felt insulted by the comment, considering all the times she had considered suicide, and then (mentally) walked away from it.

"Then," he said, apparently not seeing evidence of her own internal dialogue, "I was going to say we want to defeat it, but that is not right either. Because much of our science, our medicine, our psychotherapy and religion, it is all about defeating death."

"I suppose," Jubilee said, suddenly tiring of the conversation. He was getting philosophical with her, and she didn't enjoy that. Apparently, he was borderline crazy after all.

He sensed it. He could sense her mood changes. Perhaps they showed on her face.

"I finally realized," he said quietly, "that the word I want is *stop.* We want to *stop* death. Entirely."

"I don't," she said coldly, shifting her coat to her other arm. "There are some people who deserve to die."

And then she walked away from him, threading her way through the dogs, her heart getting heavier and heavier each time one planted itself in front of her, with a doggy smile on its face, tongue lolling, tail wagging.

She nearly made it to the edge of the park, when she had to go back.

He was still sitting on the bench, staring at the dogs as if they held all the answers.

"Why did you talk to me?" she asked as she approached. "What made you say all that stuff to me?"

He peered at her, almost as if he had forgotten her. Then his brow furrowed, and he took a deep breath—a man who was unwilling to speak, after talking so very much.

"Because I can see it," he said quietly. "On your right hand. You touched one."

Then he ran his fingers along the back of his own right hand, exactly in the place the black marks had been on her hand.

It unnerved her, but this time, she didn't want to step away.

"I didn't touch one," she said. "I *punched* one."

Hard. Hard enough to startle it. Hard enough to make it have second thoughts even as it tried again.

"Punched it," he said quietly, and then he chuckled. "*Punched* it."

He shook his head, and his smile grew with each shake. He was incredulous and yet somehow joyful, and the look transformed his face, from something broad and tough to something almost handsome.

"Punched it," he repeated.

She felt a smile building inside her. It did sound ridiculous, Jubilee, punching the Angel of Death.

"And I kicked one," she said. "Hard enough to make it fall."

He raised his head, his gaze meeting hers, and his smile, which was already broad, grew into a gigantic grin.

"You've fought the Angel of Death twice," he said.

"If only I'd won," she said.

"Oh, you did," he said. "You're still here."

"For the moment," she said, not willing to promise anything more than that. "I'm here, for the moment."

Ten

Somehow, he convinced her to have coffee. Then coffee became lunch, and lunch became dinner, and the conversations went on into the night. The people they'd known, the people they'd lost.

She shared more than he did, but she always shared more than anyone else, so she didn't think it unusual until much later, after she had joined the group and watched him with others.

They all talked about their last straws and their broken hearts and the day when everything changed for them, but he rarely said a word. He watched instead.

She had no idea what his magic was, but she knew he did have magic. It was subtle and hard to see, but it showed up, like it had when he spotted her, like it had when he ran his fingers along the back of his right hand in the same pattern as her black marks.

When he "saw" something, she learned to pay attention, although she didn't always approve.

And she didn't approve right now, of this woman, this sniper that Rodrigo seemed to think they needed.

They hadn't even decided on weapons yet. Jubilee wasn't even certain that weapons would work. They didn't even have a true game plan, just a series of ideas, wishful thinking all of it, nothing concrete.

She wasn't sure they would ever have anything concrete. She wasn't even sure concrete was possible.

And yet she was offended when the sniper woman—incongruously called Lana—stood up and declared their mission silly. Even though part of Jubilee agreed. Part of her knew that death had always been a part of life. So many ancient cultures believed—taught—told everyone—that without death, life had no meaning.

Jubilee wasn't sure she believed that. She wasn't sure she wanted to believe it. She wanted to think that life could be as precious, as fleetingly perfect, without the ever-present threat of an ending looming in the distance.

The sniper woman was staring at her. Jubilee couldn't tell if she saw disgust in the sniper woman's eyes or if the sniper woman always looked at everyone with great contempt.

Perhaps it was the sniper woman's defense mechanism. Or perhaps the sniper woman was truly as arrogant as she had sounded just a moment before, when she declared herself the best shot in her unit, the best shot in any unit she had ever belonged in, implying that she was also the best shot in any unit she *might* find herself belonging to.

"Let her go," Jubilee repeated. "We don't need attitude like that."

Usually, when Jubilee spoke here, in this office, everyone listened and agreed. This afternoon, they listened, but no one nodded. They seemed uncertain, as if they were at a crossroads none of them completely understood.

"She stays," Rodrigo said, without looking at Jubilee.

"If she wants to," Izzy added softly, her gaze on the sniper woman.

The sniper woman turned her gaze from Izzy to Rodrigo, and then back to Jubilee.

"What are you people going to do if I try to leave?" the sniper woman asked. "Kill me?"

Tru let out a guffaw. Jubilee looked over at Tru.

"Dude," Tru said, as only they could do, putting the emphasis on *dude* in such a way as to make even that word seem slightly ironic. "We're here to stop death. Dude. I mean really. We would kill you because you won't help us stop death? How dumb is that?"

The sniper woman leaned back ever so slightly, her cheeks turning a slight shade of pink. Apparently, she hadn't been put in her place in a while.

"What do you need a sniper for?" the sniper woman asked, without the edge of her earlier comments. "I mean, if there is an Angel of Death, and it is a magical creature, surely a bullet wouldn't stop it."

"Here we go again," said one of the cops from behind Jubilee. "Here we go again."

Eleven

He wasn't the kind of man to believe in magic crap. Hell, he was barely the kind of man who believed in God, motherhood, and apple pie. Lou DeMartino crossed his meaty forearms over his chest and wished he had an excuse to get the hell out of here.

Too many people, and he didn't like half of them. Okay, maybe more than half, since he hadn't even bothered to retain their names. He'd really been good at that shit once—introduce him to a roomful of people and he could cough back their names even out of order, making them all feel important.

These days, he didn't feel like making anyone feel important.

He didn't even feel important himself.

He leaned against the stupid wood paneling—if you could call that seventies crap wood—and wished he'd fixed the air conditioner last week when he'd been here, chatting up Izzy. He liked Izzy. She was no-nonsense, just as damaged as he was, and had some kind of darkness hiding behind her eyes.

Plus, she didn't judge. She knew he'd seen more than most, rejected more than most too, and had done his share of damage.

She didn't care. She would lightly touch his arm when she talked to him, smile at him without reservation (unlike the way she smiled at everyone else) and let him take his own sweet time to tell her why and how he'd found his own way here.

Everyone else assumed he'd seen something on the job, or it was some kind of accumulation of work and shootings and he let them think that. When Izzy asked her last-straw question, he'd never really answered it honestly, sometimes saying something facetious like *traffic stop,* which two of the African-Americans said, and they always looked at him or Frankie or Jose, the other cops, as if all three of them were responsible for whatever the hell other cops did all around America.

Only the African-Americans who said *traffic stop,* they never ever looked at the African-American cop, William something or other, because they never ever thought he'd be trigger happy, not at a traffic stop, not understanding that traffic stops were one of the most fraught things a cop could do.

You pull over a car, you don't know if it's a good citizen inside who will have their license and registration at the ready, who'll say *yes, officer,* and *no, officer,* and maybe, once everyone relaxed at little, might joke about having to pee or asking (sideways, maybe flirting) if they could get off with a warning this time.

You don't know if you got a good citizen or someone on the run from something, someone with a gun on the passenger seat, someone who thinks the end is near and just fucking starts shooting, like they did to Lou's friend Ron five years ago. Ron survived, but he was on disability, *real* disability, not the psychiatric crap that Lou was on.

Not that Lou disagreed with his disability. It just wasn't the kind of thing a guy like him should have agreed to, something that a guy like him should've needed. He should've toughed it out, just like he was toughing these damn sessions out, with all the people pressed around him, the rattling air conditioner that dripped more water than it put into the air, the crap-ass carpet that didn't provide any protection for his thin ass against that solid (probably concrete) floor underneath.

If he'd known that the woman they'd come to vet, Lana something or other, would ask all the same stupid questions, express all the same stupid doubts, go through the same stupid discussion about magic and bullets and could they really have power over death—not that Biblical power over death crap, in which Jesus steps out of the tomb after three days and everyone prematurely declares death defeated, not that stuff—but a very real ability to fight Death or its minions or its angels or whatever the *fuck* you wanted to call it, on its own terms.

He didn't have time to listen to those questions again. Or rather, he did have time, he had all the time in the world, because he doubted he was ever going to get cleared, considering how jumpy he was, how much he hated being around other human beings, how just leaning against this wall, his butt pressed against the floor, Jubilee's mighty ass half a turn away from his face, how much all of that just made him want to crawl out of his skin.

But he didn't, not yet, although he might, if someone—anyone—doubted that magic existed one more time.

Jubilee turned just a little toward him, put one manicured finger to her beautifully painted lips, and nodded toward Rodrigo, who was listening to everything intently, as if she was saying, *Let Rodrigo handle it.*

If Rodrigo was going to handle it, he should've handled it before summoning everyone from their houses, from their all-important afternoon channel-surfing, watching the country implode because the president was a moron and, depending on which cable news channel Lou stopped on for which length of time, either the Democrats were at fault or the Republicans, and someone was going to get impeached or go to jail or should be left alone to do his goddamn job or maybe, maybe it was all broken, and they all needed to take a pill and lie down and hope that this too would pass.

Lou let out a long breath, and apparently, it had been really audible because half the room turned and looked at him.

"You got something to add, Lou?" Carter asked from across the room. Carter was one of the professors, someone who was used to asking snotty condescending questions, particularly at those whom he perceived as less educated and therefore less intelligent than he was.

"Yeah," Lou said, half-grunting the word as he stood up, so that he could tower over the sniper (although he would never tower over Jubilee, who was tall to begin with and always wore heels that made her at least six inches taller than she needed to be).

Lou pushed his way to the front of his little section of the group, looked at the sniper and thought, yep. She had sniper training all right. Probably not as good as she thought she was, but good enough for their purposes.

"Let me put it to you in really simple terms," he said to her, "so the rest of us don't have to listen to this shit for the umptiumpth millionth time. Magic exists. But it ain't really unusual, and that's where we all make the mistake. We justify off the magic stuff as every day—the way sunshine sparkles on water or the fact that a full moon brings out all the crazies worldwide—and we normalize much too much. Like death. We just figure, shit, yeah, it happens to all of us. Death and taxes, yadda yadda yadda."

The sniper—younger than he would've thought, eyes that weren't quite dead, not yet, but were heading there. She'd seen too much and she didn't want to believe in nothing. Jesus, he could understand that. He'd been in the same boat when he got here, right after Miriam died.

"We got it worked out," he said. "To answer your questions, maybe before you ask all of them, we're not gonna use regular bullets or silver bullets or bullets dipped in holy water. We ain't really using bullets at all. We got surprise on our side, and a whole hell of a lot of rage, and what you'd be shooting, from a distance and accurately—what a lot of us might be shooting, just not from that distance—are dummy bullets, maybe rubber, maybe non-lethal crowd control. We're going for shock and awe. You don't fight magic with magic when you're a bunch of lugs like us. You fight magic with sheer determination, a whole lotta righteousness, and the courage of our fucking convictions."

"And you think that'll work?" she asked.

Apparently, he'd missed that question in his little rant. He'd thought the answer was implied. Apparently not.

"Here's the thing you should understand, Miss Windspeed, Calculus, and Impossible Angles, you don't know if anything'll work until you give it a try. And conditions on the ground might make a great attempt fail. Or they might strengthen the weakest attempt ever designed. You know, luck. It can be a factor in anything we do."

"I thought you were going to tell me that luck is magic," she said.

He didn't know how she did it—found the one thing that would shut him down—but she did. Maybe that was magic.

He felt older than he had five minutes ago, just from the words she'd uttered. Stabbed him, right through the heart. Although there was an open track to that heart, and he knew it.

"I'm beginning to think luck is the antithesis of magic," he muttered, and shuffled back to his spot. Jubilee watched him. Damn, that woman saw everything. He used to too.

She gave him a compassionate look, half-hidden by her fake eyelashes, but there all the same, and turned back toward the sniper and her stupid questions.

Luck. Lou shook his head. Once upon a time, he'd thought of himself as the luckiest man alive. Whenever he introduced Miriam, he'd say, *She agreed to marry me. I think that makes me the luckiest man in the whole entire world.*

And then...Jesus... and then her cancer and all the magical medical crap in the world didn't save her. And she made him promise. Him, promise, that he would be the one, if she couldn't have a good life after the surgeries, if she was going to decline and become one-quarter of a person, if her life wasn't going to be worth living—she made him promise that he would have the docs pull the plug.

I trust you, she'd said. *You're the strongest man I know.*

But he wasn't strong. It came to that moment, when the doctors said they couldn't make her better, they weren't even sure she would wake up from the last anesthetic, and if she did, they knew she wouldn't be herself because the freakin' cancer had eaten her beautiful brain.

He'd known that was coming, he'd *known* it when she looked at him —just the once, two weeks before—and for a half-second, she wondered who he was. She hadn't said that, thank God, because if she had, he might've wondered (ah, hell, he was still wondering) if he'd killed her because she didn't know him anymore.

But the docs talked to him, and then a whole other set of docs talked to him, and then yet another set of docs talked to him, and they all agreed that for all intents and purposes, for the purpose of the Do-Not-Resuscitate that she had signed, for the purpose of figuring out all the life and death stuff, she was already gone.

Already gone.

So he said, his voice choked with emotion, his voice barely there—the strongest man alive—he'd said, *Yeah. Do it. Pull the plug.*

And they did. They took her off life support. They let God do what God was going to do, as one of the docs said, and Lou damn near jumped down his throat.

Miriam didn't believe in God. She believed in logic and science and maybe some kind of something that humans hadn't discovered yet. She wasn't even sure there was life after death, which meant when she had told him that she wanted to die rather than live a marginal life, *she* had been the strongest person alive, because she believed that dying would probably wipe her out of existence entirely.

And she thought that was okay.

He didn't. He still didn't.

So he went from thinking he was the luckiest man alive to knowing that he was the unluckiest, because he had found the best person in the world, and then he had killed her.

Jubilee put her hand on his arm. Damn that woman, knowing and trying to alleviate other people's pain. Damn her for her compassion.

He wanted to move away.

Instead, he sniffled, and silently cursed himself, and if Jubilee hadn't been holding him down, he would've fled. He would've been done with this group.

No one looked at him, though. No one looked at sniveling former tough guys. No one, not even in this group, wanted to acknowledge that tears were possible and events in the world, in your goddamn life, could turn you into a weeping pile of worthlessness.

No one looked at him except Jubilee, and if she put one of her long arms around him, he silently swore he push her away. Hard. Noticeably hard.

He sniveled again, and wiped his nose with the back of his hand, and wished he could stop being such a goddamn baby.

Then he made himself concentrate, realizing he had lost the thread of the conversation.

"So you're saying we're going to be the Polish cavalry in World War II," the sniper was saying to the group.

Lou frowned, not knowing the reference. Jesus, his ignorance upset even him sometimes. Maybe instead of sitting on his ass and feeling sorry for himself every day, he should read a book once in a while.

"That's a myth," Carter said in his condescending tone. "The Polish did not attack German panzers with lances and swords. The Germans created myth as propaganda, and there you are, spouting it—"

Pauline, one of the few people Lou liked in the room, a teacher who had somehow survived Portage Elementary with the ability to smile and be nice even now, stepped in front of Carter just enough to shut him up.

"Yes," she said to the sniper woman. "That's exactly what we're saying. Sixteen times, the Polish cavalry faced stronger German forces, and in almost every one of those battles, the cavalry committed itself well. They succeeded at their missions. Yes, a lot of people died, but they died well and bravely, which is, I think, all we can hope for."

"Bullshit," the sniper said. She was shaking. "Bull-fucking-shit. That well and bravely thing is something someone who has never been to war says because they believe that a hero's death is actually possible."

Oh, God, Lou thought. *Here it comes. The bile that no one in this place needs right now.*

And as if she had heard his thoughts, the sniper clenched her small fists.

"Well and bravely?" she asked. "You want a sniper. You know what a sniper sees through her scope? Someone living their life—maybe talking to a friend, maybe shooting at an enemy, maybe just crossing a road. We watch, we see, we put them in the crosshairs, and when the moment is right—when *we* determine that the moment is right—we shoot them."

The room was silent. Lou closed his eyes, wishing he could close his ears.

"They explode backwards as if propelled or maybe sideways or maybe into the person they were talking to, and they don't get back up. They don't even try, if we're good, and those of us who do the job in war, we're good."

He sighed just a little and opened his eyes. He could shut his ears better with his eyes open. He stared at the open-toed shoes that Jubilee wore, her feet not pretty at all—very masculine, maybe the only masculine part about her. Except for the glitter toenail polish with the little stars in the very center, polish that matched her flowing pink outfit.

"They're not heroic. They're not brave. They were simply there one minute and gone the next. And everyone else? Yeah, maybe they have a moment where they grab a comrade and pull him aside or run in to carry out the wounded, but that doesn't negate what they did the day before, with their own rifle—"

"Enough," Rodrigo said quietly, the first words he had spoken in over an hour. "We know."

"You don't know," the sniper said. "You go on and on about being happy that you have a sniper, and you don't even know what we are—"

"We know," Lou said, before he could stop himself. "Jesus, woman, we know."

He didn't stand up this time. He sat there, the crown of his head leaning against the wall, his arms still crossed, his legs outstretched.

"You're the one who doesn't know," he said, as he pushed himself away from the wall. "You have no idea who we are or what we've been through. The person you're so rudely shouting down about heroism? That's Pauline, a school teacher—she's *still* a school teacher, although I don't know how, because I wouldn't be a school teacher after what she went through."

After all, he couldn't be a cop any more after what he had gone through. At least not until they cleared him, not until he cleared himself.

"She saved the lives of fifteen six-year-olds, did you know that?"

"Lou," Pauline said, waving a hand, trying to make him stop.

"She took three bullets getting her first-grade class away from that crazy with an automatic weapon. You remember, the one who gunned down children because he wasn't properly potty-trained or whatever—"

"Lou," Pauline said, just a little louder.

"She's a hero. She made sure her kids were safe, then went back into the school and dragged out her colleagues. You see her. She makes you look like you're Arnold Schwarzenegger. If she had died that day, she would have died bravely and well—"

"Lou!" This time it wasn't Pauline. It was Izzy, and he realized what

he had said. *If she had died that day.* God, where did these sentences come from?

He nodded, and would've shut up, if the sniper hadn't taken that moment to frown at him.

"You don't know us," he said. "You have no idea what we've been through, what we've seen, or why we're here."

"So why don't you tell me?" the sniper asked.

"Because, honey," he said, "people like you don't deserve to know."

Twelve

And with that final insult, Lou DeMartino voted with his legs. He shot one last nasty look at Lana, then pushed his way past the people in front of him, and walked out the office door.

One by one, the others followed him. A number of them gave Rodrigo perplexed looks, as if they didn't know why he had brought them to the office in the middle of such a hot afternoon.

And he wasn't sure either, truth be told. He had seen her, saw the ghost of the rifle still in her hand, knew that she had been one of the best of the best, just by the aura around her, her eyes, and the way she still held that invisible gun.

But he couldn't see her soul. He couldn't see any of their souls. He could only guess and, as usual when he tried to lead, he guessed wrong.

He tried not to let despair take him. Self-pity was a waste of time. He firmly believed that, and yet, there he was, tottering on the edge of it.

Lana stood very still as the exodus began. She didn't move as it continued, even as people around her left. Sometimes they brushed against her. Sometimes they bumped her so hard that she had to struggle to keep her footing.

Even when Rodrigo had brought in outspoken people like Lou

DeMartino, the group had never reacted like this. They almost seemed to hate her.

Maybe they did hate her.

And that surprised him.

But she was the closest thing to a pure killer that he had tried to recruit for the team. There was clearly very little humanity left inside her.

And maybe that was good.

Only a handful of people were left. Izzy still sat at her desk. Jubilee stood near the wall, Tru beside her like they always were. Two of the police officers—William and Jose—and that professor, Carter, who grated on Rodrigo's nerves, even though Rodrigo knew the man's story. His entire extended family lost the day after he left for college, in a house fire that would have taken him too, had he been home. Day two of the family reunion. The day before he left for college, he'd had fifteen family members. Two days later, he had none.

He could've given up. Instead, he'd bottled up, and used his mind to move ahead, getting two Ph.D.'s and doing some post-doc work before getting snatched up by the university here. He was thirty-five before it all caught up to him, and even then, he hadn't understood it.

A friend had brought him to the grief group, and Rodrigo, seeing the anger underneath, had brought him here.

Lana's gaze met Rodrigo's as if to ask, *What now?*

He had no idea. The group had clearly rejected her, the first time that had ever happened. Usually they accepted anyone he brought in.

Maybe they knew that with the arrival of a sniper, the plan would actually happen. Maybe that frightened them.

It was one thing to talk about killing the Angel of Death. It was another thing to actually try it.

He pushed away from the desk, feeling slightly chilled. The air conditioner failed when the room had been full, but now, its half-hearted wheeze managed to put out enough cold air to make him uncomfortable.

Or maybe, the fact that they had been close to executing his plan made him uncomfortable.

Because he had lied to all of them. He had never actually seen the Angel of Death.

He had felt the angel, over and over again. The beat of wings, the looming presence, that moment when the person, bleeding out in his arms, seemed to rally, only to smile, focus on something in the distance, and fade away.

Five tours. He hadn't lied about that. Five tours and lots of death, and that feeling just before someone left, that feeling he didn't know how to describe. When he'd been in the Arizona desert as a boy, crossing from Mexico with a group of people his mother had paid dearly for him to travel with, he could tell when someone wasn't going to make it.

Not because they gave any overt signs of illness or because they seemed to be on their last legs, but because the sun got very bright, and the air gained a chill it hadn't had before, and then the sound of flapping wings, not that he had known what that was the first time.

The first time, he had thought he heard sheets on a clothesline, flapping in the breeze, before he realized there was no breeze, no clothes line, no clean clothes.

And then the sun became so bright it hurt his eyes, and he shivered, and the next thing he knew, the slender man beside him, the one who had shared his water, the one who had egged him on, had fallen face first in the sand.

No matter what Rodrigo did—no matter what they all did—the slender man did not get up. He would never get up again.

The first of so many deaths. On that trip, another six succumbed. And then there were the people at the nursing home where he had gotten his first job. At that home, there was no sunlight. Just fluorescents that flared as if they were about to go out at the oddest hours. Only they didn't burn out. They stayed on, and didn't flare again, not until a few minutes before someone else died.

And then there were his tours. He didn't like to think about his tours. In fact, he couldn't think about them or the brilliant sunshine that seemed to coat everything. It couldn't get stronger there because it was already at full strength, something that sometimes made him wonder if he had actually served in a real place or if he had been doing his tours in a small corner of hell.

He wasn't sure; he had never been sure.

All he had done when he got home was try to find respite, try to figure out how to live with all he'd seen.

Which led him to the Meeting, and then the shooting, there.

He knew Izzy blamed him for some of the deaths, particularly young Alyssa. Because Izzy thought—maybe rightly—that he could have stopped it.

If he had seen it. If he hadn't been looking up, noting the chill on the breeze and the fact that the sun was brighter than he had seen it in years. And that surge of fear that had run through him—that had happened before the first gunshot, before Dugan had come out of the door, chasing everyone.

If Rodrigo had just looked down, he would have seen the movement in the glass panels beside the door, he would have known, he would have grabbed the rifle, saved lives.

He would have, he would have—if he had known, he wouldn't have taken the water from the man whose name he had never known. Rodrigo was younger, stronger, he could have made it through that desert on his own. And in the tours, he would have...

The air conditioner rattled, almost like the sound of flapping clothes on a line. He frowned, glanced at Izzy, who was staring in horror at Lana.

Lana, who had a handgun in her hand, her nearly dead eyes unfocused and unseeing.

Just like Dugan. Dear God, just like Dugan.

Rodrigo launched himself toward her as she raised that handgun slowly, aiming it—at him? He didn't have time to consider—and then the report echoed in the close quarters.

Out of the corner of his eye, he saw Jubilee grab Tru's neck and fling them to the ground as she went down. The police officers ran toward Lana, just like Rodrigo was doing, but Carter was staring toward the air conditioner itself.

The rattle had stopped, and the air inside the office had grown stifling.

Rodrigo reached Lana first. He tackled her, knocking her backwards, but she kept a grip on the handgun.

"Let me go, you fool," she said. "You want it dead, right? Let me make sure it's dead."

But he didn't let her go. He wasn't going to let anyone go. He had enough people die on his watch.

She was struggling beneath him.

"Let her go," Izzy said. "Rodrigo, let her go."

Jubilee was standing slowly. Tru stayed down, their head covered with their arms. The police officers were standing beneath the air conditioner, looking at the floor.

The air conditioner itself had changed color. A blackness covered it, almost an ichor—if that was the right word; it certainly wasn't one he had ever used before. The water from the broken condenser dripped down the wall, also black.

Izzy had stood, making her way around the desk.

"Let her go," Izzy repeated. "Before it vanishes. Let her go."

It. It. He didn't know what "it" was. He didn't see an it. But Jubilee was on her feet now, and Tru had let their hands slide from their skull.

He let Lana go, and she walked over to the desk, moving just beyond it, and poking with her toe.

Poking at nothing.

"Don't you see it?" Izzy asked.

"See what?" he asked.

"That shape over there," Carter said.

"The wings," said Jose.

"It's so small," William said.

"Andrew," Jubilee said.

"Alyssa," Izzy said.

"Alyssa?" It took Rodrigo a moment. The teenage girl, the one that Izzy had taken under her wing.

The one who had died at Dugan's hand.

Lana was still poking with her toe. "I didn't think a real bullet would kill it," she said.

Then she raised her head, her gaze meeting Rodrigo's. "You didn't see it?"

"I don't see anything," he said. He never saw anything. He should have told them that from the start. He never saw anything at all.

"The girl. Maybe twelve. She was—it was—" Lana shuddered. "It couldn't hide the wings. Or those eyes. All black, all pupil. No whites."

She looked at Izzy. "How long had she been coming here?"

Izzy was staring at the floor, in the space that Lana kept poking with her toe.

"I don't see a twelve-year-old," Izzy said. "It's Alyssa. Or it was, until..."

Jubilee walked toward them. "I should've known they could be hurt. The way that one ran from me after I punched it."

Rodrigo joined them. They were standing around something, only he couldn't see it. Nor could he see a bullet hole in the wall.

Just the ichor on the air conditioner, and a scent—something like rancid vanilla.

"What do we do with it?" Carter asked him, as if Rodrigo had all the answers. Although he probably deserved that. Because he always acted like he'd had answers.

"We can kill them?" he asked, astonished that it actually worked. Even though they hadn't tried.

"Yeah," Tru had joined the group. "Not that it matters. You all saw the other one, right?"

"No," Lana said. "I would have shot it too."

"You can't," Tru said. "They take lives at the right time. So if one is supposed to die..."

"Another shows up to make sure it does." Carter put a hand over his face, then staggered backwards just a little.

"It doesn't matter," William said. He normally didn't say much at all. "We sent a message. We let them know we're serious."

Lana looked at him sideways, as if to say, *You believe that?* Then she glanced at Rodrigo.

"It was here all along," she said. "Why didn't you just kill it?"

"I never saw it," he said, almost whispering. "I never saw any of them."

"Then why did you bring us here?" Izzy snapped, clearly furious. "Why did you promise us we could kill them? Why did you organize us? Why did you rent this office? Why did you—"

"Because," he said. "Some of us need more than talk. Some of us need to take action."

"Even if it's futile?" Izzy asked.

He had never seen her that angry.

"Especially if it is," he said.

He hadn't expected them to succeed. Expected one of them to succeed. Although he had known Lana was something special with her invisible rifle and her very real handgun, the one he hadn't realized she was carrying all along.

His gaze met hers, and there was something in her eyes, something livelier than there had been earlier in the day.

"It was feeding off you," she said. "Your pain. I was watching it. I saw the wings twice. And then, as everyone left—"

"The wings unfurled," Jubilee said. "I caught a glimpse of them."

"Was it coming for one of us?" Carter asked.

The bright light in the office. The chill. The sound of wings. Had that been for them? Or for the Angel of Death itself?

"How would we ever know?" Tru asked. "How would we ever know?"

Thirteen

No one wanted to leave. No one except Rodrigo.

They just kept staring at the dead creature that he couldn't see.

So finally, he walked out of the door, and sat on the cracked sidewalk, his feet extended in the ruined parking lot.

It was twilight. No more sunlight flaring. No bright day. No chill in the air. No wind. It was hotter than shit out here. Midwestern heat, filled with so much humidity that the air felt like a blanket, pressing down on him. Drowning him, with each breath.

But he kept breathing. Thinking.

He went to every Meeting. He came to this office every day. He talked about killing the Angel of Death, and then when it happened, when someone actually pulled it off, he felt as numb as he had in Afghanistan, when that last bomb exploded fifteen yards and two buildings away from where he was.

Triage was easy when you were numb. You didn't think about the tattooed limbs as part of a man you'd spoken to not thirty minutes before. They were simply parts to be gathered, a job to be done.

That was what this had been for him.

A job.

A way to get through.

He crossed his arms over his knees and rested his forehead against his wrists. Magic had happened and he missed it. The event he had been planning for occurred. Ironically, the person he had brought in to do the job had done it, quickly, efficiently.

And, as he suspected, it had made no difference. Because there had been a second angel, there to take out the first.

Voices echoed behind him. Then laughter.

Laughter. When was the last time he heard laughter? Real joyous laughter?

He raised his head, saw Tru and Jubilee, smiling at each other as they came out of the building.

Jubilee crouched beside him. "It vanished on its own," she said. "Kinda like the witch in the *Wizard of Oz.*"

"'Surrender, Dorothy!'" Tru quoted. "Guess threats like that never work."

"Judy's revenge," Jubilee said, and Tru laughed.

Tru started across the parking lot, but Jubilee stayed for a moment longer, crouching beside Rodrigo.

"What can I do for you?" she asked him.

He shook his head. He had no idea.

"It's nice to hear you laugh," he said. "Keep doing it."

She squeezed his shoulder, then stood. "You know where to find me."

"Yeah," he said, watching Tru shift from foot to foot in the parking lot. "Thanks."

Jubilee stood and headed to a car that Rodrigo hadn't seen before. More voices surrounded him. William, Jose, Carter, talking about what they had seen. They didn't acknowledge him, too intent on their conversation, perhaps, or maybe they hadn't seen him at all.

Then Lana. She sat down beside him, extended her legs and crossed them at the ankles.

"I suppose you want to hunt them," she said.

He let out a breath. Did he? Spend his entire life pursuing creatures he couldn't see? Being present at the worst moments, trying to figure out why the sun was brighter that day or the air had a chill? Did he really want to do any of that?

"No," he said. "You can, if you want."

"And be what?" she asked. "The Angel of Death for the Angel of Death? No thanks."

She wiped her hands on her thighs, as if her fingers had gotten dirty just from firing the gun.

"Your club is weird," she said. "I don't like it."

And he, he just realized, didn't like her. He let out a silent sigh, then got to his feet. He wondered if he should thank her.

But she made it easy. She just walked away from him, as if they hadn't spoken at all.

That just left Izzy. Izzy who was still inside the office. Izzy, who practically lived there.

He went inside and found her, sitting at her desk, staring at the apparently empty spot on the floor.

"What do we do now?" she asked, not looking at him. "What do we do now?"

He crouched in front of her, then leaned forward and drew her into a hug. He'd known her nearly a year and he had never hugged her before.

She leaned against him, body stiff, and then, muscle by muscle, it relaxed.

It wasn't until his shoulder felt warm that he realized she was crying. He leaned his head against hers.

"Fucking wheel," she said after a few moments.

"Wheel?" he asked.

"Grief wheel," she said. "It's not a wheel. It's a gauge."

"A gauge?" He wasn't sure he understood what she was saying.

"Yeah," she said into his shirt. "Denial, anger, bargaining, depression, acceptance. It's not a wheel."

Bargaining. Jesus. The entire group had been built on bargaining. They had been negotiating how to kill the Angel of Death. Bargaining with the way the world worked, as if they could actually change it.

"I'd been stuck on anger," Izzy was saying.

And he had been bargaining. He'd brought them all into it.

"You're not stuck anymore?" he asked.

"I don't think I am." She brought her head up. Her cheeks were wet, and her eyes should have been red, but they weren't.

He wasn't stuck anymore either. But he felt a little lost, like he sometimes did when he finished a mission. Not that he had finished this one.

Or had he? He had finally found the right person, the catalyst, who changed everything.

What had Lou said? Their mistake... *We justify off the magic stuff as every day...we normalize much too much. Death and taxes.*

Death and taxes.

And Izzy, in his arms, warm and lighter than she had been since he met her.

She was watching him. He smoothed her hair away from her face. Then he kissed her. And she kissed him back.

Not hearts and flowers. Not even Disney-fied.

But nice. And different.

There was a reason he had relied on her, a reason he had trusted her.

They understood each other. They had needed each other. Right from moment one.

He helped her out of the chair.

"There's going to be a full moon tonight," he said, the king of non sequiturs.

"You saying we all went crazy because of it?" she asked.

He hadn't been. But he wouldn't put it past them. Any of them.

"Just thought maybe you'd want to see it," he said.

"I've already seen full moons," she said.

"But not this one," he said.

She stared at him for a moment. Then she smiled, nodded, almost laughed.

"You're right," she said. "Not this one. Chance of a lifetime."

It was. It was one of those moments—like every moment, really—that would never come again.

But he didn't say it.

Instead, he led her outside, to the ruined parking lot on a crappy street in a dying strip mall. A big orange moon was rising over the dilapidated buildings a few blocks away.

Orange meant there was a lot of sunlight reflecting off it. Big meant it was low on the horizon. And yet, it felt unusual. Magic. More magic than the actual magic that had occurred in their rundown office.

He put his arm around her, and she leaned into him. And they said nothing as the light hit them, brighter and brighter.

But the air stayed warm, and nothing flapped in the nonexistent breeze.

They were alone

They were together.

And, for that moment at least, they were alive.

Newsletter sign-up

Be the first to know!

Please sign up for the Kristine Kathryn Rusch and Dean Wesley Smith newsletters, and receive exclusive content, keep up with the latest news, releases and so much more—even the occasional giveaway.

So, what are you waiting for?
To sign up for Kristine Kathryn Rusch's newsletter go to kristinekathrynrusch.com.
To sign up for Dean Wesley Smith's newsletter go to deanwesleysmith.com.

But wait! There's more. Sign up for the WMG Publishing newsletter, too, and get the latest news and releases from all of the WMG authors and lines, including Kristine Grayson, Kris Nelscott, Dean Wesley Smith, *Fiction River, Smith's Monthly, Pulphouse Fiction Magazine* and so much more.

To sign up go to wmgpublishing.com.

About the Author
Dean Wesley Smith

Considered one of the most prolific writers working in modern fiction, *USA Today* bestselling writer Dean Wesley Smith published far more than a hundred novels in forty years, and hundreds of short stories across many genres.

At the moment he produces novels in several major series, including the time travel Thunder Mountain novels set in the Old West, the galaxy-spanning Seeders Universe series, the urban fantasy Ghost of a Chance series, a superhero series starring Poker Boy, and a mystery series featuring the retired detectives of the Cold Poker Gang.

His monthly magazine, *Smith's Monthly*, which consists of only his own fiction, premiered in October 2013 and offers readers more than 70,000 words per issue, including a new and original novel every month.

During his career, Dean also wrote a couple dozen *Star Trek* novels, the only two original *Men in Black* novels, Spider-Man and X-Men novels, plus novels set in gaming and television worlds. Writing with his wife Kristine Kathryn Rusch under the name Kathryn Wesley, he wrote the novel for the NBC miniseries The Tenth Kingdom and other books for *Hallmark Hall of Fame* movies.

He wrote novels under dozens of pen names in the worlds of comic books and movies, including novelizations of almost a dozen films, from *The Final Fantasy* to *Steel* to *Rundown.*

Dean also worked as a fiction editor off and on, starting at Pulphouse Publishing, then at *VB Tech Journal*, then Pocket Books, and now at WMG Publishing, where he and Kristine Kathryn Rusch serve as series editors for the acclaimed *Fiction River* anthology series.

For more information about Dean's books and ongoing projects, please visit his website at www.deanwesleysmith.com and sign up for his newsletter.

For more information:
www.deanwesleysmith.com

facebook.com/deanwsmith3
patreon.com/deanwesleysmith
bookbub.com/authors/dean-wesley-smith

About the Author
Kristine Kathryn Rusch

New York Times bestselling author Kristine Kathryn Rusch writes in almost every genre. Generally, she uses her real name (Rusch) for most of her writing. Under that name, she publishes bestselling science fiction and fantasy, award-winning mysteries, acclaimed mainstream fiction, controversial nonfiction, and the occasional romance. Her novels have made bestseller lists around the world and her short fiction has appeared in eighteen best of the year collections. She has won more than twenty-five awards for her fiction, including the Hugo, *Le Prix Imaginales*, the *Asimov's* Readers Choice award, and the *Ellery Queen Mystery Magazine* Readers Choice Award.

Publications from *The Chicago Tribune* to *Booklist* have included her Kris Nelscott mystery novels in their top-ten-best mystery novels of the year. The Nelscott books have received nominations for almost every award in the mystery field, including the best novel Edgar Award, and the Shamus Award.

She writes goofy romance novels as award-winner Kristine Grayson.

She also edits. Beginning with work at the innovative publishing company, Pulphouse, followed by her award-winning tenure at *The Magazine of Fantasy & Science Fiction*, she took fifteen years off before returning to editing with the original anthology series *Fiction River,* published by WMG Publishing. She acts as series editor with her husband, writer Dean Wesley Smith, and edits at least two anthologies in the series per year on her own.

To keep up with everything she does, go to kriswrites.com and sign up for her newsletter. To track her many pen names and series, see their individual websites (krisnelscott.com, kristinegrayson.com, retrievalartist.com, divingintothewreck.com, pulphouse.com).

kriswrites.com

facebook.com/kristinekathrynruschwriter

patreon.com/kristinekathrynrusch

bookbub.com/authors/kristine-kathryn-rusch

Also from WMG Publishing

FICTION RIVER

Kristine Kathryn Rusch & Dean Wesley Smith, series editors

Unnatural Worlds
Edited by Dean Wesley Smith & Kristine Kathryn Rusch

How to Save the World
Edited by John Helfers

Time Streams
Edited by Dean Wesley Smith

Christmas Ghosts
Edited by Kristine Grayson

Hex in the City
Edited by Kerrie L. Hughes

Moonscapes
Edited by Dean Wesley Smith

Special Edition: Crime
Edited by Kristine Kathryn Rusch

Fantasy Adrift
Edited by Kristine Kathryn Rusch

Universe Between
Edited by Dean Wesley Smith

Fantastic Detectives
Edited by Kristine Kathryn Rusch

Past Crime
Edited by Kristine Kathryn Rusch

Pulse Pounders
Edited by Kevin J. Anderson

Risk Takers
Edited by Dean Wesley Smith

Alchemy & Steam
Edited by Kerrie L. Hughes

Valor
Edited by Lee Allred

Recycled Pulp
Edited by John Helfers

Hidden in Crime
Edited by Kristine Kathryn Rusch

Sparks
Edited by Rebecca Moesta

Visions of the Apocalypse
Edited by John Helfers

Haunted
Edited by Kerrie L. Hughes

Last Stand
Edited by Dean Wesley Smith & Felicia Fredlund

Tavern Tales
Edited by Kerrie L. Hughes

No Humans Allowed
Edited by John Helfers

Editor's Choice
Edited by Mark Leslie

Pulse Pounders: Adrenaline
Edited by Kevin J. Anderson

Feel the Fear
Edited by Mark Leslie

Superpowers
Edited by Rebecca Moesta

Justice
Edited by Kristine Kathryn Rusch

Wishes
Edited by Rebecca Moesta

Pulse Pounders: Countdown
Edited by Kevin J. Anderson

Hard Choices
Edited by Dean Wesley Smith

Feel the Love
Edited by Mark Leslie

Special Edition: Spies
Edited by Kristine Kathryn Rusch

Special Edition: Summer Sizzles
Edited by Kristine Kathryn Rusch

Superstitious
Edited by Mark Leslie

Doorways to Enchantment
Edited by Dayle A. Dermatis

Stolen
Edited by Leah Cutter

Chances
Edited by Denise Little & Kristine Kathryn Rusch

Dark & Deadly Passions
Edited by Kristine Kathryn Rusch

Broken Dreams
Edited by Kristine Kathryn Rusch

Fiction River Presents

Allyson Longueira, Series Editor

Fiction River's line of reprint anthologies.

Fiction River has published more than 400 amazing stories by more than 100 talented authors since its inception, from *New York Times* bestsellers to debut authors. So, WMG Publishing decided to start bringing back some of the earlier stories in new compilations.

VOLUMES:

Debut Authors
The Unexpected
Darker Realms
Racing the Clock
Legacies
Readers' Choice
Writers Without Borders
Among the Stars
Sorcery & Steam
Cats!
Mysterious Women
Time Travelers

To learn more or to pick up your copy today, go to www.FictionRiver.com.

Pulphouse Fiction Magazine

Pulphouse Fiction Magazine, edited by Dean Wesley Smith, made its return in 2018, twenty years after its last issue. Each new issue contains about 70,000 words of short fiction. This reincarnation mixes some of the stories from the old *Pulphouse* days with brand-new fiction. The magazine has an attitude, as did the first run. No genre limitations, but high-quality writing and strangeness.

For more information or to subscribe, go to www.pulphousemagazine.com.

EXPANDED COPYRIGHT INFORMATION

Expanded Copyright Information

Expanded Copyright Information